Knowledge of Sins Past

Lexie Conyngham

DEDICATION

To N&D for the initial shove, and M for patiently keeping up the
momentum.

Dramatis personae

The family at Scoggie Castle:
Lord Scoggie
Lady Scoggie
Major Alexander Keyes, hero of Seringapatam
Henry Scoggie
Robert Scoggie
Deborah Scoggie
Beatrix Pirrie
Charles Murray, the secretary and tutor
Naismith, the steward
Mrs. Costane, a vicariously highly qualified French chef
Grisell, the maid
Hannah, the kitchen maid
Andrew, the manservant

The occupants of Aberardour Lodge:
Philip Bootham
Jane Bootham
Baffled servants

The low town inhabitants of St. Monance (pig-haters)
Joe Baillie, leader of the fishermen
Tom Baillie, his brother
Hugh Farquhar
Richie Shaw
Mallie, an enthusiastic butcher

The uptown inhabitants of St. Monance (pig-lovers)
Nathaniel Tibo, lawyer to the Scoggie family
Cocky Leckie, his clerk
Geordie Kinkell, weaver
Mrs. Kinkell, his wife
Peter Kinkell, his son
Sandy Kinkell, his brother
Chrissie Farquhar, Sandy's wife
Don Downie, wright
A weaver from Crail, late owner of a sow
Parry the Pugilistic Chanticleer
A sow

CHAPTER ONE

If there had been anyone there to see them, they might have been hard put to say what they were up to. For one thing, the moon, full though it was, rushed from cloud to cloud like a fugitive, and showed their progress in jerky stages like a broken nursery trick. The light seemed to confuse them, as if they could not decide, in the moon's brightness, whether to hide from its glare or to take advantage of it. Worst of all, the effort to move the great sow quickly but silently – apparently an impossible combination – had struck the younger man as hysterically funny, and he spent most of his time doubled over, clutching his splutterings hard to his face, while the older man tried to herd youth and pig with a sound lashing of muttered curses.

If there had been anyone there to see them, they might have been interested enough to follow the strange trio, man, youth and sow, down the softly muddy street to the harbour, where the gentle tidal movement nudged the fishing boats against each other to tap their secret signals in the darkness. The rig cottages along the harbour glowed suddenly blue-white as the moon reappeared: all their windows were dark, deep-set and sleeping. The pig stopped abruptly, mumbling to herself. Snorts of laughter came from the young man. The pig sat down.

If anyone had followed them down there, and watched from the shadows as they took the sow to the edge of the harbour and tethered her there, leaving a few kale fronds to keep her quiet: if anyone had seen them check the tethers, then look up, startled by some distant noise, they might have noticed the similarity in the two moonlit profiles, the shape of the head and the busy hands.

They left the pig and picked their way silently back over the road to the foot of the hill they had come down. Before he began the ascent, the man glanced around, then spat firmly in the direction of the harbour. Struck by sudden solemnity the youth did the same, then caught sight of the sow again sitting in a pool of moonlight and had to gulp down his laughter. He followed his companion quickly up the hill and disappeared into the darkness.

If there had been anyone there to see them, there was nothing else to see. Anyone would be wise to go home to their beds.

Charles Balfour Murray was heir to the fine estate of Letho, and to a grand house in the New Town of Edinburgh. On a bright October morning in the year 'four, he was twenty years old, dark and handsome, and squatting in a pig trough.

'You can't just sit down,' said Robert authoritatively. 'You have to stand up so we can hit you.'

'That's not much of an incentive.'

'What?'

'I can't row if I'm standing up.' The pig trough was, if anything, cleaner than the midden it was resting in. Murray had no particular wish to leave his current perch while the alternatives were so unpromising. He was wearing his usual dark brown coat and waistcoat, the ones that showed the fewest stains, but there seemed little point in testing them further than usual.

'He's quite right, Robbie,' came Henry's welcome voice. Henry, after all, had the textbook, its leather covers increasingly tatty from much travel in pockets. 'They sat down in the war canoes, even the small ones.'

'Well, he'll have to stand up to fight, once he's rowed close enough,' Robert decided from the top of the midden wall, currently doing duty as the poopdeck of His Majesty's Ship *Discovery*. 'Row close enough, Mr. Murray.'

Murray dutifully plied the yard brush he had been given as a paddle, trying to look as if he were straining against a heavy sea. Robert watched critically, thoughtful fingers tapping his wooden sword.

'I thought Captain Cook just attended a review of the Matavai war canoes,' Murray tried. 'He didn't fight them.'

'He might have, if he'd wanted to,' said Robert quickly. 'And he'd have won.'

'Of course. How far away am I now?'

Robert considered, possibly taking reckonings on how long he could make his tutor suffer, versus how soon he could reach the interesting part.

'Mr. King!' he called to Henry by the name of Captain Cook's officer. 'How far away is that war canoe?'

'I don't want to be Mr. King,' Henry objected. 'I want to be Otoo.'

'You want to be a tribesman?'

'Otoo's much more interesting than boring old Mr. King. If I can't be Captain Cook I want to be Otoo.'

'But I need an officer!'

'Anyway, why can't I be Captain Cook? I'm older than you!'

Murray took advantage of the debate to ease off on his paddle. The pig yard was currently deserted: the pigs were rooting through the last of the windfalls in the orchard, and the pigman, if he had the sense of his breed, was somewhere sheltering from the sharp October wind. Over the wall, or poopdeck, the leaves of the orchard trees tossed, their colours tired and grey-green, many torn off before they could ever turn yellow. In the other direction, the tall towerhouse could be seen above the pig sheds, one or two windows open to demonstrate the hardiness of the inhabitants. It was his second autumn here, and he felt he knew the place well: as secretary and librarian to Lord Scoggie and tutor to his boys, there were few parts of the house or lands barred to him.

A figure appeared at one of the upstairs windows. Beatrix glanced out, then stared at the sight of the battle in the pig yard. She was some way away, but Murray could still see her shake with laughter, and he felt himself blushing stupidly. That would give Beatrix and Deborah a subject for teasing for at least a week. He was growing cramped and cold, and decided to put an end to Captain Cook's suppression of the natives. He stood up, bracing his feet against the wooden sides of the trough.

'Right,' he said, taking the boys by surprise. 'I've reached you. This is my war spear, and I'm going to throw it at you.' He hefted the yard brush menacingly, trying to ignore the chill wind reaching all the now-exposed damp patches on his breeches.

'You have to miss,' said Robert promptly, not one to allow his enemy any unfair advantage. 'And anyway, you have to play antics first.'

'I'm not playing antics, not in this weather,' said Murray firmly.

'But it *says* –' said Henry, flicking through the book.

'It also says it's one of the hottest climates,' said Murray. 'And it says I have "great judgement and a very quick eye", I think you'll find.' Preparation, as he had discovered, was the backbone of teaching.

'Come on, fight!' said Robert, a boy who knew where his interests lay. Murray sighed and waved his yard brush in a supposedly Matavai manner, then flung it hard over the orchard wall, missing Robert by a deliberate, though regrettable, couple of feet. Captain Cook cheered and waved his sword, while Mr. King-Otoo scowled at his textbook, sheltering it from the wind. Captain Cook grabbed another length of wood from his belt, and, demonstrating the careful attention to diplomatic relations with tribesmen for which he was renowned, shot his Matavai tutor from a range of five yards. Murray obligingly clutched his leg, and sank back into the pig trough, groaning.

'Got him!' cried Robert, waving sword and pistol. 'Got him! Now we have to take him to the morai to sacrifice him to Atooey!'

'The eatooa,' Henry corrected him coldly.

'How are you going to take me?' said Murray: being shot was one thing, but sacrifice to a god consisting mostly of vowels was beneath his dignity. 'I'm on a canoe, probably being washed further away from your ship with every wave.'

'I'll send a boat for you. Mr. King!'

'I'm not Mr. King,' said Henry stubbornly.

'Otoo, then.'

'Otoo's a king. Of a whole island. He's not going to take orders from you.'

Robert threw down his sword and sat on the wall.

'I wish we could play in the lake.'

'You know your father forbids it,' said Murray, taking the opportunity to leap from the trough on to the wall, avoiding the midden in between. 'Come on, up you get. It's time to go in.'

'I want to play in the lake,' Robert insisted, arms folded.

'Believe me,' said Murray, 'sometimes I wish you could go and play in the lake, too. But you can't, and there's an end to it.'

Robert's face set into one of his least attractive expressions.

'Oh, dear,' said Henry, recognising it, 'we may be here for some time.' He looked at Murray, assessing unsympathetically Murray's chances of overcoming Robert's obstinacy.

'Well, if I can't play in the lake I'm going to stay here and not go in.'

Murray stood next to him on the wall, trying not to look impatient.

'And do you imagine anyone is going to bring your dinner out to you in the pig sty?'

'Grisell won't, anyway,' Henry chuckled. He took the opportunity to poke Robert with his wooden sword, but misjudged it. Robert snatched it, nearly toppling his brother off the wall. Henry, too, sat on the wall, to avoid further mishap, but in order to differentiate his stand from his brother's, he sat the other way round, dangling his feet into the orchard. Robert tapped the sword on the wall, beating his heels on the stones, and demonstrating no inborn sense of rhythm. Distractedly, Murray hoped he would not have to teach the boys dancing. He had hoped not to teach the boys at all.

'I don't want any dinner,' said Robert.

'Now, that's a first,' Murray remarked. 'Are you sure you're not sickening for something?'

Robert treated him to a disparaging look.

'Tell my father I'm not going to eat until he lets us play in the lake.'

'Don't be ridiculous,' said Murray. 'I don't care whether you eat or not, but I'm not running messenger to your father with such an idea, particularly not on your orders, young man.'

The next few seconds were a blur. Murray had time briefly to reflect that his perch on the wall was not the most secure for provoking small boys with swords, as Robert whacked him just behind the knees, above his boots. Murray's legs gave way. There was a slither, a crack on his elbow as he tried to save himself, and the next moment he was up to his thighs in cold pond water, cleaner than the midden beside it, but much deeper.

Robert's face was churning with gratified astonishment and terror at the result of his actions. Henry's mouth had dropped open as if his jaw had doubled in weight. Murray stepped out of the pond, boots and breeches heavy with icy water, and managed to keep his face straight as he looked at Robert.

'Right,' he said. 'That's it. No more nonsense.' He swung himself over the wall and dropped lightly down into the orchard with a squelch. He retrieved the yard brush from where it had fallen, then turned and secured Robert by the ear. 'In – or it won't be lakes we'll be talking to your father about.'

Robert opened his mouth to object, but only briefly. He scrambled off the wall, followed by Henry with an air of faint disappointment. Murray let go of Robert's ear, but managed to carry the yard brush in a way that implied threat without actually having to make the effort to carry it out. Escorted by their dripping erstwhile prisoner, the boys dragged their feet along the path by the orchard wall. The pigs ignored them, and when Robert tried to rectify the situation by lifting a windfall to throw at the nearest copper flank, he found Murray's hand clamped suddenly round his upraised arm, and dropped the windfall in resignation. Then he brightened.

'Mr. Murray, did you know Parry the Pugilistic Chanticleer's coming to Elie?'

'Really?' Elie was bigger than St. Monance, their nearest village, but that did not make it particularly large. The Pugilistic Chanticleer's career must be on the way downhill. 'You're sure it's really this Elie?'

'There's another one?' asked Robert vaguely. 'No, I'm sure. He's to stay at the King's Arms, and give demonstrations and lessons. Can we have lessons from Parry the Pugilistic Chanticleer?'

'In pugilism or singing?' asked Murray, straight-faced. Robert reacted by kicking a windfall at Murray's feet.

'You're only a tutor. What do you know about pugilism?'

'Enough to know you'll have to ask your father about lessons from anyone in an inn in Elie,' said Murray, trying not to think of his own father, and the enforced sporting lessons he had hated through his youth.

'He'll say no,' said Henry, demonstrating his ability to walk, read about Cook's last voyage, and listen to the conversation at the same time. 'He'll say it's not gentlemanly.' A windfall hit him with a hard splat on the side of the neck.

'There's little enough hope that Robert will ever be gentlemanly,' Murray remarked, handing his handkerchief to Henry and cuffing Robert.

'You said his clothes were mucky anyway,' said Robert. They emerged from the orchard gate and followed the path to the drive at the front of the house. Here, you could see it for what it was: a confused series of extensions to the original tower house, crow-stepped gables like unplanned staircases ending before they were ready, turrets turning off corners as if they were paper bags twisted hastily to close them. Murray supervised the use of the boot scraper by the door, and manoeuvred the boys into the hall. The dark interior smelled of brass balls and leather soap, and glinted with the Scoggie ancestral armoury. Murray always half-expected straw on the floor.

He saw the boys to the bottom of the generous winding staircase, and listened to hear them mount at least to the first floor before he himself slipped, dripping, through the curtain to the servants' corridor, seeking the warmth of the kitchen.

'Oh, that man would give you the nyerps!' The voice was that of Mrs. Costane, the cook: she was a West Coast woman and entitled to her opinion.

'Good morning, Mrs. Costane,' said Murray warily, hoping the man in question was not him, but Mrs. Costane greeted him with a slightly frantic grin, which turned to a look of dismay.

'What in the name of all that's good and holy has happened to yourself?'

'I was attacked by Captain Cook, I think,' Murray laughed. The fire was hot for the dinner, and he edged towards it, feeling his face cooking even yards from it. Mrs. Costane and the kitchenmaid had permanently tanned faces from their daily work.

'You'd be better getting those wet things off you, or you'll catch your death,' said Mrs. Costane.

'But not in here,' added the kitchenmaid, sourly.

'Ach, you're a tedious old maid,' Mrs. Costane objected. 'Mr. Murray, you're a fine-looking young gentleman. Would you not do the decent thing and take Miss Deborah away out of this? Set up your household and I'll come and be your cook.'

'I couldn't afford you or her, Mrs. Costane, I'm afraid. You know my position.'

'By jingo, I'd nearly do it for the love of you both, for Miss Deborah is the only member of the family I've ever heard say a word of sense.'

'What about Miss Beatrix?'

'Oh, she's not a Scoggie, mercifully for her.' She scooped a dumpling mix competently into a cloth, with a look of almost audible disgust. 'Besides, she has an eye for you.'

'Miss Beatrix?' Murray's heart seemed to take a little detour off track.

'No, Miss Deborah. Miss Beatrix? If she wasn't in the Church, she could be a nun, that girl. But Miss Deborah's father would make her a good portion.' She eyed Murray wistfully. Hannah, the kitchenmaid, seized the dumpling from her listless grasp and dumped it into a saucepan boiling over the fire, kicking the fireirons into place with careless expertise. Murray waited until she had finished, then snatched himself a turn in the fire's heat, drying his damp breeches.

'What have you been doing? demanded Mrs. Costane, brushing flour from her hands but with all her attention on Murray.

'As I said, playing at Captain Cook in the pigsty.'

'Those breeches are soaking. You'd be better to have them off.' Her face turned long and bland. 'Hannah'll help you.'

'Oh!' said Hannah, 'I'd hate to get in your own way, Mrs. Costane. I doubt you have more experience of young men's breeches than I do.'

'Aye, in my young days,' sighed Mrs. Costane.

'Anyway,' said Murray hurriedly, 'what has Lord Scoggie done to offend you this time?'

'Oh, the usual,' muttered the kitchenmaid.

'Kale, kale, kale,' added the cook, dramatically. 'The man wants nothing but kale and brose, herring and brose, cheese and brose, or on a holiday beef and brose, with a wee bitty kale, maybe, for a treat. Why in the name of all that's good and holy am I here? I'm a French-trained chef!'

Murray's lips twitched as the kitchenmaid, behind Mrs. Costane's back, mouthed the last four words along with her. Hannah, nearly the cook's age, was not a French-trained chef – nor, strictly, was Mrs. Costane, but her husband had been – but Hannah usually ended up saving Mrs. Costane from the disasters that could easily have resulted from her boredom with kale and brose.

'Any worse than usual today?' Murray asked, feeling slightly guilty for his lack of sympathy. Mrs. Costane's eyes rolled.

'We have a guest coming to stay.'

'Oh, yes, I've heard. The great Major Alexander Keyes.'

'Aye, that's the one. The great hero of Seringapatam in India. You'd think a man who had travelled would take kindly to good food, and Miss Deborah and I had a whole menu worked out, and then his Lordship comes and changes the whole thing, says military men need proper food, not foreign muck, the Scots have fought on brose for centuries and fought and won, and it's brose and dumpling and boiled chicken or he won't touch it. I've kept my beetroot pancakes, though!' she added, with an air of vicious triumph.

'When is he arriving?'

'Tomorrow. You'd think it was Sir David Baird himself, the state they're in upstairs. Wee Grisell's up and down those stairs like a clockwork toy overwound, and Miss Beatrix and Miss Deborah have the hero's bedchamber spun like milk in a churn.'

'And what about Lady Scoggie?'

'What about her? Has she died off? I haven't seen her for months.'

'She's very busy,' said Murray, reluctantly drawn into defending the family. 'She does a great deal of charitable work.'

'So I hear,' said the cook, with a degree of irony.

'Och, she does work hard, though, give her that,' said Hannah, with unexpected benevolence. 'There isn't a soul in the parish she wouldn't attend to if they needed it. And I hear she's not above getting down and scrubbing a floor or making a bit of broth if it has to be done.'

'I grant you, I grant you I've heard the same stories.' Mrs. Costane was gracious. 'And she's very organised, I'll grant that, too. But why does she do none of it in her own home? The minute Miss Deborah was old enough to give an order, she was away like a bird with the cage door open.'

'She hasna looked happy this long time,' Hannah reflected. 'I've sometimes had the thought that it's the way with these fine-looking women: you reach the age when you start looking at your daughter – and so do all the men – and you realise your fine looks have faded like – like an oul hen,' she finished with a poetic flourish.

'Fine looks faded, eh?' said Mrs. Costane, her mouth tight. 'Just because you're an oul hen yourself, Hannah, you needn't think that female persons of the age of Lady Scoggie are not in the prime of their looks.'

'And, Mrs. Costane, I believe you mentioned once that you and Lady Scoggie are of an age?' Murray put in, innocently, and scooted sideways as she flailed at him with a pudding cloth.

'Anyway,' he went on, from a position of greater safety beyond Hannah. 'I don't see why everyone praises Miss Deborah's looks – though I don't say she's not pretty – and ignores Miss Beatrix. Why do you say she should be a nun?'

'Oh, the poor relation, no family, that's how the French manage matters,' said Mrs. Costane, with the authority of the widow of a man who had been to France. 'And that calm look of hers. If it wasn't for her, this household would be upside down in a week, whatever Miss Deborah's orders.'

'You think Miss Beatrix will not marry well?' Murray asked, trying to sound as interested as he would be in an academic problem.

Mrs. Costane blew through resigned lips.

'I doubt it, or not before Miss Deborah goes, anyway. You're a young man, you don't see things yet the way the world does. But you'd be surprised the difference five thousand pounds and a few fine gowns can make to a girl's beauty.'

'Beatrix seems to have fine gowns, too,' Murray objected.

'Yes, but not till they've been worn a few times by Miss Deborah first – or had you not noticed?'

Murray turned in surprise. The idea had never occurred to him.

'But –' he began, 'but –'

At that point the kitchen door opened without warning, and an extraordinary-looking man stepped in.

Murray had seen storks in Italy and Spain during his limited grand tour, and had noted the way they sometimes stood, wings tucked behind them, long grey beak thoughtfully down, crown feathers slicked back and thick black thighs dwindling abruptly to skinny legs and feet. Murray could not get it out of his head that Naismith, the butler to the household, abided by Pythagoras' notions and was in fact more used to inhabiting the body of a stork than that of a man. His thin grey hair was drawn back over a balding crown to a black silk ribbon at his collar, and his long, flat nose seemed to blend down into his long, flat chin and on down, in about the same shade of greyish white, to where his shirt and pale waistcoat made a V at the top of his coat – the tip of his beak. The tails of the same coat could easily have been tail-feathers, and his unfashionably ample black breeches and knobbly stockinged calves completed the picture. Murray always expected him to fly up and roost on the chimney.

'Ah ... cook,' he said, after some avian contemplation.

'Mr. Naismith,' said the cook, as one who draws a line in the sand.

'Preparations are going on well for the Major's visit. Are they?'

'You tell me, Mr. Naismith. I'm never out of my kitchen, as you ken.'

Hannah rolled her eyes at Murray out of sight of the others, and made a performance of checking that the dumpling was not boiling dry. Naismith regarded Mrs. Costane for a long moment with his head on one side, hands clasped behind him, then turned back to the door.

'Boy!' he called.

A young man, not much below Murray's own age, stepped quickly into the kitchen and closed the door behind him. Blond, brown-eyed and rosy, he had the look of one who would take storks and angry French chefs in his stride. Naismith nodded at him.

'A new boy for general and occasional upstairs work, cook. Boy, this is the cook, and the kitchenmaid. And – oh, I beg your pardon, Mr. Murray. This is Mr. Murray, his lordship's secretary.'

Murray nodded, slightly embarrassed at the formality with which Naismith had introduced him. He was never quite sure where the line was between him and the servants, or between him and the family. There was one, certainly: he was welcome in both worlds, and made free of the pleasures of both. Where it came, he sometimes thought, was that he could find fault with neither in either place. He could be easy with the Scoggies and with the lower servants, and was even trusted, he believed, with the secrets of each. Naismith, though, was the greatest difficulty. As one who saw himself as the legitimate go-between for family and servants, he treated Murray, particularly when he had found out from Lord Scoggie that Murray's father was not unimportant in society, with all the stiffness that he reserved for the family. That did not matter upstairs, but here in the kitchens it could be seen, though Murray tried not to be tempted, as rudeness. The new boy, however, nodded back to Murray affably. He seemed unlikely to be bothered by such niceties – until Naismith educated him otherwise.

Naismith had fallen silent, and stared for a long moment at the youth as if he had wound down. Then he stared about him, beady eyes shining, and gave a little cough.

'But this is not the whole establishment, of course. Ah, Mrs. Costane, where is Grisell?'

'I think she said she was to lay a fire in the drawing room, Mr. Naismith.'

'I shall, ah, fetch her,' Naismith announced, with a queer little smile on his face. In Murray's view it was not half as queer as the look then exchanged by Hannah and Mrs. Costane the minute he left the room. He believed he was trusted with secrets ...

There was a moment of silence, as Mrs. Costane inspected some boiling fowl and Hannah brought kale from the scullery table – there was no separate scullery in this old-fashioned kitchen, but a table, sink and buckets in a window corner served the purpose. The young man took in the great sandstone vault of the kitchen, the huge fireplace, the high windows in the cross vaults, in a manner that said that he intended one day, with all due respect, that all this would be his.

'Well,' he said eventually, 'my name is Andrew. I've been in service the last four years to a merchant in Kirkcaldy, but he died and I fancied the country life again. Mrs. – I'm sorry, I don't believe I caught your name – have you been here long?'

The merchant in Kirkcaldy had not taught Andrew not to speak till he was spoken to. The cook sighed, and resigned herself to a twisted smile.

'I'm Mrs. Costane, boy, and this is Hannah. You're not backward in coming forward, are you?'

Andrew grinned, flicking back the soft blond hair that must have broken several Kirkcaldy hearts already.

'Where would be the point in that, ma'am?'

Mrs. Costane glared.

'Maybe you'd find you knew your place better, boy. Are you serving at table?'

'Mr. Naismith said no, not for a while.'

'Then if you've nothing to keep your clothes good for, you can take these peels out to the pig midden. It's over the yard.'

'I'll find it,' said Andrew brightly, undeterred. Murray smiled to himself: Andrew and Mrs. Costane were not going to settle easily, and the battle might be amusing. Andrew started to gather scraps into a bucket, going to wipe the scullery table off with a cloth.

'Not that cloth!' cried Hannah. 'Grisell uses it for my lady's room.'

'Grisell? Is that the maid?' said Andrew, turning back. 'That's a strange name. I think my granny used to know a Grisell: she must be ancient.'

'Take that muck out to the pigs and get on,' snapped Mrs. Costane. Hannah watched him, an odd expression on her face. Murray seemed to be the only one to hear the light footstep in the passage outside.

The kitchen door opened, and Naismith entered. His wing-arm flapped protectively around the shoulders of a girl – around, but not quite touching.

'Here we are,' he said. 'This is the new boy.' He slid round her and presented Andrew by seizing him by the arm, tugging him away from his work at the scraps. Andrew still clutched the bucket. Naismith looked as proud as though his infant daughter clutched a posy to present to some great lady.

'Twenty to one, Mr. Naismith,' Mrs. Costane interrupted, nodding at the great kitchen clock.

'Oh! my.' Naismith pivoted on claw feet. 'Time for me to lay the silver.' With a sweeping beam from Andrew to Grisell, he stalked out of the kitchen.

'Is it no dinner yet?' asked Grisell.

'Oh, Grisell dear, I've hardly the upstairs dinner made, and here's Mr. Murray still down here.'

Murray suddenly realised the time himself. Hannah hurried to tip the kale into the broth in short crinkly strips of black-green. Mrs. Costane spat to test the heat of her griddle.

'You're Grisell?' asked Andrew, taking in red hair, creamy skin, quick blue eyes and a figure he had only dreamed of, even in Kirkcaldy.

'Grisell, aye. Who are you? The new boy?'

'Aye,' said Andrew weakly, and dropped the bucket of slops all over the kitchen floor.

'My, ye ken well how to make an impression on your first day,' remarked Mrs. Costane.

'Here, I'll help you.' Grisell's offer was made with a good deal of resignation, and Hannah, too, came round the table to fetch a mop and bucket. Andrew looked helpless, though Murray thought he detected a hint of practice to the look, as if it had worked well before. If it had, it was not going to here. Grisell, on her knees on the flagstones, slapped Andrew smartly on the calf with her wet cloth.

'Get down here and help, you useless hapeth!'

Laughing with Mrs. Costane, Murray made his way back to the kitchen door and almost collided with a flying figure in the doorway.

'Mrs. Costane! I beg your pardon, Mr. Murray – oh, you are not changed yet – that is a good sign!'

'But I'm late,' said Murray, and received a frown in return. Miss Deborah Scoggie did not brook impediments.

'Mrs. Costane, is there any way dinner could be stretched for another two?'

'Two, miss?' Mrs. Costane assumed a blank look.

'Well, one and a half. Is there?'

'One and a half?' Murray queried.

'Mr. Tibo and Mr. Leckie, of course,' she snapped, hardly glancing at him. 'You know Mr. Leckie has the appetite of a child.'

'Considerably less, if the child in question is Robert or Henry,' Murray agreed, and this time received a quick sideways grin.

'You hear Mr. Murray, Mrs. Costane. One and a third?'

Murray wondered if it was for the sake of Mr. Tibo that her dark hair was particularly finely braided today, and she seemed to be wearing another new gown. She held the pale skirts of it away from the slop-clearing operation continuing at the scullery table.

'One, maybe,' said Mrs. Costane finally. 'I cannot answer for Mr. Leckie's dinner.' Her lips sealed themselves up like dampened pastry pressed shut.

'Oh, then the family must all eat less,' Miss Deborah decided abruptly. 'I shall tell Father and Beatrix – and the boys, the greedy wee beasts. And I must tell Naismyth to lay two more places. With cushions for Mr. Leckie. Thank you, Mrs. Costane.'

Murray held the door open for her as she flew out, then turned to wink heavily at Mrs. Costane before following Miss Deborah back up to the ground floor. He left the kitchen reluctantly: it was vast, but somehow cosy compared with the rest of the castle.

Miss Deborah was in a hurry, and only realised he was behind her when they reached the hall again.

'Oh! Mr. Murray!' She spun round, new gown swirling.

'Miss Deborah.' He bowed, hoping that she would not notice his damp boots and breeches.

'You have heard that Major Keyes is coming to stay?'

'Yes, of course.'

She frowned and looked away for a moment, as if she had just remembered to dust the swords on the walls.

'He's been very ... heroic,' she said eventually. 'You know he lost a leg at Seringapatam?' Her mind was still on household matters, and she made it sound as if the Major had lost a button at the breakfast table.

'Yes, though I understand he is still very active.'

'Yes! Yes, he is.' She fingered a pretty pendant that she seemed to have acquired recently, but still frowned. 'Mr. Murray, you won't be upset, will you?'

Thinking she meant to tell him something further, Murray said cautiously,

'No, no, I'm sure I shan't.'

Deborah Scoggie smiled, relieved.

'Good! Thank you so much, Mr. Murray.'

With a whisk of her skirts, she vanished in the direction of the Great Hall, leaving him standing bewildered. Her voice floated back to him, but unhelpfully.

'Mr. Murray, your boots are soaking!'

CHAPTER TWO

Determined not to let the boys out of his sight again, Murray marched Henry and Robert, clean and shining as he could make them make themselves, downstairs and across the entrance hall into the Great Hall for dinner.

The Great Hall stood above the kitchen in the oldest part of Scoggie Castle, and, like it, was loftily barrel-vaulted and whitewashed, with a flag floor. Paintings dotted the bare walls as if hung on nails left over from forgotten purposes, and a few panels of tapestry dangled lifelessly between the high windows, their colours long faded into drabs and greys. Murray often felt he had never eaten food in such an uncomfortable place. From March to October, there was no fire in the huge fireplace in the middle of the day, Lord Scoggie's chosen dinner time, and the draughts blew as they had blown for centuries, unimpeded from chimney to doorway to window and on mysterious routes of their own, as if the ghosts of Scoggies long gone came and whispered over the shoulders of the dinner guests. In the winter, when the fire was lit, you had the enviable choice of freezing at the edges of the room or roasting by the fire, and whichever you chose, the draughts remained as deliberately fickle as ever.

The table was the same one that had been built in the Hall when the Hall itself was new, and could have seated a regiment. The Scoggies of today electing not to eat with their entire household, those dining usually formed a small company at one end of the board, with Lord Scoggie at the head. The original benches had, fortunately for the ladies, been replaced by chairs, hard and upright, which had scraped white channels on the grey flags since the day they had been knocked together by some ambitious local chippie. Members of the family, and guests who were familiar with the room, often brought rugs for their knees, and even squares of carpet for their feet, preferring not to be crippled by rheumatism or chilblains by the end of the meal.

Today there were nine places laid at the end of the table, from Lord Scoggie's at the head to Lady Scoggie's, set last on one side rather than at the distant foot of the huge board. Murray and his charges were the first of the family to appear: alone in the room, as they came in, were the two guests, Mr. Tibo and Mr. Leckie.

As he was the family lawyer and man of business, Mr. Tibo was not an unfamiliar guest at the dinner table. His family, likewise, had been lawyers and men of business to the Scoggies for as long as the Scoggies had had any business and the Tibos had been lawyers, so Nathaniel Tibo, descendant of uncounted generations in his place, had known the dining room since he could walk, and had run out of things to interest him in it. Nevertheless, he had arranged himself in front of a painting of Lord Scoggie's mother and was studying it closely, hands crossed aloof behind his back. The painting was in oils and did not flatter the sitter, as if the artist had felt a keener interest in the late Lady Scoggie's dentistry than in her complexion. The impression was of a country matron caught for a joke in fashionable city lady's secondhand clothes. By contrast, the lawyer examining her seemed like a sharp facet of the town cut into the country. Mr. Tibo was a man in his late twenties, discreetly prosperous and delicate of manner, less cautious than careful. Though his hair, briefly dark, had greyed completely by the time he was twenty, his complexion was fresh and his appearance distinguished, and he was generally considered, not least by himself, exceedingly handsome.

Mr. Leckie was his clerk, and therefore dined less frequently in the Great Hall, though he was well designed to avoid the worst of the low-level draughts by being very short, and having to have his chair stacked with cushions to allow him to reach his dinner. Murray had, to be truthful, never observed that he suffered a deficiency in appetite equal to his deficiency of size, and had warned Robert and Henry not to eat quite so much as they usually did, though this had involved an arrangement regarding pies later in the afternoon. Nevertheless, he was pleased to see Cocky Leckie included at dinner, for the man was the most amiable, good-humoured fellow it was possible to imagine. It was rumoured that Cocky was employed by Nathaniel Tibo to go to places and talk to people that a respectable lawyer would not be expected to know, but Murray found this difficult to believe: he could see, instead, Tibo moving undefiled amongst the lower orders, picking out what he needed with gloved hands, and returning bland-faced to his more worthy clients, while Leckie would be incapable of such deception.

Murray nudged the boys into making their bows to the guests, and approved their clean appearance following their resignation from the *Discovery*. He, too, had changed into appropriate clothes for a tutor and secretary to wear at his master's table, though he wondered if something grander would be required for the arrival of Major Keyes. As if he had read his thoughts, Mr. Tibo turned from his usual polite enquiries of the boys and asked,

'And when is our great battle hero, Major Keyes, expected?'

'Tomorrow, I believe, sir,' said Murray. He nodded to the sideboard, almost the length of the dinner table. 'I see the silver is much depleted, so I expect Naismyth is giving it a final polish.'

'Mr. Naismyth is much pleased with having a hero in the house, I think,' said Leckie, setting to with a patter of leather soles on the flag floor. 'He told me all about Major Keyes and Seringapatam.'

'Aye', said Tibo, less enthusiastically. 'I overheard the bit where he captured Tippoo Sultan single-handed. I suppose Sir David Baird must have been busy elsewhere that day.'

Murray laughed.

'But Sir David Baird captured Tippoo Sultan, didn't he, Mr. Murray?' Henry was painful in his pursuit of accuracy, and Murray hardly wanted to dissuade him.

'Sir David Baird, ably assisted and supported by your cousin, Major Keyes, and quite a number of other people, captured Tippoo Sultan's body and took Seringapatam,' he said. 'Robert, where is Seringapatam?'

'Where Sir David Baird left it?' Robert chanced. At Murray's frown he tried again. 'The Leeward Islands?'

'Um,' said Cocky, and performed a complicated little dance step.

'Not quite.' Mr. Tibo looked superior, while Murray tried not to care. After all, he had never wanted to become a tutor.

'We'll deal with that particular chasm in your knowledge this afternoon, I think,' he told Robert. 'After all, if your cousin Major Keyes had the misfortune to leave a leg there, I think we should at least find it in the atlas.'

Henry, the most literal of boys, opened his mouth, no doubt to point out that Major Keyes' leg was unlikely to be in the atlas, but fortunately at that point his sister and her companion entered the room and the conversation paused, preparing to be redirected.

Deborah Scoggie entered first, as usual, and took in in the first flashing glance the right number of places at the table, the missing silver from the sideboard, and the empty hands of the guests. She half-turned, and met the eye of Beatrix Pirrie behind her.

'You were right, Bea. You always are.'

Bea, more shy than her kinswoman, gave a little smile and edged into the room. Over her arm she had two rugs in a dull plaid.

'Here,' Deborah said, seizing them. 'Mr. Tibo, Mr. Leckie: I know the invitation to dinner was late, and you wouldn't have come prepared. Slip them on to your seats – that's right, that one – and don't let Father see, you know.'

Obediently quick, Tibo took the plaids and hid them, then turned and bowed to the two girls.

At first glance they could have been sisters, and at first Murray had taken them to be so until he was corrected. Now that he knew them better, he could see the differences. Both had, in thankfully modified form, the Scoggie family teeth. Both were pale, in Deborah's case slightly pasty, in Bea's lit, on occasion, with an inner glow which few seemed to notice. She was the poor relation: Deborah was the confident, self-assured daughter of the house. Beatrix was fairer than Deborah, though they both had blue eyes, and wore their hair in a similar way, though which of them took the lead in this was probably clear.

Deborah drew her shawl around her and threw a glance at the fireplace.

'I don't suppose Father would allow ... of course he wouldn't. What am I thinking about? Mr. Murray, I'm delighted to see you found dry clothes.'

'Oh, Mr. Murray!' Beatrix murmured. 'Did your boating expedition not go as planned?'

Murray glared at her, remembering her watching at the window overlooking the pigsty. It was not a moment to admire her voice, which, after Deborah's, was pleasingly soft. Robert, however, was more disconcerted, and watched Murray carefully out of the corner of his eye. Henry charitably kicked him on the leg.

'Henry!' snapped Deborah, then saw Robert's expression. 'Ah. I think, Bea, that we have here someone who may know more about Mr. Murray's boating accident than any other.'

'Boating?' said Tibo. 'I though Lord Scoggie did not allow the boys to play by the lake.'

'He does not,' agreed Murray mildly. 'And he is sound in his judgement, when you consider how wet we can become simply by playing in the pigsty.'

'I am sure you are too kind to my brothers, Mr. Murray,' said Deborah. They were all standing rather self-consciously around near the laid end of the table, for there were no easy chairs in the Great Hall, and family custom did not decree a meeting in any other room. It was awkward for talking, as Cocky Leckie was smaller now even than Robert. Murray could feel the cold of the flags creeping up through the thin soles of his shoes. Deborah gave a little shuffle of impatience.

'Oh, where is my father gone now?'

'We are not expecting Lady Scoggie?' asked Tibo politely.

'We gave up expecting my mother long ago,' said Deborah, taking the sting out of it with a smile.

'Years,' added Robert, trying to sound world-weary. Henry poked him. 'Ow!'

'Robert,' said Murray, 'And indeed Henry.'

'Well, she's never here,' Robert said, almost as reasonably as he had hoped. 'I think I saw her yesterday, but I'm not sure.'

'She's out doing good work,' said Henry firmly.

'Why can't she do good work at home?' Robert demanded.

'Boys ...' Murray's voice was ominous.

'But why?' Robert insisted.

'One more word, Robert, and you will regret it.' Well, Murray thought to himself, if Tibo and Cocky Leckie don't know what the family is like by now, they deserve the shock. Robert shut his mouth with a sullen snap, manoeuvred himself to where he thought Murray could not see him, and began to make faces at Henry.

'I believe my mother is visiting some families down by the saltworks today.' Deborah tried to pretend nothing had happened.

'She does a great deal of very welcome charitable work,' Tibo agreed, smiling his smooth smile at her. She glowed in its warmth.

'She certainly does not spare herself,' Murray agreed. 'She works extremely hard, and does not shirk from helping in the lowliest of places.' A quick tweak to Robert's ear stopped the rude faces almost silently.

Above them, tacked to one of the white-washed walls, was what Murray thought a very good portrait of the present Lady Scoggie, painted only that year by a young local lad called Wilkie. It showed a thin-faced woman with high cheekbones and a chin that brooked no opposition. She had truly lovely dark eyes that stared directly – no misty-eyed young girl, this, but a woman who had made firm decisions concerning her life – at the humble viewer. Her hair, curled round a pale scarf, was still dark, and thick with the kind of gloss that indicates generations of wealth and good food behind it. Firm hands, thinly disguised in lace gloves, were clasped in front of her, relaxed but at the same time giving the impression of waiting. If what she had been waiting for was her first view of the portrait, Murray hoped for the artist's sake that she had liked it.

Tibo glanced up at the distant ceiling, as if seeking some further inspiration for conversation.

'The days are drawing in fast,' said Leckie, not above resorting to the obvious if no other subject presented itself. 'Major Keyes will find it chill.'

'He is not here straight from India,' Deborah said quickly. 'He has been in England, under the care of a surgeon, and then for some time helping with barrack duties, so my father says. After all, Seringapatam was years ago.'

'Indeed,' agreed Tibo, with a smug look. 'I hope he does not find the dust settled on his palm leaves.'

'Not if Mr. Naismyth has the chance to go at them with a cloth, anyway!' quipped Cocky Leckie, and the others laughed. Before a further silence had the chance to fall, the door opened, and Lord Scoggie made his appearance at the end of the Great Hall.

'Ah, Nathaniel! "Behold an Israelite indeed, in whom is no

guile"!'

'I hope not, indeed, sir,' responded Tibo with a low bow, which almost hide his fixed smile. The joke was an old one: it had even formed part of the estate bequeathed to Lord Scoggie by his father, and had seen a great deal of wear since. Lord Scoggie, beaming, advanced into the room. With his angular legs, fulsome hair and monumental teeth, he looked like a billy goat taught to walk upright for a wager, but Murray had a good deal more respect for him than his appearance seemed to merit.

'I am delighted you could stay to dinner. We can go on with our meeting afterwards. Mr. Leckie, too, you are welcome to our board. Deborah, Beatrix ...' he nodded at each of them, though he must have seen them during the morning. 'Ah, Henry, Robert. Tell me what you have been learning this morning?'

'We were Captain Cook,' Robert volunteered, with a flourish of his sword hand.

'Both of you? Well, well: Mr. Murray, I take it this was a geography lesson?'

'Principally, yes, my lord. With sideways ventures into gravity and the theory of water displacement.'

Lord Scoggie laughed.

'I take it you managed this without going near the lake?'

'Oh, yes, my lord.'

'Good, good. Now, where is our dinner?'

He took his place at the head of the table, and waited standing while everyone else went to their places. Deborah stepped to her mother's empty place and rang a large handbell that sat there, then returned to her own place, bowing her head. Lord Scoggie cleared his throat, and pronounced grace at a solemn pace that made Murray feel dinner was being unnaturally postponed. The second he had finished, the company muttered 'Amen', and were in their seats before the echo had died away. The soup appeared instantly in front of Lord Scoggie, who spooned it into pewter bowls and passed it round the table.

Kale, kale, kale, thought Murray. The soup was of the kind you could have found in the home of a peasant two hundred years before: oatmeal, kale, salt and water, boiled until grey. Mrs. Costane had probably added curses of her own making, but apart from that, Murray felt as if he was eating liquid history. It was enough to put him off the subject.

'I was hoping to see Lady Scoggie at dinner,' said Lord Scoggie after a few moments.

'She's visiting the new families at the saltworks,' said Deborah. 'She probably hasn't noticed the time.'

'Has she visited Tom Baillie's family recently, do you know?' Lord Scoggie's eyes were on his soup. Deborah looked surprised.

'I have no idea, Father. Is it important? I could ask her when she comes home.'

'No, no.' Lord Scoggie shook his heavy head quickly. 'It matters very little, very little indeed. Speaking of visiting, though: did you know that we have new neighbours?'

'New neighbours? That's exciting.' Deborah finished her soup. 'Where have they come to?'

'To Aberardour Lodge – you know, on Sir John Anstruther's land,' explained Tibo. 'Sir John is never here and his agent is in Edinburgh, so I helped with the agency. The name is Bootham: English, a couple, no family.'

'Mr. Tibo says the man is a scholar,' said Lord Scoggie with satisfaction. 'We shall enjoy their company. Mr. Murray, you might visit them at some point: Mr. Bootham will be pleased to talk with a Master of Arts.'

Murray smiled politely, used to Lord Scoggie flourishing him as an intellectual trophy.

'And his wife?' Deborah asked. 'What is she like?'

'Very pretty,' said Tibo, confident in his judgement. 'Another ornament to the parish.' Beatrix looked at him with her slow, deep eyes, but did not say anything.

Deborah glanced round the table to see if everyone had finished their soup, and reached over to ring the bell again.

'Anyway, I was hoping to ask Lady Scoggie to visit them, of course, so that everyone else can,' said Lord Scoggie. When he spoke of his wife, his tone was wistful, and a little humble. It always surprised Murray.

'Beatrix and I shall go and visit them this afternoon,' said Deborah decisively. 'That should suffice, particularly if we take Mamma's apologies. We have had a busy few days, but we're almost ready for Major Keyes coming tomorrow, aren't we, Bea? I think we have time for a little outing.' Beatrix did not look so sure, but said nothing.

'Major Keyes is to arrive in the afternoon, I think you said, Miss Scoggie?' said Tibo.

'That is when we are expecting him, yes. His room has only to have flowers put in it. We shall visit the Boothams. If we are not scholarly enough to talk to the husband, then surely between us we'll be pretty enough to talk to the wife.'

Tibo's mouth twisted a little as he nodded acknowledgement to her, not quite sure if she meant a reprimand. Murray was positive that she did.

The door from the kitchens opened, and Naismyth appeared with boiled chickens in a serving dish. Murray sighed inwardly, longing for a little variety.

There was little variety down in the howff by the harbour, either, but on the whole the customers were more concerned about the quality – the chicken over which they were picking in the dregs of the broth served by the landlord's wife was, to say the least, athletic. Joe Baillie had expressed several opinions about it already, but his plate was cleared and he wiped round it a heel of hard bread, which he then chewed viciously. The other fishermen around him nodded obediently each time he spoke, but ate with silent enthusiasm. The wonder was that they could taste the broth at all, for the room was thick with pipe smoke intensified over several hours of dedicated smoking, and with an equally thick air of discontent.

Joe Baillie finished his bread, spat a last piece of bone from his wet lips, and leaned back, wiping his hands through his lead-grey hair. His face was weathered as rough as the skin of a dogfish, his eyes pale, brows dark and permanently rippled like sand after high tide. The others finished their broth hurriedly, one eye on him. He, on the other hand, was staring out of the low window at the harbour, and the boats scraping idly against the walls. The narrow street between was empty, everyone at their dinner.

'Aye, a fine day for the fishing,' Joe remarked, and the others nodded, reaching for their pipes again. There was no novelty in the statement. Joe alone had said the same thing round about once an hour since dawn, when they had all met by the harbour, when the day had been lost in a moment. A few seconds later the howff's great brown clock, too large for the wall, struck the same measure of time. Now that dinner was over, one or two of the fishermen looked uneasy, as if they felt they had spent enough of the day in respectful communion and could well find things to do at home. Joe, however, did not show any sign of moving from his bench, and gradually the others settled again, like yawls coming reluctantly into harbour.

It was mostly the older fishermen here in the howff, the year-round men who took the small boats out, summer and winter, four men and a helmsman, for the white fish, with lines for cod and haddock, or nets for skate. Some, the loners, or the odd men out, took the yawls out in summer for red ware cod in the rocky waters around the coast, on their own or with a boy to help and learn the skill. The younger men, newly back from the whaling, had spent the morning draped about the harbour, scuffing their toes, staring at the sea and the empty boats in the harbour, no doubt also remarking on the fineness of the day. Men who had hurried back to their home village from the slow vastness of the ocean, and the enormity of the rich whale harvest and the racked barrels of sweet oil, for the rush of the herring season, were not going to wait patiently. Now that dinner was over, one or two had gone to inspect the seaweed or to stare speculatively at the saltworks, or find girls to talk to, carefully avoiding the score of big herring boats. The few young fishermen reappearing at the harbour now, as the new smoke permeated the stale fug of the howff, stared at the sky as if willing dusk to come and allow them to go home honourably.

The howff was silent, except for the occasional suck or spit or shuffle. Joe's brother, sitting by the fire, stretched one leg out and wriggled his back, but he was allowed a special dispensation for such obvious movement. Joe looked over at him and met his eye comfortably.

Richie Shaw, bald as a seagull's egg, expelled a long channel of smoke and stared at the fire.

'Aye, my lass brought us a piece of news on the Sabbath.'

No immediate reaction came, but Richie's expression showed no anxiety. There was no rush on a day like this. Eventually Joe licensed the conversation himself.

'She'll be marrying soon, that lass.'

'It's no that.' Richie was emboldened. 'It's worse. She says Major Keyes is expected up at the Castle.'

If the room had been quiet before, it was holding its breath now. Joe was motionless, and no one else dared move before he did. It was only when the innkeeper's wife hurried in to collect the dishes that the spell was broken, and several of the fishermen set to to relight their pipes.

'Major Keyes, eh?' Joe met his brother's eye again, but this time his look was more calculating. Tom Baillie himself stayed calm, but raised his eyebrows as if asking his brother what he was going to do about it. Joe looked as if he had his plans, but was not going to air them there.

'We can't just let him walk back down here and expect to be welcomed,' said Richie Shaw, after watching the Baillies for a moment.

'He cannot walk down here that easily himself, I hear,' said Hugh Farquhar, trying to make it sound offhand. He rubbed at some fresh-looking scratches on his face. 'You'll have heard about Seringapatam.'

'Aye, well, it's you that does the reading, Hughie,' said Joe Baillie, as if Seringapatam could only exist on paper. 'You say he's lost a leg, but I doubt that would stop a man like him.'

'He's a gentleman,' added Richie, with a fine lining of spite to his words. 'He could probably have himself carried down here.'

'And why would he do that?' asked Hugh, cross that his contribution had been dismissed. 'He's a great hero now, with freedoms of this city and that, and no doubt a great fortune, and a fine pension, and maybe a grand wealthy wife, for all we know to the contrary. What in the Lord's name would bring him down to this wee back end of a place?'

'A grand wealthy wife?' asked Joe. The tone of his voice was warning enough. Hugh, who was not a powerful man, shrank into his seat. 'What could we tell a grand wealthy wife, then, about her new hero of a husband with his freedoms of the city? Would it be worth his fortune? Would it be worth his fine pension?'

'You're no saying we threaten him for money, Joe,' said Tom Baillie softly, cutting under his brother's rising voice. Joe drew breath, then caught Tom's eye once again.

'Ach!' said Joe, frustrated.

Richie grunted, and drew his pipe from his mouth to make an

apologetic gesture in the air.

'He's no married,' he said. 'My wee lassie wonders if he's to marry Miss Scoggie.'

'That would put Nathaniel Tibo's nose out of joint,' Hugh put in.

'Keyes doesn't deserve her,' said Joe definitely, then reflected. 'Though if she grows up like her mother, maybe it would be punishment enough. That woman has a nose on her the size of the kirk spire, and she's forever poking it into other people's business.'

'She been round again, then, Joe?'

Tom replied for his brother.

'Aye, she came round with some vegetables and a loaf of bread yesterday morning. She's very kind.'

Joe spat, and Tom smiled at him. When he smiled, his weariness showed through.

'Here's Mally,' Richie remarked, seeing a figure pass the tiny window. 'He's a bit late for his dinner.'

The door of the howff shot open, and Mally filled the doorway, enormous, shoulders bulging, arms at his sides like the claws of a lobster. He wore an apron, at first a pale blur as their eyes grew accustomed to his outline against the light. Then, as they focussed on it, they gasped with a collective hiss.

Mally stepped into the room, black hair brushing the ceiling, a rag tied hard around his unshaved neck, sleeves rolled high over his bristly biceps. His hands were vast, muscular, each big enough to encircle a man's throat. He stepped over to the fire, and nodded a greeting to Tom Baillie. In the firelight, everyone could see. His apron dripped with blood.

'Aye, Mally,' said Joe, his voice for once uncertain.

'Aye, Joe,' Mally said, a laugh in his deep voice. 'I've sorted it. We're fishing in the morning.'

CHAPTER THREE

Whatever business Lord Scoggie had with his lawyer and his lawyer's man – and it did not have to be anything very important for Lord Scoggie to treat it like matters of state – was lengthy enough to warrant continuation after dinner. This meant that they would all be in the library, which was where Murray had hoped to pursue undisturbed the other side of his work at Scoggie Castle. Though Lord Scoggie assured him that he would not be disturbing them, Murray preferred, privately, to see the situation the other way around. Apart from Lord Scoggie's cawing voice, he had found something oddly unsettling when he had previously worked in the library during one of his Lordship's meetings with Nathaniel Tibo. The family papers, which Murray was dusting, arranging, and cataloguing, consisted to a very great degree of correspondence involving generations of Lords Scoggie, dealing, in neat succession, with as long a pedigree of Messrs. Tibo. Murray could not avoid the impression that he was part of a large automated manufacturing machine, into which the present Lord Scoggie and the present Mr. Tibo, patterns for their own descendants, poured paper and ink at one end of the library, while he sorted and batched the finished product at the other end, like so many bales of cloth. Some of the documents had been written by Tibos and signed by Scoggies when Queen Mary was a girl, and Murray wondered if the machine would ever stop.

However, the day was still moderately fine, and he had a conviction that Robert had not suffered enough for his misdeeds of the morning. He took both boys back upstairs to change into outdoor clothes again, and led them out to the front of the house equipped with sketchbooks and chalks.

'Oh, not *drawing*,' moaned Robert. 'I'm not doing *drawing*. Deborah and Bea do *drawing*.'

'Yes, they do, and very well, too,' Murray agreed. 'But I'm not asking you to do drawing. This is engineering – and architecture.'

'Oh!' Robert looked more interested. Henry had been politely attentive all day.

'You're each going to draw the front of the house, paying great attention to each stone, and working out how the important ones, like lintels over the windows, might have been cut and built in. I want you to label your drawings with all the architectural terms you know. Then we'll see what you're going to do next.'

While they settled down and made a start on their sketches, Murray wondered what they were going to do next. He had had no idea, when he came to work for Lord Scoggie, that he would be required to tutor his sons, and the idea had filled him with a raging panic he had never previously felt. Now, over a year later, he was still surviving on a mixture of impulse, his own interests, and what he remembered learning at the High School in Edinburgh. The last had consisted mainly of how to parse Latin and avoid beatings. Occasionally the lessons were bounced along by the boys' own current interests, as in the case of what was supposed to have been a geography lesson that morning based on Captain Cook's last voyage. Sometimes he liked the boys, particularly Henry: often he came perilously close to loathing them. However, he had no choice, at present, in his career, but to face poverty and homelessness, or to stay here, obey his fairly reasonable employer, enjoy the parts of his work he could enjoy, and pray for the day when Henry and Robert would be packed off to university. Unlike many tutors, he had no intention of escorting them.

He glanced over their shoulders now and again. Robert's drawing was a fair representation of the front of Scoggie Castle, but he was going to have difficulty in fitting in all the details required. Henry, his attention drawn to the window lintels, had begun with one of those and branched out from it in painfully accurate little chalk lines, but he would be lucky if he fitted much more than the one window on the page. Still, so far they were both concentrating hard and seemed to be enjoying the challenge. Murray found he was holding his breath, and stopped.

The breeze lifted a little, and blew an echo of Lord Scoggie's voice to them from the library. Good heavens, thought Murray, the man must have the window open. Tibo and Leckie would have to be chipped off their seats like ice off a lake at this rate. From here in front of the house you could see the lake, a broken slice of sky lying at the foot of the hill with woodland beyond it, and a few trees to this side. Sheep grazed the park smooth; they were the closest thing Lord Scoggie had to ornamental gardeners, and the only flowers visible were a few late daisies the sheep had missed. What happened in the kitchen garden was closer to farming, as Lord Scoggie declined to find any vegetable good that had not come out of his own soil. Murray sighed at the thought. Another year of kale every day and he felt he might start to frill at the edges.

The dusk was hardly drawing in, but the day was turning colder. Murray looked again at the boys' work.

'My hands are blue,' said Robert, more out of curiosity than complaint.

'Yes. I think we'll go in, now. Have you finished?'

'Nowhere near, sir,' said Henry, concerned. He had outlined the facade of the castle to fit just within the edge of the paper, and was scrupulously drawing stones to fill it. He had a long way to go. Robert announced that he had completed his.

'Very good, Robert, an accurate basic shape. The doorway is quite fine, too. What about the top window in the left tower, though?'

'The what, sir?' Robert looked blank.

'You left out a window.' Murray pointed upwards.

'Oh, it's only Bea's room. It's not important,' Robert decided.

'It's important to Bea. But you can draw it in when we go back indoors. Pack up your chalks, and we'll see if we can find a fire lit somewhere.'

'And cocoa?' asked Robert, flexing his blue fingers ostentatiously.

'And cocoa. And maybe,' said Murray, with a rush of benevolence, 'those pies I mentioned before dinner.'

As the boys packed up with enthusiasm, Murray heard the front door open, and looked up to see Nathaniel Tibo and Cocky Leckie emerge from the house, their meeting finally over. Cocky skipped over to them.

'Drawings, lads? May I see?'

The boys proudly showed off their work, forgetting their cold hands. Cocky found good in both pictures and praised them, while Murray and Tibo looked on, Tibo's mouth twisted into a little smile that did not quite stretch to his eyes. Murray found himself wondering if Tibo actually had any affection for the Scoggie family at all. Then he realised that, as usual, Tibo knew he was being watched, and Murray looked away, embarrassed.

'Mr. Leckie,' said Robert, emboldened by the little man's friendliness, 'have you heard that Parry the Pugilistic Chanticleer is to come to Elie?'

'Is he? Is he indeed?' Murray was sure Leckie had already heard the news, but he was giving Robert his moment of glory in telling him. 'Is he here to give an exhibition?'

'I think so,' said Robert very seriously. He folded his hands behind his back in the way his father often did, and straightened up. 'I heard that he was supposed to have been fighting Jem Belcher, but he won't fight now he's lost an eye.'

'Very true, and sensible of him, for it is hard to judge distances with only the one eye,' agreed Leckie. Belcher's eye had been knocked out over a year ago, when the Pugilistic Chanticleer had never been heard of. As far as Murray could judge, he would not have been heard of now, for he was not in the first rank of pugilists, except for his habit of beginning and, if the fates spared him, ending each bout with a song of his own composition. A little way away, he saw Henry thoughtfully cover one eye with his hand, and stare about him at the nearest trees, head on one side.

'We want Father to let us go to see him,' Robert explained, more interested in action, and in the chance to gather allies for his argument. 'He's famous. Famous people don't come here very much.'

'That at least is true,' said Tibo with a smile. 'One can only wonder what has driven the mighty Parry to a backwater like Elie. And is Lord Scoggie disposed to allow you this outing?' His smile deepened as Robert's face fell.

'We haven't asked him yet. And Mr. Murray says he probably won't let us. Father thinks pugilism isn't for gentlemen, but lots of gentlemen in London do it. I bet Major Keyes does it, even with his wooden leg. Even Mr. Murray did it, years ago, when he was young.'

'Well, we can but put these telling arguments to your father, and see what happens,' said Murray, suddenly feeling ancient. He was not at all averse himself to seeing Parry perform: as Robert said, famous people, even mildly famous people, rarely came to any of the East Neuk villages, and Elie was not far off. He had not fought since he left university. He wondered if the boys were more likely to be allowed to go to a public exhibition or to a private lesson, and if the latter, if he was fit enough to take a lesson himself. The topic began to interest him, and he felt his hands twitch into half-fists, ready to do battle. Even if the boys were not allowed to go, would Lord Scoggie object if he himself went?

'Ah, the ladies,' said Tibo suddenly, as if it had been what he was waiting for. At the door appeared Beatrix, dressed as she had been at dinner but with a warm blue pelisse and bonnet and grey gloves, and

Deborah, in a different dress, a rather dramatic cloak and a bonnet Murray had not seen before but which was probably an old one retrimmed yet again. Her hands were hidden in a stylish muff, but she drew one out to wave at them.

'We really must go in, boys, and see if we can find that fire before you freeze,' said Murray. 'Say goodbye to Mr. Tibo and Mr. Leckie.'

The boys made the kind of bows that Murray hoped a dancing master would soon improve, retrieved their drawings from Leckie, and scuttled off towards the house. Murray made his own farewells, and followed more slowly, in order to great Bea and Deborah before they set out.

'Where are you off to?' he asked, smiling at Bea.

'To make our visit to the new neighbours, if Mr. Tibo will remind us of their name,' said Deborah abruptly.

'I shall do better than that: I shall escort you to their very gate,' said Tibo gallantly.

'The name would be more immediately practical, Mr. Tibo,' said Deborah, but softened it with a smile.

'Mr. and Mrs. Bootham. From somewhere in England, I believe.'

'It is such a lovely day for a walk, and we have had rain for so many days it seemed a shame to spend yet another afternoon imprisoned indoors with mending and letters,' said Beatrix, with her own, softer smile. Murray loved her clear skin and bright eyes, but each time he met her gaze it seemed to flicker away to Deborah and what she was doing or saying.

'And preparation for Major Keyes, of course,' Deborah added. 'We are looking forward to a pleasant stroll and an afternoon making new friends and new discoveries. Mr. Murray, my father said to tell you that the library is empty now, if you wish to carry on with the papers, but I should warn you that there is no fire laid and my father has had the windows open all through his meeting with poor Mr. Tibo and Mr. Leckie. There is a fire laid in the school room.' If her mother's constant absences had done nothing else, they had made a brisk and determined housekeeper of Deborah Scoggie. Murray bowed his acknowledgement of the information and of the dismissal that seemed to be included in the words. As he moved away, he heard her continue. 'Well, then, Mr. Tibo, let us make our merry way to see Mr. and Mrs. Bootham of Aberardour Lodge.'

Tibo confidently offered her his arm which she took as though it was to be of purely practical value. Mr. Leckie, not tall enough to offer the same service to Beatrix, fell into friendly step beside her behind his master.

The drive was not a long one, and they were soon out into the lane that led to the village. The late autumnal sun toasted the stone walls to a warm gold on either side, and the mud of the track was firm and walkable under foot, though both girls wore sensible boots for walking. The lane lay between cow pastures on one side and bare tilled soil on the other, and in the next field Bea could see little clouds of birds following the sowers at work on the wheat. Here a beech tree had begun to spill an amber pool across the lane, and there a lone hawthorn, crinkled and grasping, hunched against the prevailing sea wind, clinging on to a few late dusty leaves and blackened haws. There was a chill in the air, but the light could make you believe you were warm, and after a few minutes' walking they were, rosy-cheeked and glowing inside their warm winter clothes. Above it all, the high Fife sky glistened with sunlight, an unbelievable blue, just turning to grey at the horizon.

Before they reached the gate to Aberardour Lodge they had to pass one or two cottages, inland strays from the village itself which lay chiefly down the steep hill to the harbour. These first cottages belonged to weavers, and as they approached they heard the thump and rattle of the looms and smelled the wool on the thin air. The weaver at the first cottage, though, was not at his work: he was propped against the wall between his cottage and the bare field beyond, passing the time of day with one of the sowers as he reached the field's corner and emptied his pouch of seed. They were all a little acquainted, as people in a small place are likely to be, and Deborah stopped for a moment, taking the opportunity to release Tibo's arm.

'Mr. Kinkell,' whispered Beatrix from behind her. 'Son's in service.'

'Hello – it's Mr. Kinkell, isn't it?' Deborah called. 'How are you? And your family?'

'Miss Scoggie,' said the man, pushing himself away from the wall and straightening his waistcoat, which was his outermost garment. 'Thank you for asking, Miss: we're all as well as can be expected, praise the Lord. You see young Peter here,' he nodded to a bench at his front door, where young Peter, a man of around twenty, sat taking in the sun on his broad, happy face. Bea remembered hearing that he had never been quite right in the head. 'The wife's not so good, now, but she says she's comfortable.' He gave a little smile and a nod, as if the situation was quite satisfactory. Miss Deborah frowned.

'Has my mother been to see her?' she asked sharply. 'I had not heard that there was illness in the house.'

'Oh, no, Miss, but never fret. We're managing very nicely, and Bessie Smith next door does us a grand dinner when we cannot see our way to one ourselves.'

'And has the minister been to see you?' persisted Deborah.

'Oh, aye, Miss. He's been a few times. He's a grand man for the visiting.'

Deborah looked at Beatrix. Beatrix was perplexed. It was rare for Lady Scoggie to miss visiting any house in the village or its environs on any pretext, but sickness certainly attracted her attention. And if the minister knew of it, then Lady Scoggie would know, for the two worked as a team – the minister was young and unmarried, and could not have stood up to Lady Scoggie's legendary charity even if he had wanted to. Beatrix made a mental note to mention the Kinkells to Lady Scoggie when she saw her.

Beatrix hoped, for the sake of the village, that Mrs. Kinkell's illness was nothing infectious. Behind her, she could sense Mr. Tibo twitching with impatience: the poor bored him excessively, and she doubted he had even glanced at Kinkell since they had arrived at the cottage. Deborah was hesitating. Beatrix wondered if Mrs. Kinkell would hear them standing out here discussing her, and if so, was she wishing that they would come in or praying that they would stay outside and leave her in peace, to force her to make the effort to be polite and grateful. She wanted to do something now, to go in and see the poor woman and find out if there was anything to be done for her improvement or comfort, but she could sense that Deborah did not want to go. Deborah was wearing her best afternoon dress, and was intent on meeting new and pleasant neighbours, not trying to help old poor ones, and she could be right. Beatrix wrestled briefly with her uncertain conscience. It would be better to come back tomorrow with some soup and some medicine, and do the job properly. Anyway, it was not up to her to decide: that was Deborah's place, and Deborah had decided.

'I shall let my mother know your wife is unwell, Mr. Kinkell. I do hope she feels better soon. And your other son – in service, isn't he?'

'That's right. We haven't seen him for a bit, now, but we expect to soon, Miss.' He beamed again, showing two neat rows of even teeth. He was a handsome man, Beatrix thought, though his skin was pale from indoor work.

'We must be going,' Deborah went on. 'My mother will no doubt call soon.'

'Good day to you, Miss Scoggie. Thank you, thank you.' He went on smiling as they passed by, so that you would have thought his only feeling was warm gratitude. But Beatrix had an odd feeling that there was more to Mr. Kinkell than met the eye, and when she turned, irresistibly, to look back at him, there was a look on his face that, try as she might, she could not put a name to.

Mr. Tibo was as good as his word, and saw them to the very gate of Aberardour Lodge, a leafy entrance some distance from the weavers' cottages. Beatrix could see Deborah's relief even as the lawyer and his man bade them goodbye – no doubt she had dreaded that Mr. Tibo would decide to visit at the same time, thus linking his name with hers in the eyes of the newcomers. Beatrix laughed to herself. Deborah was very pretty, but it often caused her more trouble than it seemed to bring her benefits. Beatrix was pleased, she told herself, that no one found her at all pretty. It made life so much more simple.

After Scoggie Castle and the brisk chill of the walk along the lane, it had to be said that the Boothams' new home was at least warm. The drawing room, though small and awkwardly shaped, was glowing with a bright fire; the windows were thickly curtained and a carpet covered the floor, so luxurious that for a moment Beatrix, country girl that she was, thought she had stepped into a bog. The colours, after the faded grandeur of the Castle, were intense: new curtains and upholstery, new marquetry like rainbows in woodwork dazzled the eye. Little lamps here and there chased the October shadows, and pretty shawls were draped across the backs of chairs. Paintings, almost all landscapes, were arranged tastefully on the walls and another stood on a little easel on a table, as if for closer study. Other tables held *objets* and conversation pieces, inviting examination, asking to be touched and lifted and talked about. On the mantelpiece, pastille burners seeped sweet perfume into the air, making it feel heavy, like summer. It was all so unusual and interesting that that awkward feeling that Beatrix felt amongst strangers was altogether dispelled.

The Boothams were both taking advantage of the cosy room, with books and papers scattered about them and some lacework on a cushion. Nevertheless they rose quickly when Miss Scoggie and Miss Pirrie were shown in. Mr. Bootham stood aside as his wife hurried forward to greet them warmly.

'I am here on behalf of my mother, Lady Scoggie,' Deborah explained, sounding much less apologetic than she had over the dinner table. 'Welcome to St. Monance: it is a real delight to see new faces in the neighbourhood.'

'We feel at home already,' Mrs. Bootham assured her. 'Will you have some tea? We are about to have some.'

'That would be lovely.' Deborah established herself with elegance on a low sofa, and Beatrix sat beside her. Mr. Bootham watched them both with approval as he again leaned back into his shady seat near the fire, and his wife leaned over to tug on the bell rope. 'Do you find the house quite comfortable? Is there anything you need? Sir John is rarely here, you know.'

'Yes, the agent warned us. No, I cannot think of anything – we are perfectly comfortable, as you see.'

They certainly looked it. Mrs. Bootham's white cheeks were rosy from the fire, and her hazel eyes were bright with reflected flames. Her gown, as fashionably cut as the latest Paris fashion plate, floated as she moved, and an airy paisley shawl was draped across her shoulders. She was small and slim, and graceful, with a face like some magical woodland creature. Her dark hair curled about her pale brow and cheeks. Beatrix thought that Mr. Tibo's dismissal of 'very pretty' was not in the least fair.

'You have certainly cheered the old place.' Deborah looked about her critically. The walls had been papered, and the furniture and curtains were not Sir John's old tat. 'You'll know it was without a tenant for some time.'

'I cannot imagine why! It seems quite charming!' Her English accent drew out the last word in a musical swoop which in anyone else would have been quite irritating, but in her was delightful. Deborah's lips tightened a little, Bea noticed.

'You do not find it at all impractical? Other tenants, I believe, have found this room very awkward for fitting furniture, and the cellars are known for being rather damp.'

Mrs. Bootham laughed.

'You are very kind to warn us of these faults, but as you can see, we have managed our furniture quite well. As to the cellars, I believe the maid did mention something about them, but I am sure we shall cope very well.'

'I'm sure you will. And when you see Scoggie Castle, I assure you, this place will seem even more delightful!' Deborah relented, though Beatrix guessed she would come back to the subject later, when they were alone. 'How long are you hoping to stay in the area?'

Mrs. Bootham looked to her husband.

'For some time, I believe: some time.' Mr. Bootham's light voice came out of the shadows.

'Does it differ greatly from your previous home?' Beatrix asked, when it seemed that Mr. Bootham was not to be more forthcoming.

'The house is rather smaller. The landscape, too, is more – inspiring.'

Beatrix wondered where on earth they could have been, but left the question.

'Yes, indeed, Miss Scoggie and I often paint and draw in the park or by the shore. If you are so inclined, I am sure Lord Scoggie would not mind you doing the same.'

Mrs. Bootham glanced again at her husband, this time with what Beatrix thought was anxiety. It was hard to see his face, and anyway, when Mrs. Bootham's face was in the light it was hard to resist watching only her.

'That would be delightful. I, indeed, would be very happy to take up my pen and paper again in this countryside.'

'And how do you occupy your time, Mr. Bootham?' Deborah asked.

'In reading, of course, and in contemplation, and if I am fortunate, in a little writing.'

'You are an author?' Beatrix was thrilled.

'A poet,' he replied, and leaned forward suddenly into the light.

She found it hard not to gasp. Hair the colour of white corn, dark brows and lashes, and eyes of the darkest brown, offset a head as perfectly carved as a statue, with strong chin, high cheekbones, and a high forehead as smooth as marble. It took a second to realised that he was rather older than his wife: it hardly showed, even in his pale, perfect hands, or the firm line of his lips. Only a little loosening round the eyes betrayed him. Beatrix found herself staring, and looked away, back at Mrs. Bootham. They were an extraordinary couple.

The tea arrived, perfectly timed to distract them, and with it muffins, caraway cake, tasty little rout cakes with fruit in them, and bought iced biscuits of a sophistication rarely seen in St. Monance.

'We brought several boxes with us,' Mrs. Bootham explained. 'They are Mr. Bootham's favourites.'

Mr. Bootham, however, did not indulge, but watched with veiled eyes as the girls nibbled at theirs. His abstinence seemed to make Mrs. Bootham nervous.

'And – and is it a large family, at Scoggie Castle?' she asked, dabbing at crumbs on her plate.

'No, not really,' Deborah replied. 'My father and mother, my two younger brothers, Henry and Robert, and my cousin Beatrix here, and me. Though soon we shall be joined by another cousin, Major Keyes of Seringapatam – you have probably heard of him?'

'Oh, yes!' said Mrs. Bootham. 'He was terribly heroic, was he not? He and General Baird and Mr. Wellesley between them.'

'And rather marvellous treasure brought back, I seem to remember,' added Mr. Bootham smoothly. 'I published a sonnet at the time, on the theme of exiled beauty captured in the coldness of the English winter.'

'How wonderful! May we be permitted to hear it some time?' Beatrix found herself saying.

'Oh,' said Mr. Bootham, politely surprised. 'Would that kind of thing be appreciated hereabouts?'

Deborah laughed.

'It certainly would – at Scoggie Castle, anyway. I can't vouch for anywhere else in the neighbourhood, but my father in particular appreciates scholarly endeavours of all kinds. And we have a very clever tutor for the boys – my father's secretary. He's a graduate of St. Andrews University.'

'St. Andrews – oh, yes: that's quite near here, isn't it? I was at Oxford, myself.'

'Well, of course, we can know little about these places,' said Beatrix, diplomatically. 'Do you come from a scholarly family too, Mrs. Bootham?'

Mrs. Bootham smiled.

'Oh, not particularly, Miss Pirrie. But many of my father's friends are very clever, and the conversations at home were often very entertaining and witty.'

'And where is home, Mrs. Bootham?' asked Deborah, but at that the door opened. The maid who had admitted them earlier appeared and curtseyed. As Deborah and Beatrix had noticed to their surprise earlier, she was dressed entirely in white, though her apron now had smudges of food on it.

'Excuse me, ma'am,' she said, speaking very clearly in her local accent. 'The cook wants to know if you will kindly tell her what you will be wanting for dinner today.'

'What? Again?' Mrs. Bootham looked annoyed.

'It wants but two hours to your appointed dinner time,' said the maid. The edge to her voice was not reflected in her obediently blank face. 'The cook needs to know what you wish to eat, ma'am.'

Beatrix and Deborah looked quickly at each other. Mrs. Bootham fluttered her hands amongst the trails of her shawl.

'Oh, Mr. Bootham, what shall – what – do you have any preferences, my love?'

Mr. Bootham pressed the tips of his fingers together, and half-closed his eyes.

'Let us have simple food,' he spoke after a moment. 'Such food as the humble draw towards them in wooden dishes, when they return from the honest toil of their fields and hedges. Nourishing, health-giving, and filled only with such meat and vegetables as grow within the lands around us.'

Mrs. Bootham clapped her hands.

'The very thing! Miss Scoggie, what passes for food in these parts?'

'Brose,' said Miss Scoggie, with no hesitation.

'With kale,' added Beatrix, who felt that she had some claim to authority on the subject.

'Then tell the cook that that is what we shall have. Brose – yes? Brose, and kale. How wonderful!' To Beatrix' astonishment, she had tears in her eyes. Mr. Bootham nodded in approval.

'Brose, ma'am, and kale.' The maid's expressionless face gave nothing away for a long moment. She repeated it, more slowly. 'Brose and kale.' A look of astonishment crept from her eyes to her mouth, and it twisted, despite her best efforts. Mrs. Bootham frowned.

'Do you doubt these ladies?'

'No, ma'am. There is no doubt that the workers in the fields around us usually dine on brose and kale.'

'I am delighted to receive your approval. Now, go and tell the cook.'

The maid left the room, and Beatrix thought she heard a snort as the door closed. Mrs. Bootham looked about her with satisfaction.

'Brose and kale,' she repeated, feeling the unfamiliar words on her lips. 'Brose and kale. And what may we expect from these local delights, Miss Scoggie?'

'A kind of barley broth,' said Deborah impassively, 'and kale is a green vegetable, cut and boiled.'

'And will you be good enough to stay and enjoy our humble meal with us?'

'We should be most honoured,' Mr. Bootham added.

'I fear,' said Miss Scoggie slowly, not particularly wishing to admit to being of so unfashionable a household, 'we have already dined. My father prefers to dine in the middle of the day – so old-style, I know!'

'In the middle of the day? Indeed!' said Mr. Bootham. 'I am surprised. But we must accustom ourselves to these curious ways, my dear, now that we have settled here.'

'A little like moving abroad, is it not?' said his wife, excitely. 'What is Italy, compared with Fifeshire?'

'Perhaps a little warmer. My dear, your shawl.' Mr. Bootham rose in a smooth movement from his seat, and bent to rearrange his wife's pretty shawl with a tender gesture, which finished with a finger running across her pure, pale cheekbone.

'We must be going, I'm afraid,' said Deborah, clearly feeling a little awkward. 'Beatrix, don't you think so?'

'Oh ... yes, we must. And with Major Keyes arriving tomorrow, we still have so much to do, don't we?'

'He arrives tomorrow?' Mr. Bootham turned quickly.

'You must call and meet our tame hero!' said Deborah lightly, rising from her sofa.

'We shall be honoured, indeed,' said Mr. Bootham. Mrs. Bootham had her eyes on her husband's face, and said nothing, smiling faintly. 'Let us show you to the door, then, if you feel you must leave, ladies.'

He led his wife by the hand so that she stood, and followed her into the hallway. Miss Scoggie and Miss Pirrie adjusted their bonnets and drew on their gloves. Outside it was growing towards dusk. Mrs. Bootham shivered, and tugged at her shawl. Mr. Bootham gave the trees about the drive a distant look, as though he saw things there that no one else did. Then he turned back to them.

'Goodbye, then, ladies: we look forward to seeing you again soon.' He bowed over Beatrix' hand, looked up, and met her eye. After a second, he smiled, and she would have sworn that every ounce of blood in her body froze and melted again in the same instant. If Deborah had not slipped an arm through hers and led her off in her usual way, Beatrix did not know if she could have left the drive at all. Behind them, the Boothams stood at the doorway, waving as their first guests disappeared amongst the trees.

CHAPTER FOUR

Scoggie Castle had been a double tower house with a curtain wall to join the towers, extended once to the rear to house the Great Hall and kitchens, then again later to house such peacetime frivolities as the drawing rooms, schoolroom and extra bedchambers. Lady Scoggie and the girls slept in the ancient Lady's Tower, chambers one above the other like drawers in a tallboy. Murray and the boys slept by the schoolroom, and Lord Scoggie retired at night to the Lord's Tower, the eastmost, with its views of lake and woods and, distantly, the sea. His Lordship's room was on the second floor. Beneath it was the library. At Scoggie Castle, the library was the room which received all the attention Lord Scoggie knew how to lavish.

It was probably the largest room in the castle, after the Great Hall. The afternoon sunlight, glancing off the lake and filtered through fine trees, lit it through windows on two levels in broad bays. It filled two floors of the large east tower, the upper floor accessible from a gallery off the main staircase and also by long, unstable ladders from the ground floor. The ceiling, creamy from years of smoke from the uncertain chimney, was a dim dome. The floor was stone, polished with age and use, with a few turkey carpets scattered about as thin concessions to a weaker age. There were two long, broad tables, lying parallel to each other in the centre of the room. The walls were thick with books, collected and cared for by generations of Scoggies, who had always had a bookish disposition – young Henry was clearly destined to inherit it himself. Winking with faded gold letters, volumes of sermons looked down, with instructive books on agriculture and estate management, atlases and travel accounts, collections of military tactics, Greek, Latin and Hebrew works familiar from Lord Scoggie's time at St. Andrews and Murray's own years there, devotional diaries kept by widows and unmarried sisters, poetry and novels, new, crisp leather bindings or old soft ones, pale with age, that left tan dust over hands and cuffs. Murray had sorted out some books for the boys and arranged them on a lower shelf to try to deter them from using the ladders, unsuccessfully, but they enjoyed nonetheless Cook's voyages, selected passages from Henry Fielding and Oliver Goldsmith, and even poetry by Burns and Fergusson. On a waist-high ledge between bookshelves lay unbound volumes, either stripped by Murray for rebinding or brought home impatiently by Lord Scoggie from the bookseller to be read before they ever saw a binding. The air was thick with the dust of paper and leather, polished wood and old smoke, sunlight and firelight.

Murray had hit a period of poverty at university, and had been forced to sell some of his own books. Before that, he had thought, if he had thought at all, that books had to be owned before they could be loved. Then he realised that being among books is the true joy, not the coveting and the buying and the binding for oneself. He loved to work in the library, in its lofty peace, finding new treasures or meeting old friends. His favourite time was when the family was out and the household was quiet. Then he would climb a ladder, or go up into the gallery, and, perched in the dim heights of the silent room, would look about him, fingering the spines, sliding out something unfamiliar to examine its contents and touch the crinkled surface of coloured plates, refreshing by-heart memories of passages he loved. In the midst of the traumas of living in someone else's household, not to mention tutoring, the library was his refuge and his consolation.

It was also the business room where he carried out two-thirds of his duties for Lord Scoggie, when he could. The first task was the updating of the vast volumes of library catalogue, begun nearly a hundred years ago when the Lord Scoggie of the time had evidently felt that with Jacobite uprisings occurring around him, some notion of the contents of his library was an urgent consideration. The catalogues had been kept with varying degrees of enthusiasm since, from the meticulous son of the Lord Scoggie who had started it, who had recorded title, author, price, binding, chapter headings and any damage or marks in a book, as well as its place on the shelves, to the present incumbent who was so excited by the acquisition of a new volume that the tedious task of recording its arrival was usually forgotten altogether. These huge volumes lay on one of the large library tables, along with a few of the books currently being checked and identified by Murray, before he made a new entry or amended an old one in neat black ink.

Beside this table, perfectly placed to trip up passersby, were a number of black deed boxes of different shapes and sizes. This formed the raw material for Murray's other task, the sorting-out and listing of their contents, the family documents generated by the Scoggies, their correspondents, transactions and estate business, for the past four hundred years. In recent years Lord Scoggie had conceived the notion that he could lay a legal claim to the Marquisate of Ballavore, and when he had tried to present papers to prove it, he had discovered the alarming disorder in the deed boxes, which had not received much attention beyond an occasional shake in the whole course of their history. He had gathered all the boxes he could find about the castle and brought them into the library – a mistake, as it turned out, for several of the boxes had found permanent homes in the stables and for a long time added significantly to the otherwise pleasant smells in the library. A corner had rusted off one box, and Murray had been a little surprised one morning to pick up the next bundle of papers and find that he had disturbed a mouse-mother and her brood, snugly established underneath in a nest of sixteenth-century conveyances.

To Murray's mind, the Marquisate of Ballavore was scarcely worth claiming. The first Marquis had acquired the title pretty much by accident, stopping a sword intended for King Charles II by the simple expedient of hitting the assassin with a door that he had mistakenly opened in search of a privy. Despite his unseemly haste in accepting the King's thanks on the spot, the Marquisate followed quickly, which was probably fortunate before the King could reconsider. The second

Marquis led an unadventurous life, farming incompetently in Perthshire and fathering a series of clever daughters who had spent their lives orchestrating the careers of their husbands. The third Marquis, his father's only son, did not share in their cleverness, and nor did his own son. This fourth Marquis stumbled one day, when out with some of his kinsmen, on some kind of meeting by a loch, and the next thing he knew, after a good deal of marching, he was being attainted for supporting Charles Edward Stuart. That was the end of his title and estate: the estate was disposed of by the York Buildings Company that dealt so thoroughly with the properties of similarly disgraced gentlemen, and the fourth Marquis of Ballavore ended his days in bewilderment in France, without any clear idea of how he had arrived there. His wife had left him for a much more glamorous Jacobite in the glory-days of rebellion, and had borne him no children. The title was therefore in abeyance, and Lord Scoggie looked upon it as his own through some lengthy and possibly tenuous link to the first Marquis's younger brother. Murray was under orders to draw out any references in the papers to genealogies, births, deaths and marriages, and they formed a separate section in his list and a separate heap in an emptied, explicitly mouse-proof deed box that rested on the table itself in a place of honour. His lordship was patient: he knew the job would be a long one, for often he found further deed boxes in attics and cellars and brought them apologetically to the library, so he rarely pursued Murray to find out the state of his progress. Murray was duly grateful.

Murray had free use of the library table with the catalogues and the deed boxes. The other library table was Lord Scoggie's. It was where he held meetings with Tibo and the like, or admitted to interview a villager wishing to consult him on some matter. Like the dinner table in the Great Hall, this table had survived from an earlier age and could well have served as an example of evidence of the values of that time. It was a good foot taller than the table used by Murray, and behind it was a chair – perhaps better described as a throne – raised on a small dais. Seated magisterially on this cathedra, Lord Scoggie gave his instructions and passed his judgements, and occasionally signed documents. It was not there that he read or consulted the books in the library: the second table seemed to form a little room within the library itself, a place for duty.

Two library chairs by the fireplace were where books were read, when they could be seen through the smoke: atlases and picture books were consulted on Murray's table. The raised table was the royal reception area, ignored the rest of the time, untouched by the rest of the family except on the most solemn occasions.

Now that it was dark, the library was lit with oil lamps and the fire had been burning for a couple of hours, contributing little to the warmth of the room but thickening the atmosphere nicely. Shadows lay around the deed boxes and lurked amongst the upper tiers of the bookcases, and the gallery was a dark cave amongst them. Robert and Henry were, if they could be believed, preparing their lessons for the next day and trying to find Seringapatam on the schoolroom globe. When they were finished they had permission to amuse themselves as they wanted, which might include trying to persuade Mrs. Costane to release more pies into their custody. Murray had escaped to the library an hour and a half ago and was settled at his table over some kind of parchment document in a cramped Latin hand, weighed down at its springing corners by four books. The oil lamps tutted quietly and the fire rumbled to itself, the only noises in the tall room.

Murray heard the footsteps outside in the hall just before the door opened and Lord Scoggie walked in, a pair of spectacles in one hand and a decanter of brandy in the other.

'Good evening, Mr. Murray. I hope I am not disturbing you?'

'Not at all, my lord,' said Murray, on his feet. Lord Scoggie waved at him to sit down again, and went to set the decanter down on a small table by the library chairs at the fireplace. A number of glasses were already on a tray there, and Lord Scoggie poured himself a reasonable measure. Murray, back in his seat, noted the fact with some interest: Lord Scoggie did not often drink in the evenings, preferring to limit himself to claret at dinner time.

Lord Scoggie began to scan the bookcases for something to read. When you saw him in his library, you realised, perhaps for the first time, how ill-fitted he was to anywhere else in the world. It was as if his arms had grown long especially to reach that shelf, his pigeon chest and narrow shoulders allowed him to squeeze through just there between ladder and wall, his flat feet fitted the ladder rungs like the long hand-feet of an ape. Once or twice Murray had half-expected him to lodge a book under his huge front teeth while he returned to the floor, like a rodent with a particularly desirable trifle. Now he plucked a volume from a high shelf with his long fingers, flicked it open, and studied the contents for a moment through his little spectacles, then brought it back to his library chair. He reached out for his glass.

'Would you care for some brandy, Mr. Murray?'

Murray smiled.

'No, thank you, Lord Scoggie: I should be nervous of spilling a drop on this document.'

'Oh, what is it?' Lord Scoggie rose and came over, leaning precariously over the table with his own glass. 'Oh, it's the old charter for these lands. I'm glad you found that – haven't seen it for years. Not that anyone is arguing about the ownership, I suppose, but if they were ...'

Murray had already noticed the place names Scwgy, Ryssie and Aberwrgoe, with their strange archaic spellings, amongst the Latin scribbles, the three little estates now all known under the Scoggie title. He made a note on some scrap paper next to the charter and sat back. Lord Scoggie was still staring at it over his shoulder, and took a noisy sip of brandy.

'Where are the boys?' he asked eventually, wandering back to the fire.

'I've set them some work to do up in the schoolroom. When they have finished that, they are to play quietly until bed time.' Murray glanced up to see if his employer approved, and Lord Scoggie nodded his goat-like head, a little absently. 'They're looking forward to their cousin Major Keyes coming tomorrow, of course,' Murray added. He was surprised to see Lord Scoggie's shoulders tense suddenly at the name.

'Ha!' he said, not quite sounding amused. 'Upstairs all is in turmoil, looking forward to Major Keyes coming tomorrow. Every time my daughter says that everything is ready, something else seems to require to be done. The castle was not cleaner and more decorated for my own wedding than it is for tomorrow.'

He sighed heavily, and took another very large sip of his brandy. Murray was not sure if he was expected to respond. After all, it was not every day that a great national hero came to stay, and even he himself was looking forward to meeting the great man and hearing him discussed amongst the servants. Still, Lord Scoggie did not like to be put out of his routine, even for a national hero. When Major Keyes was settled and became commonplace amongst them, as even heroes must eventually do, Lord Scoggie could relax again.

'It's not the disarrangement,' said Lord Scoggie suddenly, as though he had been following Murray's thoughts. He poured himself another glass of brandy, and waved the decanter towards Murray. Murray, realising that it might be some time before he could work on his charter again, relented and accepted a glass. 'No,' said Lord Scoggie, handing him the glass. 'It's not the disarrangement, unpleasant though such things always are. It's the man himself. I'm speaking in confidence here, of course, Mr. Murray.'

'Of course, my lord.'

'Of course. You know that. You see, the thing is – well, Lady Scoggie thinks that Major Keyes might make quite a good husband for Deborah.'

'I see,' said Murray. In fact, he could not see why that should particularly bother Lord Scoggie. He could, however, see it bothering Mr. Nathaniel Tibo – and, for that matter, Deborah herself.

'You think it's a good idea?' Lord Scoggie asked him suddenly, with an oddly pleading voice.

'I'm not sure, I'm afraid,' Murray hedged. 'I haven't yet had the honour of meeting Major Keyes, of course, while both you and Lady

Scoggie have. I know together you must be the best judges of your daughter's happiness. But have you spoken to her? Or has Major Keyes expressed an interest in the matter?'

'That's just it,' said Lord Scoggie in frustration. 'Major Keyes would jump at the idea, of course he would. How could he not? But I'm not at all sure he's right for her. You know, the last time he came here he damn' nearly killed someone?'

Again, Murray was shocked. He had never before heard Lord Scoggie use any kind of profanity. On the other hand, he was on his third large glass of brandy already.

'Nearly killed someone? Who? How?'

'A fisherman from St. Monance. He challenged him to a fight, or the fisherman challenged him, one way or the other. I didn't feel I could trust either account, and there was no doubt more I never heard at all. But Major Keyes went wild, whatever way it started, lashing and punching all over the place, then he kicked the fellow in the knee. Lamed him completely. Fellow can't put any weight on it at all now, dreadful pain. And of course he's no use in a fishing boat, not even in a yawl round the rocks. I tried to make Major Keyes pay up some kind of compensation, but of course he was as poor as a widow in those days, barely enough to meet his mess bills. I ended up paying some support to the family on his behalf, though I don't think Major Keyes cared tuppence for them. I can tell you, I was extremely angry. Of course, it was all hushed up as far as it could be, even Lady Scoggie barely knows what happened, and now, of course, Keyes is wonderful and unmarried – unless he picked up some dusky wench on his travels – and coming here, and Lady Scoggie quite rightly points out that poor Deborah really sees very few men at all, not of her quality, and that this might be a very good opportunity.'

'Perhaps being in the army has allowed him to develop a cooler temper,' Murray suggested, trying to be tactful. Lord Scoggie seemed unconvinced.

'You know 'hero' is quite often a word that means a man who happens to lose his temper against the right people. I've a feeling that

Seringapatam was just lucky for Major Keyes, and if Tippoo Sultan hadn't shot himself first, the Major would probably have lamed him, too. You know the stories they tell about General Baird, the Major's commanding officer out there, how even his mother said dreadful things about the temper he had, and how the high heidyins out there allowed Baird to attack Seringapatam because they thought it might calm him down. I tell you, suicide is a crime in law and against our good Lord, but if I were Tippoo Sultan and I got wind of the fact that Davie Baird and our Major Keyes were after me, I'd shoot myself as fast as I could load the gun, out of self-preservation.'

'I'm sure, anyway, that if she wished to Miss Deborah could keep him in order, my lord.' Murray tried to lighten Lord Scoggie's mood, but instead he slammed his glass down on the table with a thud.

'Oh, I've just remembered why I came in here in the first place. No time to read, damn it, Murray: I have some fishermen coming to see me. Will you take notes of our conversation? I'm afraid the whole thing might come to law at some stage, and I want to be able to recall what happened.'

'Very good, my lord,' said Murray. 'You'll be at the big table?'

'Oh, aye, aye, yes, of course. They'll be here shortly, I believe.'

Murray found and sharpened his pen and a spare one, throwing the shavings on the fire, then took a notebook from his papers on the low table and brought it over to the big table. Lord Scoggie, keen to be caught at his best, climbed up on to the high chair and set his brandy glass down importantly in front of him. Murray brought him some paper, too, as he often wanted to fiddle with something while listening to people talk. He finished his own brandy and put the glass aside, feeling that a brandy glass was less impressive in a secretary than in an adjudicating lord. He wondered why the fishermen were coming here. They usually sorted matters out amongst themselves. Perhaps they were coming to protest against the imminent arrival of Major Keyes and his violent temper.

There was an unnatural pause after this sudden flurry of activity.

The hall outside was silent, and Murray looked longingly at his interrupted work. He set a chair for himself at the high table, next to Lord Scoggie's dais, and arranged a few other hardback chairs on the far side of the table, but then remained standing, trying not to shuffle his feet. Lord Scoggie tapped on the table with his long fingers, finished the brandy, and struggled down out of the chair again to refill his glass. It was while he was at this business that there came a clang of the bell at the front door, and he scurried in an unlordlike fashion back to his seat, barely into his place when the library door opened and Naismyth, beak aloft and feathers preened, announced the arrival of three fishermen from the village. They entered, two confidently, one curiously, all accompanied by the rich aroma of fish. Naismyth did not dignify them with names, but Lord Scoggie quickly made up for his omission as he waved them to sit in the chairs Murray had put out. Once seated at the high table they were all tiny, head and shoulders only visible to Murray and Lord Scoggie.

'Mr. Murray, these are Joseph Baillie, Richard Shaw and Hugh Farquhar, representatives of the fishermen down in the village. Gentlemen, this is my secretary, Mr. Murray. He will take notes of our meeting.'

'Where's Mr. Tibo?' asked Joe Baillie. Murray wrote his name down, and noted his prickly grey hair, his truculent expression, and where the last two fingers on his left hand were missing, an old injury. He seemed to be the leader of the party.

'I have not asked Mr. Tibo to attend this evening. I happen to know he is quite busy at the moment, and I was not aware that it would be necessary. Would you prefer to wait until he is available?'

'Nah,' said Joe. 'I was only asking.' There was no hostility in his tone, and Murray wondered if the truculence were simply habitual.

'And how is the season this year, gentlemen?' Lord Scoggie asked. 'Did John Walker find a sixth man for his boat in the end?'

'Aye, he did, your lordship. His son came back from the whaling after all, and not so bad as he was said to be. He had lost a couple of fingers, like myself.' He held up his hand. 'Caught in a harpoon rope, just the same. So he's back on the boats.'

A few minutes' discussion followed on the quality of the season's herring, until Lord Scoggie had been fully informed. Murray was already impressed by how much he knew of the lives of these men.

'So, gentlemen,' Lord Scoggie went on at last. 'What seems to be the problem?'

'Well, it's no our problem, or it wasn't till last night,' Joe began. Murray tried to pay attention, succeeding better than the young man with the scratched face, Hugh Farquhar, who was gazing at the books all about him with hungry eyes. Murray knew that look.

'What happened last night?' prompted Lord Scoggie. Murray had the impression that he already knew. He leaned back in his high chair, a benevolent monarch tending to his subjects. Murray, hunched over his notebook at the over-high table, felt like a schoolboy taking his dominie's dictation. Across the acreage of the table, Joe Baillie drew his thoughts together for his story.

'Someone left a pig at the end of the harbour,' he announced at last. Murray thought that this was the beginning of the story, but after a second realised that it was the highlight. A pig, of course, and these were St. Monance fishermen. A pig on the harbour was disastrous.

'When you say someone *left* a pig on the end of the harbour,' said Lord Scoggie carefully, 'do you mean you think that someone brought it there deliberately? It didn't just escape and wander down the hill?'

'*Of course* someone brought it there deliberately, your lordship,' said Joe, his anger just under control. 'Why would an escaped pig just wander down to the harbour – and tether itself? Someone brought it – and we reckon we ken who.'

'Ah,' said Lord Scoggie, not entirely encouragingly. The matter was serious. As far as fishermen were concerned, pigs were ill-bringing creatures. As far as the fishermen of St. Monance were concerned, they were the unchanciest beings on the face of the earth, devil-begotten, foul, filthy hellthings that carried with them the greatest of misfortune. Up the hill, away from the harbour and the delicate, fragile boats, pigs were just farmyard animals that had the decency occasionally to provide a nice side of bacon or a few roast trotters. The fishermen did not see it that way, and never touched a pig from their birth to their death if they could possibly help it.

'See, we think it must be someone from up the hill, your lordship,' interrupted the man called Richard Shaw. The light from the oil lamps glinted off his bare head. In his youth he might have helped to kill the whale that fuelled them. 'There are those up the hill who would do something like that, and know what it would do to us.'

'Aye, indeed,' said his lordship. 'So did any boats go out today?'

'Not one, your lordship,' said Joe, nodding. 'How could we? And the herring skipping past, and the Edinburgh boats waiting off the shore to buy them from us on the way home, and not a boat outside the harbour. You ken we can't touch them.'

'Aye, that's right,' agreed Lord Scoggie. He picked absently at his teeth, and Murray wondered if he was still tasting his breakfast ham. 'But the thing is, gentlemen, why would you think that someone from up the hill would do something like that?'

The three fishermen looked at each other in surprise.

'Just for devilment, your lordship. They're up to anything up the hill – your lordship excepted, of course,' Joe added, with a little nod of his head, which Lord Scoggie acknowledged with a straight face. Murray had a sudden vision of Lord Scoggie steering a pig down to the village, cackling through the dark – disturbing.

'But a pig is an expensive thing, Joe. Why would any of them go to the trouble of taking one down to the harbour, perhaps exposing it to harm on the way?'

'It's harmed now, anyway!' Murray heard Richie Shaw mutter

under his breath, but Joe nudged him hard.

'Well,' he said reluctantly, 'it's maybe that there's been a wee dispute. Over a wedding. You ken, mixed marriages always bring trouble.' He looked to Lord Scoggie as if to emphasise that they were both reasonable men, who understood these things. Lord Scoggie's face went blank, waiting for a fuller explanation. Joe pondered for a moment. 'It's that Hugh's sister here went and married one of the fellows from up the hill, and now she's left him, that's all, and they've lost her, and more fool them.'

'Your sister ... she married one of the Kinkell cousins, did she not, Hugh?'

'That's right.' Hugh, drawn back from his contemplation of the bookcases, nodded sharply. His face was dark. 'Chrissie was always a wee bit wilful, you ken, your lordship. She would hear no arguments against Sandy Kinkell, the wee slinking fellow. It near killed my father, letting her go to him.'

'And now she has come home, wilful once again,' remarked Lord Scoggie. There was an odd little shiver amongst the men across the table, as though something had gone swiftly unspoken between them. Richie Shaw shuffled, apparently taking something out of his pocket under the shield of the table, though Murray could not see what it was. In a moment he put a pipe to his mouth, then took it away again, not feeling comfortable smoking there. 'Tell me,' Lord Scoggie said, fingering his brandy glass, 'how does Sandy Kinkell feel about her departure?'

'We wouldn't know,' Joe explained. 'I'd imagine he's no so pleased.'

'I seem to remember that the wedding was peaceful enough.'

'Oh, aye,' said Richie Shaw with some emphasis, 'the *wedding* was peaceful enough.' Again he seemed to confine his remarks to the table in front of him, mumbling. Lord Scoggie looked sharply at him. Then he appeared to remember something.

'The first child was christened ... a month ago, was it not? A boy. I remember the minister mentioning it.'

'Aye,' said Joe Baillie, his face closed. Hugh was starting to look dangerous, a frightening thing in one so apparently scholarly. Lord Scoggie watched him carefully, and let the silence lie for a long moment.

'Am I right in thinking that the christening was *not* so peaceful?' he asked at last. The three fishermen tried not to look at each other. Lord Scoggie tapped hard on the table with the base of his glass. 'Tell me about the christening,' he said, quietly.

'They served pork,' said Joe Baillie at last, looking sick at the memory. 'They invited us all up there to dinner with them, and fed us pork. Some of the fellows didn't know – they would never have tasted it, the poor lads. They ate some. We're keeping them off our boats altogether till next year, though one of them is already dead – fell off the harbour on a windy day. John Walker's youngest, you'll have heard.' Lord Scoggie nodded sadly, but did not comment. 'Sandy Kinkell was in the midst of it, of course. He knew well enough what he had done, though he claimed he had no idea. But we could see them all laughing in the yard.'

'That was not well done,' Lord Scoggie agreed, looking solemn. 'If they agree with you or if they don't, they should not have done it. But how did young Chrissie take this insult against her own family?'

'Chrissie ...' Joe looked exceptionally pained, and Hugh had his head in his hands on the edge of the table. 'Chrissie ate the pork.'

'Willingly?'

'Oh, aye. Licking her lips and saying she loved the taste of a nice piece of pork. That's what Sandy Kinkell has done to her, see? He's twisted her round to an up the hill way of thinking, abandoning the ways of her own people.'

'My father couldna speak for a week,' put in Hugh, with tight lips. 'When he could, he said he'd never speak to her again. He said he'd rather she'd married a foreigner than a man up the hill, for foreigners had more sense of natural decency. And he knew some of them on the whaling ships, so he would know.'

Joe nodded in agreement, and Richie Shaw fiddled mournfully with his pipe.

'I doubt, then,' said Lord Scoggie, with an air of innocence, 'that you would let this insult go unavenged?'

'Well, no,' said Hugh, before Joe could poke him under the table. Hugh stared at Joe, then looked back at Lord Scoggie. 'That's to say, well, it was enough to say we'd never speak to her again.'

'But it was about this time, surely, that your sister left her husband who has such influence over her, and came home to live?'

'Aye, that would be right,' admitted Joe, not meeting Lord Scoggie's eye now. He was on a losing streak, and he knew it.

'Now, tell me, Hugh, as a decent man,' said Lord Scoggie, leaning forward alarmingly in his high chair, 'did your sister come home of her own accord?'

'She did, your lordship,' said Hugh bravely, though it did not last long. He fingered the scratches on his face. 'She sort of did. She only yelled out a bit.'

'That was before we got the bitty bag over her gob,' remarked Richie, helpfully, then looked dismayed.

'You kidnapped her, didn't you?' Lord Scoggie accused them sternly. 'You took her away without her permission or the permission of her lawful husband. I'm afraid that was not the right thing to do, either. You'll have to give her back.'

'We will not!' cried Hugh, leaping up. Murray set down his pen and stood up slowly. He was a foot taller than Hugh, and half the width again in the shoulders, and Hugh was at heart a sensible man. He flung himself back down and Murray also sat. Lord Scoggie looked away from the whole incident, as if embarrassed. Joe, on his side, glared at Hugh who had the decency to look abashed.

Lord Scoggie went on.

'Your sister Chrissie is lawfully wed, in the eyes of the church, to Sandy Kinkell, and they both seem happy with the arrangement. You can't stand against that.'

'What about the child, though? We canna let her bring up a child eating pigmeat,' said Joe reasonably. 'The boy is a grandson of Tom Farquhar, a grandson of fishermen. What if he shakes off the Kinkell taint and grows up a fisherman himself?'

'Well, consider, Joe,' said Lord Scoggie. 'If the boy is as true a descendant as you claim, he will be called to the sea and he'll eat no more pork. If he is not, and he is a true son of Sandy Kinkell, then he'll be a weaver and will eat pig with the rest of them up the hill, and you will not even desire to stake a claim to him. But in either case, he will not benefit from having his mother's folk and his father's folk at odds, for then he might not take to either of you, and run away to be a soldier.'

Joe sat back in his seat, the other two following his action. Joe considered, while Richie fiddled nervously with his pipe and Hugh sat still and tense. Murray stretched his hand out, flexing the muscles. Both his pens were blunt.

'Aye, I suppose it's right enough, your lordship. Lads, we've got to let her go back.'

'After all the trouble we went to to take her?' asked Richie in disbelief. 'She near had my eye out with her fingernails that night.'

'She's causing enough trouble in the house,' Hugh admitted at last. 'She and my father still aren't talking, and she flung a dish of stew over me last night.'

'There's your answer, then, gentlemen. I shall ask Mr. Tibo to step by to your father's house, Hugh, and see if they need for anything. Thank you for calling. There will be ale in the kitchen before your walk home.' Lord Scoggie nodded graciously from his throne, a gesture combining acknowledgement of their respect and an indication of the door. The men rose, shuffling round the chairs, suddenly tall again as they moved away from the table. Murray went to open the door for them, ready to show them out and not bother Naismyth. At the door, Joe paused and looked back.

'Your lordship, is it a true thing that Major Keyes is coming back to these parts soon?'

Lord Scoggie, who had returned his attention to the brandy glass, glanced up quickly and caught his eye.

'Yes, Joe, it is. He is expected tomorrow.'

For a moment longer, they met each other's gaze. Then Joe and his colleagues left the room, in silence.

CHAPTER FIVE

'There he is, look!'

Robert's feet performed a little tattoo on the flagstones as he pointed frantically at a movement out along the lane. Henry peered in the same direction.

'No, it's not, you fool. It's old Wyllie taking his plough horse home.'

'It's not! It's Major Keyes on horseback.'

Murray saw where they were looking.

'I'm afraid Henry's right, Robert. Anyway, I imagine Major Keyes will arrive from the main road, not from the village – don't you?'

Murray had been trying to teach history in the school room, but it had been impossible: the house was in a fluster, and at every sound, from steps on the stairs to the front door closing, the boys ran to the windows and stared anxiously down at the empty driveway. In the end, it made more sense to borrow the old brass telescope from the library, relic of some Scoggie who had served his time in His Majesty's navy, and take the boys up the west tower under the guise of learning how to survey land. Murray's memory of this was fairly hazy, but his pockets were stuffed with trigonometry. The narrow walkway around the tower's topmost spike was safe but usually out of bounds, and had the virtue of keeping the boys pretty much in one place while they watched out for their cousin.

'Anyway,' Henry was saying, in his slightly pedantic way, 'he won't be on a horse. How could he ride with only the one leg?'

'I bet he could, with practice,' Robert objected. 'All he needs is a good mounting block.'

'He'll be in a carriage.' Henry was definite.

'What kind of hero arrives in a carriage? I bet he'll be on a horse.'

'He'll need a carriage for all his luggage. Army officers have tons of luggage. What do you think baggage trains are for?'

'That's for the men,' insisted Robert, who had a strong bent towards romantic impracticality. 'The men need all kinds of things. Tents, and things, don't they, Mr. Murray?'

'Yes, they do, but so do the officers.' Robert turned away in disgust. 'Officers need all kinds of important luggage,' Murray went on, trying to soften the blow. 'They need tables to spread maps on, and clean uniforms for going to balls and revues, and a tent to have conferences in with their fellow officers, and all the comforts of home while they're in winter quarters.'

'Balls and revues?' said Henry scornfully.

'Maps?' added Robert. 'Conferences? What about fighting?'

'You don't carry much luggage when you're actually in battle.'

Henry looked as if he knew better but chose not to lower himself to argue. Robert was also unimpressed. Murray wondered how he had managed to annoy both of them.

'All right,' he said. 'Tell me what is the lowest point of land you can see from here.'

'Why would he need luggage coming here, anyway?' Robert persisted, while Henry applied himself to the telescope. 'He won't need to look at maps, and there won't be any balls or revues, and there's a table in his room that Bea's put *flowers* on, and if he really wants to have a conference there's always the library.'

'He might want to look smart while he's here, in his best uniform.'

'That would be good,' Robert admitted, 'but I don't see why he'd bother.'

'Because he's going to marry Deborah,' said Henry, handing him the telescope. Robert nearly dropped it.

'Marry Deborah? Our Deborah?'

'I heard Mamma say so.' Henry turned to Murray. 'The lowest bit of land would be the bottom of the lake, but we can't see it.'

'Why would he marry Deborah? I mean, he's a hero ...'

'She's very pretty.'

Murray's statement was regarded with immediate suspicion by the boys.

'Pretty? But she's Deborah.'

'But it might be quite good to have a hero for a brother. I mean, when we go to university it'll sound very good. The other boys won't have one. And he could help me get a commission.' Robert was already starting to see the bright side.

'Father won't let you go into the army, will he, Mr. Murray?'

'I'm not sure,' said Murray. 'It's an honourable occupation for a younger son. My brother has a commission in the Royal Regiment.'

'Major Keyes is in the 73rd. Highlanders,' said Robert clearly, with the unmistakeable meaning that it was the only possible regiment to serve in.

'Not with only one leg, though,' added Henry.

'But it *was* his regiment.'

'Of course it was, and a very fine regiment, too.' Murray tried to make peace. Surely these boys were ready for university? 'Robert, if you were attacking Scoggie Castle with a troop of infantry, which direction would you come from?'

It was effective. Robert had the telescope to his eye in an instant, back straight, in his mind already Sir David Baird debating the siege of Seringapatam – now that he had finally found it on the schoolroom globe. Murray had found accounts of the battle in some old newspapers in the library, and Robert had studied them with more attention than he usually gave to his history work. Murray was sure that through his telescope he was now seeing jungle, and ferocious natives guarding strangely-carved walls and elaborately-worked gates. Henry sighed, impatient for his turn again, and leaned over the wall of the walkway, staring into the distance, tapping the toes of his boots on the stonework.

'There he is!' he suddenly cried. Robert swung the telescope around and accidentally swiped Henry across his forehead. 'Ow!'

'Where?' demanded Robert excitedly.

'I was joking,' Henry snapped, rubbing his head crossly. It looked painful: Robert's enthusiasm could be quite dangerous.

'You idiot!' Robert cried, and used the telescope deliberately this time to whack Henry in the ribs.

'Enough!' Murray snatched the telescope and tweaked Robert's ear. 'Do you want Major Keyes' first sight of you to be squabbling on the battlements?'

'He won't come for ages,' mumbled Henry, trying to rub his ribs and his head at the same time.

'He's coming now,' said Murray. 'Look.'

The boys turned again to the wall. Just wheeling in to the end of the short drive was a fine carriage – so Henry had been right – with a riding horse trotting along behind it, ridden by a groom – so Robert had been right. On either side of Murray, the boys had suddenly gone quiet. The carriage wheels turned briskly on the gravel, and soon they could hear them echo off the front of the castle. Robert was pale. Henry said, with much less than his usual assurance,

'Do you think we could go down?'

'Do you think we should?' Robert whispered. Both of them were clutching the battlements with white knuckles, suddenly overawed. A real hero was suddenly really here, whether he was their cousin or not.

'I think you probably should,' said Murray. 'Your father will want to introduce you to him. Let's see you both? Hands? Straighten your waistcoat, Robert. Henry, just wipe the toe of your boot there where you have dust on it. Right, you both look very respectable. Fit to meet a hero.' Henry's temple was beginning to bruise nicely, but there was nothing he could do about that at the moment. Deborah would have ointment to bring the bruise out, but just now she would have other things on her mind. He patted both boys on the shoulder and pushed them gently towards the door to the winding staircase that would take them back down the tower to meet their intimidating guest.

Downstairs in the hall everything was in a fluster. Naismyth was on his knees, lifting invisible dust off the floor and hiding it in his pockets. The little maid, Grisell, gave a last wipe to a dented breastplate on the wall and vanished through the door to the servants' corridor, skirt tails flying. There was a squeal as the door closed, then it shot open again and Beatrix appeared, having just collided with Grisell. She straightened her hair and took her place at the back of the hall. Lord Scoggie stood by the stairs, apparently calm, but the twitching of his hands betrayed him, though he clutched them together. Guests, heroic or not, were not common in his rural fastness. Murray took the boys over to stand beside Beatrix, and they exchanged small smiles. There was a patter on the stairs, and Deborah appeared, slippers light on every second step as she flung herself down to stand by her father.

'Can't find her,' she gasped, just as the doorbell was clanged enthusiastically outside. Naismyth rose to his feet, face arranged into a bland expression, and straightened his coat. He stalked to the door with measured stork-strides, and opened it as if he had been practising.

It was as if a bear had entered the hall in search of honey. A large man stooped through the doorway, then swung himself into their presence, bright in his red regimental coat with a sweeping cloak tossed back over his shoulders. He pulled off his shako in a sweeping movement, and shouted:

'Scoggie! Scoggie, my friend, it is a delight to see you again! The old place has not changed one jot! And you, in the midst of your family as ever!'

Lord Scoggie had been in mid-bow, but Major Keyes seized his hand in both of his and shook it as if trying to pull a sword from the body of his enemy. Lord Scoggie's face was a picture. Robert and Henry stood with their mouths open. Only Deborah and Beatrix managed for the moment to remain smiling politely.

Finally released, Lord Scoggie brought them into the scene as quickly as he could.

'My daughter Deborah,' he presented her, 'and over there our cousin Beatrix Pirrie.'

Major Keyes made a ludicrously low bow to each lady.

'My, Miss Deborah, when I last saw you you were two hands higher than a duck and still amongst your dolls. And now look at you! You'd look well on the arm of any officer! Miss Beatrix, my respects. You'll find me a brash companion, no doubt, for I am little used to the ways of ladies.' He bowed again, while Bea and Deborah quickly exchanged glances over his back. Murray could not quite interpret them. Keyes, though, was moving quickly on as though the girls were too hot a fire to stand near. 'And who are these young men?'

Lord Scoggie nodded to Murray, who pushed the boys forward to make their bows.

'My elder son, Henry, and my younger son, Robert,' said Lord Scoggie, waiting for approval.

'Good day, sir,' said the boys politely, and bowed to perfection. Murray felt unexpectedly proud of them. When it mattered, maybe they did know how to behave. Then Robert let out a cry, and fell over, knocking Henry down against the wall. Suddenly, from nowhere, an immense white dog was on top of them, licking their heads and hands for all it was worth.

'Tippoo, down!' Keyes lunged for the dog's collar, and hauled it off before anyone else could move. 'All right, boys? He's a friendly sort of dog, but sometimes he likes a bit of a joke, eh, Tippoo?'

The boys pulled themselves up, keeping a careful eye on the dog, which now sat by Keyes' leg. Their dark coats were thick with white hairs, and they were wide-eyed with shock. Lord Scoggie stepped in.

'Tippoo, eh? Grand name for a dog, I suppose. Hey, Tippoo? Good dog.' Tippoo did not respond, but kept his eye on the boys. 'Ah, Keyes, it's not long to dinner. You'll want to change and so on ...'

'But where's Lady Scoggie? Where's my fair cousin?' Keyes demanded suddenly, looking about him as if he thought they might have her hidden amongst the armoury. Deborah met Beatrix' eye again.

'I'm afraid my mother is out at the moment. We had not expected you until later in the day, though we are delighted to find you were able to reach us earlier. My mother is very much involved in charitable work about the parish.' She looked a little desperately at her father. 'May I show you to your chamber? I hope you will find it adequate for your stay.'

'By all means, Miss Deborah – show me all the way.' Major

Keyes grabbed the hand rail and swung his leg up on to the first step of the stairs, and followed her up and out of sight. The dog, with a longing look at Robert and Henry, paused for a moment, then joined the small procession. The party in the hall listened to Major Keyes remarking loudly on the unchanging decor of Scoggie Castle and the contrasting changes in Deborah all the way up the stairs and when the sounds faded a little, they relaxed, visibly.

'Beatrix, dear,' said Lord Scoggie, 'if you have not already done so, please tell Mrs. Costane we shall not want dinner for another hour. I know that is later than our usual hour, but I am in need of a moment to catch my breath. I shall be in the library, should anyone really need me.'

Stepping carefully, as though not entirely sure of the reliability of his legs, Lord Scoggie crossed the hall and vanished into his bolthole. Naismyth disappeared outside to deal with Major Keyes' heroic luggage, and Beatrix and Murray were left with the boys in the hall.

'Well, he is safely arrived, then,' said Murray.

'Just as well,' said Beatrix, 'or the dinner in his honour would have looked a little foolish.'

'That's not today, is it?'

'No, no: it's on the first of November. The whole county will be here. You're expected to eat with the family, too, so there's no chance of getting out of it.' She sneaked a mischievous smile. 'You know how Lord Scoggie likes to show off your intellectual conversation.'

Murray scowled, and changed the subject.

'Henry has a bruise on his head,' he said. 'Could he have some ointment for it?'

'Surely,' said Beatrix, letting out a long breath. 'Was it the dog, Henry?'

'No, it was Robert. With a telescope.'

'You make it sound as if he needed it to aim with,' Beatrix smiled.

'No, just to hit with.' Henry was resigned to his brother's violence. Robert was less used to injury.

'That dog should be on a chain,' he muttered. 'It does as much damage as Tippoo Sultan himself.'

'It's probably how it got its name,' Murray said. 'We'll just have to watch out for it.' The boys had really been shaken by the incident. The dog might have been licking them on this occasion, but Murray had seen the size of its teeth. 'No dinner for another hour – go up to the schoolroom and Beatrix will bring some ointment, and I'll see if I can persuade Mrs. Costane to give us some milk to make chocolate. Stoke up the fire, and I'll be up shortly.'

'We're not *babies*, you know,' said Robert, but they went up anyway.

Lady Scoggie must have been detained in the village, for she did not appear for dinner. Deborah, with the air of someone who has decided to hold the fort for now and deal with the courts martial later, took the place of hostess with almost her usual self-assurance. The boys, fortified by chocolate, were relaxed as long as they knew that the dog Tippoo was over by the fireplace where they could see him. A fire had been lit, surreptitiously, by Deborah's orders, and Lord Scoggie had not been heard to object when he saw it, so the Great Hall was a mosaic of hot and cold patches. Major Keyes did not appear to notice.

Now that he was sitting still enough, Murray could see him better. On closer inspection, his uniform was elderly, patched and darned in places, with the lace repaired. Physically, he certainly seemed the conventional hero: his head was large, his forehead like a sloping field put to the plough, with a scrubland of reddish hair beyond it. Whiskers emphasised his solid jaw, and his eyes were pale against a shiny complexion polished hard by the climate of India and other foreign battlefields. He had a nose that had been straight and determined, but was no less imposing for having been broken once or twice. His lips were thin and red, frequently parting in talk to show very white teeth with the occasional gap. He handled his cutlery as though a fine table in Fife were no different from a camp fire two miles from Bombay, and only practice for handling an infantry sword. Sitting opposite him, Murray, used to being amongst the tallest and broadest in the company, found himself feeling small and delicate.

'No, it was a ridiculous thing, really,' he was saying now, encouraged by the boys to talk of a battle that had monopolised their thoughts for the last week. 'Of course, one can never know the moment that is going to make one's name, but to be honest the final assault was just that, the last little bit of a long campaign in which many great men were lost. My own sergeant, Lord love him, was run through in a thicket when we were ambushed by Tippoo's scoundrels, and that was a kindly death compared with the way prisoners were treated when they fell into his hands. Look at Davie Baird himself – knighted, did you notice, just recently? He was taken captive by Tippoo twenty-odd years ago, and chained to another prisoner.'

'I hear his mother had a great deal of sympathy for that other prisoner,' said Lord Scoggie, winking at Murray.

'Aye, that's a famous one. "Lord help the poor chiel that's chained to our Davie," she said. Anyway, they couldn't make up their minds whether to give the command to Sir David, or to Colonel Wellesley, but in the end they let Davie lead the final assault to take his revenge on the Tiger of Mysore.'

'Was it a duel to the death?' asked Robert, his eyes wide. It had not been reported as such in the papers, but Murray knew Robert's love of romance.

'Ach, no, son. We found Tippoo dead, after all. He had no courage when it came to the bit, the heathen. The palace was full of animals he had sacrificed to his foreign gods to protect him.'

'But why did you have to attack him in the first place?' asked Henry, slightly truculently.

Major Keyes laughed indulgently.

'It is not enough for you that he was hostile to our interests?'

'Henry is a thoughtful boy,' said Murray. 'He likes to know the ins and outs of the situation.' Lord Scoggie regarded Henry with interest.

'A strategist, eh?' Major Keyes thought for a moment. 'Well, like some of the other states around at the time, he kept harassing Company troops, which isn't conducive to trade, of course. He hated the British. There was a great clockwork toy in his palace, I saw it myself. A tiger, nearly lifesize, eating a British soldier. When you turned the handle, the tiger growled and mashed its jaws, and the soldier squirmed and groaned most horribly.'

Robert's eyes lit up.

'I heard the French were thinking of an alliance with him as a foothold back in India,' Murray suggested meekly.

'Oh, yes, the Tiger of Mysore was up to anything like that,' Major Keyes agreed, laughing again. 'He was a nasty piece of work, no doubt about it, young Henry. India is better without him.'

'How many natives did you kill, Major Keyes?' Robert asked. Mrs. Costane had made her threatened beetroot pancakes, and he speared one of the bloody-coloured discs as he spoke. Deborah just managed not to tell him off, though her hands twitched.

'Oh, dozens, I suppose. In the heat of battle you lose count very easily, you know. I remember one young fellow – but perhaps not in front of the ladies, eh? So, are you keen to join a regiment when you grow up, Robert?'

'Oh, yes!' Robert breathed, then glanced at his father. Lord Scoggie's face was impassive.

'That's a long way ahead yet, I think, Keyes,' he said lightly. 'They have their studies to think of, first.'

'Aye, studies are useful enough for an officer, I suppose,' Keyes agreed, 'though fitness and good fighting skills are better. Are they being taught fencing and boxing? I suppose they must be.'

'Mr. Murray teaches them a little fencing,' Lord Scoggie said. 'I have not yet been convinced that pugilism is a fit sport for a gentleman.'

'Not a fit sport for a gentleman? I am amazed!' cried Keyes, banging his knife down on the table. 'It's all the rage in London. And anyway, gentleman or not, if you drop your sword in battle and you can't get at your knife, a good crack on the jaw is enough to stop many a murderous fiend in his tracks.'

At the very thought of it, Robert glowed with excitement.

'Father, the Pugilistic Chanticleer is coming to give an exhibition in Elie. Please can we go? It would be very good to know how to stop a murderous fiend in his tracks, because you never know when you might meet one, even in Fife.'

'We are fortunately short of murderous fiends, even in Fife,' Lord Scoggie remarked, with a thoughtful hand on his long chin. 'I take it the Pugilistic Chanticleer is some kind of professional pugilist? I seem to have seen his name mentioned in the *Courant* from time to time. Usually as the vanquished, I seem to recall.'

'I think you could say he has been unlucky in his friends' choice of opponents,' began Keyes, in the manner of a connoisseur. Lord Scoggie clearly did not want to pursue the subject in that much detail for now.

'I shall consider the matter,' he told the boys. 'I make no promises at this stage. And perhaps, too, we should consider an appropriate outing for the ladies, while you are here. They so rarely have a suitable escort.' Lord Scoggie looked down at his plate as he said this, not quite sure if he wanted to say it at all. The Major looked startled.

'Oh, of course. I shall be glad to escort you anywhere you please, ladies – I have brought my own horse if you wish to ride – or driving would be equally, er, delightful ... whatever you desire, of course.'

'What a kind offer, Major,' said Deborah, while Beatrix looked firmly up at the wall above the Major's head. 'We must consider carefully before we impose on you. My mother may have some interesting ideas on the matter.'

'Of course.' Keyes bowed his head again, but Deborah had already looked away, so he turned back to Lord Scoggie. 'Did I mention Davie Baird was given a knighthood this year? Of course in the barracks they're all wondering who will be next.'

He grinned generally round the table, his white teeth glinting. Up on his feet again at the fireplace, the dog Tippoo heard the tone of his master's voice, and barked.

After dinner, Murray left the family to talk in the parlour, and retreated to the kitchen. The servants were seated around the fir table at the far end of the great vaulted room: it was so large it had to serve as their dining room as well as the cooking kitchen and scullery. There, there was a smaller fireplace, less ferociously stacked, and more regularly lit than that above it in the Great Hall. The servants' table still had benches on either side, and Mrs. Costane waved Murray down to join them, even though he had already eaten. He accepted a tankard of ale, and sat down.

'So what do you think of the great Major Keyes?' she asked at once. 'Did he eat my beetroot pancakes? And the curry – did he like that? That's my own receipt for curry powder, you ken. I didn't buy that.'

'It was delicious. And yes, Major Keyes ate it all. The boys liked the pancakes, too, I think.'

Mrs. Costane looked satisfied. She had not asked about Lord Scoggie's appetite, but she would have known that he had concentrated on the steamed fish (from the village harbour), the beef (from their own cows), the carrot pudding (grown in their own garden), and the baked apples (from their own orchard). The artichoke tart, the curried chicken, and the raisins in the dumpling had all been rigorously ignored by him, though he urged them contentedly enough on his guest. The dishes had come down empty: the carrot pudding being consumed by the servants was an extra one, and the curried chicken was a beast that had seen more of the world than the plump youngsters that had gone upstairs.

'He is a very fine gentleman of refined tastes,' said Naismyth, then seemed surprised when Mrs. Costane thanked him for the compliment: he had not intended it for her.

'He's very handsome,' put in Grisell, with a wink to old Hannah, the kitchenmaid. 'He'd do you nicely, Mrs. Costane, if you thought of taking a second husband. Though I might fight you for him myself,' she added thoughtfully.

Andrew, the new boy, scowled.

'I saw nothing out of the ordinary in him. He's a rough-looking specimen.'

'So would you be,' retorted Grisell, 'if you had done all the things he has, fought and travelled and led men to victory, instead of combing his hair back and trying to look ornamental in some master's house.'

'There's a great deal more to service than that, and you know it,' said Naismyth, with dignity. Andrew grinned up at him.

'Aye, you hear that, Grisell? Anyway, there's plenty of us in service could fight and travel if we wanted to – we just know how to face up to our responsibilities here.'

'Oh, aye,' Grisell responded sarcastically.

'Anyway, I don't think much of his dog,' Andrew went on. 'A filthy-natured, white creature, with too many teeth for his mouth.'

'It's a fierce thing, a dog fit for a hero,' Naismyth insisted ponderously.

'It nipped me twice before I had the soup as far as his Lordship.'

'Aye, it knows its master when it sees him,' said Naismyth, and Grisell laughed.

'Well, I'd follow the colours for him if he asked me nicely,' she said. Andrew did not respond, but concentrated on removing the last of the meat from his chicken leg with surgical persistence.

'You'll need to put something on those bites, Andrew,' said Murray sociably. 'I don't think that dog's too fussy about its food.'

'Aye, Miss Beatrix has some salve for me when I've finished here,' said Andrew, without looking up. Grisell's grin faded slightly.

'Anyway, you saw more of him than we did, Mr. Murray.' Mrs. Costane struck in again. 'What was he like?'

'Much as you would expect, Mrs. Costane,' Murray said. 'He's large and full of himself, very handsome, well-informed, I think, about current gossip in London, a little shy with the ladies, and keen to tell his stories as any old soldier might be.'

'Less of the old, Mr. Murray,' said Naismyth sternly. 'He is not of any great age.'

'I beg your pardon, Mr. Naismyth, I meant merely a man who has formerly been a soldier, not necessarily one of any age.'

'The man is a hero to his nation, Mr. Murray. His deeds may have aged him before his time, but they are deeds of which any gentleman might be proud. Yes, Andrew, service is a grand way to live if you can do no better, but the army is the only true profession there is.'

'Apart from the Church, Mr. Naismyth,' said Hannah primly.

'And the law,' added Mrs. Costane, who liked Nathaniel Tibo.

'My brother is already in the army, Mr. Naismyth. I was brought up instead to manage my father's estates when he is gone.' Murray felt he had heard enough in praise of the army for one day. Naismyth, who had briefly forgotten that Murray was not just another servant, immediately turned unctuous again, to Murray's disgust.

'But of course, Mr. Murray, the responsibility of an estate, with all its workers and families, that is a great thing. I had meant by profession the need to go out and earn one's pay of course, nothing like the true occupation of a gentleman, like Lord Scoggie, or like your honourable father, of course.' And nothing at all like a tutor or a secretary, Murray added silently to himself. He already regretted speaking.

'Why is the garden door open? he asked, trying to change the subject.

'Ugh,' said Mrs. Costane, remembering. 'One of the fish from the village was off. The place was stinking.'

'You'd think it would be easy enough to buy good fish, this near the sea,' said Andrew, still working the last scraps off his chicken.

'Oh, you're new to the place, aren't you?' said Mrs. Costane. 'The best of the fish never even touches the land. It's taken by the Edinburgh boats from our boats, and off down the coast before we even know it's caught. You have to tell them well ahead if you want any of it.'

'There's a bit of a draught now, though, isn't there?' said Hannah grimly. 'I'll close the door again.'

She slid off the bench and stepped over to shut the door. The servants turned back towards their good fire, and rubbed their hands together as Mrs. Costane and Hannah took away their plates and brought the baked apples.

Outside, the closed door cut off any further sounds from the kitchen. Tom Baillie had been sitting quietly behind a water butt, his legs stretched out on the ground in front of him. He had been listening, but he was at peace for the moment, for the spot was sheltered and dry, and he was distracted by the patterns of the movements of some slaters up and down the rough stonework of the castle wall beside him.

He felt weary, sleepy almost, but just now the kitchen garden was empty, for the gardeners were at their dinner too, and he had to move before they came back. He pushed himself up to crouch on one leg, the other out straight in front still. The strong bent leg lifted him, helped with one hand pressed against the wall and the other pulling the top of the water butt. It wobbled and he froze, muscles tense as wires. The butt settled again, and he breathed. He managed to straighten up, and pulled his crutches from behind the butt where he had hidden them. He swung them under his armpits, into their long-accustomed place, and began the long walk back to the village road through the orchard. The road was as quiet as the orchard and garden, and no one stopped to help him on to the back of their cart, or shortened his journey with talk as he hobbled down the steep hill to the village. In the distance he could see the herring boats, dots on the pigeon-grey sea. He was past regretting such things, but just for a moment the smile he caused to inhabit his face when he was in company faded a little as he stopped to gaze at them. Then he tugged his crutches back into place, and picked his way carefully down over the mud and cobbles of the village street, smiling blankly at the ground ahead of him.

CHAPTER SIX

'Excuse me,' said Murray, poking his head around the door of the drawing room. 'It's time for the boys to have their walk.'

He had not been able to resist pausing for a moment before he opened the door. There had been only the barest trace of conversation from inside: a sentence or two from Lord Scoggie, a few words from Deborah, and a pause before a response from Major Keyes. Even so, the atmosphere did not seem to be affecting the boys. When Murray looked in, they were sitting side by side on two low stools, gazing reverently at their hero – though keeping him between them and the frightening dog. They seemed disinclined to leave him for something as pedestrian as a walk, but their father was more enthusiastic.

'Yes, of course, Mr. Murray. Henry, Robert, go along now.'

Major Keyes watched them push themselves reluctantly to their feet, then appeared struck by an idea.

'I could fancy a little exercise after my carriage ride, and after that fine dinner,' he said. 'Would you mind if I joined you, lads? Ladies, would you be good enough to excuse me?'

'Of course,' said Deborah, just a little too quickly. 'You must have some fresh air, and the walks here are very pretty.' She stood to encourage him, and Major Keyes pulled himself up out of a sagging chair. 'Perhaps, Mr. Murray, you might like to show Major Keyes the lake walk.'

Murray met her eye, surprised but trying not to show it. The lake walk was the longest on the estate, and on a day like this they would be lucky to be home before dusk. She nodded briskly at him, and he took the hint. It might take some persuasion on Lady Scoggie's part, he thought, to marry her daughter to Major Keyes.

The two men and the boys met in the hall in a few minutes in their outdoor boots and coats, and Murray led the way out on to the drive. While he saw to it that the boys had their hats and gloves on, Keyes took a few deep breaths of air with marked appreciation.

'You have no idea how good it is to breathe in like this, this damp, salty air, cold and healthy,' he explained. 'Even the south of England is too warm for my liking.'

'And India?' Murray asked, pushing the boys off ahead of them towards the lake. Robert gave a longing look to Major Keyes, but could not resist the pull of mud and trees. He ran off down the slope.

'A filthy climate. We lost more men to disease than to any native assault.'

'That must be very wearing.' He wondered if Major Keyes had any other topic of conversation: if not, it was going to be a long walk, and a long winter ahead. Fortunately, the major almost immediately proved him wrong.

'Do the boys walk every day?' he asked.

'Well, if the weather permits it. Lord Scoggie is very enthusiastic about fresh air.'

'Aye, all the windows in Scoggie Castle always seem to be painted open! And what other exercise do they have?'

'I teach them a little fencing,' Murray said, slightly apologetically, feeling he was talking to a professional. 'In fine weather they run races and steeplechases over hurdles, and of course they have ponies which they ride a few times a week. Archery is a little more difficult: there is nowhere around that is suitably flat that does not usually have a howling gale blowing across it.'

Major Keyes smiled.

'And pugilism?' he asked. 'I noticed an air to Lord Scoggie's remarks at the dinner table.'

It was Murray's turn to smile.

'Lord Scoggie does not consider it a fit sport for gentlemen.'

'But the boys are keen on it?'

'Robert is, or thinks he would be if he could try it. Henry would verify that Robert is keen to practise with his fists. Robert,' he raised his voice, 'keep away from the edge, or your father will skelp you.' Robert's scowl was visible two hundred yards away.

'Do they swim in the lake?' Major Keyes asked, as the surface of the lake came more clearly into view through the trees. 'It's a fine body of water.'

'It is, and to my regret they do not. Lord Scoggie does not permit it. In the summer, however, we often walk down to the sea and bathe there.'

'You are a strong swimmer yourself? Then what is his objection?'

'He lost a dog here once, and he is convinced that there are weeds below the surface that trap swimmers. He may well be right, for I do not believe that it has been dragged for several years. There is a boat here but it is rarely used.'

They paused for a moment to survey the length of the lake in mutual sorrow at the waste of it. As the boys reached the trees ahead, they disturbed a flock of pigeons which rose with a clatter like falling playing cards, and shot up towards the house and the doocot, wings whistling as they went.

'What's your background, then?' Keyes asked. 'Apart from being a Master of Arts from St. Andrews University, which of course is enough for Lord Scoggie.' A grin took away any offence in the remark.

'My father is laird of Letho, near Cupar. He saw to my early training in fencing, boxing, riding, and so on, but my inclination was more to reading, I'm sorry to say. We had a falling out while I was at St. Andrews, and Lord Scoggie kindly employed me to enable me to support myself independently.'

'I see. Perhaps Lord Scoggie would allow me to involve myself in the boys' physical training during my stay,' Keyes suggested. 'It was very notable in the regiment which men had had a good upbringing and were well used to physical exercise. They were better at coping with the diseases as well. I shall put it to him.'

'You are very welcome to try,' said Murray, 'though I am not sure that an argument based on its usefulness for military service will carry much weight with him. Robert would very much like to join a regiment, but I am not sure that his father will let him.' He tried to remind himself that he was not that keen on overseeing the boys' exercise himself, and should not feel that Major Keyes was treading on his property.

'But I am astonished that he feels that way: he has certainly never said as much to me.' Major Keyes pondered for a moment. 'It is extraordinary that someone as keen on the traditions of North Britain as he is should forbid his son to join the army. Soldiers are one of our greatest exports, are they not?'

Murray laughed.

'I had not thought of them that way, but perhaps you are right.' He paused to allow Keyes to negotiate a kissing-gate that led to the lake path, which he did awkwardly, shuffling on his wooden leg which otherwise did not seem to hold him back. 'My own brother is in the Royal Regiment, but I am not sure he is much of an export at the moment. I had hoped, perhaps, that scholarship was something we were better known for. Hume and Adam Smith, for instance, to speak of recent times, though Europe used to be flooded with scholarship from this part of the world.'

'I don't know much about scholarship, but the Royal Regiment is a good example. If your brother's with them, you'll know their nickname: Pontius Pilate's Bodyguard. We've been exporting soldiers for a good long time. And the French king's archers were all Scots.' The major freed himself from the gate, and called to Tippoo who scrambled efficiently over the adjacent wall. 'India is full of Scots, both administrators and soldiers. I remember a day I was invited to dinner in Bombay – that's a town on the east coast, one of the headquarters for the East India Company. It was not long after 'Patam, and I was still a little unsteady on my foot. So was everyone else after the dinner ended though, eh? Two days of drinking, then we went out to hunt wild pig. Aye, grand days! But every man at that dinner, and there were forty of them, was a Scot.' He laughed at the memory, then cocked an eye sideways at Murray. 'I talk about nothing else, do I?'

Murray, surprised to have his thoughts suddenly echoed, made awkward, non-committal noises, and Keyes grinned sheepishly.

'I can't help it,' he said. 'For one thing, I spent three years out there, and it was a marvellous place. Terrible, and marvellous. The sights I saw ... they haunt my dreams, you know. For another, since 'Patam no one has asked me about anything else. I was given the freedom of cities in England I'd never even visited till the presentation, and honours and medals and who knows what, and invited to all kinds of clubs and dinners, and all the time people just want to know all about India and the battle and what did Tippoo Sultan look like and did he have a harem, and half the time you don't even know what their names are because they are much keener to tell you that they know who you are. It's a bit monotonous, to tell you the truth, Murray.'

'It must be.' Murray had not thought of it before: it was as if Keyes' life had frozen the day of the taking of Seringapatam, and he had not been allowed to progress since. He did not envy him.

'And to be honest,' Keyes went on with diffidence, 'it's easy enough to be a hero when you're from North Britain. People almost expect it of you. Like Davie Baird – now, I wouldn't want to take anything from him, for he's a grand soldier, but there he was offered the chance to take his revenge on Tippoo. The other officers were just standing back letting him charge ahead, so how could he not be a hero? Now there was a fellow out there called Wesley, an Irishman. You may have heard of him? He's a grand man for the baggage train, a kind of quartermaster general by birth. He's not one for charging ahead with fifty kilted Highlanders behind him, screaming curses on the enemy and slaughtering all before him. He's a good man, but he'll never be a hero. All David Baird had to do – all I had to do – was to be ourselves.'

'What have you found, Henry?' Murray asked suddenly. The boys were just in front of them now, and Henry was poking something delicately with a stick.

'It's a bird's nest,' said Henry, using what Murray liked to think of as his Royal Society voice, employed for gentle lecturing of his regrettably stupid tutor. 'I think it's a crossbill's. Yes, look: here's a bit of eggshell, white with bits of red and brown on it.'

'Let's play football with it,' urged Robert.

'No! I don't have a crossbill's nest in my collection.'

'Well you're not a crossbill,' Robert pointed out, reasonably enough. 'Why do you need that mouldy old thing?'

'For scientific purposes,' Henry explained grandly. He clutched the ball of moss and lichen to his chest like a new-born lamb, and looked up into the fir trees they were passing under. 'It must have fallen from the very top ...'

'Maybe the crossbills thought they were under siege, and dropped it on the enemy,' Robert suggested, with the barest glance at Major Keyes.

'If you're under siege, you don't drop your whole fortress on the enemy,' said Henry disdainfully. 'Mr. Murray, will you carry it for me? And please be careful.'

'I'll do my best, Henry.' Murray reluctantly took the nest as the boys rushed off again. 'And there,' he added with a smile to Major Keyes, 'are both our arguments regarding North British exports proved. Henry is the scholar, and Robert the soldier.' And the sooner we can export them both the better, he thought, shifting the nest to a safer hold. It would probably have fallen apart by the time they reached the house, and no doubt he would be to blame for the loss to science.

They strolled on. The path was lightly muddy, and Major Keyes seemed to be managing very well. Tippoo jogged along beside him, and a little ahead when the path was too narrow, rarely distracted by the interesting smells along the way, as if he had a greater purpose in mind. Here there was no salt odour, for they were in a hollow: the air was scented instead with earth and decaying leaves, fir bark and the damp shallows of the lake. When the sun showed itself a little through the clouds, the light was muddled with shade under the trees.

They had gone a little way in silence, listening to the shouts of the boys up ahead, when Keyes cleared his throat and folded his hands behind his back.

'Ah, would you mind if I asked you something about the family? I understand you're in a difficult position, so if you don't want to answer just say so, but I'm a clumsy fellow, and I don't want to put my foot in it, so to speak.' He grinned, glancing down at his wooden peg. Murray said:

'Go ahead.' He expected something about Deborah, and was surprised when Keyes began.

'I asked earlier after Lady Scoggie, and though the explanation given – that I had arrived before I was expected – is quite natural, I thought I sensed something more to the matter. Tell me, is she ill?'

'Oh! no, not that I know of.' Taken aback, he thought quickly. 'If there is a little tension, it is perhaps that they were embarrassed. Lady Scoggie spends a great deal of time in charitable work, and because she cannot always predict when she will be at home she has handed much of the running of the household over to Miss Deborah, who is very good at it.'

'Charitable work, eh? That was not always her way.' Keyes thought for a moment, as if remembering. 'I used to know her well before her marriage to Lord Scoggie. She's my cousin, you know, and we met often when we were growing up. She was not brought up to it, and she never had much inclination towards charity, preferring balls and routs. But perhaps there are few of those in this neck of the woods.'

'Certainly that is true,' said Murray. He could not remember the last time he had danced, and he missed it. 'I think Miss Deborah would prefer more of a social life sometimes.'

'Miss Deborah, eh? Now she has changed greatly since I last saw her. She's a fine figure of a lass, is she not?'

'She is considered very much of a beauty, indeed,' said Murray.

'And is she spoken for?' Keyes gave him an odd look sideways. 'Is there a man lucky enough to claim her for his own?'

'Not as far as I know,' said Murray carefully. It was possible that Nathaniel Tibo thought he might some day have that privilege, but Murray did not think he had received much encouragement from Deborah herself. It was probably best not to mention it. 'I think, of course, that Lord Scoggie would like to marry her into an old Scottish family, people who would match the Scoggies for history and standing.' He looked round at Keyes, intending the idea partly as a joke, and was surprised at the expression on the major's face. It could best have been described as blank, wiped clean. Murray was about to say something when the expression cleared, and Robert ran up to them.

'Mr. Murray, will you carry this? It's a magic stone!'

He handed Murray a flattish stone with a natural hole worn in the middle.

'Who told you that?' Keyes asked.

'Henry. But I think it would be brilliant to put in a catapult. Think about it, Mr. Murray: you'd have a stone that would come back every time after you'd hit something!' He ran off again, leaving Murray with the muddy stone.

'Um,' said Murray, balancing it on top of the nest, then thinking better of it and slipping it into his pocket. 'I think people hide them in their thatch for luck, or am I thinking of something else?'

They were more than halfway round the lake now, passing the icehouse half-buried in the bank amongst the trees, with, at that moment, Robert trying to fling himself off the door lintel, while Henry investigated a clump of dangerous-looking toadstools by the path.

'Mr. Murray, will you – ' Henry began.

'No, I'm not carrying one of those, Henry. It would either fall apart on the way home, or rot overnight when we got there.'

'Then I want to draw it now.' He squatted down beside them and drew out his notebook and pen. They had each been given them, but Robert's was probably reduced to paper darts by now. With a sigh, Murray found a fallen log and led Keyes over to it so that they could wait in comparative comfort. Robert came to sit beside them, and began to work quietly at a stick with his pocket knife. For a little while, all was peace.

In front of them, the lake was the shining brown of a mountain pool, flecked with golden beech leaves floating at peace where they had fallen. Beyond it, the far shore was softened by trees starting to turn yellow, willows trailing into the water, and the green lawns stretching up to the castle with its outbuildings on the top of the rise. The sky, high above, was grey-white like limewash.

Suddenly Murray heard voices approaching and footsteps on the path coming from the other direction. For the moment they were invisible to the newcomers, and Murray was surprised to see a couple he did not know strolling hand in hand by the side of the lake, and stopping to look over at the castle. The woman was small and neat, in a beautiful blue cloak, and pointed with a tiny gloved hand across the lake.

'I suppose that must be Scoggie Castle,' she said. 'How unpicturesque it is, quite what one expects of its name. It is irregular enough, I suppose, for beauty, but it is hardly part of its landscape, is it?'

The man, who from the back was most remarkable for his tight-fitting breeches and delicacy of movement, looked where she was pointing.

'I disagree, my dear. The castle is indeed picturesque, but in the absolute sense of the word, almost Gothic in its intensity. See how it stands out against the sky? It is like a great nail hammered in to the landscape to subdue it, as Presbyterian as the nail with which Martin Luther drove his declarations into the cathedral door at Wittenberg. I expect Lord Scoggie to be a most interesting type of gentleman, do you not?'

'Most interesting!' she agreed, turning to him with laughter – and caught sight of their audience. There was an awkward pause, but only for a fraction of a second. The man turned quickly and came towards Murray and Keyes, who rose from their log with some attempt at dignity. The man removed his broad-brimmed hat, which made him look like a minister, thus displaying his extraordinary blond hair, which did not. His face was calm and serious.

'Forgive us, gentlemen, if we have caused any alarm or offence,' said the man. 'Do I gather that one of you must be Lord Scoggie?' He looked expectantly at Major Keyes, but he shook his head without smiling.

'Alexander Keyes, sir, kinsman to Lord Scoggie, and this is Mr. Murray, Lord Scoggie's secretary.'

'Philip Bootham, gentlemen.' Bootham bowed beautifully, reminding Murray suddenly of an actor he had once seen in Edinburgh. 'May I present Mrs. Bootham?'

The lady came forward at that and made her curtsey. When she looked up, Murray temporarily forgot to breathe. Hazel eyes met his. Her white skin was flushed with the fresh air, or perhaps with embarrassment that they might have overheard her comments, and ebony curls framed her face. Around it, her bonnet seemed almost out of place, for he found himself irresistibly thinking of dryads and wood nymphs, and creatures that flitted through forests at dusk, evading human eyes. For a moment, he was lost for words. Then the boys ran up, and the spell was broken.

'I beg your pardon,' he managed to say. 'You must be the new tenants of Aberardour Lodge. Are you intending to visit the Castle this afternoon?'

'Yes, we had hoped to,' said Mr. Bootham. 'Miss Scoggie was kind enough to suggest yesterday that we could walk in the grounds, but we wanted to ask Lord Scoggie himself if this would inconvenience him in any way. Mrs. Bootham has a talent for watercolours, and is always eager for inspiration.'

Watercolours ... water under the trees, flowing brown and shining through the woodland, and this woman beside it, bending over it, hair sliding to kiss the dancing surface ... Murray shook himself inside. This woman inspired fantasy. What was she – a witch? Fife had a good tradition of witchcraft, but surely this woman was English? Whatever she was, she was muddling his thoughts like strong ale on a sunny day.

'Then you must come with us up to the castle,' Keyes was saying to Mr. Bootham. 'We are returning there soon, are we not, Mr. Murray?'

'Directly, though it is still some distance, as you see. Come on, boys: are you finished, Henry?'

'Yes, I suppose so.' Henry looked down at his notebook, then noticed that Mr. Bootham was also gazing down at it. He snapped the notebook shut instantly. Murray noticed that, fortunately, this amused Mr. Bootham, rather than offending him. The party set off, back the way the Boothams had come, so that Keyes could complete his circumambulation of the lake. Keyes offered Mrs. Bootham his arm and they went ahead, led by Tippoo the dog. Murray and Mr. Bootham followed, and the boys kept their usual chaotically varied pace around them.

'You teach the boys science, I see?' said Bootham, waving a graceful hand towards the nest in Murray's hands.

'Henry is a keen student. He is the elder boy.' Murray nodded in Henry's direction. 'Robert, the younger, prefers history and geography.'

'You are lucky to teach such scholarly pupils. I understand that such a situation is much more rewarding than striving to drum a few useful facts into more reluctant heads.' He smiled gently. Murray did not reply. Ahead of them, Mrs. Bootham's long cape trailed through the fallen leaves along the path, tumbling at the edges like a wave on the beach.

'And has Lord Scoggie other children? I have already met Miss Scoggie and Miss Pirrie, of course.'

Murray felt ashamed that he was not playing his part in the conversation, and tried to concentrate more.

'No, just Miss Scoggie and the boys. You are right, they are comparatively rewarding to teach, and two is not a great number.'

'Miss Scoggie is a charming girl,' Bootham went on. 'Lord Scoggie must be eager to find her a suitable husband soon.'

'I suppose he must,' said Murray discreetly. 'It is usually the aim of fathers to see their daughters suitably attached.' And what about Beatrix Pirrie? he thought. Why were all of them so interested in Deborah? She was energy and brightness, certainly, but Beatrix – surely other men could see her large, calm eyes, with such depth; her smooth complexion, the colouring so subtle on her cheeks and throat, her ready intelligence. Why was it not her marriage that people enquired about? Money, he knew, played a key role: Bea was the classic poor relation. He felt drawn to her often, for to him they seemed to be if not in exactly the same position in the household, at least in similarly anomalous ones: she was of the family but not quite accepted by outsiders as such, while he was not quite of the family and not quite of the servants' hall, and seen by each as a spy and informant.

He struggled to return to the conversation again.

'Do you find yourselves happily settled at Aberardour Lodge?' he asked.

'Oh, yes, very much indeed,' said Bootham in his calm way. 'It feels like home already.'

'And where was home before?'

'In England,' Bootham replied. 'But we are very fond of North Britain. We find being near the coast, too, a very refreshing experience. Already we have been able to walk along the shore most days.'

'You'll find that increasingly refreshing as the winter comes on,' said Murray with feeling. 'Take care you are not blown away.'

Bootham laughed lightly.

'We are not so hardy that we insist on sea air every day. I think we shall be wise, Mr. Murray.'

'I'm glad to hear it. And when you are not walking, how do you amuse yourselves? I'm afraid there is little entertainment in the neighbourhood, but we try to be sociable.'

'Social activities are not essential to my happiness, Mr. Murray. I had thought perhaps Miss Scoggie might have mentioned that I am, in fact, a poet.' Murray turned in surprise, and Bootham smiled, a sweet smile, as of an angel to a mortal. For a moment he reminded Murray of a cat in Lord Scoggie's stables, who seemed to smile this way, beneficently, usually just before he brought in a particularly large rat. He looked away, and glanced about to see that the boys were in no danger and causing none to anything else. Robert had found a large stick to trail behind him, and Henry was picking moss off a tree trunk.

'Lord Scoggie did say that you were a scholar: I had no idea that you were also an artist. It is quite a privilege for the neighbourhood.' He thought he had managed to sound quite sincere. 'Lord Scoggie has a fine collection of volumes of poetry, which he would be happy to inspect with you, I am sure.'

'Lord Scoggie sounds like a most generous neighbour.' Murray was sure that Mr. Bootham also thought that he had managed to sound quite sincere. He grinned to himself.

They rounded the far end of the lake in a gentle curve, passing over the little bridge that crossed the outflow stream. Mrs. Bootham paused for a moment on it, watching where the stream trickled down through woodland, into which sunlight was suddenly filtered as though for her especial delight. The glow reflected in her face, or it may simply have been her smile, responding to some remark made by Major Keyes, that seemed to illuminate the scene. Murray looked away, automatically checking again that the boys were nearby.

'We go through the kissing gate up ahead,' he said generally, hoping that the party would move on.

'Oh, how does the poor dog manage a kissing gate?' Mrs. Bootham asked in concern.

'You'll see, very readily,' replied Keyes, and led her on. Murray paused before following, to leave Keyes time to manoeuvre through the gate without everyone standing watching. Tippoo leapt the wall again, to light applause from the Boothams.

The grassy slope was an easy end to the walk, and they arrived at the front door with plenty of breath. Murray sent the boys upstairs, with intact nest and magic stone, to change into indoor clothes, and asked Keyes to take the guests up to the drawing room while he went to find Deborah and Beatrix and Lord Scoggie. As he went to the library door, Beatrix appeared from the Great Hall.

'We have guests,' he said quickly. 'The Boothams. I've sent them up to the drawing room.'

'Oh, Deborah's there,' said Beatrix, looking pleased. She and Mrs. Bootham must have liked each other's company, Murray thought. 'Lord Scoggie's in the library. Where's the Major?'

'With the Boothams.' They heard a bell: Deborah must have rung for tea.

'I'd better go up and rescue her,' said Bea obscurely, and smiled at Murray as she darted away up the stairs. Murray knocked gently on the library door, and went in. He found Lord Scoggie in easy conversation with Nathaniel Tibo.

'The Boothams? Delightful,' said Lord Scoggie, as soon as he heard. 'I wonder if he would like to see my library. Did you speak with him? Tibo here says he is a scholar.'

'A poet, apparently.'

'A poet, eh? I wonder should I have heard of him? Always such a difficult question to ask, but one must be interested – and indeed I am. And his wife – is she a well-informed woman?'

'Major Keyes may be able to tell you better than I. I had no conversation with her.' At that Tibo met his eye with a cynical stare.

'Will you join us for tea?' said Lord Scoggie, oblivious to this exchange. 'Where are the boys?'

'Upstairs. Yes, I should be happy to, thank you, my lord.'

The drawing room had a ladylike character compared with the rest of the public rooms of the castle, with chintz curtains and china, and the walls hung with the family's watercolours and embroideries. The Boothams, when Murray, Tibo and Lord Scoggie reached the doorway, were relaxed and perfectly at home: Major Keyes, though he knew the room of old, sat in a manner usually reserved for pickpockets hanging around on street corners. He had an odd habit, Murray noticed, of leaning forward to scratch the side of his leg – the wooden one. Murray wondered if he was haunted by his real leg. He had heard of such things happening.

Mr. Bootham rose gracefully when Lord Scoggie entered the room, and bowed, and after the preliminaries were over he made his excuses for arriving without invitation.

'Miss Scoggie very kindly said you would allow us to wander around your charming park in order to find subjects for Mrs. Bootham's watercolour sketches, and we came, eager as you see, to ask for formal permission.'

'Of course, of course, there is no obstacle to that, Mr. Bootham. I hear you are a scholar? And a poet? Then perhaps you would also like to make some use of my library – poor, perhaps, compared with what you might be used to – I believe you hail from London?'

Mr. Bootham smiled.

'I should be honoured, of course. We are already delighted by the beauty and scholarship of the area, are we not, my dear?' He turned to his wife, who caught his eye and smiled – a little absently, Murray thought.

'I see there are already many watercolours of your lovely estate, Lord Scoggie,' she said, rising to indicate the paintings on the walls.

'Oh, yes, indeed!' Mr. Bootham stepped past her to examine a group of watercolours by the fireplace. When he moved or spoke, it was easy to forget the age his face occasionally betrayed. Murray saw Beatrix looking anxiously towards him: one of the watercolours was hers, and she was a girl always more ready to receive criticism than compliments.

'I'm afraid those are our own poor amateur efforts, Mr. Bootham,' said Deborah. Major Keyes levered himself out of his chair, too, and took a closer look.

'You did these, Cousin Deborah, did you, by Jove?'

'Some are mine, some Beatrix's, and some my mother's. From

before she was married, of course: married ladies seem to have no time for such amusement!'

'Your mother's, eh?' Mr. Bootham peered more closely at one of the paintings, a study of a pet rabbit now long dead. 'Quite a talent, don't you think, my dear?' He nudged his wife and pointed to the rabbit. Mrs. Bootham seemed less convinced, but said nothing.

They were poised like this, with the Boothams and Major Keyes by the fireplace, the ladies and Lord Scoggie seated on the pretty sofas and chairs, Tibo arranged by a window and Murray tucking himself to one side out of the way, when they heard steps on the stone stairs outside the door.

'Ah, the tea,' said Deborah, arranging her skirts to allow her to serve. The door opened, and a small figure came in, neat to the point of thinness, hands to her chin to undo her bonnet ribbons, a woollen shawl in the *à la Nelson* fashion of half a dozen years ago slipping from her shoulders, her skirt hem muddy to a height of six inches from her boots.

'Mother!' exclaimed Deborah. 'You're back! We have our visitors, Mamma.'

The Boothams and Major Keyes swung round from the paintings. Nathaniel Tibo stepped forward from the window embrasure.

Lady Scoggie, with a faint squeak, sank to the floor in a deep faint.

CHAPTER SEVEN

Murray tried to concentrate on the document on the table.

Written in flaking black ink on a crisp slice of vellum, it had spent a century or so folded in four, and now had to be pinned flat with a book and a couple of candlesticks. The handwriting was aged, but Murray had difficulty in believing that it had ever been easy to read.

'Be it known - to all present ...' he managed, mouthing the words. A shadow passed over the vellum. He did his best to ignore it. 'that I, Jacobus Scoggy, Lord Scoggy of Scoggy, being seik in bodie but of haill mind ...'

He felt a movement behind him, a soft scuffle amongst the books to go to the binder. Blinking, trying to refocus, he glanced up at the high ceiling and then down again to the document. Up in the gallery, which was simply part of the first floor landing, he could hear Beatrix and Deborah hurrying past, Deborah laying out the plans for the day. The windows were open, and from outside, distantly, came the scrape and tap of fencing foils and the large voice of Major Keyes, instructing the boys in their lesson.

'Knowing no thing more certain than the judgement of our Lord and no thing more uncertain than the day of our own death ...'

'Mr. Murray!'

He jumped, and spun round in his chair.

'Yes, Lady Scoggie?'

She smiled rather weakly at him.

'I wonder if you would mind helping me to open this deed box?'

He looked at it. It was one of the heap drawn into the library for him to work through. Nothing about it signified, to any useful extent, its contents, and Lady Scoggie had never previously expressed the least interest in his work amongst the family papers. In fact, he was fairly sure he had never even seen her in the library. However, why should she not look?

'Certainly, my lady. Some of them are a little rusty.' He knelt beside the deed box and applied his long fingers to the lock at the front. Lady Scoggie continued her uneasy perambulation of the library.

Deborah had let it be known that her mother's faint had been the result of missing both breakfast and dinner, and it seemed that she had managed to win a battle of wills that ensued, for Lady Scoggie was reluctantly confined to the castle for the day, and barred from her usual charitable visits in order to rest. Neither woman was now in a particularly good mood, and Murray had had to suffer, for the last hour, Lady Scoggie's presence in the library, poking, scuffling, sighing and meandering, while being enjoined just to ignore her. It would almost have been easy, physically: Lady Scoggie was always small, but seemed now to be shrinking, and Murray wondered how many other meals she had missed recently. Her old brown gown was loose across her shoulders, and she huddled around her the same shawl she had worn yesterday. Though he himself saw a change in her appearance, he could have read it just as easily in the look of complete shock that had passed over Major Keyes' face when he had seen her in the drawing room before her faint.

'Are these all the boxes Lord Scoggie has given you?' she asked, returning to stand beside him.

'So far, my lady. He adds to them from time to time when more are found. I think these are from the gun room, the east tower room and the stables – be careful you don't go too close to that one, for instance, my lady. I think some of the top floor rooms have still to be examined for others.'

'Good Lord!' said Lady Scoggie. 'I had no idea this was such a great task.' She perched on the edge of his chair, watching his progress. He had taken a piece of wood he sometimes used for the purpose and was gently knocking the corners of the deed box, trying to break the seal or to knock the lid back into shape: this particular box looked as if it had been used as a step up to some well-used high shelf. 'And what age are the papers you have discovered so far?'

'Around the time of Queen Mary and King James VI, most of them. It was around that time that the Lord Scoggie of the time was building up the estate, so there are lots of deeds transferring land to him. But the one on the table there is his will.'

'His will? Really?' She turned to study the document, touching the old vellum with her pale little fingers. Murray watched her for a second. She was really extremely colourless. He thought of Major Keyes asking him if there was some illness in question, and wondered if there actually was.

After a moment she looked away from the will again and stared away at the fireplace, contemplating something much more distant.

'I seem to have spent so little time with the family recently,' she said. 'Major Keyes arrived yesterday before dinner, I gather.'

'That's right. Rather earlier than expected, but not quite early enough for Robert and Henry.' He looked up and smiled at her, and she smiled back.

'I can imagine. It's so difficult for little boys to be patient.'

'And they do not stay little for long,' Murray added, seizing a small opportunity. 'Soon they will be ready for University – or I think

Robert would prefer the army.'

'Goodness,' was her only response. 'So soon.'

Murray managed to lift one corner of the lid a quarter of an inch, but it slid down again when he tried the other side.

'I'm afraid this is taking some time,' he said, to fill a silence.

'Perhaps I should have asked for some other box ...' A confused look passed over her face.

'Not at all – they all have to be opened some time.' He applied the blade of a paper knife delicately to the edge of the lid.

'And the guests who were here yesterday when I arrived home – '

'Yes?'

'I don't think I have had the pleasure.'

'Mr. and Mrs. Bootham. They have taken Aberardour Lodge, and had come over to ask Lord Scoggie for permission to walk in the park. It seems she is quite a painter, and he is a poet. They are English, though I am not sure from where.' He had spent some time the night before thinking about the Boothams, or at least about Mrs. Bootham. She was a witch, he had decided. She was beautiful, a wood-elf, certainly, but there was something altogether too unsettling about her. A married woman should not have that effect, surely. And her husband, with his fair hair and sculpted face – there was something not quite human there, too, surely. He would have to ask Major Keyes what he thought.

'It will be pleasant for the girls to have some other female company,' said Lady Scoggie, without expression. 'Bootham, you say?'

'That's right.' With a snap, the paper knife broke, the point flicking backwards to embed itself in a leg of the table with alarming force. At the same moment, to his surprise, the deed box opened enough for him to insert the broken knife and lever the lid up fully. Inside were about a hundred bundles of thin paper, rolled into tubes but tossed into a heap. Not one that Murray could see was labelled.

'Oh, well done!' cried Lady Scoggie. 'Now, what do you suppose all those are?'

'I haven't the remotest notion,' said Murray, trying to keep the irritation out of his voice and not quite succeeding. Lady Scoggie glanced at him, and settled down quietly to the papers, allowing him to return to his will.

She took a few bundles of the papers from the deed box and sat opposite Murray at the table, delicately unrolling the tubes and trying her best to read the spidery writing inside. Murray could not help glancing over, partly for a change from his Stuart papers: the bundles from Lady Scoggie's box could not have been more than fifty years old, and were comparatively clean. His fingers were filthy with dust from the charters, whose box was rusted through on one side.

For ten minutes or so, they worked opposite each other in silence. Lady Scoggie quickly examined each of her papers, and soon piled her side of the table with discarded rolls, as if she were looking for something. Murray worked on, reading through the early Lord Scoggie's mundane bequests and inventory. 'Ten milch cows, at six shillings the cow. Ane old sheep at fourpence. Ane red nagg, ane pound ... My old clothes, hats, wiggis and teeth to my daughter's spouse William.' Was William suitably grateful, Murray wondered? Maybe fashions did not change so quickly then. Still, teeth were always useful, he told himself, grimacing.

'So what is your opinion of Major Keyes?' Lady Scoggie's question came suddenly. Murray looked up at her, momentarily stuck for something to say, wondering what she was after. An opinion on Keyes' suitability as a son-in-law?

'I walked round the lake with him yesterday,' he began. 'He appears a very interesting gentleman. He spoke at some length over dinner on the battle of Seringapatam and the officers there.' He thought that Keyes was not finding it easy to return to civilian life, but decided to keep that to himself for a little. Certainly he had seen nothing of the aggression that Lord Scoggie had hinted at here in the library before Keyes' arrival.

'And what do you think Deborah thinks of him?'

Here was more difficult ground.

'She was a little overwhelmed by him, I think, at first,' he ventured, and looked at Lady Scoggie to see how that had been received. She was rolling up the documents she had examined, eyes on her own fingers.

'Does she prefer him to Mr. Tibo, for instance?' she asked. She looked up at him. 'I might not be here all the time, but Lord Scoggie misses less than you would think.'

He nodded, acknowledging the statement.

'I cannot say, I'm afraid, my lady. I have not had much chance for comparison yet.'

'But –' Whatever Lady Scoggie was about to say was lost for good. At that moment the door opened, and with a swagger that was mostly due to his wooden leg, Major Keyes entered the library, Tippoo the dog pattering behind him. Lady Scoggie leapt from her seat.

'Livvy!' Major Keyes cried, holding out his arms to her. Livvy? thought Murray, never having heard her called anything but Lady Scoggie or Mamma. He vaguely remembered reading amongst the papers that her Christian name was Livia, a name he could only, in his mind, associate with the livelier members of the Roman imperial family. Watching Lady Scoggie's prim acceptance of Major Keyes' hug, he found it easy to put the parallel out of his head. He turned back to the will.

'I'm delighted to see you looking so much better,' Keyes was saying. 'I had not expected to see you this morning at all. Good heavens, Livvy, what a scare you gave us all yesterday!'

'I'm so sorry, Alec. What a way to welcome you! But as you see, I am at home today and quite well.' She did not seem entirely well: now that he had released her, she was edging towards the library door.

'Then we must sit together and talk of old times, my dear cousin. But what are you doing in here? I never had you in mind as a lover of libraries!'

His cheery familiarity was having its slight effect in Lady Scoggie's pale face, the beginnings of a flush of amusement.

'No, no, you are quite right. I was looking for Lord Scoggie, but as you see I have missed him.' She took another step, backwards, towards the door.

'I, on the other hand, was looking for Mr. Murray, and have been more successful,' said Major Keyes. Murray, his head bowed over the will, grinned a little to himself at their eagerness to find excuses for being seen near books. 'I have been teaching your lads a little swordplay. Young Robert has the makings, you know.'

'Has he?' Lady Scoggie looked aghast.

'I suppose you would like me to take my charges back now?' Murray asked hurriedly.

'Actually I was going to ask you if I could take the boys out for their ride before dinner,' said Major Keyes. 'My own horse needs exercise today, and I would enjoy seeing how they are coming along in that activity, too.'

'I have no objection, if Lady Scoggie does not mind,' said Murray, though he would have liked a ride himself. Lady Scoggie, not usually consulted over her sons' activities, shook her head quickly.

'Where are the boys?' she asked suddenly. 'I have not seen them this morning.'

'I sent them to fetch their coats and hats,' Major Scoggie admitted. 'I had great hopes of having my wish granted.' He grinned at Murray.

'Then I shall go and say good morning to them before they go,' Lady Scoggie said. She snatched at the door handle. 'I shall send them down to wait in the hall when I have spoken to them.'

Left alone in the library, Major Keyes and Murray sat for a moment in silence, taken aback at the speed of her exit. Tippoo sniffed his way around the room, his claws tapping lightly on the hard floor.

'Keep an eye on Robert, won't you?' Murray said quickly. 'He's inclined to go galloping off and he's not as good a rider as he thinks he is.'

'I'll bear it in mind. Look, Murray,' Major Keyes' voice dropped. 'Can I have a quick word? I'm not sure who else I can talk to.'

Murray looked up in surprise.

'If I can be of assistance at all,' he said, without much encouragement. People who were half-family, half-servants, ended up with a lot of confidences, not all of them welcome.

'It's this,' said the Major, without further preamble. He reached into his pocket and set down on the table a rough piece of paper, folded into a letter. 'Go on, open it.'

Murray opened the paper, and read the careful writing.

"Yew wer not wyse to com back to St.Monance, Major Keys. Yew wuld doe well to kep looking beind yew. A freind."

He turned the paper, but the only mark on the outside was Major Keyes' name.

'Where did this come from?' he asked.

'I don't know. It's anonymous,' the Major snapped.

'I mean where did you find it? How did it arrive with you?'

Major Keyes slapped the table lightly, looking frustrated.

'Naismith brought it up to my chamber earlier. He said he had found it on the hall table – apologised for hours about missing it before. Man's a nuisance.'

'Why show it to me?'

'Well, I can't show it to Scoggie, or Livvy. It seems a bit ungrateful, a guest complaining about this kind of thing.'

'I'm sure Lord Scoggie would be only too pleased to try to get to the bottom of the matter for you. After all, who could it be? There can't be many candidates.'

'That's what I was hoping you'd help with. Do you know if there's anyone locally who was – who doesn't like me?'

He leaned his bad leg against the table, sounding suddenly rather pathetic. Murray contemplated the note. Whatever the Major's complaints about his universal popularity after Seringapatam, it must be easy to fall into the habit of being liked, and difficult to face anything different.

The note was quite poorly written, but not, he thought, deliberately so to deceive. The care taken with each letter implied writing in desuetude: the paper was old, but had been folded neatly. Whoever had done this had taken time over it. He could only think of one candidate in the neighbourhood, but he felt he had to be careful how to phrase the suggestion.

'It was mentioned to me – I heard it somewhere – that the last time you were at Scoggie Castle you had a – an altercation with one of the fishermen.'

'Did I?' Major Keyes looked vague. 'I may have done. I was a fighter in those days, eh?' He laughed.

Murray cleared his throat.

'This was one you injured quite badly. You apparently kicked his knee.'

The Major frowned.

'Oh, that sounds faintly familiar. A young lad. With a pretty wife, I think?'

'I believe so.'

'Oh, I don't expect he can write.' The Major wandered about the library for a moment, swinging his wooden leg with a deliberate swoop as he went along. Back at the table again, he poked around amongst the documents that Murray had carefully arranged, then discovered the copy of *The Siege of Seringapatam* that the boys had been consulting and had of course not put away. He picked it up and flicked through it, smiling dismissively.

'You know the troops went a bit wild after the walls had been breached,' he said. 'There was a lot of looting in the town – well, the soldiers had been waiting around for months, and once they were over the river and in there was no holding them. No reason to, really – they have to have their reward, too. Wellesley was a real killjoy, protecting Tippoo's family, hanging and lashing. He just doesn't understand. After a battle a man needs a drink, a meal, and a woman, and if he doesn't get it he'll take it. You have to be there to know. They've made him a General now, you know, but he's still in Mysore, tedious young paper-pusher.'

Murray did not know quite what to say. It seemed that the Major did not really want help with his anonymous letter: he had just wanted someone else to know about it. He contented himself with pushing papers for a moment, thinking that General Wellesley sounded like a sensible man.

'So what keeps you busy in here?' Keyes asked eventually.

'Sorting out the family papers, constructing a genealogy of the Scoggies – the fashionable thing.' If Lord Scoggie wanted Major Keyes to know about his claims to the Marquisate of Ballavore he could tell him himself.

'Genealogy, eh?' Major Keyes had the air of someone who had heard all the rude jokes there were about genealogy. 'Any dark secrets, ha ha?'

Murray smiled.

'Sadly, no.' There were one or two, perhaps, occasional arrangements for payments to local women inconveniently supporting children of a coincidentally Scoggie-like appearance, one or two accounts of illicit duels or correspondence concerning raiding parties and their results, but it was not his business to discuss them, however distantly past they were. 'There's the library catalogue as well – I'm revising and extending it.'

'Oh, Scoggie and his books!' Keyes came round and looked over Murray's shoulder at the will in front of him. 'What's that mouldy old thing?'

'It's the will of the Lord Scoggie who died in the reign of James VI.'

'A will? Anything juicy in that?' Scratchy tapping told the progress of Tippoo, who followed his master round the table. A white nose appeared over the table edge, sniffing at the document and Murray's hands. Murray kept still.

'Not much, to be honest. He lists his various children and what he wants them to have, and there's an inventory of his animals and crops and so on.'

'I don't know how you can read that stuff. It looks like Hindoo writing to me.'

'It takes a while to adjust, true. And you can't do too much at a time, or you go cross-eyed.'

'Ha! Hardly worth it.' Keyes tapped his hand on the table, making his point, and in a blur of white movement Tippoo lunged and seized the will. The candlesticks crashed over, the book holding down one side fell to the floor. The dog ran off with the document to the shelter of the other library table. Keyes swung over, face scarlet with anger.

'You stupid creature! Give that back at once, sir!' He gave a few sharp pokes with his stick under the table, and was answered with muffled yelps. 'Genealogy! I'll tell you a few things about your genealogy, you cur!' He stretched in under the table, struggled for a moment, and at last produced the will, handing it back to Murray. Another struggle produced the dog, which he laid about with the stick without ceremony. Between him and the dog, the noise was terrific.

Murray examined the will. The vellum was tough, and was stretched, rather than torn. Some of the writing, though, in its flaky ink, had broken away altogether, and there were parts of the document that could no longer be read at all.

'I'm desperately sorry, Murray,' said Keyes at last, breathing heavily. The dog cowered at his ankles. On his back at least one weal was visible through the thin white coat: Keyes had drawn blood. Murray swallowed.

'It's all right. The thing is made of skin: maybe it still smelled of animal.'

'Skin, eh? I'd never have known. It looks like thick paper. Clever dog, eh? Spotting something like that.'

'I'm sure I heard the boys coming down the stairs,' said Murray. 'They'll be waiting for you. I'd recommend a ride across the park and through the woods to the left of the lake – there's a good gallop beyond there.'

'A grand idea.' Keyes grinned at Murray. 'We'll go at once. Come along, Tippoo.' Subdued, the dog followed him out into the hall. The door closed. Murray leaned back against the table, feeling sick. He had wondered about Keyes' violence, but no longer. Now he wondered instead how he could help to persuade Lady Scoggie not to marry her daughter to that man.

The answer to many of life's problems lay in a cup of tea. He listened for a moment at the library door, waiting for the sounds of the boys and Keyes departing for the stables. Then he slipped into the silent hall, and across to the door to the servants' corridor. In a moment or two, he was within reach of the refuge of the kitchens and the natural bustle of preparations for dinner.

But as he approached the half-closed kitchen door along the flag passage, it quickly became clear that all was not normal in the kitchen. He could hear banging, rhythmic, metallic banging, and the slap of hands, and hurried steps. In a moment, he heard upraised voices. It took a few seconds for him to recognise the noise as singing.

He pushed the door fully open, and gaped at the scene. Mrs. Costane, skirts and apron flying, was dancing an improvised military two-step with the new man, Andrew, the length of the kitchen, a look of vicious pleasure on her face. At the big fir table, Hannah beat time with a wooden spoon on the base of a copper saucepan, accompanied by Grisell with a rolling pin on the table. All were singing, but not perhaps the same tune. Even Naismyth, sitting in a porter's chair near the fire, was tapping his fingers on the chair arm.

Mrs. Costane, spinning violently halfway up the kitchen, suddenly caught sight of Murray.

'Another couple! Hannah, quickly!'

Hannah, with unaccustomed enthusiasm, seized Murray's hands and dragged him off to join in the two-step, finding her feet surprisingly quickly, with a lightness that consorted oddly with her usual sour expression. Grisell, laughing through her singing, took over the wooden spoon and saucepan drum. Murray walked Hannah and wheeled her, in step with Andrew in front of him, twice more up the kitchen and down again. Then, exhausted, Mrs. Costane broke away laughing and returned to her table, followed by a demure Hannah. Andrew tossed his blond hair back from his face, looking as if he could take anything in his stride. Mr. Naismyth rose from the chair and paced up and down, smiling a satisfied smile.

'What on earth is the occasion?' asked Murray, helping himself to tea from the pot by the fire.

'Lord Scoggie has been kind enough to offer us a ball,' Mr. Naismyth announced. 'He is a most generous employer.'

'On Hallowe'en!' Grisell added. 'Less than a month away!'

'And a great deal to do before then,' added Mrs. Costane, reprovingly. 'Look what you've done to my milk saucepan, you young vandal! That'll have to be re- coppered when the man comes round.'

Andrew caught Grisell's eye: the percussion had been Mrs. Costane's idea. Grisell looked away.

'You'll come, won't you, Mr. Murray?' she asked. The tone was innocently friendly, but the look of incredulity that Andrew shot him before he could reply was enough to show him that he was not accepted without question in this world.

'I'm not sure ...' he replied.

'Mr. Murray has duties too, you know, Grisell,' put in Mrs. Costane, mercifully. 'But you'll come if you can, Mr. Murray, won't you? You've showed yourself a good enough dancer, and I can tell you, we'll need you. You should see the way some of the gardeners hirple round the floor.'

'The gardeners come too?' said Andrew, slightly dismayed.

'Well, it wouldn't be much of a ball with just the six of us, now, would it? The gardeners, the laundrymaids, the kitchen and house staff, the girls in the brewhouse and the pig and cattle men in the mains farm, the stablemen and grooms and any of their families. There'll be upwards of forty of us, if past years are to go by. And it's all very well to say it's an evening's holiday, but who'll be making the supper?'

'Aye,' Hannah nodded, knowing that whatever drama Mrs. Costane made of the evening, she herself would really be making the supper.

'Where will it be?' Andrew asked.

'We use one of the barns, lad,' Mr. Naismyth explained.

'We're allowed to decorate it, with paper things and branches and flowers, if we can find any,' Grisell added.

'Apples would be nice,' suggested Mrs. Costane, 'if we could take a branch or two from the orchard.'

'Neep lanterns,' said Hannah suddenly.

'I'm not sure Lord Scoggie would allow such paganry,' said Mr. Naismyth, meaning, as they were all well aware, that he was not sure about it himself.

'What about the food?' asked Murray, leaving the subject of neep lanterns until Mr. Naismyth was elsewhere.

'Ices,' said Mrs. Costane, 'and jellies. Cold meats. Breads. I hear there's a new recipe for rout cakes in the neighbourhood, brought along with the Boothams at Aberardour Lodge. I'll speak to the cook there: I warrant I can handle a rout cake better than she can.'

'But this is not a rout, Mrs. Costane,' put in Mr. Naismyth reproachfully.

'I think we're all aware of that, Mr. Naismyth. I'd like to see the rout at Carlton House that has neep lanterns mouldering away amongst the plasterwork.'

'Is anyone invit from the village?' asked Hannah. Grisell looked up at this. Mr. Naismyth smiled.

'I don't think so,' he said primly, as though she had just made a slightly indecent suggestion.

'There was a deputation up from the village the other night,' said Murray, assuming that they would already know.

'A deputation? Who would that have been?' asked Hannah. She

was not from the village herself, but from Elie, down the coast, and therefore considered herself more of a local expert than either Mrs. Costane or Mr. Naismyth, with their foreign Edinburgh ways.

'Some fishermen,' Murray explained. 'They had a complaint about a pig.'

'What about pastries?' asked Andrew suddenly.

'What?' Mrs. Costane glared at him.

'Pastries. My employers in Kirkcaldy always had pastries at balls. They said they were easy to eat standing up, if there weren't enough seats for the men to sit down to supper.' He cast a look, not quite at Grisell, but enough to see if she was impressed.

'Well, now, who's the expert?' said Mrs. Costane, standing back with her hands on her hips.

'I'm just saying what I've heard,' said Andrew.

'Pastries, young man, are my speciality. No one can cook pastries like a proper French-trained pastry chef. Of course we'll have pastries, sweet and savoury. It's just a pity,' she added, half to herself, 'that it's the gardeners and the laundrymaids that'll appreciate them a lot more than certain higher born people upstairs.'

'I like pastries,' said Andrew.

'What are you doing from now to dinner, young man?' asked Mr. Naismyth, whose mind seemed to be elsewhere. Andrew turned to look at him.

'Miss Deborah wants me to help Miss Beatrix dust out the carpets in the schoolroom floor, because the boys are out.'

'Well, someone will have to go and fetch the mails from Elie today.'

'He'd never be back before dinner now, Mr. Naismyth,' Mrs.

Costane pointed out. 'It's gone eleven – and young men are incapable of visiting a town and coming straight back, even if a good dinner is waiting for them.'

'I'll go,' said Murray suddenly. He was finding the kitchen almost as overwhelming as upstairs this morning, and he could obviously not retreat to the schoolroom floor, where he also slept.

'But you'll never be back before dinner either,' Mrs. Costane pointed out. 'Your dinner is even earlier than Andrew's.'

'Ah, but I have the use of a horse,' said Murray, 'and since Major Keyes has taken the boys out for their ride himself, my usual mount needs her exercise. Will you let me go, Mr. Naismyth?'

'We should, of course, be honoured, Mr. Murray, if you would be so good.' Mr. Naismyth gave a little bow.

'Give me the mail bag, then, and I'll be off.'

As it turned out, the ride down to Elie was not perhaps quite as enjoyable as Murray had hoped.

At the stables, he discovered that Robert, ever with an eye to opportunity, had persuaded Major Keyes that he normally rode Daisy, Murray's usual mount. Daisy was not a mare keen to live up to her gently floral name: she was tall and powerful, and far too much for Robert to handle safely. As Henry had taken his usual pony and Keyes had his own horse, Murray was left with the choice of Robert's pony, far too small for him, or Lord Scoggie's idiosyncratic gelding. The groom, apologetic over Robert's daring, saddled the gelding without meeting Murray's eye, mumbling soothing noises as the horse stood sullenly still.

The stillness was deceptive, as Murray knew. Half of Fife also knew. One of the reasons Lord Scoggie kept the horse, Murray was sure, was that with its distinctive brown dappling everyone recognised it and knew to give it a wide berth. It was a grand horse in motion, smooth and elegant, changing pace effortlessly, sound on every hoof. People at a distance, usually strangers to the area, had been known to remark on the beauty of its movement. However, the main problem was keeping it moving, for it was not in its body that the difficulty was – it was in its mind. The gelding was known for shying. It was known for shying at hens, ox carts, soldiers in uniform, women in blue cloaks, babies, small girls, sheep with horns, toll bars, canal boats, the doors to unfamiliar stables, and, obscurely, copper fish kettles – saucepans did not have the same effect. Occasionally it shied at other things, just for variety. Nursing the gelding through these alarming experiences could prolong a journey by a third again, and Murray did want to be back for dinner.

On the other hand, it was a pleasant morning, and he was glad to have the chance to be alone for a change, even in the company of the gelding. Gloves and a scarf were necessary, but the air was as clear and fresh as dawn, and he moved in a mist of his own breath and the steamy breath of the gelding. It was only a couple of miles to Elie, enough to get the blood moving, and enough for the gelding to shy five times, once particularly violently at nothing at all. Murray finally dismounted and led it from the outskirts of the village to the post office, which was a room in one of the inns. Sympathetic glances followed him down the street as people recognised the gelding, and he realised he had no hope of finding a boy to hold the gelding's reins while he went in to the post office. He found a post to tie the horse to, sure, at least, that no one was going to steal it. Nearby, a boy was holding the reins of a pretty pony, white as limewash, mane unbraided and long. He looked at it while he detached the castle's mail bag: he was sure it was not one he had seen before.

The office was dark, and he had to stoop beneath the lintel. The interior was lit by three greasy candles and the luminous presence of Mrs. Bootham.

'Ah – Mr. Murray, isn't it?' she said, turning with an expression of pleasure.

'Good morning, Mrs. Bootham. What a pity we did not know you were coming here, or I could have collected your mail along with the Castle bag.' He handed the outgoing bag to the scruffy clerk behind the table, and waited while he searched for the bag for him to take back.

'Oh, but I enjoyed the ride. Elie is a pretty little village, is it not?'

The clerk came back with a single letter.

'Miss Jane Croft,' he read slowly, as if picking his way through the writing on the cover.

'That's right.' Mrs. Bootham snatched the letter, and Murray noticed a faint blush colouring her perfect face. Either the clerk had seen it too, or he had also fallen under her spell. He was staring at her, mouth open.

'Miss Jane Croft?' repeated Murray automatically, though it was none of his business. It was her fault: she took away any reason in a man standing close to her.

'My maiden name,' she said hurriedly. 'My poor father – he's a little confused, you know? Sometimes he forgets that I'm married!'

'Mm,' said Murray politely. 'Yes, I used to have an aunt with that problem. She was always losing things.' He turned, with an effort, and managed to catch the eye of the clerk. The clerk's gaze broke and he scuttled off, coming back directly with the Scoggie Castle bag. Murray took it, and tried to speak again to Mrs. Bootham without actually looking at her. 'May I escort you back to St. Monance?'

'Oh! it is very kind of you, but I have a little shopping to do. Female things, you know, very tedious to men, or so Mr. Bootham tells me!'

'Then I must hurry back to dinner.' He smiled sideways at her, part disappointed, part relieved, and let her precede him out of the office.

Outside he bade her farewell, and turned to untie the gelding. On the wall of the inn was a bill which caught his eye.

'At the Royal Inn, Elie, 25th to 30th October, 1804 appears The Famous FIGHTING CHANTICLEER, visiting from the Principality of

Wales. The FIGHTING CHANTICLEER will demonstrate the finest points of the Pugilistic Science, and perform his Own Works. (Private classes in Pugilism available to Gentlemen and Others on Application)'

Thoughtfully, he mounted and rode away. The gelding shied at the inn sign, and backed gracelessly down the street.

CHAPTER EIGHT

The road from the village to the Castle was invisible in darkness thick with the necessary sounds of small animals preparing themselves for winter. Above the branches of the quiet trees, one or two stars pierced the edges of clouds. In a nearby field, a fox silenced a rabbit with a sharp squeal. In the distance, round the corner, the sound of footsteps gradually came into focus.

As the footsteps came closer, the men at the gateway of Aberardour Lodge stirred themselves a little, only to stand, tensely still in the darkness, not speaking but aware of each other and of the men coming up the hill. In a moment, the glow of a lantern could be seen, then the lantern itself, swinging a little with the easy pace. The men at the gateway watched it approach. No speech came from either party. The animals in the hedgerows grew silent. The only sound was the soft padding of boots on the muddy road.

'So you're off to see his Lordship, then, Geordie Kinkell?'

The voice came like a pistol shot through the silence. The footsteps stopped, and the lantern swung violently, till it was steadied by a black hand.

'Show yourself, then, whoever you are,' came a voice from behind the lantern. With an easy step, the men hiding at the gateway emerged until the raised lantern lit their faces. Joe Baillie, Richie Shaw and Hugh

Farquhar stood across the road. Behind them, Tom Baillie hoisted himself on to his crutches and tried to look their equal.

'I smell fish,' said a man behind Kinkell.

'And we smell pig,' said Joe Baillie, with emphasis. 'Are you hoping his Lordship will take your side? Because I can tell you – you're too late for that.'

'I heared you were up the other day,' Kinkell acknowledged. 'You always were the one to run to your mammy if anyone birled you.'

'We're no here to prevent you going up to the Castle,' said Joe graciously, ignoring the slight. 'It's just we felt we should tell you he's heard our side of the story already, so there's no point in you making the effort. I wouldna like to see you struggling for words to say to his Lordship when you don't have to.'

'You're awful kind.' Kinkell had taken the same lofty tone. In the lantern light his ginger hair looked almost green. 'And very decent of you to do it and come all this way, leaving your boats unprotected when the least wee thing can disrupt your fishing. Is he no a grand fellow, lads?' There were mumbles from behind him. In the lantern's variable light, the fishermen could identify Kinkell's poor son Peter, standing grinning blankly, as well as a few of the other men of the upper end of town, a wright, another weaver, a cordiner, and, at the back, Sandy Kinkell, Geordie's brother, the one who had married Hugh Farquhar's sister Alison. It was a wise thing for him to stay at the back. Tom Baillie could see Hugh Farquhar's fists twitching.

'If anything else disrupts our fishing,' he said, 'I wouldn't like to say what might happen to other people's looms, or their stock.'

'Is that a threat, Hugh Farquhar?' said Geordie Kinkell, in a shocked tone.

'Ach, he could never carry a threat through from here to the end of the road,' said Sandy Kinkell, and pushed his way to the front. 'Sure his sister's a better man than he is.'

'Well it's sure you've changed her from the good young lass she was, Sandy Kinkell,' snapped Hugh, 'but I didn't know you'd turned her into a man.' His fists were already up in front of his thin chest.

'Let her come back to me and I'll show you how much she's a man, and how much a woman and my wife!' cried Sandy.

'Now, lads, enough,' said Joe Baillie, not wishing to bring up the subject of returning the inconveniently kidnapped Alison. He barred Hugh's way with an authoritative hand outstretched. 'I'm sure Alison will be in her rightful home as soon as possible.' Whichever end of town that might be, he added to himself. 'We'll let you get on your way, then, Geordie. I wouldn't want you to be keeping Lord Scoggie's supper waiting.'

'Aye, I hate to inconvenience my host,' Geordie agreed, with a hard nudge in his brother Sandy's ribs. 'We should be going on. We'll be seeing you, gentlemen.'

He stood by with the lantern held high while his companions went past, in case the fishermen tried anything in the dark. The two parties passed in silence, until Richie Shaw, glancing back at Geordie Kinkell, remarked,

'By the way, have you seen the gentleman at Aberardour Lodge here, Geordie? A Mr. Bootham, they say.'

'Why should I have seen him?'

'No reason. It's only – it struck me when I saw him yesterday.' He scratched at the woollen cap covering his bald pate. 'He's awful like your son.'

'Oh, aye?' Joe Baillie overheard this. 'Is he indeed? Is this his first time in the parish, do you know?'

'Less of that, Joe Baillie,' snapped Geordie Kinkell. 'I won't have a word said against my wife.'

'Aye, well,' said Richie Shaw. 'But take a look when you next have the chance, Geordie - just a word to the wise.'

His tone was not unfriendly, and as he vanished into the darkness Geordie Kinkell, mouth open for a forgotten retort, stared after him, holding the lantern dangling loose by his side.

Lord Scoggie was already established on his high chair in the library when Murray was summoned to take the minutes of his meeting with the next delegation.

'This will be the other side of the argument,' he sighed as Murray came in, pen and paper at the ready. 'The time these people take up with ridiculous quarrels that should never happen in the first place. I don't mind sorting out real problems – it's my duty, of course – but petty squabbles like this – ah, yes, Naismyth, show them in, I suppose.' He remained seated, while Murray arranged chairs for the five men at the raised table. They bowed to Lord Scoggie and settled themselves.

'I'll just make sure my secretary knows all your names,' said Lord Scoggie. 'Mr. Murray, this is Geordie Kinkell with the red hair, and his son Peter, and this is his brother Sandy. You caused all the trouble in the first place, didn't you, Sandy? Why could you not do your courting up the hill instead of down it?'

Sandy, also red-headed, looked defiant, but his brother Geordie seemed inclined to agree.

'Mixed marriages are always fraught with difficulties,' Lord Scoggie went on. 'Now, you I know,' he nodded to a lean, strong looking man with thin hair. 'You're Don Downie, aren't you? You helped fix Lady Scoggie's pony trap last year when the spring went.'

'That's right, your lordship,' said the man, gratified. 'I have a wright's workshop up from the kirk.'

'Yes, indeed. But you are new, I think.'

The fourth man nodded.

'Well, speak up, man, who are you?'

'He's a weaver like me, your lordship, but from Crail,' explained Geordie Kinkell. 'He has a stut, so he doesn't like to speak much.'

Lord Scoggie waved his hand, permitting such an eccentricity for the moment.

'Now, what do you have to say?' he said. 'I'll have you know that I have already heard the fishermen's side of the matter, but I shall listen to you, too. I have already advised them on some action, and I'll tell you that I don't approve of some of their actions. Speak, then, and let me hear how you see things.'

'They stole my wife!' Sandy burst out. 'They have her locked away!'

'Steady, now, brother,' said Geordie. 'It's true, your lordship. They came in the night and took her from her hearth, leaving her bairn behind like a fish they didn't fancy, and carried her away down the hill. Now, we could have been impetuous men and gone to snatch her back, but instead we come to you to plead our case.'

'You're very virtuous, Geordie,' Lord Scoggie allowed. 'I'm impressed. You'll be anxious to get her back, no doubt, Sandy, and your bairn will be missing his mother terribly. When did this happen? Last night? The night before?'

'A week ago!' cried Sandy. 'They've had her a whole week!'

'A whole week, eh?' Lord Scoggie tutted through his enormous front teeth. 'That's a dreadful state of affairs. A week, and you haven't tried to rescue her yet?'

'Yes! No,' added Sandy hurriedly.

'You don't seem very sure,' said Lord Scoggie.

'Well, of course we had to go down there straight away, your Lordship,' said Geordie, trying to make his sudden inspiration sound reasoned. 'We had to make sure that they were treating her well, though of course we could not just burst in and snatch her back. We might have hurt someone.' It was quite clear to both Lord Scoggie and Murray that they had in fact tried to burst in and snatch her back, but that something had gone wrong. Perhaps the someone hurt had been one of them, rather than the fishermen.

'And were they treating her well?' asked Lord Scoggie, mildly.

'They had her locked in,' said Sandy, 'and her hands were tied.'

'I heard,' said Lord Scoggie, without quite meeting Sandy's eye, 'that she tried to scratch Ritchie Shaw's eyes out. Would that be some reason for tying her hands?'

A complicated look passed over Sandy's face, in which Murray thought he could read, swiftly, alarm, pride, and possibly even sympathy – for Ritchie, not for his independent wife.

'Aye, maybe,' he conceded thoughtfully.

'So, having decided – wisely, I agree –' Lord Scoggie went on, 'not to attempt a violent rescue, how did you spend the rest of the week? For I must say, that for a man anxious to get his wife back and not entirely assured of her fair treatment by her captors, and for a man seeking my help in the matter, you have left it a long time to come up here.'

'Of course we don't ask for your help lightly, your lordship,' Geordie said hastily, glaring at his brother. 'It takes us time to sort out our arguments so that we waste none of your valuable time when you are good enough to see us.' He looked forthright and in all respects the honourable and thoughtful tenant. It was quite a good act, Murray thought. In the mean time, Geordie's son, Peter, leaned back in his chair, gazing up at the chandeliers high above him, mouth open and dazzled, quite oblivious to the proceedings. Murray remembered seeing him warming himself on the bench outside Geordie Kinkell's cottage, staring up at the sun in much the same way, or waving happily at any passer by. It would have been difficult not to like him.

'And while you were sorting out your arguments so considerately,' said Lord Scoggie, 'what else were you doing? I cannot imagine that relations between the upper village and the lower village have been good for the past week.'

'They k-killed my pig,' said the weaver from Crail suddenly. Geordie's face fell.

'You were supposed to be saying nothing,' he hissed at him.

'But they k-killed my pig,' protested the man, eyes wet. 'They did, your l-lordship. They k-killed my pig.'

'That's a terrible thing,' agreed Lord Scoggie. 'A dead pig is not as useful as a live one, I suppose. Was it a sow or a boar?'

'A sow,' moaned the man, almost sobbing. 'I had hoped to b-breed of her next year.'

Lord Scoggie tutted again. Geordie looked up at him warily.

'A sow,' repeated Lord Scoggie. 'I should be very upset if any of my sows was killed, I must say. On the other hand, it must be said that I do not put my sows to any great hazard. I keep them, or my pigman does, in their sty, or perhaps let them root in the orchard. I don't often take them for walks. Perhaps they would fancy the notion, but even if they did, I think I would probably not take them out at night. Not at night, not down a steep muddy hill, and not to a harbour. And even if I did, even if I paid as little regard to the welfare of my sows as to do all this with them, I would not abandon them on the harbour to the mercies of the local fishermen who, let it be acknowledged, do not appreciate pigs, sows or boars, as we do.'

'Oh,' said Geordie Kinkell after a moment.

'Indeed, oh. You left that poor sow down there by the harbour, in the middle of the night. What did you expect them to do with her? Give her an apple and send her home?'

'I told you,' muttered the weaver from Crail. Peter Kinkell

straightened up and looked at Lord Scoggie.

'Poor sow,' he repeated. 'Poor sow.'

'They sent her back in joints,' said the weaver, now openly crying. 'Mally the flesher b-b-butchered her. Joints!' He wiped his nose on his sleeve. Peter Kinkell stared at him.

'Poor sow,' he said, and began to cry, too. Geordie, his father, looked desperate.

'It was only a joke,' he said. 'It was just a joke,' he turned to Lord Scoggie. 'It just went wrong.'

'They're savages,' added Sandy, not in the least likely to cry. 'If they butcher my Alison I'll slaughter every one of them with my bare hands.'

'I'm sure you would,' said Lord Scoggie drily, 'but you'll acknowledge there's a fair difference between a wife and a sow.'

'Poor sow!' sobbed Peter.

'She was as dear to me as a wife!' the weaver wept. Geordie caught Lord Scoggie's eye, his mouth twisting.

'You canna cut a wife up and expect good bacon, for example,' he said.

'I'll mention it to the fishermen at their next visit,' said Lord Scoggie, now beginning to look cross. 'Now, listen. I have told Joe Baillie and Hugh Farquhar to return your wife, Sandy, and mind you look after her better this time. And have more sense than to anger her family by serving ham the next time you're lucky enough to be celebrating the birth of a bairn. If Alison does not reappear in the next few days, come and tell me. As for the sow, I'm sorry for your loss, but you were extremely foolish, the lot of you. You know they can't fish if there's a pig about the harbour, and it's the herring season. Do you want them all claiming poor relief off the parish? You should consider yourselves lucky they sent you back the meat, and didn't burn it. Smoke it and salt it and enjoy it over the winter, reckon up the feed you've saved yourself, and save up for a new pig in the spring, and take better care of it this time. All right?'

There was a moment of shuffling and sounds that did not quite constitute speech. Murray waited, pen poised, for a response. Peter and the weaver sobbed on.

'Aye, well, I suppose,' said Geordie eventually.

'And you've told them to send Alison back, your lordship?'

'I have. She may even be waiting for you when you get home.'

'Thank you, your lordship.'

The two brothers, ruffling their red hair in a gesture that emphasised their family resemblance, stood up and bowed again to Lord Scoggie. Geordie urged the weaver and the wright to follow them, while Sandy took his nephew Peter by the arm and led him towards the door, wiping his face as they went. Geordie nodded at them, and looked up at Lord Scoggie.

'I'm sorry I had to bring the lad, your lordship,' he said. 'My wife's no well, and I didn't want her bothered around the house while I was out.'

'That's all right, Geordie. I'm sorry to hear about your wife. Nothing too serious, I hope?'

'I'm feart it might be, your lordship,' said Geordie, blushing at such an admission. 'She's very frail.'

'That's very bad. I shall ask Lady Scoggie to – to take her some soup, perhaps. Has the doctor called?'

'Ach, no, your lordship, we can get on well enough without that.' He turned away.

'I know how you feel,' said Lord Scoggie. He rose from his seat and returned to ground level, and went round the table to Geordie. 'Doctors can be very intrusive, can't they? But I know a man would go along and see her just as a favour, and she can send him away if he bothers her.'

'Do you, your lordship?' Geordie looked torn, moving from one foot to the other, unsure whether to abandon this hope. 'Do you know, would he be prescribing all kinds of fancy medicines?'

'Well, now, I don't know. But you can always say no, come the time.' He paused, giving Geordie space to break away. 'Shall I send him round?'

'Aye, I suppose you could do worse, your lordship. Thank you, now,' he said, and followed the rest of his party from the room. Murray, who had been trying to pretend he was absent during this tactful conversation, looked up at his employer.

'I don't suppose he can afford the doctor,' he said.

'I don't suppose he can,' Lord Scoggie agreed. 'But he won't have to.' He went to the table and opened a book that lay there, and removed some coins from inside it. 'Here,' he said to Murray. 'Take these to that weaver fellow. He doesn't deserve it, but I hate to see a man deprived of his pig.' Murray, with a grin, took the coins and hurried out.

In the hall, the men were being shown across to the servants' corridor by Naismyth, to take the ale that was always on offer to visitors from the village. At the same moment, Lady Scoggie, small and shabby, was ascending the stairs, accompanied by Mr. Tibo who seemed extraordinarily well turned out beside her. The weaver, the wright and Sandy Kinkell looked up at the couple, but Geordie, concentrating on the servants' door and possibly the ale beyond, kept his gaze down and chivvied his flock through. Murray followed, noticing that Tibo had turned at the noise, and was gazing down at the party with some intensity. For a second, they paused on the stairs, Lady Scoggie with her eyes still on her feet, as if she expected to miss her footing. Beyond them, Murray suddenly caught sight of Andrew, the new manservant, who had almost run them over in his hurry down the stairs. He paused, also staring at the party from up the hill, then unexpectedly turned and ran back up the way he had come.

Murray managed to complete his duty with the coins discreetly in the servants' corridor before they reached the kitchen, and turned back to the hall. It was almost supper time, so presumably Tibo was to stay for supper. He often did, for want of other company in the parish of the level he thought he belonged to, though as always Murray was almost convinced that Tibo despised them all, except, of course, for Miss Deborah. Perhaps now that the Boothams were nearby he would spend more time with them – or perhaps the hero Major Keyes would prove the bigger draw. Tibo did not seem like the kind of man who appreciated heroes: poets were probably more to his taste. Oh, well, time would tell.

He glanced at the long case clock in the hall, and went upstairs to look for the boys: he had set them some sentences to render into something approximating Latin before their morning class. Climbing the stairs to the second floor, he could hear Tibo and Lady Scoggie talking, with the girls, too, he thought, in the drawing room on the first floor. At the top of the narrower flight of stairs, he turned left, past the rounded wall of the east tower room, and down the dog-legged corridor to the passage that served the school room, the boys' bedchambers, and Murray's own room. It was silent.

With a feeling of resignation he opened the school room door, and found it empty. On the two desks were the Latin exercises he had set, mostly, he conceded, complete. He decided not to give himself indigestion by looking at them now. He returned to the passage and glanced into first Henry's room, then Robert's, then quickly into the other rooms in the wing, including his own, just in case. Then he went searching further afield.

The usual indoor place to find the boys, after the kitchens, was the tower room that topped the west tower. While the east tower housed the bedchambers of Lady Scoggie, Deborah and Beatrix, the west tower, above the two storey library, held only Lord Scoggie's bedchamber, and the top room was a sort of box room into which things were placed which might require attention more urgently than the things placed in the rambling attics. To get to it, Murray wriggled past the east tower again, past the stairs, and out into the Long Gallery.

It was a slightly eerie place at night. During the day, with its line of windows giving views over the drive and park, and lighting the solemnly hideous portraits of earlier Scoggies, it provided a respectable exercise ground on wet days. The floor was long enough for bowls, the ceiling high enough, so Deborah told him, for skipping games, the portraits loathed enough for racquet games to be permitted. Off to the side opposite the windows were the doors of spare rooms, usually given over to female guests when there were any, but as Major Keyes was the only guest at present, he was the only resident. As Murray passed along the gallery, with its shadows at the uncurtained windows and the scanty candles, the sound of Keyes mumbling fondly to his dog was quite reassuring. The dog itself was quiet.

At the far end of the gallery, the door to Lord Scoggie's room stood closed beside the tiny winding stair that encircled it and led up to the tower room. Murray paused at the bottom, listening. For a moment, he thought he heard a slight noise, a quickly released breath, or someone brushing softly against a wall. Then there was nothing. He trod on the first step.

Yells burst from the door above him. A barrage of missiles was hurled down at him, beating him back even as he put his hands up to protect himself. As the missiles tumbled around him, he looked up through crossed arms to identify his attackers. Robert and Henry stood at the top of the stair in the doorway, waving their wooden swords.

'You're Tippoo Sultan,' screamed Robert, 'and I'm Davie Baird, and you're trying to attack our camp, but we've just caught you!'

'I can't help feeling that it would be fairer if I knew that I was attacking your camp before you caught me. Couldn't you let me know what my plans are in advance?' He looked about him and with relief saw that the missiles were mostly old cushions, some burst and leaking feathers.

'Then you might come armed,' objected Robert.

'But I'm armed now,' said Murray. 'Look, you've armed me!' He grabbed an armful of cushions, and started hurling them back up the stair at the boys. They shrieked, and backed through the doorway, but he sprang up and caught the door handle just before they had time to close it in his face. There was a moment's frantic struggle, before Murray managed to manoeuvre himself entirely into the low tower room, laying about him with cushions as he went. In a few seconds it became a three-sided fight, as Robert started to beat off both brother and tutor with his sword, and Henry blamed him for the failure of the Tippoo assault.

'And anyway, why can't *I* be Davie Baird? You never let me be anything!' he cried, slashing indiscriminately at Robert and at Murray's leaking cushions. No one noticed the heavy footsteps on the stair until the jovial voice came from the doorway.

'Oh, aye, lads, heave away there!' called Major Keyes. Henry dropped his sword in surprise, and Murray quickly snatched it off the floor and out of his reach. Henry attacked Murray's ribcage with his fists, and Robert, the method appealing to him, dropped his sword as well and laid in bare-handed. The noise was unbelievable, yelling and laughter, until Murray got Robert by the collar and dragged him off, and Keyes caught Henry's flailing arms, pulling him backwards.

'These lads need teaching in their fighting,' said Keyes at last, as Murray helped the boys tidy the tower room. 'We shall have to see about that pugilistic display you mentioned.'

'Oh, yes!' cried Robert, dropping the cushions he was holding.

'Only if your father says so,' Murray reminded him sternly. 'Come along, it's supper time.' He blew out the candles the boys had lit, and chased them in front of him back down to the Long Gallery. Keyes let them pass and followed more slowly with Murray.

'I'll try and persuade Scoggie to let them go,' he carried on, more quietly. 'It would do them the world of good.'

'Will you go anyway?'

'I think I might. There is little enough entertainment for men around here, and I thought of having a lesson, too.' He looked sideways at Murray. 'If I can't persuade Scoggie, would you like to come on your own?'

'I'd be delighted,' Murray admitted, slightly surprising himself. 'If Lord Scoggie has no objection, of course.'

At some earlier stage in the Scoggie family history, someone – Murray suspected some strong-willed Lady Scoggie – had insisted that the Great Hall was not suitable for comfortable suppers, and had moved supper to the parlour next to the drawing room. It was an informal meal, and when Murray, Keyes and the boys arrived, Tibo, Cocky Leckie and the ladies of the family were already half-seated, chatting, around the table. Henry hurried over to greet his mother, while Robert dawdled after.

Murray and Keyes followed and paid their respects to everyone.

'Was there some kind of riot going on upstairs?' asked Deborah. 'I thought I heard an invasion.'

'No, not an invasion: Tippoo Sultan was rash enough to venture an attack on Sir David Baird's camp,' Murray explained.

'I don't remember that from the newspapers,' Deborah remarked, and Beatrix smiled.

'I hope Tippoo Sultan was not badly injured,' she said.

'The missiles were fortunately fairly soft,' he grinned back. Keyes' dog, hearing his name, pushed round his master's legs and sniffed optimistically at Beatrix' lap. She pushed him gently away.

'Boys, you are so violent!' Lady Scoggie sighed over her sons. 'What am I to do with you?'

'It's just because we're men,' Robert explained to her kindly. 'We have to be strong and hit people.'

Tibo pushed his chair back.

'Not necessarily,' he said. 'Not all men hit people.'

Robert shot him a look in which disbelieve mingled with derision.

'All *real* men do,' he said clearly.

'Well,' said Tibo, looking round at all the grown-ups with a half-smile, half-sneer, 'I seem to have been put in my place.'

'Robert, you are very rude,' said Lady Scoggie.

'Well, I thought he was being silly,' said Robert, not quite clear what he had done wrong.

'There's nothing else for it,' said Keyes, standing behind Tibo with a hand on his shoulder. 'You'll have to come with Murray and me to see the Pugilistic Chanticleer. And the boys, if Lady Scoggie and my host will let them come with us.'

'Oh, I don't think so,' said Tibo, his sneer-smile growing broader as he looked across at Deborah. He ignored Keyes' hand. 'It seems to me a foolish way to spend an evening.'

'And a dangerous one!' said Beatrix. 'Must you all go?'

'Certainly not,' said Tibo, still watching Deborah.

'Oh, I think you should go,' said Deborah, surprisingly.

'You do?' Tibo sat up. 'It seems to me that there are better ways of taking exercise.'

'But Major Keyes is right: it is a very manly way,' said Deborah. 'Think of it: you will never be able to hold your head up in front of the boys again if they are allowed to go and you decline such an opportunity.'

'And we should support people who come all this way to entertain us, shouldn't we?' added Cocky Leckie, with half a knowing eye on Deborah. 'Even if you do not choose to fight, you can at least come and see the exhibition.'

'And if you're going too, Father will have to let us go!' added Robert.

'Go to what?' asked Lord Scoggie, coming into the parlour at that moment.

'To the pugilistic exhibition in Elie,' Tibo sighed.

'You still want to go, eh?' Lord Scoggie asked the boys. He stood like a goat in judgement, hands behind his back. They broke away from their mother and stood straight, recognising this as a solemn moment.

'Yes, Father.'

'*Please*,' added Robert fervently.

'Then if Mr. Murray is willing to escort you, you may go.'

'Hooray!' cried the boys, leaping up and down. 'Thank you! Hooray!' They dragged Cocky Leckie, who was nearest, off his seat, and danced around the room with him. 'We're going to see the pugilist! We're going to see the pugilist!'

'We shall be quite a party, then,' said Keyes happily. Beatrix smiled anxiously, but Deborah looked not the least concerned.

'Now you cannot refuse, Mr. Tibo,' she said persuasively.

'No, indeed!' cried Cocky Leckie, escaping from the boys and scrambling back up on to his chair. 'It will be the greatest entertainment this whole year! You cannot possibly miss it!'

Tibo smiled, but the smile was more like a wince of pain.

CHAPTER NINE

Dear Father,

I am now well settled at Lord Scoggie's house, tutoring his two sons and acting as his Lordship's secretary. Henry, the elder, is a bright intellectual lad, with a strong bent toward science and literature. His father encourages this in him, and we hope that he will soon go to St. Andrews. Robert is a boy more to your taste, active and energetic and good at all manner of sports, just like George at the same age. There is some talk that, like George, we will make an army officer of him.

My dear father, it is now eighteen months since we last spoke at St. Andrews, and I have heard from neither you nor George since then.'

Murray stared at the last sentence for so long that the black letters seemed to lift off the page, hovering above it, casting little shadows beneath them. Then he leaned back in his chair, changing his gaze to the ceiling and its shallow coffers.

He stroked out the words, and wrote:

'I have settled very happily here, and am on terms of mutual respect and liking with the whole household, I believe. I am allowed to ride and walk when I please, and have full liberty to use Lord Scoggie's extensive library ...'

Libraries would not interest his father. He broke off again. The coffers tempted his absent scrutiny. In his mind, the ceiling above him was turned from the pale oak squares of Scoggie Castle's upper floors to the bare black beams of his old student lodgings in St. Andrews, and he lived again, as he had so many times, through that last argument with his father.

It had all been his father's fault, that much had always been clear. His father had been bullying, selfish and unimaginative, and cared nothing for what mattered most to his elder son. He hoped his father realised that, that he had lived to regret it, skulking on his own now in Letho, stamping around the big house with no one but the servants to reprimand and despise. It would serve him right. After all, here Murray was writing to the man, finding the words to communicate to him when he certainly went to no effort to write to his son. He no longer wished to have anything to do with Murray, and that was the end of it.

The trouble was, he thought, as the coffers came into focus again and the back of the chair dug into the nape of his neck, that when it was a matter of family there was never an end of it, not even, he suspected, with death. He missed his father, and even more he missed his brother George, following his career second or third hand, asking any officer he met in Elie or in Cupar if they had heard of his brother, heard tell of a George Murray in the First of Foot – was he well? was he happy? was he a success? There was enough he could reproach himself with, too, when it came to it: he should not have been selfish, either, should have thought more about what mattered to his father and to his family, not just about his own pleasure.

He was happy enough in his present life, but on so many levels he regretted what he had done. He wondered if his father did, too, or did he deal with his past sins by ignoring their crouching presence on his shoulder, or did he struggle to think of an atonement? He looked down again at his own attempt at atonement, the letter on his desk. Sighing, he folded it, and slid it into the drawer of his desk, incomplete. He would have to find a bigger drawer soon: that one was full of incomplete letters, not sent to his father.

'Mr. Murray, sir! Are you coming? We're all ready to go!'

Robert stood at the door, jiggling with impatience. Murray pushed himself out of his chair and snatched up his coat and hat from the bed where he had them ready. It was time to leave for Elie to see the famous Pugilistic Chanticleer.

Lord Scoggie had not the least interest in such displays, and had left his sons in the hands of his kinsman and his tutor for the day. Even so, they made quite a procession starting off from Scoggie Castle: Major Keyes had elected to take his carriage, which could also accommodate the boys and Cocky Leckie, who had no horse. Nathaniel Tibo sat gracefully on a grey gelding chosen, Murray suspected, because the grey was flatteringly the same as Tibo's own hair. Murray was on his usual mount from the Scoggie stables, Daisy the mare, and not, thankfully, on the embarrassing gelding. They had started early, expecting the road to be busy, but it was almost empty, and the cottages they passed along the way had an abandoned look, instead of the usual weekday bustle.

'Do you think the French have invaded, gentlemen?' Cocky called from the carriage.

'If they have, they've left the place unusually tidy for an invading army,' Keyes remarked, casting an expert eye over the countryside.

'Maybe they've just come to see the pugilism,' Robert suggested, half-seriously, but Tibo was dismissive.

'Pugilism is not to the sophisticated European taste,' he said. 'It's only the British that find one man hurling another around a chalk ring a suitable way of spending an afternoon.'

'And that's why we'll defeat the French in the end, my lads. The British fighting spirit,' said Keyes, grinning broadly. Tibo looked disgusted.

The day was bright, with an unstable kind of brightness that lurched in a sharp wind from glowing to glittering, whipping dust off the road and into their dazzled eyes. Tibo and Murray came off worst, the shine taken off Tibo's glossy boots before they had gone far. As they neared Elie, the wind also carried sounds – cries, groans and cheers, sweeping around them as if the wind itself had a voice.

'It's the public display,' cried Robert excitedly. 'It must still be going on!' He struggled to turn and look out of the carriage window, eager for the first possible sight of his hero.

Parry the Pugilistic Chanticleer aimed to make the most out of his visit to Elie, whatever it was that had brought him to such a small town. His afternoon, taking advantage of the daylight, was to be given over to a public display in the town's wide main street, outside the inn, where he would take on all comers for a small consideration, pausing during the bouts to comment on technique. The evening was to be spent in the inn's upper room, in private coaching for wealthier folk. The Scoggie Castle party had booked themselves in for the first of these evening sessions, hoping to be home for the boys' supper, but the quiet road had allowed them to arrive early.

Major Keyes' skilled coachman drew the carriage up at the back of the crowd, and hurried to pull the hood down so that the Major, the boys and Cocky could stand and see the ring over the heads of the crowd. Tippoo the dog barked and nosed up on to the seat, tail furiously wagging. Murray and Tibo were not the only ones watching from the vantage point of horseback: every farmer in the countryside who had the use of a nag with more than two legs formed a tight ring around the crowd, like dragoons at a public hanging.

'Watch out for pickpockets, boys,' Murray called, but he was ignored. Already Robert and Henry were entranced. Murray turned back to watch.

A ring had been roughly roped off in the middle of the street, and boards had been laid across it. Murray could just see part of a square chalked in the middle, though most of it had been rubbed over by the bare feet of the fighters. There were two in the ring just now, and a few others, stripped and sweating, stood about at the ring's edge, their bouts over for the day, rubbing their bare arms down with sacking. One had a broken nose, Murray could see clearly, and blood had flowed freely down round his mouth. Another favoured his right leg, leaning against the inn wall. In the ring, a stocky man with fair hair seemed to be trying to obey his opponent's instructions in intervals between punches: he had his fists up defensively, but was looking down at his feet, fidgetting with their position as if he was learning to dance, pink with concentration and embarrassment in front of such a crowd of watchers. His bare shoulders were red and wind-bitten, with a sandy scuffmark on his shoulder to show where he had already been thrown. His opponent, then, was Parry, short and tidy in his movements, pale-skinned to his waist and buff breeches. Parry was evidently pleased at last with his pupil's feet, and the pair took on more seriously the pose of those about to fight. A man designated referee stood forward, and dropped a red handkerchief. The bout began.

Parry gave his pupil the first three hits. One grazed his arm, hardly touching him. One missed him altogether. The last caught him on the jaw, and the crowd cackled with laughter as he stepped back and shook his head as if to clear it. Then he launched himself at his pupil.

It was a more even fight than you would have expected, for the pupil was a good couple of stone heavier than the professional and was clearly used to a certain kind of brawling. But Parry had technique and endurance on his side, and though few of his blows were particularly heavy, they had a relentless regularity to them that was wearing even to look at, let alone to endure. They landed about the pupil's ribcage and throat, restricting his breathing, making him gasp for air when he could instead of using his energy to finish Parry off. He tried to stop the blows by seizing Parry around his thin shoulders, trying to trap the flying fists in a crushing embrace, but Parry squirmed away, poking his pupil in the eye as he went. The pupil cried out, echoed by the crowd. One hand to his face, he lashed out at Parry half-sideways, hitting him near the kidneys but not with quite the devastating blow he had hoped for. Parry was impressed, though, and skipped away, then used the pupil's momentary loss of balance to thump him in the stomach. The crowd drew breath collectively, and as the man fell slowly to his knees, they let out a vast sigh. He doubled over, one hand still to his face, the other clutching his stomach, while the referee stood over him, counting. His friends, gathered at the side of the ring, began a chant of encouragement, gradually taken up by the rest of the crowd. For a moment, it looked as if it might be enough to lift him again – his head moved a little, and he started to sit up, but in a moment it was clear that it was only to shake his head in defeat. He was helped to his feet and out of the ring, his friends crowding round him, slapping him on the shoulders, wrapping him in coats. Parry watched him go with a kindly smile, then turned back to the crowd with a bow. They cheered loudly, but he waved down their enthusiam, and in a second they were silent. Here was the second part of the performance. Parry the Pugilistic Chanticleer smiled from ear to ear, and drew breath to sing.

> *Come lads and ladies, girls and all,*
> *And gentlemen, come hear my call:*
> *A tale of triumph you will hear*
> *From the Pugilistic Chanticleer.*

A great cheer went up at the name, and his grin increased as he sang on, conducting the crowd as they joined in the last line of each verse.

> *For on a fair and breezy day*
> *I faced the great Black Sam Hannay.*
> *For what, I thought, had I to fear,*
> *The Pugilistic Chanticleer?*

> *We faced each other, black and white,*
> *And slow began the famous fight,*
> *And foolish Sam, he thought to jeer*
> *At the Pugilistic Chanticleer.*

He beat me up, I beat him down,
We beat each other round the town
Till one great clout about the ear
Felled the Pugilistic Chanticleer.

The expected cry of outrage went up, and Parry looked suitably solemn.

And down and out and cold I lay:
They knelt beside me on the clay,
The ladies shed a lovely tear
For the Pugilistic Chanticleer.

But yet I rose, ere count was done,
And standing up against the sun
I caused the Black to shake and fear
The Pugilistic Chanticleer.

And while he stood in fear and awe,
I went and socked him on the jaw.
His eyes did bulge, his lips did leer
At the Pugilistic Chanticleer.

He did not rise, he did not speak:
He barely came round in a week,
While the crowds raised, with a mighty cheer,
The Pugilistic Chanticleer!

The crowd went wild, as Parry bowed again and again, and the referee stepped forward to wrap a white robe around him. Waving, Parry retreated into the door of the inn, and though the crowd cheered and called for another five minutes, he did not reappear. Slowly, they began to disperse, and at last Major Keyes' coachman could lead the horses up to the inn's archway and through to the stableyard, where the boys,

Cocky and Keyes dismounted, followed by Tippoo the dog. Murray and Tibo left their horses in the coachman's care, and the party entered the inn.

The hefty landlord barred their way until they identified themselves as Parry's first customers of the evening, when they were shown to the inn's upper room, which turned out to be the best bedchamber. The landlord surveyed it with satisfaction.

'King James Five slept here, gentlemen, ye ken. Though that was before my own time.'

'I assume it's out of respect you haven't decorated since,' Tibo remarked. The room was panelled and dark, with a low ceiling. A four-poster bed, wider than it was long, stood at one end of the room, and was presumably where the Pugilistic Chanticleer was expected to retire to at the end of the evening. The rest of the room was evidently usually cluttered with ancient furniture, black carved wood and worn leather seats, but these had been pushed back against the walls to make a rough square in the middle of the floor, just in front of the huge fireplace. The oil-lamps were perhaps not part of the original comforts offered to James V, but the only new-looking piece of furnishing was a large cheval-mirror, set to one side of the fireplace. In front of it, as they came in, the famous pugilist, now dried off and in a clean shirt, was throwing punches towards his own reflection, and noting them with approval.

'This is a dreadful place for the purpose!' snapped Major Keyes. 'There is no room at all! Have you never seen boxing rooms before?'

The landlord, bewildered, shook his head.

'It is our best room, sir. There is no other as large.'

Tibo smiled.

'Come, Major Keyes, let us not stand on ceremony. If pugilism is as manly an art as you say, surely as men we may pursue it anywhere?'

'King James Five slept here, sir,' pleaded the landlord, sensing support.

'But I doubt he boxed here. Thank you, landlord, we shall be quite all right.'

As the landlord retreated, Parry feigned to have noticed them for the first time, and came forward to greet them, bowing low.

'Do I have the honour of addressing the heroic Major Keyes?' he asked, in a voice that almost sounded as if he were still singing. Robert and Henry stood in awe, their mouths open, watching the two mighty men meet and bow to one another.

'Saw you boxing in London a few years ago,' Keyes was saying. 'Better conditions than here, anyway.' He looked round sourly at the room, taking in the fraying carpet and the awkward fighting space.

'Ah, well, the London gentry are as a whole more appreciative of the pugilistic art than elsewhere,' said Parry fluidly, a little sideways bow showing that he did not include his present audience in this. He had a quick, dark face, ready with any expression as required. 'I have been delighted, though, with the way I have been received here in Elie.'

'These are my guests this evening,' said Keyes, turning to indicate them. 'Mr. Tibo, Mr. Murray, Mr. Leckie, and Henry and Robert Scoggie, my kinsmen.' Henry and Robert grew two inches each at this description. Kinsmen to a hero!

'There is some claret over yonder, beside the bed,' said Parry, after bowing to each of them in turn, 'for those watching. I take it you are all here for a lesson? Who is to start?'

'Mr. Tibo?' Keyes suggested.

'If you don't mind,' said Murray quickly, 'I think the boys should go first.' Robert looked round at him quickly with an expression of the deepest gratitude on his face. Keyes nodded, and the boys, looking as if they were in a dream, stepped forward.

'Coats off, then, boys, and your cravats too. Then come over here, and I'll show you how to bandage your knuckles.'

'Robert would have burst if he had had to wait any longer,' Murray explained apologetically, as they retreated to the bed and the claret.

'You are quite right, Murray,' Keyes agreed. 'Come on, Tippoo, out of that.' The dog was keen to fight, too.

They sat in a row on the wooden chest at the end of the bed, and passed the claret bottle amongst them, filling ancient glasses with chips off the rims and feet. The boys, in stocking soles, were learning footwork already, though Robert's fists were clearly itching to punch. Tippoo, looking wistful, rested his chin on Nathaniel Tibo's knee, and was batted off.

'Tippoo, come here,' said Keyes indulgently. 'I cannot leave him anywhere or he'll scratch the door down waiting for me.' He scratched the dog affectionately behind the ears. Murray looked away, unable to banish from his mind the awful beating Keyes had given to the dog the day before. You could still see the red welts through the dog's thin white hair.

'Oh, well done, sir!' cried Cocky, holding up his glass in recognition of Robert's first punch, a neat jab to Parry's outstretched hand. Robert laughed, confident now and happy. Henry was biting his lip, face pale, waiting for his turn. The men watched now as Henry stepped up to the mark and, concentrating hard, punched firmly in the direction of Parry's hand. The blow was straight, but all the strength was out of it before it hit its mark. Cocky still cheered, and Henry, flushed, looked pleased enough.

'A good pair of lads. Active and strong: sons to be proud of,' Keyes remarked, not loudly enough for the boys to hear.

'Lord Scoggie has reason to be proud of all his children, I think,' said Murray, not wishing to be drawn into his own opinions of the boys.

'Indeed,' Keyes agreed. 'The daughter, too, is a very lovely young woman.'

'She is,' Tibo agreed, but there was a warning note in his voice. Cocky whistled a tune suddenly, and knocked his heels in time against the wall of the chest.

'I think I may mention my kinswoman without reproof,' Keyes went on, still watching the boys.

'Miss Beatrix, too, is very pretty,' said Murray hurriedly.

'Is she?' asked Tibo, genuinely surprised.

'Oh, yes, sir, she is indeed,' said Cocky, leaving off whistling. 'She has fine eyes, and a lovely smile, and a friendly disposition, which adds beauty to the plainest face.'

Murray and Cocky exchanged pleased smiles in discovering each other's appreciation of the same object. Murray had always thought Cocky a sensible man.

'And what is your opinion of Miss Deborah, Mr. Murray?' asked Keyes. Murray's heart sank. In an effort not to create anything like the wrong impression, he found himself growing pompous.

'She is a very fine young lady, and has always treated me with friendliness and consideration, and is all one in my position could expect from my employer's daughter.'

Tibo smirked. Catching his eye, Cocky winked at him reassuringly. Keyes was quiet.

'This really is an extraordinary room,' Cocky tried to change the subject. 'I have never been in it before.'

'There was a dance here last summer,' said Murray supportively. 'They had removed all the furniture for that – I wonder why they did not do it tonight.'

'I was not at that dance,' Cocky remembered.

'I was,' said Tibo, with a malicious look. 'You danced with Miss Deborah, I remember, Murray.'

'So I did,' said Murray, and could not think of anything else to say. He took a deep sip of claret. Cocky began to whistle again.

'Well done, young gentlemen!' cried Parry at last. 'Who is to be next?'

'I may as well get it over,' said Tibo, and rose gracefully to take off his coat and boots.

The evening followed an informal pattern, with each of them taking turns as they tired or caught their breath, and fighting each other as instructed by Parry. Cocky fought with the boys, and there seemed to be much laughter from their group which was sadly lacking amongst Tibo, Keyes and Murray. Keyes, despite his wooden leg, turned out to be surprisingly agile, hopping back and forth as required and quick with the punches, particularly to the body. Tibo's mind was quick, seeing how his attacker would react, but his fists could not keep up, and his blows, when they arrived, were weaker than he would have liked. Murray started badly, but found himself remembering his lessons more and more, and by the end had a few words of praise from Parry himself, which he rather hoped the boys would have overheard. Parry sprung about amongst them, correcting here, praising there, landing a punch or two himself to show how it was done. Robert was in his element, and even Henry was enjoying himself.

The fighting grew wilder as they grew more tired, blows flailing, footwork sloppy, gasps of laughter or irritation coming more loudly as they crowded around the small square by the fire.

'Now, careful, gentlemen, or there'll be injuries!' cried Parry, experienced in these things, but no one paid much attention. The two groups became tangled by the fireplace. Robert tried to hit Henry through a gap between Tibo and Keyes. Tibo stepped back, elbowing Murray. Cocky rushed through to counterattack Robert, and tripped on the frayed carpet, falling forwards hard towards the fireplace and the foot of the cheval mirror. Murray, nearest, lunged to save him. Cocky hit the bottom of the mirror and crumpled. The top of the mirror swung heavily down, and hit Murray solidly on the back of his head. There was a blurred moment of confused movement, a glittering shimmer before his eyes, and darkness descended.

'Careful,' said Keyes, 'watch how you move him. I can't kneel down.'

'Blood,' said Henry, looking sick. 'There's blood. All over him.' Wide-eyed, Robert said nothing. Tibo, helped by Parry, turned him. His jaw was awfully slack. His eyes were open, but saw nothing.

'He's dead,' said Tibo finally. Henry turned quickly away, and was shamefully sick in the window embrasure. No one noticed.

'I'd better take the boys home,' said Keyes after a moment.

'You can take Murray in your carriage, can't you?'

'I think so. Though he looks out for a week. What will you do?'

'I'll take his body back to St. Monance.'

'Gentlemen ...' Parry was lost for words. Expressions ran like water over his face. 'Nothing like this has ever happened to me before.'

'It wasn't your fault,' said Tibo, though he looked as if he wanted to blame someone. 'He tripped on the carpet.'

'There will be no fee, of course, no fee at all,' Parry gabbled. Tibo looked at him for a moment in silence. 'It's never happened to me before.'

'Ring for the landlord, would you, Major?' Tibo asked. 'I shall need a cart, and a blanket.'

The landlord had to help carry Murray down the stairs, too, while

Tibo carried the little body of his clerk. Keyes and the boys followed, Robert carrying Cocky's hat as if it was a sacred object. Keyes hurried the stablemen into preparing his carriage, keeping the boys held in a net of pointless, shocked conversation about anything but what had just happened. Murray was laid on the floor of the carriage, his coat over him and the carriage blanket under his head, and Keyes and the boys scrambled in after, trying not to step on him. The carriage set off. Henry, facing backwards, could not take his eyes off the figure of Tibo standing in the midst of the busy stableyard, still as ice, holding Cocky Leckie lifeless in his arms, waiting for a cart.

Murray began to feel the motion of the carriage when it turned into the drive of Scoggie Castle. He opened his eyes briefly, but saw only a puzzling view of knees and dusky sky. A surge of pain and nausea made him close them again almost instantly, and a blissful unconsciousness swept back over him.

When he half-returned to life again, it was to find himself being carried into the front hall of Scoggie Castle. The coachman and Naismyth clearly had firm ideas about how far they wanted to carry him, and laid him down on the hall table, where the impact of the wood on the back of his head was enough to send the contents of his mind whirling again. He was vaguely aware that he had been left alone: the boys had scampered up the stairs, Naismyth and the coachman had melted towards the servants' corridor, and Keyes had gone away somewhere – he could distantly hear the tapping of his wooden leg, but could make no sense of it and soon gave up. For a while there was a luxurious silence, and he lay motionless, appreciating the stillness of the table after the jerking carriage. Outside he could hear gulls crying, high over the castle, then swooping low. There must be a storm coming, he thought. In the distance he could just hear voices, the girls, perhaps, upstairs, then Robert's voice, excitedly telling his story. Lord Scoggie's craik came in response, disapproving, surely, would he be angry with Murray? Was he going to be blamed for what had happened? What had happened? Closer at hand, he could hear Lady Scoggie, talking urgently to someone. The voices melted together, different tones, different volumes, tangling and extracting themselves ...

'And then the mirror fell!'

'Where have you left the poor man?'

'I knew something like this would happen. This is always what comes of –'

'Stay away from my daughter!'

The last voice puzzled him, and he strained to hear more, but there was a hurry on the stairs and in a second Deborah and Beatrix were upon him.

'Oh, you poor man! We must get you to your room. What a bruise!'

He was about to resign himself gratefully to their care, smiling in what he hoped was a heroic fashion through his pain, when he realised that someone else was in the hall. In a swirl of magic, Mrs. Bootham was among them, and leaning over him as if with a simple spell she could take away all his pain. He found himself struggling to sit up, and swung his legs over the side of the table.

'I'm fine, really,' he said groggily. 'I can manage.' There was nothing on earth that was going to cause him to allow Mrs. Bootham into his bedchamber, should he have to crawl to his bed on his own. For a moment sickness swept over him again, and he clutched a hand to his mouth, but it passed. 'I have a hard head. But you have heard about poor Cocky Leckie.'

'Robert told us. It's a dreadful thing, dreadful,' said Deborah.

'Poor Mr. Leckie,' agreed Beatrix, who was touching the back of his head with gentle fingers. 'But we must fetch you a poultice for your head, you know. But you can wait here for it if you do not want to go to bed.' She smiled at him, as if she understood just why he did not want to go upstairs. He smiled back, feeling warm inside, and eased himself off the table to stand up.

'Oh, Mr. Murray! Good heavens! Look at your back!' cried Deborah. Involuntarily Murray turned back, but as he could neither see his back nor feel anything wrong with it, he tried to keep his head still instead. Beatrix and Mrs. Bootham hurried to look.

'My goodness, Mr. Murray, we must deal with this. Look at yourself in the – in the mirror,' Beatrix told him. He edged over to the large pier glass amongst the armour and twisted awkwardly to look. In the reflection he could see Beatrix and Deborah, hovering anxiously, and Mrs. Bootham, a curious little smile on her face, her face glowing as if she was the only one the candlelight found. There were candles lit around the pier glass: their light caught the back of his shirt, grubby with sweat and striped with dark lines of dryish blood. The light twinkled and shone, and for a moment he thought that blood was still flowing from the odd little wounds. Then he realised what it was. Through his shirt, sparkling down his back like silver armour, were hundreds of shards of mirror glass, glittering as he shuddered at the sight of them.

CHAPTER TEN

Lord Scoggie's custom was to read family prayers each morning at the break of day in the Great Hall to the whole household, his great teeth picking through well-phrased concerns which he wished to bring to the attention of the Almighty, while edifying the family and servants. The merciful exception to this practice was Sunday, when he conceded the privilege to the professionals and led his household to church.

The whole population of the parish, pig-lovers and pig-haters, had but one church to attend, a great dark louring presence on a low outcrop to the south of the village. The Scoggie household left in good order to walk there, regardless of weather, each Sunday morning, and the day after Cocky Leckie's death was no different, except that Nathaniel Tibo, who usually attended church in the company of his most prominent clients and their daughter, was absent. Instead Major Keyes took Miss Deborah's arm with a hearty smile, and followed Lord and Lady Scoggie down the drive. Murray followed with Beatrix, needing eyes in the back of his hat for the boys behind him, and after that followed Mrs. Costane with Mr. Naismyth, Hannah and Grisell, and finally Andrew taking up the rear, stiff in his new best livery.

The wind was sharp and blustery, knocking them about in the narrow lane and threatening to tumble hats and whip shawls away. They were making slow progress, what with Major Keyes' swinging gait and Robert having to run back after his wide-brimmed hat as if he was chasing a hoop, and as they reached the gate of Aberardour Lodge, Mr. and Mrs. Bootham appeared, wrapped up in coats and cloaks and scarves as if it was midwinter. Mrs. Bootham smiled generally at the party, and Murray felt himself try to turn away involuntarily, as if avoiding the impact of that smile. Beatrix on his arm, however, broke free and stood smiling back. Murray saw with admiration that her complexion was quite pink from the cold wind.

Lord Scoggie and Mr. Bootham were greeting each other cordially, though there was more warmth, perhaps, on his Lordship's side.

'And will you walk with us, Mr. Bootham?' Lord Scoggie was asking.

'But you are clearly on a family expedition, Lord Scoggie – we would not intrude for the world, would we, my darling?'

'We are simply off to church, Mr. Bootham!' Lord Scoggie looked surprised. 'I had assumed that you would be heading in the same direction.'

'Oh!' Mr. Bootham seemed to grow an inch, taking on a rather superior air. 'I'm afraid my wife and I do not attend.'

'If you are thinking of an Episcopalian chapel, sir,' said Deborah, 'I do not think there is one nearer than Edinburgh.'

'You mistake, my dear Miss Scoggie: my wife and I do not attend church at all. Religion is an antiquated and meaningless ritual. We do better to shrug off its pointless bonds and return to mankind's true freedom.'

Murray turned discreetly to catch Beatrix' eye at this amazing statement, but to his surprise she seemed to be thinking about something else. Lord Scoggie had temporarily lost control of his jaw, and even Deborah seemed unable to think of anything to say. Only Lady Scoggie seemed unshocked.

'Then you had better not go anywhere at this time of a Sunday,' she suggested. 'In this part of the country, you will be opening yourselves to criticism and censure.'

'I would expect such an attitude from a place so far from the centre of modern thought and attitudes. It is not the fault of these poor people – they lack only the proper education.'

Lady Scoggie's mouth tightened in a moment of characteristic impatience.

'I think you underestimate the intelligence of these people – and the ridicule to which you might subject yourself.'

'Ridicule, eh?' Bootham paused, a more thoughtful expression on his beautiful face. 'Perhaps, my dear, we should avoid giving any offence locally, and take our little walk later.' Mrs. Bootham looked surprised, and opened her mouth as if to protest, but Lord Scoggie had found his voice again.

'I believe it would be best, sir. That is, if we cannot persuade you to join us?'

'I fear not, sir.' Bootham removed his hat to bow once again to the party. 'I hope we shall meet again soon.' He smiled smoothly at the family, and led Mrs. Bootham back towards Aberardour Lodge.

'Extraordinary,' said Lord Scoggie, when they had moved on out of earshot. 'Of course one reads about such people – poets, in particular, of course – but who would have thought that they really exist? You dealt with it very well, my dear,' he added to his wife, though she seemed to be thinking about something else.

'Does Mr. Bootham *never* go to church?' asked Robert interestedly from behind Murray.

'Don't even think about it,' said Murray. He was not much surprised to find that Mrs. Bootham did not go to church. He could not see her following the precentor's drab voice amongst solemn stonework and the devout of St. Monance Kirk. He pictured her instead bearing honey and wine to the woodland shrine of an ancient Roman deity, hair loose and barefoot ... he shook his head sharply, but when he looked at Beatrix he thought she needed shaking, too.

By the time they reached the harbour to walk along the shore to the church, there was quite a crowd heading in the same direction in Sabbath solemnity of dress and expression. A certain deference was paid to the Scoggie Castle contingent, and their formation was not disturbed, though people walked beside them and before them. At the end of the village was a little burn, flowing at this time of year but with nothing like its spring energy. They crossed from bank to bank at a rudimentary ford, the gentlemen helping the ladies up and into the kirkyard on the other side.

What stones there were were dark sandstone and almost instantly weathered away on this exposed site, so that local memory and the beadle's books were the only reliable record of burials on this rocky headland. The wind hurtled across the pale grass as gulls swooped and shrieked around the tattered spire of the church itself, deceptively solid looking against the white sky. Closer inspection revealed black holes amidst the slates and gaping windows, stonework battered and torn, the great west door hanging half off its hinges as if in dismay at the ruins about it. Major Keyes stopped and gazed about him with interest.

'This is even worse than it was ten years ago. Cousin, your kirk is a wreck. I've seen better in sacked cities.'

Lady Scoggie surveyed the building with a frown.

'There is little enough money in the parish,' she said crossly, 'and what there is is better spent elsewhere, as long as we have somewhere to worship in safety.'

'But you cannot possibly worship in safety in there!'

'We don't. We confine ourselves to the east aisle.' She noticed the minister approaching them, his black gown flapping as if trying to parcel him up. 'The manse is in a worse state, and we have no schoolhouse at all, should you happen to have any rich friends of a generous disposition, cousin.'

'Come, Murray,' said Keyes, 'there is time yet before the service. Let us see the ladies in and examine these ruins more closely.'

There was not, in fact, long before the service, but Keyes was fascinated: the stone inside the building dripped with damp, green and fragrant as an old well. Dim light seeped down from the high roof and empty windows. A few broken chairs rotted soft as cheese in the middle of the rough floor, amidst fragmented slates and anonymous lumps of tracery. Boards shielded the precious east aisle from this abandoned wreck, built up with broken stones so that there was little noise from the gathering congregation beyond. Keyes prowled about, pausing at every step to see that his wooden peg was safely perched before he put weight on it, Tippoo only ever a step ahead of him and sniffing at everything. Murray stood near the middle, looking around him.

'You stand very still,' Keyes remarked suddenly. Murray was taken aback.

'I like to see what I can from one point,' he said after a moment. 'If I move around too much I miss things.'

'I like to move around,' said Keyes. 'Look – what's here?'

He had found a door, grey-greened to the colour of the walls and low in the side of the church. An old iron latch, red with rust, held it shut, but when Keyes lifted it the door opened with only a little effort, and Keyes said he was sure that the green would brush off his coat later. Inside was darkness: they could see the bare stone floor dimly for a couple of feet, and then nothing.

'I think it's where the minister used to keep the communion things and the registers, in a kist,' said Murray. 'They're at the manse now, I believe. The registers were getting damp.'

Keyes had drawn a flint from his pocket and dashed out a light, but all it revealed was a plain stone room built small into the thick walls of the old kirk.

'We'd better be going,' Murray added. 'I think the service is about to begin.'

Keyes let the flame go out, closed the door again and gave one last look around the gloomy space.

'Aye, well,' he said at last. 'I suppose. Is it still that precentor that sings flat?'

Murray grinned.

'That's the one.'

Keyes sighed.

'Sometimes, you know, it's tempting to be one of these modern unbelievers.'

Murray's head was still hurting on Monday morning, and his back, stiff from being pressed against the back of the pew for so long on Sunday, stung. In the hours before breakfast and after morning prayers, he set the boys a lengthy Latin passage to translate and made his way down to the kitchen to crave a cup of tea. Mrs. Costane instructed Hannah to pour him one, and looked at him with concern.

'You're still not right, Mr. Murray. I hope you're not off to the funeral today.'

'I think I have to, Mrs. Costane. Everyone else is going, and I was one of those who was there when it happened.'

She sucked her teeth sharply.

'A terrible thing to happen to such a pleasant wee man. Andrew, lad, come here and help Hannah lift the ham off the fire, would you?'

Andrew pushed his blonde hair back off his face and looked up from polishing boots in one of the window embrasures.

'I thought helping with the food was Grisell's job?'

'Did you ever read in the Bible about a job given to one person and no one else? Grisell's off doing the fireplace in the Great Hall.'

'Thank heavens,' Murray remarked. 'You could use that room as an icehouse.'

'She's only polishing the brass bits, not lighting it.' Mrs. Costane said absently, supervising the lifting of the ham. 'On to this ashet, that's the way. There, good: now take it over to the table in that window and let it stand.'

'Grisell hates that job anyway,' Hannah remarked.

'Why?' Andrew was always keen to find out more about Grisell: the servants had been marking with interest the confident town man's clumsy courtship which Grisell had so far not deigned to take under her notice.

'She doesna like ham, of course,' said Hannah, impatiently.

'Why of course?'

'Oh, well,' said Hannah, with mock respect, 'since you're from the worldly metropolis of Kirkcaldy, you wouldna ken our little local customs. In the village, the fisherfolk dinna like pork and pigs, and the uptown folk like them. It's as simple as that.'

Andrew stared at her in disbelief.

'And Grisell is from the fisherfolk, then?' he stuttered.

'Aye, of course. Her father's a man named Richie Shaw, one of the high heidyins down yonder, and a great pal of Joe Baillie, the king of them all. Aye – I hope you like the smell of herring, young man, and can give up your breakfast bacon.'

Murray thought Andrew looked rather pale, but he was so fair it was hard to tell. He looked, for a second, as he stood in the middle of the kitchen, like an echo of someone else Murray had once met, but the impression was fleeting and Murray's mind lost its grip of it in a moment.

'Well, when's this funeral?' Andrew asked abruptly.

'You're no going, you never met the man,' said Mrs. Costane.

'I know that,' said Andrew quickly. 'I only wanted to know when you would all be off.'

'Straight after breakfast.' Naismyth stalked into the kitchen and made them all jump. He paused and looked about him slowly, as if taking angles of the room by the length of his beak. 'You may stay here,' he went on at last, 'and keep a pot boiling for tea when we return.'

'Thank you, sir.' Andrew returned dutifully to the shoes, kneeling amongst them with an admirable regard for the knees of his breeches.

'Ah, Mr. Murray,' said Naismyth, turning his head, a little to one side, in Murray's direction. 'I hope this morning finds you improved.'

'A little, thank you, Mr. Naismyth.'

'Will the boys be attending the funeral?'

Murray frowned. He had discussed this with Lord Scoggie yesterday but their conclusion had satisfied neither of them. Lord Scoggie felt that neither of them was old enough: Murray thought that Henry was, but not Robert. Both of them, however, thought that attending Cocky's funeral would be of value to both boys. Henry had been deeply upset since the carriage ride home with his senseless tutor on Saturday night, and the funeral might help him to put an end to it. Robert, on the other hand, seemed completely unmarked by the incident, and displayed only a greater zeal for pugilism. As no one had the heart to fight with him, he was reduced to boxing pillows, doorways and trees, but Murray and Lord Scoggie both found it disturbing.

'Yes, Robert and Henry are both to attend the funeral.'

'And Major Keyes will lend the occasion a heroic dignity, no doubt,' Naismyth added with satisfaction. 'Is the breakfast nearly ready to go up, Mrs. Costane?'

'It is, Mr. Naismyth.'

'Then let us proceed.' With his features arranged into the likeness of a benevolent smile, Naismyth nodded roundly at the company, and Murray took his cue to leave his tea and hurry back to the Great Hall to join the family for breakfast. It was served, inasmuch as breakfast was ever served, by Naismyth and Grisell, and Murray noticed that she avoided even touching the ham plate. Richie Shaw was one of the fishermen who had come to speak to Lord Scoggie last week ... well, well.

The family were already in mourning, and when the table had been cleared Murray checked to see that Henry and Robert were properly turned out for their first funeral. Henry was pale, though Robert seemed more excited than distressed. Gathering in the entrance hall, they waited for the carriages to come round, and Keyes took the boys, Murray and Tippoo in his, while the others climbed into the Scoggie carriage. Knowing the servants would follow directly, they set off.

The funeral was well attended, the mourners squeezing into the little house that Cocky had lived in alone. Nathaniel Tibo was the chief mourner, and looked more genuinely upset than Murray had ever seen him. He seemed to have provided the funeral meats out of his own pocket. The crowded rooms were warm, and people busied themselves with eating, drinking, and saluting Cocky's little coffin, reluctant to leave for the cold outdoors and the interment in the bleak kirkyard.

Up the hill, Geordie Kinkell's cottage was quiet and the loom stood still, for Geordie was at the funeral – Cocky Leckie had been an uptown man, but in any case was a popular one. His wife was not well enough to attend, and was lying in the kitchen bed, dozing fitfully and then waking at the unaccustomed silence. Above her she could hear gulls screaming, and the wind was getting up: in her broken dreams she was battered by storms and blown over cliffs, only to be caught up by the strangling bedclothes again. The pain was not bad today, for which she gave thanks in a whispered prayer, as fervently as she often prayed for relief, or simply for the ability to stand it and not distress her poor son Peter, who had not the mind, poor lad, to understand why his mother was always abed, or to stand her greeting.

At first the sound at the door was just a part of her dreams, the sound of trees cracking in a high wind. A brighter light shone, and for a moment her dreams took a strange turn, the gates of Heaven opened and she gasped herself awake, to find that the cottage door was open. Even in that moment, it closed again, and she could see a dark shape in the kitchen with her.

'Mother?'

'Oh, son, is that you? Is that you? I haven't seen you for so long!'

'Mother, why did no one tell me you were so ill? What's the matter?'

She shrugged a little, looking away from him.

'It won't be for long, anyway, think of that,' she said. He seemed to allow this ambiguous statement to comfort him for a moment. He drew a creepie stool over from the fireplace with his foot, and sat beside her bed, taking her hand in his. She could feel his shock at how thin it was, how his automatic grasp had to tighten a little to find her papery hot skin. He looked round him at the dim kitchen, exploring with his eyes, noting the familiar and the changes since he was last there. She watched him, her own eyes half-closed, as he examined the hams hanging to smoke in the rafters, the family Bible on a high shelf with a yellowed print of John Knox, the fire tamped down so that she would not have to worry about it while she was in the house on her own, the table with the branderback chairs around it, at which, when he was small, he would have had to perch on a roll made out of his father's greatcoat to reach his bowl of brose, the low doorway through to the room where his father had the loom. Even as she watched him, she could see the fond rejection in his eyes – he remembered, but he could pass beyond these humble beginnings: his life now would not involve brose, she was sure. She smiled a little, proud of him, but that did not stop the tears coming to her eyes. She tried to blink them away before he looked back at her, but did not quite succeed.

'Are you in pain, mother? Is there anything I can do?'

'Oh, there is pain, my dear, but as to what you could do ... If you would be willing, I could fancy a wee cup of tea. I have a powder here from that woman in Elie that takes away some of the worst of it.'

He had already stood up to move the kettle over the fire when he heard the rest of her speech. He was shocked.

'That old woman by the harbour? Is she not a witch?'

His mother laughed, a shadow of old laughter.

'Aye, she looks it, but she's kind enough to those in need. Here, help me to sit up a bit.'

He was an inexpert nurse, but between them they managed to manoeuvre her up the bed to lean against its wooden head. He pulled the covers up to her chest and on her instruction fetched her a shawl to put around her shoulders. He seemed cheered by this change in her appearance, as if someone sitting up was further from death than someone lying down. He grinned at her in the old way, and she smiled back.

'My golden boy,' she said fondly, and his grin spread as he brought the kettle to the boil and made tea for both of them.

'How long are you able to stay?' she asked.

'Not long, mother. I might be missed.'

She tried to hide her disappointment in a little fluster over pouring her powder into her tea. He watched her in concern.

'Why don't you ask Lady Scoggie for help with the pain? I hear she knows a fair bit about illness and such.'

'Oh, aye, she's the great one,' she said, 'but I doubt she'd visit the likes of me.'

'I don't know why not,' he argued. 'She was visiting the families at the saltworks the other day. Why wouldn't she visit a respectable weaver's wife?'

'I don't want her to.'

'Why not? I could get a message to her, I'm sure –'

'You will not, son. There's no need to bother Lady Scoggie or involve her in our troubles. The end will be the same whether she comes or not. There!' she said, as if suddenly relieved, 'that's these powders. Who needs Lady Scoggie when you have the witch woman of Elie at your disposal?'

The powder really seemed to have helped, for she became more alert and at the same time calmer, and he could convince himself that she was not so bad, that she would last a good while yet. He answered her questions about his life and doings with readiness, and made her laugh a little with some of his stories, till she seemed to tire again, and the questions tailed off, though she kept her eyes on him. They sat in companionable silence for a little while, listening to the wind outside.

'It'll be a storm tonight,' he said at last.

'Aye, them down the hill will have to stop the fishing for a bit. That'll not please them.'

At the mention of the fisher folk, he looked thoughtful, but she did not question. She wondered if he had a girl yet: she would have been surprised if he had not, for he was a charmer, there was no doubt about it.

'Well, mother, I'd better be going now.'

'Aye, before the storm sets in,' she agreed, with regret.

'Do you need anything else before I go?'

'Will you light the lamp there? It's getting gey dark.' She watched while he touched the wick with a taper from the fire, and replaced the glass. His movements were neat, almost – she laughed to herself – gentlemanly. He bent to kiss her.

'Come back again when you can, dear,' she whispered.

'I will – when I can. Tell him to send to me if – if I'm needed.'

She nodded. The powders made her sleepy, and already she was slipping away from him, seeing him as a blur against the lamp.

'Goodbye, dear,' she mumbled.

'Goodbye, mother. I'll see you again soon.' She was already asleep, jaw slack, sliding down the bed again. He opened the cottage door as little as possible, thinking of the draughts, and stepped outside, closing it firmly behind him. He looked up. In the little time he had been there, the sky had turned a greyish yellow, an unhealthy, bruised colour. He pushed his hat hard down on his head, and turned his collar up. The wind caught the tails of his scarf as he wound it round his neck, then he hurried off. Above him, the seagulls swept and cried, woven like pearls into the sick sky, and into his mother's drugged dreams.

Cocky's coffin disappeared beneath the rocky earth of the headland just as the first heavy drops of rain began to fall. The diggers, fuelled by whisky, muttered curses at the sky and dug more quickly. Eager to see the formalities finished with, the mourners passed the traditional bottle of brandy amongst themselves as they stood with their backs to the wind, feeling the hot spirit send their blood flowing. They shook hands quickly, gave a nod in the direction of the muddy grave, and scurried back towards the street, slithering down the rocky slope to the ford over the burn, clutching hats and scarves, racing to beat the weather home. Back at Cocky's cottage, the women had already dispersed, seeing the weather worsen, leaving the minister on his own to stare out at the sky and wonder at the state of the manse roof. The servants of Scoggie Castle, sent ahead, found that Andrew had been busy heating water and lighting fires, preparing the place for receiving cold, wet travellers. The ladies had a less certain passage home, for already the lightning had begun to stitch the land to the black sky, and the horses dithered and skittered over the rough road. The gentlemen followed not long after in Major Keyes' carriage, rolled by the thunder along the lanes and up the drive at a gallop. Lord Scoggie paused at the door, staring up at the sky, then down east, towards the sea.

'The good Lord be with the fishermen tonight,' he said, half to himself, but Murray found himself responding with a heartfelt Amen.

In Aberardour Lodge, the servants huddled by the kitchen fire, while Philip Bootham and his wife stood arm in arm in an upper window.

'Look at the grandeur of it, my love,' he murmured. 'What is man or his puny God, beside nature in all its glorious strength?'

Geordie Kinkell came home with Peter, to find his wife sound asleep with a cup in her hand, and the lamp mysteriously lit.

In the lower reaches of the village, lamps were lit in the windows facing the sea, and in more than one cottage a shawled figure stood by the lamp, or in the doorway, distant gaze on the sea as it rolled and broke.

'It's not at its worst yet,' Richie Shaw's wife called along the street to Hugh Farquhar's mother. Mrs. Farquhar shook her head.

'If they get in now, they'll be grand.' The wind snatched her words, laughing at her. Richie Shaw's wife waved to her in a gesture that meant everything, reassurance, companionship, acknowledgement that this was not the first or the last time they had talked like this, and went inside her own cottage again. Mrs. Farquhar waited, though, propped against the doorway with her arms folded over her plaid, immune to the cold and the rain. In the dim distance she thought – she was sure – she could see the shapes of the herring boats slipping and bouncing over the waves. If they came back now, if they could slip into the harbour before the worst of the storm caught up with them ...

'We must turn back now!' cried Joe Baillie, one arm hugging the gunwale as if it was a lifelong friend. The wind whipped and cracked about them, as if the darkness around them were some huge black sail, shrouding them in stiff canvas folds. His crew were turning before he had even given the order, for these half-dozen men knew these seas almost as well as he did. Dotted about them, sliding in and out of sight as if in some huge magic lantern, were the other herring boats, nineteen of them, captained by the senior fishermen of the village, manned by their boys back from whaling in greater seas than these. Joe glanced over them, counting them again in his head, knowing every boat like a mother seal with her pup. In the open hold, the silver darlings slithered and spilled as if the boat were already under water and the herring were swimming free. The heaped nets bundled and tumbled about, kicked aside by frantic feet as the crew toiled and fought and ploughed hard for the harbour.

Joe counted again, and again. John Walker's boat vanished for a long second, then reappeared from beneath a wave, untouched. There was Richie Shaw ahead, never one to take a risk these days, holding a steady course for his home berth and a warm dish of stew by his fire. Joe smiled to himself, feeling the salt crack on his face. He counted again. Nineteen. Who was missing this time? He counted more carefully – had he remembered to include Richie up ahead? He had. Twenty. Twenty small boats, daring to confront the might of the sea.

'They that go down to the sea in ships, that do business in great waters.' The words passed through his head, as familiar as the surging deck beneath his feet, his mind holding them as firmly as his arm clutched the gunwale. 'These see the works of the Lord, and his wonders in the deep.' The boat plunged down a long, steep wave, and he leaned back, keeping his balance, losing sight of all the other boats. Up they swept again as if they would fly, and one by one all the others fell and rose again in the same wave. Another boat was perilously close as they came clear: Hugh Farquhar, standing in his father's old place, waved to Joe. He put his hands to his mouth.

'Riding .... Out,' he cried, the words coming muffled to Joe's cupped ear. Joe shook his head, waving his free hand flatly.

'Mad!' he shouted back. 'Come Home! Stay Together!'

'Waste of time,' came back the words in a sudden flat calm moment. Joe could see Hugh's crew were not racing like his own, like the others. In a second, it seemed, he was away, back far behind them. Joe stared, aghast. It was mad, it was. A stupid risk to take. Hugh was young, and daft.

He counted again. Nineteen boats, and the twentieth sitting back on the wide sea.

'For he shall give his angels charge over thee, to keep thee in all thy ways,' he cried into the wind, willing his crew on. 'They shall bear thee up in their hands, lest thou dash thy foot against a stone.' On nights like this, he could feel the hand of the Lord, scooping up his little fleet, gathering them up in His mighty hand, casting the lightning and thunder to either side of them. It was a rough ride, but that was what happened when little men dealt with God. He counted again. Nineteen boats, and the twentieth – where was the twentieth?

He turned, changing his grip, searching the seas behind him. Where was the twentieth? He watched for deep waves, for anything that might hide a herring boat. He watched, and watched, and saw nothing.

Breathless, he turned back again. Nineteen boats. Richie, up ahead, was almost at the harbour mole, almost to the last quick manoeuvre into the harbour. In he went, slick as a fish, and the next boat followed him. Nineteen boats. Now he could see the lights in the windows along the main street, and even the figures in doorways. They would be counting, too, the wives and mothers who knew the boats as well as he did. Nineteen, they would count. Another five boats slid into the harbour, and Richie was tying up, and scrambling on to the harbour.

Joe's boat would be last in, but that was his duty. Nineteen. He turned again, staring back into the darkness, lit by sudden lightning into an oily, mountainous landscape, bare of life, bare of boats. Hugh had turned back, and had left God's mighty hand, and had left them.

When he left off looking, his own boat was taking her turn to slide into the harbour, the first out and last back, the twentieth out and the nineteenth back.

As he scrambled up on to the steady harbour, he could see Hugh Farquhar's mother, standing motionless in her doorway, Richie Shaw's wife hurrying towards her. He watched for a moment, but Hugh's mother did not move, even as Richie Shaw's wife embraced her.

Joe turned away, and surveyed the sea, as the men around him scuttled in out of the storm.

It was the fault of that damned pig, he was sure of it. And the uptown folk were going to pay.

CHAPTER ELEVEN

Outside, the rain fell unremittingly. Inside, the castle had another occupant: lurking, feeling its way around the doorways, fingering the tapestries and carpets, lingering on the stairs, the smell of the solander goose they had had to eat for dinner was an evil presence that it seemed only exorcism would ever remove.

Mrs. Costane said that Lord Scoggie had appeared in triumph with the bird just before they had all left for Cocky's funeral, and when she had recovered from the shock, and had suggested, with heavy sarcasm, that it would be nicely matched by a bit of herring, Lord Scoggie had agreed with enthusiasm.

'You'd never find either on an Edinburgh dinner table,' she told Murray bitterly, when he came downstairs in the morning to find out what had died. 'The man must have no sense of smell in his head.' Hannah had a cloth tied over her face as she roasted the bird, and even

Andrew, used to the exotic dishes of Kirkcaldy, was looking distinctly green.

'Henry might like the skull for his collection,' Murray suggested hesitantly. 'If it's well boiled, anyway.'

'He'll be lucky,' said Hannah indistinctly. 'As far as I'm concerned, there's not a fragment of this bird that's staying in the castle for longer than it takes to whisk it off the dinner table.' Indeed, he noticed, she was flinging handfuls of white feathers into the roaring kitchen fire, where they added a sugary taste to the overwhelming fishy reek. He did not feel inclined to argue, and left.

The texture of the goose, which was the size of a reasonable turkey, left nothing much to be desired. Lord Scoggie had set to with every appearance of enjoyment, but on most of the plates the goose meat was abandoned at the first attempt, and Deborah actually excused herself from the table until it had all been taken away. The herring went down with greater ease, though it was true that Murray had not seen it on a polite table in Edinburgh for years. To object to its offensive smell seemed petty after the goose.

After dinner, Beatrix and Deborah hurried about the castle opening windows, but somehow the rain outside seemed to form an effective curtain, preventing the smell escaping. As they went they flapped at their shawls and their skirts, as if afraid that the smell would be clinging to them just as effectively – to Murray, discreetly flicking at his coat tails and catching Major Keyes doing the same, it seemed far from unreasonable. It was too wet to take a walk or a ride outside, though Lady Scoggie could not resist wrapping herself in several layers and setting off in a trap for some sickly victim, and at last in desperation the girls, Murray and his charges, and Major Keyes retreated to the gallery, as far up the castle as they could go, and dug out the carpet bowls. The rain darkened the room despite the high windows, and they lit some of the candles in the brackets along the gallery. Even in half-daylight, the place seemed to have a memory of dark deeds. The smell of the goose did not help.

'I wouldn't mind so much,' Deborah said, as she bent to roll one of the striped china balls down the rush-matted floor, 'but the Boothams are coming to tea, and staying to supper – or that's the intention. If I arrived in a house that smelled like this, I don't think I would stay any longer than I had to.'

'Let alone to eat,' added Beatrix, with an anxious look. 'Did you close the drawing room door, Deborah?'

'Oh, no!'

Beatrix hurried away to try to keep the smell out of one room, at least.

'Where does Father find such things?' Deborah went on in despair. 'He's worse than a cat, dragging in dead birds and expecting us to call him a clever puss!'

'I heard him say one of the fishermen had brought it to him, knowing he liked a bit of solander goose,' said Major Keyes, grinning at Murray.

'It should be a hanging offence,' Deborah muttered. 'Your turn, Major.'

Beatrix reappeared, breathless from her run.

'I'm sure the smell is spreading,' she said. 'You did tell Mrs. Costane to burn all the leftovers, Deborah?'

'I don't think she needed to be told,' Murray put in. 'I think if she had had the chance she would have burned the whole bird before it set foot in the house.'

'I wonder how long it had been dead?' Deborah said.

'Several months, would you say?' Beatrix said drily.

'It's your turn, Bea – you're on Mr. Murray's side.' Deborah seemed disposed to be friendly towards Major Keyes today, Murray thought: it was hard to know from one day to the next where her heart lay, or even if she had allowed it to stray at all. Deborah and the Major formed one team, the boys another, and himself and Beatrix the third – probably doomed to lose, for neither of them felt as driven to win as the others, but likely to enjoy themselves more than anyone.

She was looking particularly pretty today, he thought: she was wearing a pale green spencer over a white gown sprigged with the same green, and it brought out the gold in her hair, which she seemed to have done differently today. The candlelight reflected off little plaits and curls that had a not-quite artless look. How, he wondered, could anyone compare Deborah to her?

He had to be careful, he knew. He was attracted to Bea, and found her very congenial company, but he was fairly sure that part of that attraction was the lack of much other suitable female companions. He knew she was not the woman he wanted to spend the rest of his life with, and taken on a practical level, as he had been taught by his father was a good thing to do, if he was reunited with his father, his father would not approve of her or her rather limited portion, and if he was not, he could not afford to support a wife for years yet. He had heard all the stories that young gentlemen of his age did – the friend of a friend who had been trapped into marriage by false witnesses, or after a moment of careless talk in front of untrustworthy acquaintances. He knew Bea would never behave like that, but at the same time he wanted to treat her fairly: a poor relation would have few enough opportunities of marriage offers, and he wanted neither to make her think he was going to make one, nor to pay her so much attention that he would prevent some other man from stepping in and claiming her. It was easier in Edinburgh, or even in St. Andrews, where one could chat with one young lady, dance with another, sit with a third at supper, and rarely arouse comment, but here, where people were thrown together, he had to be careful, indeed.

Robert hurled a bowl down the gallery, and the cries of protest from Deborah and Henry brought him back from his reverie.

'This is supposed to be a quiet indoor game, Robert,' Deborah groaned.

'But that's no fun,' Robert objected. 'They bounce a

bit, if you throw them hard enough.'

'I imagine the same could be said of you,' said Deborah, with some menace.

'Do you think the rain will ever stop? Look at it,' Beatrix, trying as ever to be the peacemaker, drew Murray over to one of the windows. The grey light gave her blue eyes a clear luminosity.

'Miserable,' Murray agreed.

'You know what's worse than having to suffer this appalling stench,' said Deborah, abandoning any hope of reforming Robert today. 'It's the suspicion that we'll get used to it, and long before it has actually faded we'll think everything is all right and we'll be going about reeking and not realising it.'

'I'm sure you could never be anything but fragrant, my dear cousin,' said Major Keyes, winking at her with heavy gallantry.

'That's no use coming from you, Major, for you will be just as used to it as the rest of us.'

'In that case, we had better all stay together, and abandon the rest of society,' said the resourceful hero. Even Deborah smiled at his efforts.

'I'm not sure I want to abandon the rest of society.' Beatrix bowled her turn and returned to join Murray at the window. 'I like having visitors.' She scanned the drive below the window, as if willing a visitor to appear, and as if by magic, one did.

'Here's Mr. Tibo arriving already, Deborah,' she called. Deborah came up to see.

'Oh, dear: he's so fastidious. But he knows what Father is like.'

'Is he here on business?' Murray asked.

'Not really, though I'm sure Father will drag him away for some obscure purpose or other. It's just after Mr. Leckie's funeral yesterday – and he's all on his own now, for Mr. Leckie was the closest to family he had, I think. Mother asked him to try to cheer him up, but I'm not sure that a castle infested with the remnants of solander goose and herring is the best place to cheer up.'

'It might put his own problems into perspective,' Beatrix suggested, straight-faced.

'Oh, well – of course Mother isn't back yet. We'd better go down, Bea. Boys, will you put the bowls away? All of them: the last time there was one left behind, and Grisell nearly broke her ankle.'

Tibo, too, was so well wrapped up against the weather that by the time Murray had overseen the boys' disposal of the carpet bowls, he had only just appeared in the drawing room. He apologised at once for his muddy boots, but looked blank when Deborah countered with an apology for the smell of the goose. Deborah was about to explain when Lord Scoggie himself, the villain of the piece, arrived to greet the guest.

'Behold an Israelite indeed, in whom is no guile!' he cried. Tibo smiled weakly, and bowed. It occurred to Murray that he did not look as if he had slept easily: the precision of his clothing and hair looked like the frame of a painting which was unaccountably smudged. His ankle, hurt at the boxing lesson, still seemed to give him pain.

'The weather as bad as ever?' Lord Scoggie persisted, as they all sat down.

'Indeed – the wind has dropped, but the rain is as heavy as ever.' He looked awkward at having echoed Lord Scoggie's own phrase, and stopped.

'Perhaps you should have stayed at home,' suggested Major Keyes. 'For your own health,' he added, a little too slowly.

'Oh, but I was out anyway. I have been – all over the village.' He looked somehow confused.

'Oh, have you been to see the Farquhars?' Lord Scoggie asked quickly. Tibo met his eye.

'Aye, I have.' A little nod passed between them, and Murray, thinking back to the meeting with the fishermen in the library, deduced that the Farquhars must have sent their daughter back to her pig-eating husband. Then he saw Tibo's face changed, preparing them for what he had to say next. ' Hugh Farquhar's boat did not come back last night.'

'Oh, no,' Lord Scoggie breathed. 'He was out in the storm?'

Tibo nodded.

'The fleet was turning back, making a run for home, but he decided to stay behind. Joe Baillie says he felt he had lost time over the matter of the pig. He was trying to make up for it.'

'Young fool,' said Lord Scoggie sadly.

'How are the family?' asked Deborah, her mother's daughter.

'How you would expect them to be,' said Tibo, his face drawn. 'He was their only steady moneymaker – old Mr. Farquhar has not been able to go out for a few years, now, and the next boy is young yet.' He sighed, watching as one of his hands flicked at a mote of dust on his breeches. 'I spoke to Joe Baillie: there were five others on the boat, the usual crew. He has a list of the names for the minister.'

'I'll speak to him, and to Joe, myself, too.' Lord Scoggie, whatever his faults, always did his duty, though he did not expect to take any pleasure from it. 'And the village will be a boat down, too, for anyone else fishing. A bad day, a bad day.'

'Worse, too, in that Joe Baillie blames the bad luck on the matter of the pig left by the harbour. I doubt things will get worse between uphill and down before they get better.' Tibo seemed to be able to find nothing to cheer himself today, but there was still a look behind his eyes that said he did not have his mind wholly on this conversation: he was still confused by something,

something to do with the village, and on one level at least he was trying to sort it out.

The rest of the company were silent, waiting for the tea to arrive and break the spell of melancholy. The two girls sat disconsolate on the sofa, their needlework abandoned on their laps. Murray sat on the window seat, unable to think of anything to say or do. Major Keyes made an effort to break the silence.

'Joe Baillie, eh? Is he still on the go?'

The look Lord Scoggie cast him at this point would have stopped a lesser man, but that at that point the drawing room door opened and Lady Scoggie came in, pushing at her hair to rearrange it after its confinement under a damp bonnet. Murray remembered Major Keyes mentioning that in her youth, Lady Scoggie had been one for routs and parties, and wondered if she had been so careless of her appearance then – he somehow doubted it.

'Ah, Mr. Tibo, already. You'll have brought the bad news, then, I take it?'

'About Hugh Farquhar's boat? Yes, my lady.'

'Terrible, isn't it?' She sat, drawing her shawl around her. 'I went to see the Crichtons – you know their middle boy was on the boat – to see if they were in want of anything, but they barely know, yet. He was to be married at the end of the season. And I visited the Farquhars – very tense, all of them. It was almost as if they expected him back. Very sad.'

'Is there no good news in this part of the world?' Keyes asked, of Tippoo as much as anyone else. He held the dog's chin and patted its head affectionately. The dog gazed up with devotion. Murray looked away.

'Oh, mother – I meant to say, but we seem to have been so busy,' Deborah said suddenly. 'I spoke to Geordie Kinkell the other day outside his cottage, and he mentioned that his wife is not well. Have you been to see her?'

'Not well, really?' Lady Scoggie was unusually vague. 'I think the minister mentioned something of the sort. I shall find time to call in, no doubt.'

'I could go instead, if you have too many others to attend to, Lady Scoggie,' Beatrix offered. 'I am not sure that there is much that can be done for her, from the way Geordie Kinkell spoke of her.'

'No, it's good of you to suggest it, dear,' said Lady Scoggie, 'but I should be able to manage. A bad case, you say?'

'I think so. You had the same impression, didn't you, Deborah?'

'Yes, I think so, too.'

Lady Scoggie looked, for a moment, almost wistful. Puzzled, Murray looked away from her and over to where Lord Scoggie and Tibo were sitting near the fire. They were not looking at each other, but in such a way that Murray had the clear impression that it was deliberate.

Lord Scoggie knew of Mrs. Kinkell's illness – Geordie himself had told him in Murray's hearing – but he made no comment.

In the distance the doorbell rang.

'That will be the Boothams,' said Deborah, jumping up and then remembering that her mother was there, for once. 'Did you notice – any kind of smell in the place when you arrived, Mr.Tibo?'

'A smell?' He looked completely bewildered.

'A fishy sort of ... stench.'

'Deborah!' said her father. 'Are you referring to that excellent goose?'

'Father ...' But before she could think of anything to say, the Boothams were announced.

The room lit up with their presence, and even the boys, who had been playing cards at the table, stood of their own accord and did not have to be glared at. Lady Scoggie reminded Naismyth about the tea.

'A filthy day to be out,' Bootham remarked when they were all seated again. 'You have heard the bad news from the village?'

'Our maid has been inconsolable all morning,' Mrs. Bootham added. 'She was betrothed – handfastit, I believe she called it: would that be right? – to one of the dead fishermen. Such a tragedy!'

'Very much so,' agreed Lord Scoggie warmly. 'They were to marry at the end of the season. There is such a risk with these things.'

'She was really quite beautiful in her grief,' Bootham remarked, 'sitting all in white, her black hair loose, apron to her wide eyes.'

There was an awkward little silence at this, as no one seemed quite to know how to respond. Fortunately the tea arrived, and Lady Scoggie took her place beside the urn to pour. It was probably her unaccustomedness to the position that caused the cups to rattle more than usual on their saucers.

'And I hear another sad accident happened in the neighbourhood on Saturday,' Mrs. Bootham began again. 'I am sorry neither of us said anything when we met you on Sunday, but we had no idea at that time. Mr. Leckie, was it not? Your assistant, Mr. Tibo.'

'Quite right. A very unfortunate accident, though it occurred during some foolish activity,' said Tibo.

'When is the funeral to be? We should like to pay our respects.'

'It was yesterday.'

'Oh!' Mrs. Bootham blushed and looked very surprised.

'Such matters are attended to more swiftly here than they are in England,' Lady Scoggie explained to her.

'Then I am heartily sorry we missed it,' said Mrs. Bootham.

'Aye, extraordinary the length of time they wait in England,' Major Keyes came into the conversation, though if he had hoped to ease Mrs. Bootham's embarrassment he was unsuccessful. 'I remember when I first lived down there – well, I was quite shocked. And in the summer, too, in all that heat down in the south.'

'Where have you been stationed, Major?' Bootham asked smoothly, aiming to divert Keyes away from any more intimate detail of English funeral practices.

'Oh, here and there, here and there,' he said. 'I've been in Dover for a fair while, and before that Chelsea, of course, getting myself patched up, and before that India, for a few years, though of course that was a bit hotter, but then they burn their dead there, before they even have time to cool. They say it's religion, but half of it is disease, you know.'

'And before India?' Beatrix put in hurriedly.

'London, Miss Beatrix, at the Tower. That was the time you were there, too, wasn't it, Livvy?' He grinned at his cousin. 'You'd have been the toast of the town, too, if my lord Scoggie here hadn't had the sense to marry you before you visited the capital.'

'You flatter me, cousin,' said Lady Scoggie, with a very pale imitation of a smile in return. 'Lord Scoggie was very busy travelling between Edinburgh and London at the time, weren't you?' Lord Scoggie smiled and nodded. 'I stayed with your mother, I remember, Alec.'

'I should love to visit London,' said Deborah. 'It must be so exciting. I saw Edinburgh once, but that was when I was a child, and barely old enough to appreciate it.'

'There is no glory in London, my dear,' said Lady Scoggie with a sigh. 'It is in the end a very wearing city, and very dirty.'

'I think you can have forgotten the galleries, and the society, and the gardens and the river,' said Philip Bootham, and smiled at her. She did not meet his eye.

'No, not at all, Mr. Bootham, though I doubt they are all very different from my day. No doubt you and Mrs. Bootham know it well, but I no longer have the inclination for such things.'

'Then perhaps one day your husband will take you, Miss Scoggie,' Bootham turned his smile to Deborah. 'If you find yourself there, be sure to let me know, and I shall be happy to guide you amongst the best of artistic sights.'

'You are very kind, sir,' said Deborah, blushing appropriately at the suggestion that she might have a husband in the foreseeable future.

Murray was a little behind Mr. Bootham, and could not see his face, but as he looked over at Deborah his eye was caught by Beatrix beside her on the sofa – Beatrix who had been immersed in the bow wave of Mr. Bootham's smile. He caught his breath. Her face was illuminated, bright as the moon reflecting the sun's light.

Oh, no: he suddenly realised. She is in love with Mr. Bootham. Oh, dear Beatrix, he thought, and if he could have shouted it he would have. Don't make a fool of yourself, dear Beatrix.

Mr. Bootham had glided on, impervious, and was now deep in conversation with Lord Scoggie about poetry. Tibo was listening with half an ear: Keyes, Murray noticed, was torn between feeling shy with the ladies, and feeling unread with the gentlemen. He sat somewhere in between, feeding titbits of cake to Tippoo under the table.

'What verse do your boys read?' Bootham asked Lord Scoggie, nodding in their direction.

'Not a great deal at this stage, truthfully,' said Murray, drawn in by Lord Scoggie. 'They know Burns and Fergusson, of course, and Shakespeare, though Robert prefers the more violent bits. Milton, Dryden, and Spenser we have studied together. The usual, along with some Latin verse.'

'And what of the modern poets?' Bootham asked, as if he had expected no better.

'Oh, yes, but you *are* a modern poet, are you not, Mr. Bootham? Like Shelley and Southey, perhaps,' said Lord Scoggie eagerly.

'It is a great time to be a poet,' said Bootham. 'The worlds of art, science, politics, all in turmoil, all crying out for reform, for cleansing – it is thrilling.'

'You'll have come across the new *Edinburgh*

Review, then?' said Tibo, cutting across the look of shock that always appeared on Lord Scoggie's face when political reform sneaked into the conversation.

'There's a review in Edinburgh? How splendid!' said Bootham happily.

'A little Whiggish, perhaps.' Tibo tried to sound balanced. 'I hear it's growing very popular, with a certain class of intellectual.'

'My dear,' Lady Scoggie interrupted gently. Lord Scoggie turned courteously to his wife. 'Mrs. Bootham turns out to be an accomplished performer, as well as an artist. Shall we ask her to play and sing for us?'

'Oh, delightful, delightful!' Lord Scoggie managed to look pleased, though it was generally recognised amongst the family that there was more music in the library fireirons than there was in him. The rest of the family were not much better, to Murray's perpetual sorrow, and he heard of Mrs. Bootham's talent with mingled joy and dread. He had managed not to look at her directly since she had arrived, and that would be all the harder if she were seated centrally at the pianoforte.

Family and guests rearranged themselves to look attentive. Out of the corner of his eye, as he pretended to make sure that the boys were sitting still and behaving themselves quietly, he saw a flurry of pale silk as she made her way to the piano stool, and Beatrix hurried to turn the pages for her. She felt quickly over the notes, as if greeting the keyboard, charming it, then began to play and sing something by Mozart.

Murray closed his eyes. It was beautiful. He could feel something inside him, parched from want of music for over a year, stretching and growing again and basking in the cool, quenching draught of notes, filling every part of him, making him alive again.

But at the same time it was frightening. She sang like a siren, alluring, tempting, telling him to open his eyes and gaze at her again. He felt the need to see her, to hear her sing again and again, for the rest of his days. Oh, where was Odysseus with the wax and a sturdy mast when you needed him?

He made himself open his eyes as the song came to an end, and glance around him at the others. Lord Scoggie was nodding his head in time to some rhythm heard only in his head, and Deborah was not much better, however carefully taught. Tibo had the decency to sit still with a blank look on his face that could be interpreted in almost any necessary way. Major Keyes looked as if he thought it was all very well, but where were the drums? Only Lady Scoggie gazed as abstractedly at Mrs. Bootham as she would have expected, though it did not look as if her mind was on the music.

'Please, please delight us with something more!' said Lord Scoggie, and Tibo echoed the plea. Mrs. Bootham needed little encouragement, and sang a tune from the Beggar's Opera, with similar effect. Murray listened to around five bars, before he could bear it no longer and rose to walk over to the window, where he tried to find something to distract himself.

A cure was effected by Deborah's performance straight afterwards, while Mrs. Bootham retired in triumph. Deborah played just as much as she had to, with as much feeling as an automaton and considerably less accuracy. Murray tried very hard not to be seen wincing, though he was by now well used to the Scoggies' performances. He knew, too, what would come next. It did.

'Mr. Murray? Mr. Murray is very musical, you know, much more so than I can appreciate!' said Lord Scoggie. 'You will play and sing for us, too, Mr. Murray, will you not? I'm sure the ladies would like a rest.'

There was never so much attention given to male soloists, anyway, in society, he reminded himself, as he dug through the music books on the piano. And when you can command the singer to perform, as if it is part of his normal work for which you employ him, then why should you pay any attention? You simply set him going, like the automaton he had thought Deborah, and turn away to play cards.

He knew the Scoggies preferred Scottish tunes to foreign composers like Mozart – they were not alone in that – and so he ferreted out 'The Yellow-hair'd Laddie' as a compromise. It was a folk song, but J.C. Bach had written variations on the tune, and he could perform both unexceptionally as a background to the general conversation. He sat at the piano and began.

It was a pleasant tune, and his only qualm, once he had begun and it was too late, was that the yellow-hair'd laddie who, according to the song, sang so beautifully that 'silvans and fairies unseen danc'd around', conjured up visions of the Boothams again. He seemed to be the only one who thought so, though, and as he had expected the music was not much listened to. Playing his way quietly through the variations, he found himself watching the company again, seeing how they had split into further conversation.

Beatrix was playing cards with the boys, keeping them amused, though he saw again that her attention was really on Mr. Bootham. His hair was as pale as if he powdered it: only the shine as the light slid on it from newly lit candles said that the colour was real. Mrs. Bootham indoors did not wear a married woman's cap, but her hair, too, glinted. She was talking with Lady Scoggie, or seemed to be answering Lady Scoggie's interested questions. Bootham himself was now talking with Lord Scoggie and Major Keyes, though what subject they could possibly have in common was beyond Murray's imagination, and he could not quite hear them. Keyes was doing a good deal of the talking there, but in turn he was watching Tibo and Deborah, who, despite Tibo's painful ankle, were standing by the window, a little aside from the rest of the company, and appeared to be in the middle of a very serious conversation. When Murray glanced round, both were frowning, and he caught, briefly, Beatrix' eye as she noticed the same thing. She looked puzzled: it was enough to distract her for a little at least from the dangerous Mr. Bootham.

Dangerous? What made him think that? Did he think that Mr. Bootham, a married man – a married man with a captivating wife – had deliberately set out himself to captivate Beatrix?

He sighed to himself. In a musical Edinburgh house, his father's, for instance, the gap between tea and supper would be filled with more than a tutor's meandering performance, and almost certainly with some country dancing. He loved dancing almost as much as he loved music. On the other hand, he remembered suddenly, tomorrow was Hallowe'en, and the servants' dance, to which he had been invited. He hoped with sudden violence that the boys would behave themselves and he would be able to go.

After a while the whole company joined together again to play word games, at which they were mostly very clever, even the boys. Words were Lord Scoggie's music, and his gift to his family, and they all enjoyed it to the full. When supper finally arrived, an unexpected level of hilarity had set in, and everyone had relaxed: Tibo had left Deborah to be attentive to his hostess, Keyes had bravely taken on a conversation with Deborah, and the Boothams had fallen in with Robert and Henry, playing some ridiculous card game with them. Supper passed with great pleasure, and to his surprise Murray was quite disappointed when the time came for the guests to leave. Everyone came out on to the landing, and made their way down the stairs in the midst of various conversations: Murray found himself talking with Keyes about Indian food, and behind them on the stairs came Deborah and

Tibo. Keyes completed a description of a particularly hot curry, which Murray thought sounded wonderful, and they laughed together. As their laughter died away, Murray distinctly heard Tibo's voice a few steps behind them.

'So that's arranged. You'll meet me tomorrow.'

'As soon as I am free from the servants' dance, yes,' she replied, quietly businesslike. Murray, who had started to glance around, tried to look as if he had heard nothing, but as he turned back he could see quite clearly on Keyes' face that he had heard exactly the same thing, and was far from pleased. Murray, reaching the hall, was casting about quickly for something to say to distract Keyes, when Lord Scoggie bounded down the stairs beside his daughter and caught Keyes by the arm.

'Can we have a quick word when everyone has gone? In the library, I think.'

'Certainly,' said Keyes, and then the Boothams descended the stairs and everything was cloaks and hats until they had been seen into their carriage, along with Tibo, to whom they had offered a lift as far as their gates. Goodbyes echoed around the hall, the family waved their guests off happily, and at last there was quiet.

'Well, that went very well, I think,' said Deborah to her mother, as Keyes and Lord Scoggie disappeared into the library.

'Is everything arranged for the dance tomorrow night?' Lady Scoggie asked, and they moved away, discussing it. The boys ran up the stairs to finish their cards tournament before they were sent to bed, Beatrix followed Deborah and her mother, and suddenly Murray was left alone in the hall.

His throat was tired from singing, and he went to the servants' hall to beg a spoonful of honey in some warm water. The servants were quietly excited, and Hannah and Grizell were busy with their needles over a candle in far corner, doing their best to hide their work from the others. Murray asked a few polite questions about the preparations, making it clear that he was still looking forward to the event himself. He took the water and honey, and wishing them all a good night he headed back up the passage to the hall, and up the stairs to the first floor.

He could hear voices coming from the library along with a dim light from perhaps no more than one or two lamps down below. The gallery was faintly outlined. The voice he heard first was Lord Scoggie's.

'So Lady Scoggie and I were wondering, Major, if you would be interested in considering marriage at this time.'

There was a pause. Murray stopped too, not to listen, but because he remembered from earlier that the carpet was loose around here and he did not want to trip, but he could not see it in the dark. Keyes was evidently thinking.

'I cannot say that the attractions of Miss Scoggie have not been very clear to me this week, and she has been kind enough to pay some attention to an old soldier. Do you think she would take on someone with this?'

'I don't see why not,' Lord Scoggie said amiably, probably alluding to Keyes' wooden leg. Murray found the loose carpet, and was about to step clearly over it and make his way to the next floor when he noticed a figure standing, near enough to the library gallery to overhear, but far enough away from the edge not to be seen from below. He squinted through the dim light: it was Deborah.

She saw him, and with a glance at the library below hurried across to him.

'What are you doing here?'

'Watching my step on the carpet and going to my room,' he said, slightly defensively. 'And you?' They were whispering.

'I think I have a right to hear this conversation,' she replied. 'Do you know what they are talking about?'

He waited a second before saying,

'Yes.'

'Well, there you are, then.'

He looked at the dark outline of her determined chin as she glanced back again at the gallery.

'And will you? Will you take him on?'

She turned back to him, slowly. To her surprise, she took his hand.

'Oh, Mr. Murray,' she said, with surprising compassion. 'This is the deal we make. Poverty and labour, and a chance to make our own choice, or wealth and comfort, and a husband chosen for us. There is nothing to regret: there is merit in both schemes.'

He squeezed her hand sympathetically, and released it.

'Then you had better go back and hear your fate. Good night, Miss Deborah.'

'Good night, Mr. Murray.'

So Lord Scoggie had made his choice, he thought, as he climbed the stairs to his room in the school wing. He thought about Keyes' temper, and wondered why, and when, Lord Scoggie had changed his mind, and whether he had any right to comment on it himself.

CHAPTER TWELVE

'It just seems a wee bit strange,' said Mrs. Costane, without pausing once with her rolling pin. 'I mean, I'm looking forward to the dance and all, but I cannot say I've given it much thought, not with poor Mr. Leckie's awful accident and then his funeral, and then the storm, and a boat lost, and now here we are making supper for a dance in the same week, never mind the grand dinner the day after tomorrow. It just doesn't feel right, though I wouldn't stop it, of course. It's awful hard to disappoint people. What do you think, Mr. Murray?'

Murray, hovering in the kitchen to obtain pies to bribe the boys, made a noncommittal noise. He wanted to dance, but he took her point.

'I think not,' added Hannah. 'It's rare enough we get a wee dance to ourselves and a nice wee bite of supper. Anyway, is there any sign of you putting young Andrew out of his misery tonight, Miss Grisell, and dancing with the poor wee lad?'

Grisell, chopping apples for a jelly, had the grace to blush a little as she smiled.

'I might just,' she said. 'If he behaves himself.'

'I doubt you'll have him eating out of your hand by the end of the evening,' snapped Mrs. Costane. 'You've let him chase you long enough for you to catch him. I wonder are there any more in Kirkcaldy as good looking as him?'

'If there are I'm away there,' said Hannah, with unaccustomed flightiness.

'You'll stay where you are, you daft oul hen,' was Mrs. Costane's kindly advice. 'Leave the flirtings to the young ones who have the energy for it. I hope you've every inch of peel off those apples, Grisell Shaw.'

'The pigs will like them,' said Hannah, and laughed when Grisell winced.

'I suppose you've been eating them in front of the looking-glass in the passage, anyway,' said Mrs. Costane, not bothering to look up. 'To see if you see an image of him coming up behind you.'

'That would gar me grue,' said Hannah, shivering.

'Whether I did or I didn't,' said Grisell, shifting the apple peelings with her finger to hide a discarded and much chewed core, 'I couldn't tell you. That one has to be done in secret.'

'Well, you can't use the barn to see him,' said Mrs. Costane, thinking through other possible means of Hallowe'en divination, 'it's full of gardeners.'

'What about peas?' cried Hannah. 'At least that brings no unnatural apparitions.'

'Peas it is, then!' Mrs. Costane. She dropped the bowl of pastry filling she was working with on to the table, and dispatched Hannah to the bag of dried peas under one of the long benches.

'Oh, not in front of Mr. Murray!' Grisell was squirming, but not unpleasurably. Murray laughed.

'I won't tell!'

'Don't worry about him,' said Mrs. Costane. She already had the girdle heating over the fire, and was smelling it to see if it was hot enough. 'Give me the peas.' Hannah handed over two peas. 'This one with the mark on it is you, girl, and the other is himself. Now, let's see if they stay and roast together, or roll apart.'

She set the peas on to the girdle. Hannah and Grisell bent down to watch, and Murray, irresistibly, came closer.

The peas sat quietly together on the hot metal for a long moment. Then, with a crack, they leapt apart, rolling wildly around the girdle. Hannah gasped. The peas swerved, crashed and spun, then, with a final hiss, ended up together in the middle of the girdle again.

The three women stared at each other.

'Well, you'll get him in the end,' said Mrs. Costane eventually, 'but it'll be a wild courting, that's for sure.'

'And I thought you women just knew from birth how to ensnare men. I didn't realise you enlisted the help of vegetables,' said Murray, grinning.

'There isn't a thing in creation that's on a man's side when a woman is after him,' said Mrs. Costane sourly. 'Just you remember that, now, Mr. Murray. Now, enough of this nonsense: let's make sure there's a supper tonight.'

Every surface in the kitchen was covered in food, mostly prepared by Hannah, though it was of course Mrs. Costane who was showing signs of dramatic nerves over the whole performance. There was a side of beef, roasted and cooled, and there were bowls of potted mushrooms, fresh from the orchard, and baked onions in big square dishes keeping warm by the fire, and hard-boiled eggs shiny white on creamware plates. Hannah's activities at a side table echoed with the vicious crack of crab shells and promised further delights. Mrs. Costane herself had contributed two huge piles of pastries, savoury and sweet as she had promised, which were flashing in and out of the hot oven in batches, baking swiftly from cream to gold and cooling on wire trays under the high windows. A number of gardener's boys – and indeed gardeners – had appeared at odd moments throughout the morning, drawn by the smell like bees to a flower, hoping, in vain, for a quick foretaste of the evening's delights. Instead they reported on the state of the barn, the branches they had arranged on the rafters, the apples in heaps, the neep lanterns they had been carving for the last two days. One of the men had a knack for weaving wreaths from corn stalks, and had turned them into golden chandeliers on every ledge. It was hard to tell who was the more excited about the others' work: the women longed to see the barn, and the gardeners longed to eat the food. The kitchen door was blown back and forth by heavy sighs of impatience.

Murray thanked Mrs. Costane for the pies – everyday ones, not dance food – and carried them carefully back up the passage to the hall. Deborah, Beatrix and Naismyth were in the Great Hall, examining cutlery with the door open.

'That should do,' Deborah was saying as she left Beatrix and the steward with the cutlery. 'Give it a quick clean, and take it down to the kitchen for moving to the barn. Oh, Mr. Murray!'

'Miss Deborah.' They began to climb the stairs together. 'I hope everything is going according to plan?'

'I feel Major Keyes should be doing this,' she sighed. 'It feels like the invasion of a small country.'

'Is he not helping you?'

She met his eye with a sideways glance.

'I'm not sure that he's *that* eager a suitor,' she said quietly. 'Are you going to the servants' dance?'

'I hope so, if the boys settle early enough.'

'Do, do go. I know how much you love to dance,

and it will help to keep some of the unrulier elements quiet if they see someone respectable like you there. We all have the two dances with them, of course, but then we leave, and I might not even be able to manage that long for I have something else to do. It can go a bit wild after we leave, particularly when the punch has flowed for a bit. And I remember one year we had to rebuild most of the barn afterwards. Something about a pig, I think.'

'Most likely,' Murray agreed. 'I'll try to keep an eye open for trouble, if it will help.'

They were about to part on the landing, but she stopped him, folding her arms into her shawl, a little frown denting her forehead.

'Tell me, did you hear Father last night ask the Boothams to supper again tonight, to see the dance?'

'I think I did.'

'Oh, dear: another two to supper, and Mrs. Costane already like an overwound clock.' She leaned back suddenly against the wall, looking tired. 'I really don't understand what everyone sees in these Boothams, anyway. I haven't a notion why they ever came here. They don't like the weather, and they think we're all peasants. She seems to know nothing about housekeeping, and he seems to think his only function is decorative, though with his funny white hair I'm not even sure he qualifies for that. Oh, Mr. Murray, you haven't by any chance seen my mother in the course of your travels, have you?'

'Yes, as a matter of fact, I saw Lady Scoggie in the

hall about twenty minutes ago. She was going out.'

'Did she say where to?'

'To the Farquhars and the other bereaved families, I think.'

'Not to Mrs. Kinkell?' Her frown deepened. 'How very odd. But as usual she is not here, when we need her. She had better be here on Friday for the grand dinner. Oh, dear! Now, what was I up here for? Oh, yes: cushions.'

She marched off along the gallery to the tower room, where Murray hoped she would find some cushions still in one piece after the boys had used them as weapons. Feeling the sudden calm of the landing after her passing, he took a long, deep breath and paused for a moment, eyes closed, before venturing back along the schoolroom corridor to face his charges.

The schoolroom, as he approached, was ominously quiet. He trod carefully on the wooden floor, making no noise himself, and stopped just outside the door. From within, he could hear only the occasional scuffle, and some remarkably heavy breathing, of the kind Robert did when he was concentrating very hard. Murray counted to ten, and with a deep sense of foreboding, opened the door.

There was an almighty crash, and Murray flung up his hands to protect his head as books fell around him like autumn leaves, only with harder corners. When he opened his eyes again, the boys were still dumbstruck, standing on the table on which they had evidently been building a book tower. In a flash, they were down and back in their seats again.

Murray brushed flakes of pastry off himself from the battered pies, and looked at the mess.

'It's good to see you both so eager to get back to your lessons,' he remarked, 'but you needn't think anyone else is going to clear up all this mess. Pick them up quickly and put them back on the shelf, and show some respect for books – and next time, don't build a tower so near the door.'

'Well you shouldn't walk round so quietly, or we could have shouted out and warned you,' Robert objected, but Henry kicked him with all the force of an older brother recognising a hole when he saw it. They reluctantly cleared the books up off the floor, and put them back on the shelf, some upside down or back to front, though Murray decided not to pursue it.

'Thank you,' he said heavily when they had returned to their form. 'Now, it's Tacitus this morning – do you have your slates ready?'

'Robert's is broken again,' said Henry flatly.

'Another one, Robert?'

'It's only a bit off the bottom. I can still write on it,' Robert insisted, glaring at Henry.

'Then do so. Tacitus. At the top, write "Book

Fifteen, Chapter Forty-two".'

'But we did that last week, Mr. Murray, sir,' said Henry.

'No, we didn't.'

'Yes, we did, sir.' Robert was eager to support his brother.

'What was it about, then?' The question was directed at Robert, but his face went blank. 'Henry?'

'About Nero, sir.'

'Doing what?'

'Burning Rome!' cried Robert, who was easily excited by such happy pastimes.

'And?'

Henry thought hard, but eventually had to shake his head.

'So even if we did do it last week – which I gravely doubt –' said Murray, 'we'll do it now to make sure you remember it this time. Now, write down: "*Ceterum Nero usus est patriae ruinis exstruxitque domum*". He finished slowly, allowing them time to transcribe the phrase. He was growing to hate the squeak of stylus on slate, which in his own school days he had not minded in the least. 'Now, Henry, parse *extruxitque*, please.'

'Well, the "-*que*" just means "and",' Henry began.

'Sir,' said Robert with sudden urgency.

'And the rest is a verb, third person singular, perfect tense, meaning ... out of something.'

'Not bad, Henry. Think again about the possible meaning. What does *struxit* remind you of?'

'Sir!'

'Do you know, Robert?'

'Sir, no, but I do know something else!'

'Shut up, Robert, I'm trying to think,' hissed Henry.

'What do you know, Robert? It had better be useful.'

'Well, it's more sort of interesting,' Robert conceded, as one who had subjected it to close analysis. 'It's just that Deborah is going to meet Mr. Tibo tonight, after dark!'

Murray sighed.

'And are you going to explain why this is in the least interesting?' he asked, not at all sure he wanted to know.

'Well, if a girl meets a man after dark, they must be going to get married!' said Robert with certainty. 'And that won't please our cousin Major Keyes, will it, sir?'

'Robert, this is North Britain. In the winter it is dark for about seven-eighths of the day. Would you have your sister kept indoors like a nun?'

'But he's right, sir,' said Henry, making Murray feel suddenly betrayed. 'She is meeting him after dark, and it won't please Major Keyes, will it, sir? Even if Mr. Tibo doesn't marry her.'

'I don't think Miss Deborah is going to commit any errors of etiquette with Mr. Tibo. In fact, if it's this evening, it's almost certainly to do with the servants' dance. Miss Deborah has time for nothing else today. Now, *extruxitque*, Henry, if you have no further objections.'

'But we do, sir!' cried Robert. 'We want her to marry Major Keyes! Then we'll have a hero for a brother, and I'll get a commission and go and kill Hindoos and Frogs!'

'What an honourable ambition, to be sure, Robert,' said Murray drily. 'Even if Miss Deborah is meeting fifty men after dark this evening there is nothing you can do about it, particularly just now. So I suggest you turn your attention back to Tacitus, who has so far put much more effort into this lesson than you have, however many centuries dead he is.'

The next twenty minutes went by slowly and painfully, and Murray began to think wistfully of an hour he had spent as a boy having a tooth drawn. Tacitus' account of Nero's reconstruction of Imperial Rome seemed to be taking as long as the original building work, and probably with as many false starts.

'"*Namque ab lacu Averno navigabilem fossam ...*"' Murray dictated.

Robert, propped on his elbow, sighed heavily.

'Couldn't we have a ghost story, Mr. Murray? It's Hallowe'en.'

'No, we couldn't. Evening is the time for ghost stories. *Namque ab lacu –*'

'Do you think Mr. Leckie will be walking tonight, sir?'

'What?'

'Cocky Leckie, sir. Do you think he will be walking tonight? He's not long dead, and he died a violent death.'

Murray could honestly say that the thought had not crossed his mind.

'Mr. Leckie died in an unfortunate accident, Robert. I can't see why he would walk.'

'But he might walk to get his revenge, sir.'

'On what? A cheval mirror?'

'On us, for making everyone go to the boxing lesson,' said Henry suddenly. He looked a little pale.

'You didn't make everyone go. Major Keyes was going, and the rest of us were kindly invited. And Mr. Leckie liked you, and he was a good man. I don't see that his ghost would want to cause you any distress.' He picked up the book again. '*Namque ab lacu –*'

'But what about Hugh Farquhar, sir?'

He gave a frustrated hiss.

'Don't tell me you think he's going to haunt you now! Why, this time? Did you decline a plate of herring?'

Robert and Henry exchanged glances.

'Father told him he had to send his sister home. He was cross about it. Grisell said so.'

Murray had hoped that Grisell might have had more important things on her mind at the moment.

'So you think he's going to haunt your father?'

'Well, he might.'

'He's more likely to haunt his brother-in-law, I would have thought. He respected your father.'

'But ghosts don't have to respect anyone,' said Henry, with some perception.

'I assure you,' said Murray with finality, 'that if either of you can prove tonight that you have seen the ghost of either Cocky Leckie or Hugh Farquhar, I'll give you a guinea out of my own money.'

'If we see both do we get two guineas?' asked Henry, pedantically.

'And is that a guinea each, or between us?' added

Robert.

'It'll be neither if you don't finish this passage today,' said Murray ominously.

'Couldn't we do something about ghosts instead?'

'No.'

'But we could sing something for Mr. Murray,' Henry suggested quickly. 'Mr. Murray likes music, don't you, sir?'

'*The Twa Corbies* would be good for Hallowe'en, wouldn't it?' Robert sat back in his chair. 'Come on, Henry, let's sing it.'

And with an excruciating failure to establish a mutual key, the boys began to sing something reminiscent of *The Twa Corbies*. Murray sighed, and shut his book.

CHAPTER THIRTEEN

At six o'clock, at last, there was a flurry at the kitchen door and the indoor servants, in an untidy procession, bore the first of the supper dishes across to the barn, to arrange them on the tables set up ready to receive them. Miss Deborah oversaw the operation, smoothing the last wrinkles on the table cloths, making sure the splinters and rough wood were not visible, directing the arrangement with the great side of beef in the centre and the other dishes laid around in a pattern suitable for the table of gentry. The gardeners were putting the final touches to garlands of beech leaves and apples around the walls and along the tables themselves. Beatrix, frowning, was counting at one end of the barn, seeing that they had laid enough places, all provided with cutlery and plates and chairs, checking a list of guests in her hand. The floor was already smooth and sanded for the dancing later, and at one table by the door was laid a ladle and glasses, ready for the arrival of the big bowl of hot punch. In the yard outside, a concentrated flurry marked where various guests, prematurely in their best dress, tried to busy themselves rather than looking as if they were queuing to get in, always with one eye on the great door of the barn. At last everything was organised according to Deborah's plan, and the girls took a final look around the barn where Andrew was lighting the rest of the candles. It looked perfect. Beatrix could feel her feet itching, longing for a dance, just as the players appeared at the door. She pointed them towards a little dais at the end of the barn, and turned back to find that Deborah was leaving.

'We have to get changed for supper, I suppose,' said Beatrix, following her.

'Yes, the Boothams will be here shortly, again. We'll have our supper and let the dancers have their first few dances before we come down to greet them, as usual.'

'Oh, yes. I must hurry, for I have a new ribbon for my hair and I want to arrange it properly.' Deborah held the kitchen door open for her and examined her face as she passed.

'Beatrix, you will be careful, won't you?'

'Careful? What do you mean?'

'I don't quite know. There is something odd about the Boothams, don't you think? I'm not sure we should encourage them too much as our friends. Or make too much of an effort to please them.'

'I like them,' said Beatrix, for once in her life disagreeing with Deborah. 'I think they are very agreeable guests. I should like to see them every day if I could.' She marched on before Deborah towards the passage back to the hall, and Deborah stared after her, a worried expression on her face.

The Boothams arrived just as Beatrix finished arranging her hair, and she hurried downstairs to find that she was in the drawing room before Deborah.

'Ah, the lovely Miss Pirrie,' said Bootham, bending over her hand. 'Where is Miss Scoggie this evening?'

'She should be down in just a moment,' Beatrix explained, nervously. 'She's been so busy, you know, today, with things. With the dance. For the servants.'

Bootham smiled, and Beatrix could feel herself blushing. Just then, Murray and the boys arrived in the room like a small tornado, and Major Keyes followed soon after. By the time Tibo had arrived, too, the family had just about assembled, Deborah unusually plainly dressed for someone about to attend a dance, Lady Scoggie giving as always the impression of passing through in a hurry, and Lord Scoggie actually quite excited at the thought of seeing his servants enjoying themselves. For Murray it was an awkward meeting, for though he was expected to stay to supper with the family, he was also expected in the barn. He picked at his food, and hoped they would all go down soon.

In the barn, the company was almost completely gathered, and an odd jittery quiet spread around the barn, as they stared about them at the decorations and the supper, and at each other, strangely dressed, the girls splendid in the best their needles could do in a fortnight, the young men with their shoes polished and their hair brushed into submission, the old men powdered and tidied, looking for comfortable seats with their cronies round the walls. Grisell arrived with Hannah and Mrs. Costane, head held high, a demure smile on her face. Mrs. Costane was to act as hostess for the evening, in a lace cap like a knitted chandelier, and she bowed to left and right in gracious recognition of the attendants before taking up a position near the supper table, the better to survey the room and make sure that everyone had a partner for the first dance. The musicians struck up, tuning wildly for a moment while a little thrill ran round the barn, then gave the first few bars of the first dance and paused, letting the couples arrange themselves. Grisell looked about her, still smiling, peering between the hurrying dancers. She nudged Mrs. Costane.

'Have you seen Andrew?'

Mrs. Costane frowned, looking quickly around.

'No. Were you expecting him?'

'Well, yes. Well – '

'Will you dance with me, Grisell?' asked the eldest gardener's boy, with a lopsided bow that allowed him to keep looking at her face.

'Ah ...' she said, now staring frantically about her.

'Go on, dance with the lad,' said Mrs. Costane firmly. 'You can find yon blondy one later. If you still want to,' she added, with a wink at the gardener's boy.

'Oh ... all right, then,' Grisell conceded, and allowed herself to be led off, though whether she even knew who she was dancing with was a moot point.

'So are we all ready?' asked Lord Scoggie eagerly. 'We want to be down there before they sit down to their supper, really.' He had not been able to sit at peace since their own supper was finished, and had a very fine waistcoat on in honour of the occasion.

'Yes, my dear, I think we could go down now. Mr. Murray, do you want to take the boys up to their rooms, and then follow us down?'

'Certainly, my lady.' Murray nodded to the boys and began to shepherd them towards the door.

Deborah rose and smoothed down her dress.

'I feel a little headache coming on,' she said. 'I think I shall just take a little air first, if nobody minds.'

'But it's dark, dear,' said Lady Scoggie. 'And you'll have some air on the way over to the barn.'

'I shan't be long, Mamma,' Deborah said, almost as if she had not heard her. She seemed to have her mind on something else, something distant. 'I shall just fetch my shawl, and I shall see you all shortly.' Murray pulled the boys back to let her leave the room before them.

'You don't need me to attend this dance, do you, Livvy?' asked Major Keyes, as Mr. Bootham helped Mrs. Bootham with her shawl. 'I have an awful lot of letters to write - the price of fame, don't you know?' He laughed, but without much conviction.

'Well, if you insist, Alec,' said Lady Scoggie, frowning. 'At this rate we shall make a poor appearance in the barn. Come, Beatrix, you at least will come with us, and dance with someone, will you not?' She took Beatrix' arm firmly, as if expecting her to escape, too.

'We are certainly in attendance,' said Philip Bootham reassuringly. 'We are greatly looking forward to witnessing this rustic sport, are we not, my dear?'

'Come on, Henry,' said Murray. 'Pick it up and bring it upstairs.' Henry reluctantly gathered together a box of bones he was trying to articulate back into the form of a hedgehog.

'Can't we go to the dance, Mamma?' Robert asked, dragging his feet dramatically on the floorboards.

'I thought you didn't approve of dances,' Murray pointed out.

'But it's *Hallowe'en*,' Robert objected, 'and we're not having a party.'

And I won't have a party either, thought Murray, if these two don't hurry up and go to bed. 'Come on, Robert, don't hold Lady Scoggie back.' At last he managed to manoeuvre both boys out of the parlour and up the stairs, and oversaw, perhaps with less exactitude than usual, their preparations for bed.

'Why can't we have a ghost story, Mr. Murray?' pleaded Robert, once he was in bed. 'Go on – it's Hallowe'en.'

'Please,' added Henry, appearing in the doorway.

'Bed, both of you,' said Murray firmly, and immediately he saw their faces he felt awful. He had always loved Hallowe'en when he was small. 'Oh, all right – just this once. And only the one ghost story.'

Henry came dancing into the room and bounced on to Robert's bed, and pulled the eiderdown back to crawl underneath it. Murray cast a glance down at his dancing shoes, pulled a chair over to the bedside, blew out all but one candle, and waited until the boys were settled, eyes wide and gleaming in the dim light. His mind was racing, trying to think of a story that could not possibly involve either fishermen or lawyer's clerks. He let a silence creep in for a long moment, then began.

'This is the story of the headless horseman that rides the road to Elie. Have you heard of him?'

The boys shook their heads. Murray could see them calculating just how near the road to Elie was to the castle.

'Well, I've not only heard of him. One night, not so long ago – two years ago to this very night – I saw him with my own eyes.'

'Oh, you've decided to turn up, then, have you?'

Andrew spun round, but he already knew her voice. Grisell was behind him, hands on hips, her face flushed with anger.

'I didn't think you'd be fussed either way,' he said, but he lacked the teasing tone she had been encouraging for weeks. She frowned at him. He seemed paler than usual.

'Well, no, I'm not for myself. But there are some who have a higher opinion of you who might be concerned, I suppose.'

'Well, if you're not bothered, you won't want to dance with me, I suppose,' he said, pulling himself together.

'I don't – well, I might. Out of pity, you understand.'

'I understand.' He smiled at her at last. She was extraordinarily pretty this evening, he thought. The music stopped, and the dancers left the floor in a flurry of applause. The band struck up the first few bars of the next dance. 'So are you going to dance with me, then? This seems like a good time to decide.' The idea of slipping his arm around her neat waist suddenly seemed irresistible.

'Well, all right, then.' She smiled back. The idea of

the feel of his strong arm around her waist suddenly seemed irresistible. She took his proffered hand, and stepped with him out on to the floor, which was turned to clouds under her feet.

Murray softly closed the door of Robert's room and tiptoed down the passage. The boys were not asleep – if he had done his job properly they would not sleep for hours, he reflected with a grin, listening for the hoofbeats on the drive until the small hours – but he did not want to break the spell.

There had been some confusion over Mrs. Bootham's cloak in the hallway, and by the time Murray arrived in the entrance hall the party were just about to leave.

'Mr. Tibo was quick to get his cloak on. I let him go ahead to tell them we were going to be a little late,' said Lord Scoggie, full of excitement.

'I hope Deborah is all right,' murmured Lady Scoggie. 'Now, are we all set?' Without further ado, she took her husband's arm and led the party out of the front door. The Boothams followed, and Beatrix and Murray brought up the rear, closing the door after them.

Mrs. Costane came to meet them at the door of the barn, along with Mr. Naismyth in all his avian glory. The gentry smiled benevolently, and Mrs. Costane politely found them partners for the two dances for which they would stay. The music was stopped, and in a moment Lord

Scoggie led Mrs. Costane out to great applause, followed by Lady Scoggie and Mr. Naismyth.

'Miss Pirrie, will you do me the very great honour of dancing with me?'

For a moment Beatrix thought she was imagining things, but no: Philip Bootham really was leaning towards her, the light bright on his white-gold hair, his dark brows drawn together with just the faintest anxiety that she might say no. She looked, only for a daring second, into his dark blue eyes, until she thought she would swoon.

'Of – of course, Mr. Bootham.'

She had no idea how they reached the middle of the floor – flew, perhaps, for all she knew – but there she was, facing him beside Lady Scoggie, waiting for the dance to begin, praying it would never end.

Murray, too, had little idea how he had ended up facing Mrs. Bootham, much against his better judgement. He had planned to dance with Hannah, harmless enough and a good dancer, he knew, after their practice in the kitchen. Failing that, he would willingly have danced with Beatrix, of course. But there she stood, smiling at him, a little toe tapping in time to the band as they played the first few bars. He was pleased, irrationally, to see that she was wearing gloves, as if the touch of her bare flesh could somehow complete the spell that he was trying to escape. He shuddered.

Hannah joined them with the chief assistant gardener – the head gardener was no longer up to dancing, and was among the cronies along the wall, nearest the punch. That was the set complete, and the dance began.

Neither Murray nor Beatrix could have said afterwards how long the dance lasted. For Murray, trying not to touch Mrs. Bootham any more than was absolutely necessary, or to meet her eyes, it took an eternity. The very swirl of her skirts seemed designed to snare his feet. For Beatrix, it only seemed to last a mad, giddy minute. His eyes seemed always on her, and the warmth of his hand through her glove seemed to flow through her veins. The little voice in her head that told her, night after night, that he was married, was strangled now. She was alone with him in a magical instant, and nothing would ever be the same again.

Soon Lord and Lady Scoggie were politely returning the courtesies of their partners, and preparing to leave again. The Boothams, smiling at their spellbound partners, drifted back together again. Murray shook himself. He wished he had a bowl of cold water to splash on his face, and looking at Bea, he thought he ought perhaps to splash her, too. She was blindly following Lord and Lady Scoggie out of the barn, looking as if she were sleepwalking. It took Murray a moment to extract himself from the crowd to follow them to the door and wish them goodnight, and so they and the Boothams were some distance ahead of him, and for a moment he could not work out what was happening.

There was a lot of shouting, and some sound of running footsteps, and the crowd around the doorway suddenly ebbed and flowed as if some force had hit it hard.

He pushed his way to the front, and found himself beside Lord Scoggie, staring at the Kinkell brothers.

'Where's my wife?' Sandy was demanding. 'Where's Chrissie? Where've they got her?'

'I'm sorry, my lord,' Geordie Kinkell had his brother somewhat half-heartedly around the waist, pulling him back. 'He's had a bit of drink taken, and he misses the woman, dear help him.'

'There's no sign of her yet?' Lord Scoggie was concerned. 'I did tell them to return her.'

'Hugh Farquhar's missing, though, isn't he?' said Geordie, trying to sound reasonable. 'They're saying he's dead. Maybe he forgot.'

'No, no,' said Lord Scoggie, trying to draw them away from the goggling crowd at the doorway. 'I had Mr. Tibo go down to check that she had left. He assured me – Mr. Tibo? Where is the man?'

Mutters ran round the crowd, but no Mr. Tibo appeared. Murray relaxed a little, thinking that the Kinkells were no longer violent.

'I haven't seen Mr. Tibo all evening, my lord,' said Naismyth helpfully, from two rows back in the mob.

'Anyway, he said she had gone.' Lord Scoggie cast an expert eye over Sandy. 'I think it would be best if you took him home to rest tonight, Geordie,' he suggested, with heavy emphasis. 'In the morning we'll all be in a better position to do something about it.'

But Sandy was not paying attention. He had caught sight of someone in the crowd, and was loping towards them.

'I smell fish!' he cried, pointing an offensive finger – straight at Grisell.

The crowd drew back, leaving Grisell standing in a small open space.

'You're Richie Shaw's girl! I smell fish!' Sandy lurched closer. Murray stepped to stop him, but she was looking round for help from a different quarter.

'Andrew?' she called. 'Andrew? Where have you gone?'

Murray caught up with Sandy, and put a long hand across his chest. Sandy swung round, focussing with difficulty on Murray's face.

'Come on, now, Mr. Kinkell,' said Murray softly. 'It's not the girl's fault. Come along, now, and take a seat over here.' He propelled Sandy gently, using the man's own weight, and propped him on the side of the horse trough in the yard. 'What'll happen if he has another?' he asked Geordie over his shoulder.

'He'll likely fall asleep, sir,' said Geordie.

'There's a bowl of punch by the door, there. Fetch us a couple of glasses over here.'

'You can manage all right, then, Mr. Murray?' asked Lord Scoggie, pitching his voice so as not to disturb Sandy.

'Yes, I think so, my lord.' Geordie brought the punch, and he and Murray sat on either side of Sandy, propping him up.

'Then I think it's best if we just ...' Lord Scoggie took his wife and his guests, and slid off to the front of the house. Grisell, white in the face, disappeared determinedly back into the crowd, and they were left alone like three crows on a fence.

By the time he had seen the Kinkells on their way home and managed to return to the dance, cold and annoyed, Murray had only time for one more set before the company were to sit down to supper. He escorted a farmer's daughter to the supper table and saw to it that she had a full plate, then excused himself to go and see if the boys were settled.

Outside the air was fresh and crisp, the moonlight drenching the park's smooth slopes as he came round the corner of the castle on to the drive. He paused for a moment, enjoying a few seconds of solitude, letting his gaze run over the silver trees, the steely lake in the hollow, smelling the sharp frost-scents of the night.

Suddenly he thought he caught a movement, down near the trees by the lake. He squinted hard, but it had gone. An owl, perhaps, he thought. He stopped, though, and watched for a moment. The cold bit at his face and hands. Then, out of nowhere, there was a figure near the trees. It left a patch of shadow, limping awkwardly, and stepped into the moonlight. A chill ran through him, as he thought of the boys' ghostly expectations. The figure was dressed as a fisherman.

As soon as he had appeared, he vanished again.

Of course he should go down there: some fisherman prowling around the lake at this time of night was on no rightful business. It was his duty to go and see, to challenge the intruder. Somehow, though, he did not. He waited, but there was no further sign of the limping figure. There was no sound in the clean air, and it seemed like desecration when at last he stepped forward and crunched across the gravel to the front door. A little squeal came from nearby.

'Who's there?' he demanded at once, trying not to sound as alarmed as he felt.

'Is that you, Mr. Murray?'

It was Deborah, her shawl clutched around her, shivering.

'Good heavens! Miss Deborah! Have you been out all this time? Since the end of supper?'

'Yes. Please don't tell my mother, will you, Mr. Murray?'

'But you'll come in now, won't you?'

'Oh, yes.'

He hurried her up to the front door and opened it for her. She nearly fell over the threshold, clutching at the doorpost for support, and pulled off her gloves. She fumbled at her bonnet strings with frozen fingers.

'Here, let me, if you will,' said Murray, and started to disentangle the strings. 'I hope your headache is better.'

'My headache? What do you – oh, yes, of course. So completely better, you see, that I had forgotten I ever had it.' Her teeth were chattering: her lips looked blue. He undid the strings as quickly as he could, his own fingers cold, and she lifted the bonnet off, flinging it down clumsily on the hall table. 'I must find a fire,' she muttered, and headed for the stairs. He followed her into the parlour, and then into the drawing room, but both fires had been allowed to die down. They went back to the parlour.

'I'll try and chivvy some warmth back into this,' said Murray, 'if you will sit down and pull some more shawls around you.' The parlour was full of odd shawls, used to fight off the castle's perpetual chill. He knelt by the fireplace and found there was still a glow in the midst of the ashes. He set to to spread it.

'Was I missed?' she asked after a while.

'I couldn't say,' said Murray diplomatically. 'The dance was going well, though there was one distraction.' He told her about the Kinkell brothers, and the missing wife.

'And she has been gone all this time?' she said, in an odd tone. 'That's strange.'

'Indeed. Particularly since Mr. Tibo has been down to see if she is still at the Farquhars, and she is not.'

'Mr. Tibo seems to have been doing a great deal in the village recently.'

He sat back on his heels, letting a flame catch on some twigs.

'It was to meet him that you went out this evening, wasn't it?' he said. She looked up in alarm. 'I overheard you making the arrangement. The boys knew about it, too.'

'Well, if you all know so much, maybe you can tell me where he is,' she said bitterly. 'Yes, I did go out to meet him, but I never found him. I've been waiting for over an hour.'

'Well, he wasn't at the dance. Do you want me to fetch you anything? The fire has caught, now.' He stood up slowly.

'No, no. I'll be quite all right now. Thank you, Mr. Murray.' She held her hands out to the fire, pulling her gloves off. At the hem of her gown he could see her toes wriggling in the heat. He smiled, and turned to go, when she spoke again. 'You haven't seen your father for some time, I believe.'

He was brought up abruptly.

'No, I haven't.'

She looked up at him.

'Forgive me, Mr. Murray. That was an impertinent question. But please tell me, if you can: do you miss him?'

He thought for a moment, making sure that he was going to tell the truth. His father was bullying and opinionated, and never understood his interests.

'Yes, I do,' he said at last.

'What an odd thing parents are, are they not?' she said. 'And after all, in the end what does it matter?'

'I can't see Lord Scoggie taking that point of view,' he said lightly, and she laughed.

'You're quite right: he has a very firm opinion on the subject of parents and children. Firstborn sons, anyway.' She stood up and pulled her chair closer to the fire. 'Ah, well, never mind.'

She said no more, and feeling himself dismissed, Murray left the parlour.

Upstairs, all was quiet. He listened at the door of Robert's room, then of Henry's, then quietly turned the door handle. Henry's bed was empty, and did not look as if it had been slept in, but it was possible that he had stayed with Robert after the ghost story. Murray grinned to himself. Then he tried the handle of Robert's door.

Robert's bed was also empty. Moonlight streamed

across the tumbled bedclothes, and for a moment in its colourless light Murray did not realise a salient point: the blankets and eiderdown were there, but the bedsheets were not.

'Oh, damnation!'

He took a quick look around the room, particularly behind the curtains, a favourite hiding place, but there was no sign of them. Then he checked each room in the corridor, the schoolroom, Henry's room, and his own chamber, but without result.

The west tower was a strong possibility, he thought, hurrying back towards the gallery. The moonlight flooded it, and he stopped, uneasy, not liking the feel of the place. He listened. Halfway along the gallery he could hear Tippoo the dog scratching inside Keyes' chamber door, but apart from that there was silence.

He made himself walk the length of the gallery, and up the little stairs to the tower room, but it was locked with the key on the outside, and even when he went in to check, thinking that each was quite capable of locking the other inside, it was empty. The door to the attics above the gallery rooms was also locked, and the dust on the key showed that it had not been used for a while.

They must have gone to the barn, he thought. They had felt left out of the party, and had probably decided to invite themselves. He went back down to the ground floor and out through the front door, and looked around at the ground, but the gravel showed no footprints even in the frost. He strode swiftly round the corner of the castle, back towards the barn.

The dancers were back on the floor again, the devastated supper tables pushed back against the walls, but fewer were standing now for each dance and the crowd of cronies along the sides of the dance floor was growing greater. Andrew was dancing with a laundrymaid with great red hands and a style of dancing that was very reminiscent of the washtub. The gardener's boy could not believe his luck: Grisell was back as his partner, and very deliberately giving every sign of enjoying herself. The dance ended, and by chance the two couples met by the punch bowl.

'Will you give me the next dance, then?' Andrew asked her, not smiling.

'Why should I? I have a good partner.'

'That penny dog? He's no worth dancing with. Does he have to stand on your feet, like a wee lad?'

'I canna see anyone here who looks any better to me.' She would not meet his eye.

'Well, I'm no interested in dancing with a girl with no taste. You can keep your wee lad, if you fancy being a nursery maid.'

'At least he's here when I want him!' she snapped, but Andrew had turned away, and was already asking another girl to dance. He spun away with her on to the floor, and Grisell watched, irresistibly, fighting back hot tears.

'Grisell! Have you seen Robert and Henry?' She turned to find Mr. Murray at the doorway.

'No, I have not,' she said. 'Will you not dance with me, Mr. Murray?'

He gave an absent smile and a bow, looking urgently about the barn.

'I'd be delighted, Miss Grisell, but I'm afraid I have to find the boys.'

'Isn't that them there?'

She pointed behind him. In the doorway were two small figures, almost entirely swathed in white sheets.

'Robert! Henry! What on earth do you think you're doing here?'

'We were being ghosts –' said Robert, before Murray noticed that both their faces were white and even, he suddenly realised, tear-stained.

'What's the matter?' he snapped.

'Mr. Murray, we found something,' said Henry, with a gulp.

'What?'

Henry looked at Robert, and they moved a little

closer to each other.

'It's the headless horseman,' he said. 'He must have been down by the lake. He's got a victim.'

The lake? A memory of the mysterious fisherman flashed through his mind.

'Who is it?'

Henry and Robert both bit their lips, then looked up at him.

'It's Mr. Tibo.'

CHAPTER FOURTEEN

'Aye, right,' said Grisell sharply, but then she was not in a good mood. Murray, seeing the set of her arms, looked beyond her into the barn.

'Mr. Naismyth!' he called, trying to sound as if there was nothing out of the ordinary. 'Would you mind? And Andrew, too, perhaps.'

'Well, you're welcome to him,' said Grisell, in a tone that implied she was about to flounce off, but she stayed still.

'Grisell, will you keep an eye on the boys for a moment while I have a word with Mr. Naismyth?'

Grisell swung round to them, arms still folded. Her stare was acid.

'Aye. I'm used enough to looking after wee lads.'

When Robert did not even flinch at this description,

Murray knew there was something wrong. Naismyth managed to extract himself, slowly as usual, from the crowd, and Murray gestured him over to one side of the doorway. Naismyth bent gently from the waist to angle his ear towards Murray's mouth.

'The boys say that something has happened to Mr. Tibo, down by the lake.'

Naismyth considered.

'How would they know? As I understand his Lordship's instructions, they are not permitted to play by the lake.'

'Well, with little boys, 'not permitted' does not always mean 'not able'. Anyway, I'm sure something has upset them. Will you come with me to look?'

Naismyth's head tilted to one side, thoughtfully.

'Yes,' he said at last. 'And I think I shall summon Andrew.'

'Here he is,' said Murray. 'He must have heard me before. Andrew?'

Andrew, however, was heading more towards Grisell and the boys than towards them.

'Look, Grisell,' he was saying.

'Why should I look at you? There's not a thing about you that would be pleasing to my eye.' She turned her back on him, pretending to be attending to the boys.

Andrew pushed a hand through his golden hair, but the gesture lacked any of the self-confident flair he had once shown.

'Please – there's something I have to tell you – '

'I'm sure it'll keep. Mr. Naismyth and Mr. Murray want you.'

Andrew turned, surprised to see them behind him.

'Something seems to have happened down by the lake and we need to go and see,' Murray explained quickly. 'We should take lanterns. Will you fetch some?' The night was starry bright, but by the lake the trees could cast long shadows. Andrew hurried off, with one longing glance at Grisell, and returned in a moment with three lanterns.

'We cannot take those,' said Naismyth, after a moment.

'They're lanterns,' said Murray reasonably.

'They were the only ones handy,' said Andrew. From his hands dangled three grinning neep lanterns.

'Oh, come on: let's see what we can do.' Murray seized a lantern, and gathered the boys back from Grisell.

'I'll talk to you later,' Andrew said urgently as he passed her.

'I might not be here,' she said, and turned with a swirl of her best skirts back into the barn.

The boys led the way back to the great dark front of the castle where not long since Murray had met Deborah. As they left the gravel of the drive, he could see her little footprints on the frosted grass, and the prints of the boys, but as the slope steepened down towards the lake the frost lessened its hold, and though they slithered in their hurry, he could see no distinct prints at all. The starlight showed the boys' faces, pale and set, lips pressed hard and eyes wide as they showed where they had gone. The land flattened again a little as they neared the lake and the beginning of the woodland. The trees, stripped of their leaves by the storm, stretched glittering fingers up to snatch the stars, silver and grey and white, the skeletal ghosts of themselves. Beneath them, though, was darkness: dead, frosted leaves, the shadows of branches and thicket, the ground still half-damp, half-frozen, underfoot.

'We were going to frighten the people at the dance,' Robert explained, his teeth chattering only a little.

'That's why we had the sheets,' Henry added. Here the ground had been completely disturbed by the trailing sheets and the boys' panic. 'We were going to be ghosts.'

'And I said if we were ghosts we could go down to the lake on our own and no one would know it was us,' said Robert.

'Of course not – just any two small boys under bedsheets,' said Murray grimly. 'Go on.'

'We got to here, and Robert thought he heard a horse snuffle,' said Henry, with a shiver. 'And of course we knew it was the headless horseman, so we ran towards the trees to hide.'

'To watch him from a place of concealment,' Robert corrected. 'But then we tripped over – that.' He pointed, and he and Henry drew together, stopping where they were. Andrew went to hurry forward, but Murray put an arm out to stop him. He wanted to see clearly first, before the crowd gathered.

As he focussed on it in the wavering lantern light, it looked as if the cloaked figure had been lying face down when the boys had found him, but they must have pulled at his shoulder to see who it was or whether or not he was all right. Now he was lying half-flat, his left arm tucked awkwardly under his chest, his head slumped on his outstretched right arm, legs splayed out, giving the unpleasant impression of an unequal struggle lost. He was bare-headed, and even from a few paces away Murray could recognise Tibo, and see that he was indeed dead.

He had seen dead bodies before, of course, but still the sense of shock was almost palpable. There must have been some part of his mind, of all their minds, that had not believed the boys, or had thought that they had exaggerated, but even Robert and Henry could not have mistaken the white, glazed face for anything but the mask of death.

'The headless horseman must have got him, Mr. Murray,' breathed Robert.

'It seems unlikely, Robert,' said Murray. It was time to stamp on that, or there would be nightmares for months to come. 'Headless horsemen traditionally behead their victims. It would be a pretty poor headless horseman that only managed to knock a man's hat off.' Indeed, Tibo's tall hat was several feet away, already showing traces of frost on the upturned brim.

'Was it an accident, then?' asked Henry. 'Like Cocky Leckie?'

'Quite likely,' said Murray briskly, though he was wondering that himself.

'What should we do?' asked Andrew, turning to Naismyth. The steward had one hand pinned hard over his mouth, and over the clamped fingers his eyes goggled.

'I think,' said Murray hurriedly, 'that Mr. Naismyth should tell Lord Scoggie what has happened.' Naismyth nodded, without looking in Murray's direction. 'His lordship would take it badly from anyone else. Andrew and I can stay here with Mr. Tibo. Mr. Naismyth, would you mind taking the boys with you when you go in?'

Naismyth removed his hand for just long enough to say,

'Come along, boys,' before slapping it back in place, and the boys scuttled after him in their clumsy sheets as he strode with long stork strides as fast as possible back up the hill. They could see the jerking grin of the neep lantern, nodding and bouncing up through the bright darkness.

'I think he's going to puke,' said Andrew, with a nervous laugh.

'Are you?' asked Murray.

Andrew shook his head a little too quickly, but he seemed to be all right. Murray inspected his face briefly with a raised lantern.

'So what happens now?'

'I think Lord Scoggie should see what has happened here. Then I expect we'll take the body into the castle for now – we can't leave him here. While we're waiting, I'll just take a closer look ...' There were no clear traces of anything amidst the leaves around Tibo's body: his own cloak had swept some of them along to tumble around his legs, and the rest were heaped or scattered about, damply crisp. Murray took the lantern closer to Tibo, and knelt on one knee beside the body.

The light from the lantern flickered orange, making Tibo's features seem to stir, and Murray's heart skipped a beat. Blood dried black where Tibo had bitten his lip, and his teeth gleamed secretly in the dark hole. His eyes were white slits, as if they had been cut to the bone, but the real wounds were on the side of his head. His temple and the skull above it were broken like an eggshell, with what looked like one long blow. Murray traced its line with his eye, seeing how it ran downwards towards the back of the neck. Blood had run from the wound through the neat grey hair, down the side of his face, and must have formed a dark stain on the ground, but it was dry now and tight across the sagging white skin. When the boys had turned him, he must already have been cold.

There was no frost, or even leaves, on his back. Murray noticed this with a start, seeing the clean lines of the dark grey cloak as if for the first time. The wound was on the back of his side of his head, but he had fallen on to his front, and not rolled. Could he have hit his head on a branch? Murray looked up and tried to assess the height of the trees nearby, but none was really close enough, and there was no branch that Murray would have ducked for. It was beginning to look as if Tibo's death had been no accident.

Murray glanced around, but he could not see anything that might have served as a weapon. Tibo's hat, as he had noticed, was a little distance away, as though it might even have been dislodged by the blow. His gloves and cloak, however, were still in place. Murray tried to think when he had last seen the lawyer. At supper, was it not? He himself had gone to settle the boys, and when he came down Tibo had already gone ahead to the dance, to let them know that Lord Scoggie's party was going to be a little late. Had he done so? Had anyone at the dance seen him? Murray had no idea. He tried the nearest source.

'Andrew, did you see Mr. Tibo appear at the dance?'

'At the dance?

'Yes, he was supposed to go over to the barn before the rest of us appeared.'

'Ahm ... I'm not sure.'

Murray glanced up at him. Andrew looked distinctly cagey.

'You were there, weren't you?'

'Ahm, yes, of course! Mostly.'

Murray continued to stare at him. Andrew shuffled, swinging his lantern.

'I sort of had my mind on other things, you see.' He stopped again, but Murray did not look away. 'Och, it's Grisell, you ken. I suppose everybody kens. I've been after her for weeks, but as soon as she shows a bit of interest in me – well, it's not as easy as I thought it was.'

'Not easy? What's so difficult about it?'

Andrew's handsome faced screwed up like a wrung-out cloth.

'Things have changed a bit, that's all. I found out – and she doesn't know – and ...' He seemed to be completely twisted up in his thoughts, and Murray decided to let him off the hook for now. He looked away, and thought back again to the scene in the hall as they had left the castle for the barn.

Though there had been so much fuss trying to find Mrs. Bootham's cloak, the gentlemen had not bothered with outdoor wear for the short walk over from the castle to the barn. He himself had come out without coat, gloves or hat, and was feeling the lack of them. Had Tibo been particularly feeling the cold, or had he planned to stay outside longer than the others?

Behind him, Andrew stirred uneasily, and Murray realised that his own knee was starting to freeze.

'I think my neep's going out,' said Andrew, peering at it disconsolately. 'Are we to be here much longer, do you think?'

'You know as well as I do,' said Murray, standing up and brushing mud off his leg. He stared down at the body. A familiar sensation came over him. Here was Tibo, helpless, defenceless, and, which was probably worst for Tibo, not looking his well-groomed best. He had been out here for some purpose, and someone had come between him and that purpose, and struck him dead. Murray felt the writhing sense of injustice inside him, his stomach uneasy with the unfairness of the taking of a life. He knew what would happen now. He could already feel his mind starting to tick over with possibilities. Who had wanted Tibo dead?

'Look!' cried Andrew suddenly. 'I see a light!' He waved his lantern enthusiastically at the distant gleam, and his neep finally gave up the ghost. The crooked grin glimmered, and died.

'Wave yours,' said Andrew, 'or he won't know where we are.'

Murray lifted his lantern more cautiously, and the other lantern could be seen to jiggle slightly in response. Its bearer made slow progress down the long, frosty slope towards them, and Murray's neep was almost burned out by the time it showed itself to be a proper lantern, with Major Keyes attached. Tippoo the dog scuttled at his side, paws uneasy on the cold ground.

'Hallo, there,' he said, presumably to Murray and Andrew, though his eyes were already drawn to Tibo's body on the ground. 'Naismyth said there had been some kind of accident. Of course I came at once.'

'We'll have to wait for Lord Scoggie,' said Murray. 'Tibo's dead.'

Keyes nodded, his mouth hard.

'That's what Naismyth said. Come away from that, Tippoo!' The dog had sniffed once in the direction of the body. 'What happened him?'

'It looks like a blow to the head,' said Murray, pointing with his lantern.

'And he's definitely dead?' asked Keyes.

'See for yourself.'

'It's just – with head injuries. I've seen men walk around for hours afterwards, sometimes. They're funny things. I'd hate him to be –

'I don't think he'll be walking around anywhere.' Just like Cocky Leckie, he thought. But Cocky's death was definitely an accident, he had seen it himself. And this – this was surely not. Unless Tibo had wandered after hitting his head on a branch. As Keyes had pointed out, head injuries were funny things, but it would be impossible to tell until daylight.

'So was Naismyth fetching Lord Scoggie, then?' he asked at last, aware that he had been a little abrupt.

'Aye, he was beating at Lord Scoggie's door. That's what roused me to come out and see what the matter was. I think my cousin Scoggie must be getting a wee bit deaf in his old age! It took me a wee while to ready myself, for I had to strap my leg back on.' He grinned, slapping the appropriate thigh. Andrew, steady at the sight of a corpse, looked a bit queasy at this. 'Then the cloaks downstairs were in some disorder. It took me a while to find mine. All in all, I expected Lord Scoggie to be here with me, if not before me.'

'Maybe he's waiting for Mr. Naismyth to throw up,' Andrew suggested helpfully.

'Are you one of the servants?' Keyes asked, studying him with lifted lantern.

'This is Andrew. He only arrived a day or so before you, didn't you, Andrew?'

'Sir,' said Andrew, without much sign of subservience, though he had his eye on the dog.

'You've had a fine welcome to the neighbourhood, then,' said Keyes. 'Three men dead in a week! You might as well have joined the colours.'

'I'm maybe thinking of it,' said Andrew, partly to himself. Murray, thinking of Grisell, smiled. Keyes, unable to resist any longer, turned and stepped carefully towards Tibo's body.

'It really is him, then,' he said, bending down to peer more closely against the half-seen face. 'I suppose one always hopes that it is some stranger, though that is only to move the tragedy to others' doorsteps.' He straightened, his eyes still on Tibo. 'You believe that this is a deliberate act, then?'

'I think so,' said Murray, 'but it will be up to Lord Scoggie to make the decision.'

'The body will be difficult to move soon,' said Keyes contemplatively, with the expertise of the professional. 'And we should consider the safety of the ladies. If there is some violent miscreant wandering the neighbourhood, they should be warned.'

'That's a good point, Mr. Murray,' said Andrew unexpectedly. 'Whoever it was, they could be planning an attack on the house. Burglars, or French forces, or anything!'

'Or headless horsemen,' Murray could not resist adding. 'No, you're right: Tibo might well have disturbed someone who was going to try robbery, or perhaps someone who robbed him and hit him a little too hard.'

'My cousin Scoggie wouldn't be best pleased to think that footpads came this close to the ancestral fortress,' said Keyes. 'Is that him, now?' He turned at a noise, and waved his lantern in the direction of the castle. In response, another light winked and bobbed as two figures made their way down the slippery slope to the lake. In a moment, they resolved themselves into Lord Scoggie and Naismyth, frost-white in the face and smelling very slightly of brandy.

'Let's see, now, let's see,' said Lord Scoggie briskly, as though he had to fight his way through a crowd of bystanders. Keyes and Murray drew back: Andrew was already at a decent distance. Naismyth held the lantern for his master, but did not look anywhere near the corpse. Lord Scoggie, hands on his knees, braced himself to examine the body of his lawyer.

'Behold an Israelite, in whom is no guile,' he murmured softly, greeting Tibo and pronouncing his epitaph in one breath. For a long moment no one spoke, and only Lord Scoggie moved, slightly, as he looked from the top of Tibo's head to his toes, scraped into the damp leaves. At last he straightened.

'Mr. Murray, have you looked at this?'

'My lord, I have looked at the wound on his head, and the cleanliness of the back of his cloak, and the way he has been moved long after he stopped breathing. I think that was done by Robert and Henry, my lord.'

'Aye. You have some experience of such things.'

'Of poisonings, my lord, to my regret, yes. Of head wounds I know very little.'

'Of brutal deaths, untimely deaths, deaths without mercy – you have knowledge of them.'

Murray thought of the men he had seen lying dead before their time, and the dreadful urge he had felt to find their killer.

'Yes, a little.'

He felt Andrew and Major Keyes eyeing him, and hoped it was too dark for them to see him blush.

'What would you do, then, Mr. Murray?'

'I would bring the body indoors, and send word to the sheriff.'

'That cannot be faulted.' He looked away finally from Tibo's corpse, and glanced about him. 'I see no sign of a struggle.'

'He could have hit his head on a tree, cousin,' Major Keyes pointed out. 'Head wounds are strange beasts. He could have wandered some distance ...'

'But he only seems to have bled in one position,' said Murray suddenly, realising that his own thoughts on this were wrong. 'See his collar? It is quite unstained. The blood flowed only down his cheek, as he lay face down, until it dried. Surely if he had still been on his feet after he was injured he would have bled down over his ear and into his collar.'

'You are quite right, Mr. Murray,' said Keyes in admiration. 'I had not thought of that. Poor Tibo.'

'Well, then,' said Lord Scoggie, 'we must get him indoors. Can we carry him between us, do you think?'

'Not without a hurdle, my lord,' said Naismyth hurriedly, horrified at the thought of having to touch the body.

'We can use his cloak as a stretcher,' said Keyes. 'I have often seen men do it on the battlefield. If we roll him over on to his back and roll the edges of the cloak up tight, then hold it each with both hands ... I'll show you, it's hard to explain.'

'Then by all means show us, Alec,' Lord Scoggie urged. 'It's too cold to stand out here discussing it. Naismyth, give Major Keyes the lantern. Now, Mr. Murray, help me to roll him over ...' Tibo was already stiff, but fortunately was lying fairly straight. With a little difficulty about the legs, Lord Scoggie and Murray managed to manoeuvre him on to his back. Murray tugged the cloak straight under him.

'Now roll the edges in towards him, tight. That's right,' said Keyes, watching from the foot end of the body. 'Now if two of you stand near the head, and two down here, one on each side – that's the way.'

'Who are you?' Lord Scoggie asked suddenly, and everybody paused, and stared at Andrew.

'This is Andrew, my lord, the new boy,' said Naismyth quickly. 'I mentioned him last week. We have been busy, or I would have brought him for you to see him.'

'Oh, all right. Andrew. I'll take a better look at you in the light. Now, then, Keyes: what next?'

'You bend and pick the cloak up, cousin. But do it all at the same time. Your hand that's nearest the end of the cloak goes well to the end, to support his head and feet. Where you hold it in the middle, cross your hands with the man next you. Aye, that's the way! Grand! Now, easy up the slope.'

'Go you ahead with the lantern,' Lord Scoggie nodded at him, 'and show us the way.'

Keyes swung his wooden leg about and slithered round to head the little procession up the hill, closely shadowed by Tippoo. Murray, walking crablike next to Naismyth, kept his eyes on the limping, cloaked figure with his swinging lantern. So did Naismyth, who still could not look down at what he was helping to carry. Andrew and Lord Scoggie, their wrists crossing on the other side of the stretcher, were also concentrating hard, on clenching their fists on the thick cloth rolls of Tibo's cloak, and on not slipping on the frosty grass. In silence they carried him up the hill, and in silence Major Keyes limped ahead to light the way.

At last they reached the front door, and Keyes fumbled with the handle, then stepped back to let them into the candlelit hallway.

'We'll lay him on the library table,' said Lord Scoggie, who must have been thinking about it on the way. Keyes made his way awkwardly past them to open that door, too, and they clumsily edged through the doorway into darkness. Keyes hurried round, lighting some of the sconces and candlesticks, allowing the great high business table to come into view. It was empty, and with a little effort they lifted Tibo higher, and slid him on to the old oak surface. Lord Scoggie drew a handkerchief from his pocket, and after a second's consideration, laid it gently over the lawyer's dull white face. The relief of no longer seeing the slit eyes was considerable.

'There is brandy in the Great Hall, my lord,' said Naismyth, with some urgency.

'Then let us avail ourselves of it. Go and bring it in: we cannot leave poor Tibo on his own.'

Naismyth looked as if that had not been entirely what he had intended, but was grateful for small mercies. He scuttled off, wings flapping, and was back in slightly longer than he might have taken: there was a dampness around his lips, Murray noticed, and the smell of spirits off him was stronger than before.

'Now,' said Lord Scoggie, with a hollow authority. 'Does anyone have any idea who might have done this terrible thing?' He glanced down at the covered face of Tibo on the table beside him, as if Tibo himself could have answered. For an awkward moment, it seemed they were all waiting for it. Then Naismyth spoke.

'The laddie there wasna at the dance the whole evening.' Everyone turned to look at him. Naismyth's narrow brow was shiny with sweat, and his lower lip trembled unaccustomedly. He jerked his head at Andrew, and pointed a long finger. 'Him,' he added, for emphasis.

'Were you, lad?' asked Lord Scoggie, for want of

any other response.

'Eh ... I was in and out, my lord.' Andrew seemed as surprised as any of them. 'But I was never far from the barn or the kitchens, I swear.'

'What reason would he have for killing Tibo, my lord?' asked Murray. If everyone who had not been in the barn all evening was to be accused, Tibo's solitary murder would start to look like an Edinburgh street riot. Andrew flashed him a look of – no, it was not gratitude. Amusement, perhaps? Murray put it aside in his mind for later.

'A boy like that needs little reason to cause an aff-ff-fray,' said Naismyth, with a curious ferocity. He was glaring, not at Andrew, but at Lord Scoggie, with an odd twitching and jerking of his thin eyebrows. It was baffling. Naismyth had never before shown much concern over Andrew, or why would Andrew still be working in the castle? Naismyth had only to give him his notice.

'Well, Andrew, I think you must spend a night in the cells, I'm afraid,' said Lord Scoggie. Murray stared at him in surprise. Lord Scoggie, who suddenly seemed inexpressibly tired, was also looking not at Andrew, but with concern towards Naismyth.

'In the cells, my lord!' Andrew no longer looked amused.

'Aye, you'll find that any soldier accused of any crime, innocent or guilty, will flee given the chance,' Major Keyes put in. 'Much better, my lad, to jail you now, and we can think the matter over more clearly in the morning. It's fairer for you.' Naismyth tried to nod his agreement, and wobbled on his stork legs.

'Aye, lad, for your own safety, if nothing else,' added Lord Scoggie. 'Naismyth will take you down there.'

'Aye, my ...' Naismyth tailed off.

'I think –' said Murray, who had been watching Naismyth's gradual decline, 'I think someone else had better do it, my lord.'

'Oh, I'll take myself down there,' sighed Andrew. 'Where are they?'

'Under the kitchens,' said Murray. Naismyth's legs gave way gently and he sagged on to the floor, a slow look of surprise on his beaked face. 'Shall I show him, my lord?'

Lord Scoggie looked with shock at Naismyth.

'It's the brandy, cousin, I reckon,' said Keyes with his usual authority.

'He was very shocked when we came on Mr. Tibo's body, my lord,' added Murray, in Naismyth's defence. Naismyth, half-leaning on a chair, was now snoring very softly.

'I – brandy?' Lord Scoggie had a desperate look, as if he were a general whose officers were being picked off one by one. He sipped at the glass Naismyth had poured him before passing out, and looked down at it suspiciously. 'What ... Look,' he said, pulling himself together. 'Mr. Murray, will you and – Andrew, isn't it? You and Andrew carry Naismyth off to his bed. Then, Mr. Murray, will you lock Andrew in one of the cells – with a blanket, of course. Then see to the boys, if they are still awake. Cousin Alec ... come, we must arrange for poor Tibo to be watched over. I fear you and I must do it until morning, if you are ready for it.'

'By all means, cousin.' Keyes settled himself comfortably in one of the fireside chairs, pulling his cloak around him and propping his good leg on a stool, Tippoo curled beside him. Lord Scoggie, with a last glance at Tibo, followed suite. Murray caught Andrew's eye, and, with a shrug, bent down to haul Naismyth to his feet. Andrew took the other side, and they staggered towards the door, trailing Naismyth's long legs behind them in their aged dancing slippers. Murray scowled to himself – for all the dancing he had managed to do, it had hardly been worth polishing his own slippers. They were almost at the door, when Lord Scoggie stopped them with a sudden question.

'You – Andrew, isn't it?'

'My lord.'

'Andrew who?'

'Kinkell, my lord. You'll ken my faither.'

'It's a wise child that kens its faither,' responded Lord Scoggie automatically. 'You're Geordie Kinkell's younger boy?'

'That's right, my lord.'

'Come here.'

Murray tried to take the full weight of Naismyth, while Andrew stepped across to the fireplace. Lord Scoggie lifted a candle, and stared hard at his face, beckoning him to bend closer.

'The world is a strange place,' he said at last, his voice suddenly faint. 'Go along, then. And take care of that man – "I would not have him miscarry for the half my dowry".' He lapsed backwards into his chair, suddenly ten years older than he had been at supper.

Murray and Andrew struggled through the doorway, an odd mirror image of carrying Tibo's body into the library earlier, and dragged Lord Scoggie's own personal Malvolio away to his austere quarters, to sleep off his shock.

CHAPTER FIFTEEN

'How are Henry and Robert? Did they sleep well at all?' Lord Scoggie asked Murray, as they set out at Major Keyes' steady pace down the frosty slope to the lake. Murray tried not to grimace.

'No, they did not, my lord. Henry had a nightmare, and Robert was unsettled, too.'

'Then you did not sleep well, either. I regret that.' Lord Scoggie was a thoughtful employer. 'How are they this morning?'

'I left them to lie late, my lord. They seemed to be sleeping well.'

'Good, good.' He used his stick to ease himself down a particularly slippery part, and Murray and the Major slithered after. 'I worry sometimes about Henry's delicacy. Do you think he is too imaginative?'

'Not at all, my lord.' Murray was quick to jump to the defence of his favourite. 'All boys will work themselves up around Hallowe'en. It is simply that they have had a good deal of upset besides that this year, with the deaths of Cockie Leckie and Hugh Farquhar. And it would disturb most people, I think, to happen upon a dead man in the dark.'

'What I think is impressive,' added Major Keyes, 'is young Robert's hardiness in the face of all of this. Why, the morning after Cocky Leckie's death he was asking me for a sparring match.'

'Yes,' said Lord Scoggie, notably not meeting Murray's eye. There was silence until they reached the place, just under the beginning of the trees by the lake, where Tibo's body had lain. Lord Scoggie stopped, and the other two halted on either side of him, surveying the scene without really knowing what they were looking for.

'He was facing that way, wasn't he?' asked Lord Scoggie, pointing with his stick.

'His head was there.' Murray pointed in turn. He could just see the dark patch on the smeared frost where Tibo's battered head had lain. 'And his feet were there, and his arm was out in front of him, with the other hand underneath. I think it gave me the impression that he had made a half-hearted attempt to save himself as he fell, but lost consciousness too quickly. And given that the blow was to the side of his head, falling slightly sideways wouldn't be that surprising.'

'So you think he was struck from behind, but on the side of the head?' asked Lord Scoggie.

'Let me think ...'

'Where's the weapon?' asked Keyes, scouting about. He limped over to the edge of the woodland, looking amongst the low undergrowth for anything out of place. Tippoo snuffled about around his feet, clearly finding a number of interesting smells but unable to communicate them very usefully to the humans around. Murray, holding his own stick in his right hand like a club, swung it experimentally, trying to see angles in his head. Lord Scoggie turned about, surveying the land as it sloped down to this place, as if he was trying to picture his lawyer's last walk to the place of his death.

'It mustn't have rained last night, anyway,' said Keyes. The trodden frost was the same as it had been last night, after all.

'So if the weapon is still here, it would be covered in blood still,' Lord Scoggie followed.

'There's no sign of anything here,' said Keyes, resignedly, whacking the brown bracken with his stick.

'I think he was hit from behind, my lord,' said Murray. 'The blow lay up the side of his head, the left side, rising from the back to the front. Either the assailant was above him, striking from right to left, which seems unlikely –'

'Unless Tibo was bending over, or on his knees,'

said Lord Scoggie, who was following this closely.

'I'll come to that – or he was hit from behind, by an assailant using his right hand and swiping the weapon from left to right. If he was bending over, he wouldn't have fallen so flat, I think. And if he was kneeling down, there would have been more frost on the knees of his breeches, and there wasn't, I'm sure.'

'So the assailant either struck him in a cowardly fashion from behind, creeping up on him unexpectedly,' said Lord Scoggie, 'or they had an argument and Tibo turned away, and the assailant leaped after him.'

'And the weapon does not seem to be here,' added Major Keyes.

'So we may still find he has it, or has hidden it,' said Lord Scoggie.

'Or he may just have tossed it into the lake.' Major Keyes turned and they all stared into the still, unspeaking waters.

Murray suddenly remembered an impression he had noticed the night before.

'I think I have a point against the argument theory, my lord,' he said suddenly. 'Mr. Tibo was wearing a long cloak, was he not? And he was still suffering some discomfort from the knee wound he received at Cocky Leckie's death.'

'I believe so. He was still limping last night.' Lord

Scoggie was frowning.

'Major Keyes, you and Mr. Tibo were of much the same height, weren't you?' The Major shrugged and nodded. 'And you are accustomed to wearing a cloak, and you walk, forgive me, Major, with a limp. I wonder if there is someone nearby who thinks, this morning, that Major Keyes is dead, not Mr. Tibo?'

Lord Scoggie looked sideways at his cousin, fiddling with the handle of his stick. Murray could almost see the Major's history going through his mind, as if he were totting up the men who would like to see Keyes dead. The Major, frowning, leaned to stroke Tippoo's head.

'Maybe, maybe,' he said, more quietly than usual. Murray wondered if he was thinking of the anonymous letters he had received. Had he mentioned them at last to Lord Scoggie? If not, would he tell him now? Should he himself tell his employer?

'I wish we knew, anyway,' said Lord Scoggie with a deep sigh, 'who it was he came out here to meet. There he was, with his cloak and gloves and hat. He quite clearly intended to go out, to go further than just to the barn for the dance.'

'The same thing had occurred to me, my lord,' Murray admitted. He had a fairly clear idea who it was that Tibo intended to meet, but he wanted to speak to her before he mentioned it to Lord Scoggie. Who knows what she might have seen?

'I don't think there could be anything else we can

learn here,' said Lord Scoggie, with a final look around at the trees, the lake, the crushed grass. 'I don't know if there ever was anything. I just wanted to see ...' For another moment he gazed at the place where Tibo had lain. Then he turned and strode up the slope, faster than Major Keyes could manage. Left behind, Murray and the Major took it easy up the hill, with Tippoo running circles round them to keep warm.

'Anyway,' said Murray after a moment, 'I think you should take care. If it was you the killer intended, he may well strike again.'

Keyes scowled, but he looked worried.

'I think it might be time for me to tell Lord Scoggie about the letters I showed you,' he said reluctantly. 'I'm not convinced that the writer really had any intention of carrying out any threats, but it might be as well for him to know what's been going on.'

'A very wise idea, I think.'

'Any sign of Naismyth this morning?' Keyes asked, with a grin.

'I haven't seen him. I doubt he's feeling well. He really isn't accustomed to drink: seeing Tibo's body must have been an awful shock to him.'

'Do you think there's anything in his accusation of young – Andrew, wasn't it?'

'That's right. Well, I was surprised, put it that way,

but then Andrew hasn't been here for long. I don't know him. But nor, I would have thought, does Naismyth. I must go and see if anyone has taken Andrew any breakfast: the other servants will be wondering where he is if Naismyth isn't awake.'

They had reached the door of the castle, but Lord Scoggie was nowhere in sight. Both Keyes and Murray looked instinctively towards the door of the library.

'I'll go and find the surviving letters,' said Keyes, limping towards the stairs, 'and take them to him.'

'I'll go and see Andrew. See you at breakfast.'

The castle's cells, intended anciently for the convenient accommodation of local criminals, recalcitrant servants and acrimonious wives, were reached by means of a narrow stone staircase under the kitchen, lit only by whatever poor candle could be found to be carried. The staircase was worn, though that was probably less indicative of the number of prisoners kept there over the years than of the fact that the last three lairds had kept their wines in the nearest two cells. The third cell, the only one with a scraping of window to let in what sunlight found the corner of the yard outside, was where Murray had locked Andrew the night before, provisioned with three blankets and his coat, a chamberpot, and a stump of tallow candle, lit. When Murray returned, Andrew was already sitting up in the nest he had made of the blankets, rubbing his eyes and peering up at the slit window. Murray unlocked the door, and Andrew pushed his blond hair back and stared up at him, blinking.

'That's the best night's sleep I've had since I came here. You ken Mr. Naismyth snores like he's practising for the Last Trump, and he's just through the wall from me.'

'I see you're in a repentant frame of mind,' said Murray lightly. Andrew stretched.

'I've nothing to repent. Not concerning the lawyer, anyway. I scarcely knew who he was – I think last night was the longest I've ever laid eyes on him.'

'So what do you repent, then?' Murray propped himself against the doorway, waiting for Andrew to rise and straighten out the clothes he had slept in. Andrew laughed.

'There's a lot of schoolmasters go on to be ministers, aren't there? It might suit you well, Mr. Murray. Ah, but there is something I repent, indeed.' He suddenly looked older, and anxious. 'Have you seen Grisell? Does she ken I'm down here?'

'Not as far as I know.'

'I've something to tell her.'

'Something to do with the fact that you're Geordie Kinkell's son? I thought Geordie only had the one son, Peter.'

'Peter's my big brother, though he hasn't the mind of a wean.'

'Why did you not mention this in the servants' hall? All you said was that you had worked in Kirkcaldy.'

Andrew gave a quick grin.

'I didna want to be thought to be some country lad. And I did work in Kirkcaldy – I was there since I was eight. I think I ken enough of town manners not to have to say my faither's a weaver in a wee cottage down the road. And then there was Grisell ...'

'You could be playing with fire there, my friend.'

'And all the more when she finds out I'm from up the town, and her father's a fisherman. Up the town you'd as well marry a Hindoo as a fisherman's daughter. In fact she'd be made more welcome. And the same could be said of how I'd be greeted by her family.' He had been folding the blankets with quick competence, but now he sagged back, leaning on an empty wine rack. 'I can't fathom what I'm going to do. I cannot tell her, or she'll kill me. If she finds out herself, and I haven't told her, she'll kill me, too, only she'll make it longer and more painful. And if I leave her, I'll just have to kill myself. I've known a good few girls in my time, Mr. Murray, of all shapes and makes, but this one – she has me caught, without even words passing between us.'

Murray considered.

'I think you'll have to tell her. Lord Scoggie knows, now, and you know how gossip runs around this house.'

'And around the village, even up and down the hill.

I didn't even tell my faither I was back. He heard it from one of the fishermen. I think he actually heard it from Grisell's faither. Now isn't that a neat thing?'

'I came to ask you if you wanted some breakfast,' said Murray. 'I'm afraid I haven't had any instructions to let you out. But what I could do – I'm sure Grisell would bring you breakfast, if I asked her nicely.'

'Would you?' Andrew looked half-pleased, half-fearful. Then a note of warning crept in. 'But you wouldn't ask her *too* nicely now, would you? As a friend?'

Murray laughed.

'I don't think I'd have much hope with Grisell. I'll send her down to you as soon as I can. But make sure you tell her.'

'Aye.' Murray locked the cell door, and took a last look in at Andrew, sitting on the wine rack. He tossed his hair back. 'At least it'll be a quick death.'

He did not know if he was wise or not, but he did not tell Grisell the identity of the prisoner in the third cell, merely that he needed feeding and was unlikely to be violent. Mrs. Costane was a little agitated as to the whereabouts of Mr. Naismyth and Andrew, but she and Hannah had already heard about Tibo's death: the gardeners who had been summoned to help Lady Scoggie escort the corpse home were already back, and spreading the news around the house.

'There's always a third,' said Mrs. Costane, and Hannah nodded grim agreement. 'What did he think he was doing, wandering round in the dark walking into trees? Foolish man, for a lawyer,' she muttered, but there were tears in her eyes. She had always had a soft spot for Mr. Tibo.

Up in the Great Hall, Major Keyes was already sitting over a plate of ham and boiled onions.

'Any sign of the boys yet?' Murray asked, helping himself to ham from the sideboard.

'No, nothing. And before you ask,' he added, huffily, 'I haven't told Lord Scoggie about the letters yet. I brought the last one downstairs, but I couldn't find him.'

He was very touchy about these letters, Murray thought.

'He wasn't in the library?'

'No.'

Murray started on his ham without saying anything further. After a moment, the door opened, and Robert, looking washed out, came in, followed by Henry, who looked even worse. They said good morning with worrying courtesy, and helped themselves to breakfast, sitting quietly at the table and eating with thoughtless care. It was only when Robert had cleared his plate that he said,

'Where is Mr. Tibo?'

'He's been taken home. Lady Scoggie has gone to

watch him until his brother arrives to arrange things.'

Henry and Robert exchanged furtive glances. Henry muttered something, and Robert dropped his knife noisily on to his plate.

'What was that?' Murray demanded.

'Nothing,' said Robert quickly.

'Try again.'

Henry swallowed loudly. His eyes were red.

'If the headless horseman comes back and his victim isn't here, he'll take another one, won't he, Mr. Murray?'

'Don't be ridiculous. I told you it wasn't the headless horseman, anyway. You saw for yourself that Mr. Tibo was not beheaded.' He did not meet Major Keyes' eye: he did not think he was dealing with this very well.

'How do you know? You said yourself he could have missed. He could have seen Mr. Tibo's hat roll off and thought he had got him.' Robert was breathless, half-angry, insisting that the grown-ups should admit what he was sure was the truth.

'He's right,' said Henry. 'That's what you said. And we saw dead-candles before he died. That's a sign of a bad death. The headless horseman got him.'

'The headless horseman,' said Murray, 'did not get him, for the very good reason that the headless horseman does not exist. I made it up.'

'You made it up?' The boys were horrified.

'You wanted a ghost story. I made one up.'

'So you made him come. It's all your fault!' cried Henry.

'Right, I think we've had enough, Henry. The pair of you go upstairs and copy out the hundred and nineteenth Psalm in your best handwriting. I'll be up after breakfast. And no more talk of headless horsemen.'

'You think the Bible will protect us, that's what it is,' muttered Henry.

'Of course it would, if there was anything to protect you from.'

'You're lying!' cried Henry, and pushed his chair back hard. He and Robert ran to the door, flinging down their napkins, and blustered through, running hard into Deborah in the doorway.

'Good heavens, Mr. Murray, couldn't you find some kind of harness for those two?' she asked, smiling.

'I do apologise, Miss Deborah. They're rather upset, and neither of them slept well last night.'

'Nor did you, by the look of it. Dancing long into the night, I suppose?'

Murray and Major Keyes exchanged glances. Major Keyes shrugged fractionally.

'You haven't heard the news?' Murray asked, trying to warn her with his tone.

'What news?' She could not have heard.

'It's Mr. Tibo. He has – met with an accident.'

'An accident?' She had heard the warning at last, and took hold of the back of the nearest chair, staring at him. 'A ... bad one?'

'A very bad one, I'm afraid. He is dead.'

'Oh, no! You're sure?'

'Positive. The boys found him late last night. We brought him back to the house, and this morning Lady Scoggie escorted him home.'

'Oh, no ...' She braced herself with both hands on the chair now, her head lowered. Murray had the odd impression that she was as much annoyed as shocked. A poor failing in a family retainer, to find himself dead.

'Please, sit down, Miss Deborah. Let me pour you some coffee.'

She did as she was bid.

'What kind of accident?' she asked, after the first sip of coffee.

Murray looked at Major Keyes. He was supposed to be her betrothed, after all: surely this kind of thing was his responsibility. Major Keyes did not return his look: he had his eyes firmly on Deborah's face.

'He was struck down by – an assailant. We don't know who, yet.'

Deborah stared at him.

'He was murdered? Where? You said the boys found him – was he inside the castle?'

He wanted to put a reassuring hand on her arm, but knew he could not.

'No, he was down by the lake. Just beside the trees.'

'By the lake ... but ... that is still near the castle.'

'Yes. The reason I told you is that you must take care, and not go out alone in the dark, and try to keep near other people at all times.'

'Oh ... I'm sure no one else will be assaulted.' She drained her coffee and he poured more. 'I must hurry: Mamma will need help, and there is a great deal to do here after last night.'

He thought afterwards that it was an odd thing to have said, that no one else would be assaulted. Beatrix had already heard the news from the servants, and when she appeared in the Great Hall, Murray excused himself and left the girls to comfort each other. Crossing the hall to the library, he wondered if she had known what she was saying, or whether it was just the shock. He must speak to her soon, but on her own, not with Major Keyes there. Perhaps he would be able to catch her after dinner.

In the empty library, he went to the shelf where he knew he had seen a copy of Buchanan's Latin psalms, but it was not there. He knew he had not sent it to the binder's, nor taken it up to the schoolroom. Perhaps Lord Scoggie had been reading it. He walked round the high table to the fireplace where the two library chairs sat opposite each other. There was the book, on the table with the brandy glasses. He bent to pick it up, and noticed that scraps of paper from Lord Scoggie's earlier fire had drifted on to the hearth. Crouching to pick them up, he could not help noticing that the papers had writing on them, in Nathaniel Tibo's unmistakable clerkly hand. He turned the paper round. There was one word remaining on the half-burned scrap, and even it was a little damaged. Still, it was easy to read. 'Kinkell', it said.

It must have been something to do with the dispute between the fishermen and the up-town men. Tibo would not have concerned himself with the hiring of servants, so it could not involve Andrew. But why would Lord Scoggie have been burning it, just after Tibo's death? Particularly when he so rarely lit a fire anyway.

Buchanan's psalms did not go down well with the boys. They sulked all morning until dinner time. Murray was angry with them. They were foolish, and lazy, and they had shown him up in front of Major Keyes. He was angry with Major Keyes, too, who had so signally failed to back him up with the boys. When he thought about it, he was angry with Naismyth for accusing Andrew so unexpectedly, and with Andrew for so obviously hiding something, and with Lord Scoggie for behaving out of character, burning bits of paper and then vanishing. He left the boys working their way through Buchanan's short Psalm 150, and made himself close the schoolroom door softly before he stamped off into his own bedchamber. He strode over to the window, glaring out at the back of the Great Hall, and kicked the window seat not quite as hard as he would have liked. He was angry with himself. He should not have lost his temper with the boys – he should not have told them the ghost story in the first place. He should be better able by now, at his age, with his experience, to deal with this odd position he held between family and servants' hall. He kicked the window seat harder, and punched the windowsill, feeling the echo of the blow singing up his arm. What a miserable few weeks it had been. Poor Cocky, broken and dead. He could still feel the pain in his own back from the glass fragments, and sometimes his head ached where the mirror had hit him. The quarrels between the fishermen and the uptown men, and now between Andrew and Grisell, and then the death of young Hugh Farquhar, who had looked so hungrily at the library bookshelves, a look Murray had felt on his own face. And now, Nathaniel Tibo, and all the nasty, insidious ways that things would happen now that a man had been murdered. He had seen it before. Murder made the whole place twist and contort, small things swell and grow like cancers, people seem sharp and dark, devious beyond their means, until even the natural seemed wrong and sick.

He needed to get out.

CHAPTER SIXTEEN

He managed it, but only, he thought, because Deborah was still not thinking quite straight. His excuse was taking a basket of provisions to Lady Scoggie in her vigil over Mr. Tibo, and paying his respects to Tibo at the same time, a task that could have been done as easily by almost anyone else. There was, he admitted to himself, a slight edge of panic to the speed with which he managed to arrange the basket with Mrs. Costane, and to the way he found himself running up the servants' passage to the front hall, seizing his coat and hat, and hurrying outside on to the drive. Once in the fresh air, he felt his heartbeat calming, but he walked briskly down the drive, and did not look back once at the castle.

Of course it was only to be for an hour or so, but it was better than nothing. He drew a deep breath, and relaxed enough to look around him. It was frosty still, the sunshine hardly making an impression on the hard ground. He breathed out, feeling the fog of his breath on his face as he walked, seeing out of the corner of his eye sparkling droplets forming on his scarf and hat brim. He increased his stride, stretching his long legs, feeling the tension leave him.

Tibo had lived in the upper end of the village, not because of any strong feelings about pigs, but more because it allowed him to be close to his most valued clients, the Scoggies and one or two prosperous farmers, and usually whatever tenant took Aberardour Lodge. The house was new, built by his late father to look almost like a town house, with the usual dining room and one bedroom on the ground floor and the drawing room upstairs. Murray had not been there often, and today he was shown by a maid straight into the ground floor bedchamber, where Tibo's body was laid out on the bed.

Technically speaking, he had not in fact been laid out. Blood still coated his face, and the clothes he wore were the ones in which he had lain on the frosty grass last night. A sheet had been pulled over him, but just as Murray arrived, a woman from the village and her daughter had drawn it back, preparing to wash and tidy the corpse. Lady Scoggie, who had her sleeves pushed up to help, set down her cloth and bowl of water and led Murray back into the dining room, leaving the village women to carry on without her.

'I brought some provisions from Mrs. Costane,' Murray explained, holding out the basket.

'Very kind of you, Mr. Murray.'

He half-expected some remark about food delivery being more the provision of footmen than tutors, but it did not happen. Lady Scoggie was biting her lip, the basket half-forgotten in her hands. He looked around, pulled out a chair for her from the table, and took the basket back.

'Please allow me to pour you a glass of wine, my lady. You seem tired.' The keen points of cheekbone and chin were still there, the determined lips and brows, but it was as if a veil of fatigue had been thrown over her face. He wondered again if she was ill, as Major Keyes had suggested. She seemed worse every day.

She said nothing in response, so he drew out the bottle of wine from the basket and found the means to open it, as well as a glass, on the sideboard. It was red, and for a second or two he warmed it between his hands before setting it down in front of her. Rummaging through the basket, he found bread and cheese, and unwrapped them on to a napkin. Then he drew back, allowing her some space. She took the glass between her own hands, and sipped as much as a bird would.

Perhaps she had not slept well, he thought: perhaps that was all. He tried not to look as if he was watching her, and went to stand by the window, hands screwed up behind his back, suppressing a yawn himself. None of them had slept well last night, he was sure of that. But what had they all been doing earlier in the evening? Could anyone from the family, or from the household, have seen anything remotely useful, down by the lake? At least he could find out who had been the last to see Tibo alive, and how he had seemed.

He wondered how useful that would be if he was right and Keyes had been the intended victim. Had he told Lord Scoggie about the letters yet? Had he told Lady Scoggie? Was that why she was upset? Would he have confided in his cousin rather than his cousin's husband? But when he thought about it, Keyes was the kind of man much more likely to rely on another man to keep his confidences, not a woman, however related.

Lady Scoggie was not touching the food, but the wine glass was nearly empty. He stepped over and refilled it, cautiously, expecting any second to be waved away with her old briskness, but she accepted it silently. Indeed, the silence was becoming very weighty, settling over the room like a shroud. If one of them did not speak soon, he had the strange impression that neither of them would again, condemned to soundless eternity in this fashionable but blank dining room.

'I shall only remain until Mr. Tibo's brother arrives from Kirkcaldy,' she said, so suddenly he felt his heart jump. 'He should not be long.'

'Is there any way in which I can be of service, my lady?'

She looked up at him at last.

'Should you not be with the boys?'

'They had an unsettled night, my lady. I was disinclined to push them too hard this morning, but I have given them some reading to do. With Naismyth indisposed and Andrew in a cell, there was no one else to bring the basket over conveniently, and Mrs. Costane was anxious that you should not be hungry.'

Lady Scoggie's gaze had wandered a little again.

'She was very thoughtful.' She poked around in the basket. 'I see she has sent bannocks as well as cheese. I wonder does she mean them to be kept for the funeral?' She let the cloth fall back over the bannocks, and took up her wine glass again.

'Have you seen Deborah this morning, Mr. Murray?'

'Yes, my lady.'

'Does she know – about Mr. Tibo?'

'Yes, my lady. She heard the news at breakfast.'

'From whom?'

'From me, my lady.'

'Was Major Keyes present?'

'Yes, my lady.' This was like one of her old interrogations. Oddly, it put Murray more at ease.

'Then why did he not tell her?'

'He did not seem inclined to, my lady.' He tried to make it sound as uncritical as possible, though he was still quite cross with Keyes. 'He has still to find –'

'What?'

Murray squirmed inwardly. He had started to think out loud.

'He has still, I believe, my lady, to find himself entirely at ease with Miss Deborah and other young ladies.' He braced himself, ready for the reprimand he deserved for his intrusion. But Lady Scoggie looked thoughtful.

'I am anxious about Deborah, I confess,' she said, setting down her glass, looking at the floor. 'My cousin is – I know Lord Scoggie spoke to you of this. He trusts you, I believe, to be discreet. My cousin had a reputation for a very hot temper when he was young, and we would not have encouraged his suit if we had seen any evidence of it still. But all the same, although he has been given permission to woo her, Deborah has not yet given her consent.'

Murray was surprised. Deborah had seemed resigned to her fate, and he would not have seen her as someone who would postpone the inevitable. He managed not to say anything this time, and after a moment Lady Scoggie continued.

'I believe, you know, that she preferred Mr. Tibo to Major Keyes, which makes me anxious that she will be more upset by Mr. Tibo's death than we expect. I must see to it that she is all right. But in the end it will make things less complicated if poor Mr. Tibo is not around ... poor Mr. Tibo.'

'Do you have any idea, my lady, who would have

wanted to kill him?' Murray asked, taking advantage of her open mood. She frowned.

'That I do not know,' she said at last. 'I suppose the inclination is to hope that it is some vagabond or chance criminal who assaulted him for his purse, but I should rather that it was someone local and obvious who is caught quickly and cleanly. Then the problem is at an end.'

'And would you be surprised, my lady, to find that he had been killed in mistake for, say, Major Keyes?'

She looked sharply at him for the first time.

'Why do you ask?'

'They were both tall, and inclined to wear cloaks rather than coats in this weather, and last night Mr. Tibo was still limping badly from his injury at the boxing lesson. I wondered if there was any chance that, in the dark, perhaps someone had made a mistake.'

'Do you know,' said Lady Scoggie, 'that seems infinitely more likely than someone wanting to kill Mr. Tibo. As I said, Major Keyes used to have a bad temper. Who knows how many enemies he must have made in his life? One of them could have followed him here and, as you say, made a mistake.'

There was a tap at the dining room door, and the maid came in.

'Mrs. Spence says she's done, my lady.'

'He's ready?'

'Aye, my lady.'

Lady Scoggie sighed.

'I shall go back in now.' The maid bobbed and left. 'Beatrix said she would come and keep me company later, if Mr. Tibo's brother is delayed.'

'She is a kind girl,' Murray remarked.

'Yes.' Lady Scoggie eyed him briefly. The words 'And too good for you, my lad,' seemed to him to snap through the air after. He tried to look suitably servile.

'Shall I take the basket back, or leave it with you, my lady?'

'Leave it: there is plenty in it yet.' She rose, and he opened the door for her, following her into the bedchamber to pay his respects to Tibo. The village woman had done a fair job, though the lawyer would never look as spruce in death as he liked to in life. He touched Tibo's hand to ward off his ghost, bowed to Lady Scoggie, and left.

Tibo's short carriage drive decanted him on to the main road again. He stopped and spent a moment wondering whether to go straight home to the castle, or whether to take a walk down to the village. These days he often only saw it with its Sunday face, and he wondered just how it was that Lord Scoggie came by all his information on village happenings and gossip, knowledge that he had shown so clearly during the interviews with the fishermen and the Kinkells and their associates. He wished that Keyes would tell Lord Scoggie about the anonymous letters: he was sure that Lord Scoggie would be able almost at once to say who was sending them. And how did they arrive? That was a question he should have asked before now. It was all very well for Keyes to say that Naismyth handed them to him, but where did Naismyth get them? Murray was in a good position, halfway between servants and family, to find out: at least, that was, if Naismyth was now in a fit state to speak. He liked his theory of mistaken identity, and was unreasonably pleased that Lady Scoggie had not poured scorn on it: quite the reverse, in fact. If he could explain it to Lord Scoggie, perhaps without breaking Keyes' confidence over the letters, perhaps everything would be cleared up quickly, as Lady Scoggie wanted and as presumably everyone else did, too. It would be difficult for the ladies to go about as freely as they did if there was a murderer loose in the neighbourhood, and the boys would never really calm down until someone was caught – preferably not a headless horseman, or other kind of ghost.

Ghosts ... he suddenly remembered the figure he had seen in the distance last night, just before he had met Deborah outside the front door, frozen and miserable. The figure had looked like a fisherman, but with a bad limp – another limp. It could not have been Tibo, not dressed that way, nor even Keyes, for the same reason. Who else in the neighbourhood had such a limp? Not, he insisted to himself, Hugh Farquhar's ghost.

He was just about to push himself away from the gatepost and continue down to the village in pursuit of his thoughts, when they took a sudden turn from ghosts and spun in the direction of elves. Just turning the corner, walking towards him, was Beatrix, coming, no doubt, to sit with Lady Scoggie. With her were Mr. and Mrs. Bootham.

They were more soberly dressed than usual, so he assumed that they had already heard about Tibo's death. Under her blue cloak, he could see that Mrs. Bootham was wearing a gown of a deep brown like autumn beech leaves, so that he expected it to rustle as she approached him. The frost had pinched her cheeks berry-red, and her eyes were bright.

'Mr. Murray! How are you on this beautiful morning?'

'Quite well, thank you.' He bowed, trying not to remember the feel of her hand in his as they had danced last night. 'I hope you are well.'

'Very well, but much saddened to hear of Mr. Tibo's death.' She pursed her lips into a solemn look. 'We have learned from our mistakes, and are here as quickly as possible to pay our respects.'

Mr. Bootham, who had been a little distance behind with Beatrix on his arm, tipped his hat, letting the frosty sunshine melt over his white-gold hair. For just a second, the angle of his head seemed very familiar.

'Good day, Mr. Murray. A sad day, is it not?'

'Very much so. But I am glad to see that you both reached home safely.'

'I think we must have left long before the drama began,' said Bootham smoothly. 'We left directly after our visit to the servants' dance.'

'We huddled together safely in our little carriage,' said Mrs. Bootham, with a sweet look at her husband, 'and guarded each other all the way home. But do you think we are all in danger?' She turned quickly back to Murray. 'Is it some dreadful gang in the neighbourhood, robbing people?'

Murray smiled.

'I don't believe so, but Lord Scoggie will be the best person to ask. In the mean time, perhaps it is best to be wary when at all possible, and particularly at night.'

'Then it is as well that we found you, Miss Pirrie, and were able to escort you safely here.' Mr. Bootham bent over Beatrix in an intimate way that turned Murray's stomach. He glanced at Mrs. Bootham, but she seemed unconcerned, smiling at them both. Beatrix, on the other hand, was glowing, and it was not just the effect of the cold, bright air. Bootham glanced back at Murray.

'We were concerned when we saw Miss Pirrie on her own, for we wondered if Miss Scoggie was unwell. I didn't remember seeing her at the dance, or afterwards, last night.'

He ended on a slight query, to which Murray did not feel like responding.

'She seemed quite well this morning, though of

course shocked at what has happened,' he answered.

Mrs. Bootham gave a quick little skip.

'Oh, Miss Pirrie, why will gentlemen talk so when it is so cold outside? Come, let us at least go and find a comfortable fire, and show them how sensible people behave!'

She seized Beatrix by her free arm and snatched her away from her husband, hurrying her away up the drive to Tibo's front door.

'A charming girl,' Bootham remarked, absently straightening his sleeve. 'Really very sensitive. Yet it is Miss Scoggie who really interests me, don't you think, Mr. Murray? A very great deal of pent-up emotion in her, I believe.'

'As Lord Scoggie's private secretary I cannot, you will understand, make such profound observations. Please excuse me: I must return to my pupils.'

Murray stalked off. He was convinced that behind him, Bootham was laughing at him, but he did not turn round. If he had done so, he knew he would have gone back and hit him.

The boys, when he found them, were in Robert's room, playing pachisi with listless venom. They had completed the work he had left for them with such exactitude that he knew they were still angry with him even before they glared up at him from the carpet and the pachisi board.

'Where have you been?' demanded Henry.

'We thought you might have been murdered,' added Robert, sounding slightly disappointed.

'I went to take food to Lady Scoggie.'

Henry at least looked as if this was a reasonable excuse. Robert looked more dubious.

'Is he all laid out and everything?'

'Yes.' He sat down on the edge of Robert's bed, watching the progress of the game without much interest. 'Lady Scoggie intends to remain there until Mr. Tibo's brother arrives to take over.'

'Do you think,' said Robert, in a dangerously even tone, 'that if one of us was dead, she would sit with us at all, or would she find some better things to do?'

'Of course she would,' snapped Henry angrily. 'She's very good.'

'Oh, aye,' said Robert. Henry snatched up a wooden sword that was lying on the floor beside them, and hit him hard.

'Henry!' cried Murray. 'Stop that!'

'I've stopped,' said Henry sullenly.

'Mr. Murray,' said Robert, rubbing his new bruise,

'we were talking to Father about you.'

'Oh, yes?' Murray was guarded. Would Lord Scoggie take any of their complaints seriously?

'He said you'd caught a murderer before. When you were a student.'

'Oh.' A serious of thoroughly unpleasant memories sped through his mind. 'Well, I didn't exactly catch the murderer.'

'Father says you did.'

'There's no arguing, then.'

'Are you going to catch this murderer?'

'I have no idea.'

'Father says you might.'

'He's very kind to think I might.'

'Why wouldn't you?' asked Henry. 'It must be easy to find a murderer. He would be all covered in blood and he would be desperate.'

'Um. Maybe not, Henry. Think about it:' he wondered if this was sensible, but he might be able to appeal to Henry's scientific leanings. 'We think that Mr. Tibo was hit on the head with a stick or some similar weapon. It might have been quite long. It is quite possible that no blood splashed on the killer at all, and he probably threw the weapon into the lake. You said he would be desperate: well, he would indeed, but he would be desperate to hide his deed. He might not be all wild-eyed and terrible. He might just be keeping very quiet, and trying to act as if everything is just as usual.'

Henry looked thoughtful. Robert, on the other hand, looked slightly frightened.

'So we don't have any idea at all who it is?' he asked.

'At the moment, no.' He stood up, stretching his back from leaning over for so long. 'I don't suppose for a moment that either of you can help.'

He glanced back just in time to see Robert and Henry meet each other's eye, and sighed.

'Well ...' said Robert, poking at the dice on the board.

'You won't like it,' added Henry. 'Or you won't believe it. Grown-ups don't believe anything they don't want to, but they expect us to believe all kinds of things.'

'That's cheeky, but quite perceptive,' said Murray, beginning to forgive the boys. He smiled at Robert. 'What is it you think I won't like?'

Robert sat back on the floor, leaning on his hands, and not looking at Murray. He sighed heavily, and looked to Henry for a little support. Henry shrugged.

'We saw a ghost,' said Robert. 'I know you say there aren't any, but we did.'

'If you mean the headless horseman –' said Murray, annoyed again.

'No, not the headless horseman. It was someone else – I mean, it was really someone.'

If the boys could place someone near the lake around the time of the murder, the information could be invaluable.

'Who?'

'We saw Hugh Farquhar's ghost. He was in his fisherman's clothes, and he was limping.'

'He must have been hurt when the boat sank,' added Henry. They had obviously been discussing it in some detail.

Murray remembered the figure he himself had seen – and over which he had drawn the same instinctive conclusion. He could hardly blame the boys for believing in ghosts. But he had only seen it for a second: perhaps the boys had more information.

'What was he doing, then?' he asked. Robert and Henry both examined his face, estimating the degree of scepticism there, and were satisfied.

'He was walking across the grass.'

'We thought he was heading towards the village road, to that bit where you can climb the wall, and save having to go all the way round to the drive.' Murray knew the place they meant, that was constantly being mended and just as constantly mysteriously tumbled again. It would have let the figure out of the park near the woods that bordered the lake. When he had seen it, it had been heading towards the castle, if a little lower down the hill. Perhaps the boys had seen it going back the way it had come, when it had done whatever it had come to do. The thought made him shiver.

'Are you absolutely sure it was Hugh Farquhar?' he asked.

'See? I said he wouldn't believe us,' said Robert, rolling over to lie with his back towards Murray in a gesture redolent with disgust.

'No, no. I only mean – I'm sure you saw a figure, in fisherman's clothes, with a limp. That's fine. I'm not arguing, Robert. But I just want to know if it was definitely Hugh. Did you know him?'

'Who else could it have been?'

'One of his crew, for instance. They all died.'

The boys looked at each other, uncertainly, with Robert squirmed round like a prawn. Then he sat up properly and faced Murray.

'There could be ghosts all over the place,' he said, shakily.

'There are a lot more people dead than living, if you think about it,' said Murray.

'We didn't see his face,' Henry admitted at last. 'He

was going away from us. We just saw his back and his clothes.'

'But you believe there was someone there?' Robert asked hurriedly, needing to know.

'Oh, yes, I do, Robert.'

Robert, not needing a reason, sat back and grinned. But Henry, who needed his scientific evidence, watched Murray anxiously as he left the room and headed for the stairs.

There was no sign of Lord Scoggie in the library. In the hall, Murray met Andrew, and stopped him in surprise.

'You've been released!'

'Aye. Mr. Naismyth changed his tune when he came round. Maybe because he didn't want word getting round of the state he was in last night.' Andrew grinned as he lowered his voice.

'Well, we couldn't quite see why he turned you in in the first place,' Murray admitted. 'Why do you think he did?'

'Oh, that's easy! Grisell,' said Andrew, with a laugh, in which there was a good deal more of ease than there had been the last time he had mentioned Grisell to Murray. The conversation through the cell door must have been a profitable one. Andrew was about to head towards the door to the servants' corridor, but Murray stopped him.

'Any idea where Lord Scoggie is?' he asked.

Andrew tilted his head towards the door of the other room off the hallway.

'In there,' he said, 'with Mr. Naismyth. I think he was looking yourself earlier, too.'

The other door off the hallway led to a room with no name. In his time at Scoggie Castle, Murray reckoned he had been in there twice. The room took up the ground floor of the Lady's Tower, but did not accommodate much that would interest the ladies of the household: in the days when the castle was built, the ladies would have retreated to the upper floors for safety and this room would have contributed to the castle defences, with its slit windows and narrow doorway. In some ways, it still did: when Murray knocked and entered, he found Lord Scoggie and Naismyth cleaning guns from the cabinets against one wall.

'Ah, Mr. Murray.' Lord Scoggie did not greet him with his usual smile. 'Where have you been?'

'Taking provisions to Lady Scoggie, my lord.'

Lord Scoggie nodded sharply.

'I take it you know how to fire a gun?'

'Yes, my lord.' His father had made sure of that, with both handguns and shotguns, till their hair had smelt spicy with powder and their shoulders were stiff with the recoil.

'I want each of us to carry handguns, and Naismyth is to make sure that all the shotguns in here are loaded and ready.'

'Just the three of us, my lord?'

'Keyes has his own pistols. Try the weight of those?' He handed over a pair of pretty Spanish pistols. 'No, you need something heavier, don't you? Naismyth, you take those ones. Yes: I've released Andrew,' - Naismyth had the grace to look sheepish – 'but he's young and has no experience of firearms. I'd ask you to keep it fairly quiet, though: I'm sure Deborah will want some if she knows we have them.'

'She can shoot?'

'Moderately well. Lady Scoggie insisted she learn when she was old enough. It's not an unuseful skill. I think we have a muff pistol in here somewhere that is hers.' He looked around the room. There was a billiard table in it, but it was not a billiard room, and gun cabinets, though it was not a gunroom. The stone floor had patches of oiled cloth on it, but no carpet, and the hearth had not seen a fire for many years, to judge by its cleanliness and the damp air. One or two family portraits of the kind no one wanted to see hung about the panelled walls, as if they had been barred for some social indiscretion. The three armchairs in the room were ill-assorted and looked uneasy, caught walking into the wrong room. A stopped clock lurked in the darkness between the slit windows. Murray shivered involuntarily: there was something in between about the room.

'What are the boys doing?'

'Playing pachisi. They've worked quite hard this morning.'

'Do they need your attention?'

'Not at present, my lord.'

'Good. There's something I want you to do. Naismyth, will you finish in here, then bring me the keys? Come into the library, Mr. Murray. I don't like this room.'

Murray followed him across the hall. A fire had been lit again in the library hearth, and there was no trace of the papers he had seen there earlier. Lord Scoggie went to sit in the high chair behind the business table. Murray wondered if for some reason he was about to be admonished, but when he looked at Lord Scoggie's face he decided that the use of the high chair was Lord Scoggie's effort to take control of the situation: probably a futile attempt.

'Have you reached any further conclusions about Tibo's death?' Lord Scoggie asked, once he had arranged himself.

'No, I don't think so, my lord. Except that I think there is a chance that he was killed in mistake, with the killer intending harm instead to Major Keyes.'

Lord Scoggie raised his eyebrows.

'You mean, perhaps, some enemy he has made in the past?'

'Yes, I think so, my lord. I put the suggestion to Lady Scoggie and she thought it was more likely than Mr. Tibo being the real target.'

'Hmm ...' Lord Scoggie frowned down at the table. It looked like a new idea to him: Keyes could not yet have told him about the anonymous letters. Murray could have shaken him.

'I met the Boothams on my way back. They say they left straight after the dance in the barn. I presume you saw them leave, my lord?'

'Yes, yes, I think so. You think they might have had something to do with it?'

'They were around at the time, that's all, my lord. I don't suppose they knew Mr. Tibo very well. I was trying more to find out who last saw Mr. Tibo, apart from his killer.'

'Anything else?'

'Not at the moment, I think, my lord.' He was not sure why, but he was still reluctant to tell Lord Scoggie that his daughter had been, if not the last person to see Tibo, at least the last to arrange a meeting with him, on her own, in the dark. Whatever he had said to the boys, it was indeed suspicious behaviour, particularly for a girl engaged, or almost, to someone else.

'Well, let's leave Tibo for the moment, Mr. Murray. We have another problem, as you know, and I'd like you to go, now that I can no longer send either Tibo or Cocky Leckie,' he sighed heavily, 'to find something out for me. How do you feel about a walk to the village?'

'I should be happy to help, my lord,' said Murray, wondering what was coming next.

CHAPTER SEVENTEEN

'Another basket of food?' demanded Mrs. Costane. 'Has Lady Scoggie finally acquired an appetite?'

'It's not for her,' said Murray. 'It's for a couple of families in the village.'

'You're taking on her charitable duties, then?'

'Something like that.'

Mrs. Costane looked down at the intended contents, and frowned.

'Why did I put the bottle of wine out? That's a bit more than she usually takes.'

'Because I asked for it.'

Mrs. Costane sighed with annoyance and continued mixing whatever she was mixing in a pan over the fire.

'My head doesn't know what my hands are doing today, I'm that busy.'

He watched Hannah's busy hands loading up the basket with bannocks, wine, soup in a tin with a lid, and cold chicken, by habit avoiding any ham or bacon. She added some leeks from the scullery table, arranging them like a bouquet around the top, then draping the lot with a cloth and presenting the finished basket to Murray with a deeply ironic curtsey. He replied with a solemn bow, and hurried out of the kitchen.

Outside, the sun had gone in and the air felt dull. He walked quickly, hoping that he might have the task he had been given completed before dark. He had a stick, Lord Scoggie's pair of pistols, and a sword, and felt he was clanking as he walked, but after dark he knew he would feel much more vulnerable. He glanced up. The sky was definitely clouding over, and it would be a very dark night.

He was halfway down the drive when he saw a cloaked figure walking up from the woods on a path to converge with his. The figure waved: it was Keyes. He sighed: he wanted to be on his own to consider how he was to proceed, but it looked as if Keyes was determined to join him. He waved back, trying to look busy.

'You've been elusive this morning, Murray!' Keyes cried when he was near enough. 'What have you been up to?'

'I've been at Tibo's house, and now I'm off on a confidential errand for Lord Scoggie.' He laid a degree of emphasis on the word 'confidential', hoping that Keyes would take the hint.

'I'll walk along with you for a little, then,' said Keyes comfortably, swinging into step beside him.

'Did you find Lord Scoggie this morning? You were going to talk with him, I think: I left him in the library ten minutes ago.'

'Ah, well, I don't think I need to talk to him now,' said Keyes, glancing at Murray out of the corner of his eye.

'But the letters – the possibility that you were the intended victim –' Murray struggled to keep the impatience from his voice.

'I can't see that anyone would be going to kill me, honestly, Murray. What would be the reason? And as for the letters – well, I don't think I'll be getting any more now.'

'Why not?'

'Well ...' They had reached the gate, and Keyes looked about him to make sure they were alone. 'I don't know why, but I always thought that the person who sent the letters was Tibo himself. That's why I was so uneasy about telling Scoggie about them. I know he thought a great deal of his lawyer, and he would have been upset. I like old Scoggie.'

'You thought the writer was Tibo?' Murray stared at

the Major. 'Why on earth would Tibo have wanted to write you anonymous letters?'

'Well, he seemed to be trying to warn me off, wasn't he? He probably thought my being here would bother some of the villagers. You maybe know I had a bit of a rammy with one of them the last time I was here, and maybe Tibo was just being sensitive.'

'But doesn't that mean that there is someone around, in the village, even, who has a reason to kill you?'

'Ach, don't be daft!' Keyes, laughing, had no notion of being afraid. 'The fellow I fought will have forgotten it long ago.'

'I'm not sure that Lord Scoggie would agree with you –'

'And that's exactly why I won't bother Lord Scoggie with the matter. Don't you think he has enough to worry about?'

Murray closed his eyes. Murdering Major Keyes was briefly very tempting indeed.

'The thing is,' said Keyes, oblivious, 'there was one more letter last night. I found it on the hall table, on my way out to see what was going on – when Tibo was found.'

'The same as the others?'

'Aye, much the same. Take a look.'

He dug in his pocket, and produced another folded paper. Murray took it and stopped to read it.

'Yew will not heed my warnning. Yew must goe, and goe nowe. A freind.'

The breeze lifted the corner of the letter suddenly, and Murray thought he noticed something. He held the letter up to his nose, and sniffed.

'It smells of fish.'

'Maybe Tibo had fish for his dinner.'

'And the spelling?'

'A blind. Good spelling would have cut down the possible writers considerably.'

Murray looked down, past the letter, and thought hard. He tried to picture Tibo as an anonymous letter writer, attempting to disguise his identity. It was much easier to picture him drawing Major Keyes aside and giving him the warning in person. Why would Tibo have hidden behind these yews and goes? It made no sense.

'Where were you anyway, last night? Did you see where anyone else was?'

Keyes laughed.

'I was as safe as could be. When you all left for the dance, I went upstairs to my room, took off my old leg, and wrote letters to my admirers for what seemed like hours. The first I knew anything had happened was when

Naismyth, already, I believe, the worse for brandy, battered on Lord Scoggie's chamber door to rouse him. If the murderer was after me, he was in the wrong place altogether.'

There was a clatter of wheels and hooves behind them, and Murray stepped up on to the bank to allow a carriage to squeeze its way past Keyes, balancing his peg leg in the ditch. The curtain on the near window was down, showing the passenger to be a neat man, dressed in mourning.

'Tibo's younger brother, then, I suppose,' Keyes nodded after it.

'Lady Scoggie will be able to come home soon, then.'

'You won't have to take her her dinner.'

'What?' Murray looked down at the basket he was carrying. 'No, it's not for her. It's for someone else.'

'Who?'

'It's this confidential work I'm doing for Lord Scoggie,' said Murray, again with emphasis. They were not far from his destination now, and he was wondering how he was to shake Keyes off. It was less difficult than he expected.

'I'll walk as far as Tibo's house, then, and maybe I can escort Cousin Livvy home. I hear Scoggie has you armed to the oxters, too?'

'Oh, aye,' Murray smiled, flipping his coat back to show the sword. 'I'm sure she'll be grateful for the security.' He stopped outside the row of cottages on the brow of the hill. Keyes looked at them curiously. 'Here's where I stop. I'll see you later, I expect.'

'Keep safe,' Keyes said cheerfully, giving a little bow, and continuing down the road. Murray waited until he had disappeared round the corner before selecting the cottage he wanted to enter. From inside, he could hear the hum and rattle of the loom, until he knocked the door. The work rattled to a halt, there was the scrape of a stool on an earth floor, and the door opened. It was Geordie Kinkell.

'Oh, aye?' he said, after a second recognising Murray from the servants' dance.

'I'm here from Lord Scoggie.'

'Well, I never thought you were representing the Moderator of the General Assembly. You'd better come in.'

Murray stooped through the door, finding himself in the kitchen. It was smoky and dark: the lum was not well built, like many of these cottages. The earthen floor was well trampled and seemed to have been swept, but evidently not by the lady of the house. When his eyes had grown accustomed to the dim light of the crusie lamp he saw her, no more than bones beneath the blankets, propped up in the recess bed.

'Mrs. Kinkell.' He bowed, clumsy under the low rafters. Geordie was a big man himself, but had the habit of walking about his kitchen with his head a little on one side. Above the rafters hung what seemed to be a small ham and some cheese in cloth, and odd tools and boxes. The mantelpiece held the requisite Bible and nothing much else. On a creepy stool far too close to the fire, his son Peter sat, head right back to smile up at the visitor. Murray smiled back irresistibly.

'Will you sit, before you crack your head?' said Geordie, nodding to a Windsor chair that had pride of place on the other side of the fire. Murray, feeling he was in the way, sat.

'I brought a few things for you from his lordship.' He held the basket out, but at Geordie's nod set it down beside him.

'From his lordship?' Geordie gave him an odd, sideways look. 'No her ladyship?'

'It was his lordship that sent me.' What was Lady Scoggie's reason for failing to visit this house, when there was not another door in the village she did not darken?

'I see.' He watched as Peter grabbed the basket and snatched off the cloth, then rescued the bottle of wine tenderly from his starfish hands. 'He's awful good to an old household in trouble.'

Murray tried to find irony in this statement, but could not quite.

'I hope your brother Sandy saw himself safely home last night.'

Geordie grinned, though his eyes seemed sad.

'Aye, I think so. His feet usually find the way, even if his head hasna a clue.'

'It was difficult to deal with the matter last night, but Lord Scoggie wants to know if it's true: has Chrissie not appeared yet?'

Geordie looked surprised.

'Well, it's like Sandy said: she hadna by last night, anyway. His lordship said long ago her brother had let her go, but he mustn't have at all.'

'Mr. Tibo went to see them after Hugh Farquhar's death, and she had gone, he said.'

'He said, or they said? I wouldna put anything past that lot.' He spoke with easy, accustomed bile. 'Likely they have her stowed in the fishloft, or wherever. She was no at Sandy's, anyway.'

'Who's looking after his child?'

'Our mother. She lives with them – well, it was her house.'

'But you haven't seen him today.'

'No! I've enough to do without tying him to my apron strings.'

'I'd best go and see him myself, then.' Murray made to stand up, but Geordie scrambled to his feet first.

'Give me a minute and I'll come with you. Here, Peter, get your hat and scarf on, and we'll go and see Uncle Sandy.' Instead of fetching his own coat, he stepped quickly over to the recess bed, murmuring something Murray did not try to catch. He took a knife from his pocket and quickly opened the bottle of wine, pouring a little into a cup by the bed.

'Try it anyway,' he said. 'Are you warm enough?'

She nodded, though her head seemed too heavy for her fragile neck. The smell of her disease wrapped the room about, taking hold on all their lives. There was nothing that could be done. Yet that never stopped Lady Scoggie. Why did she not come here?

'I'll wait outside,' he said, giving them a moment of privacy. Seconds later, Geordie and Peter joined him, and led the way across the road and into a lane that ran between the fields opposite.

'I take it Mr. Tibo is too busy again to do his lordship's work for him?' said Geordie with a sarcastic smirk. 'You seem to be getting all the jobs these days.'

'You haven't heard, then?' Murray saw the answer in his face. 'Mr. Tibo died last night. He was murdered.'

Geordie stopped in his tracks.

'He never was!' He stared at Murray, testing his face for honesty. What he saw seemed to satisfy him in some small way. He blew out hard through narrow lips. 'Did they get them?'

'Who?'

'The fellows who did it. The fishermen.'

A limping figure passed across the frosty slopes of Murray's memory.

'Why do you think the fishermen did it?'

'Ach, they'll do anything!' The words were similar to his earlier remark, but something about the tone was not quite right, nor was the way he avoided Murray's eye. 'How did they kill him?'

'A blow to the side of the head.'

'I'd have expected a knife. He was in his house, I suppose.'

'No. He was beside the lake.'

Geordie stared again.

'On the laird's own land? My, they're braw!'

'Braw!' cried Peter, making them jump. He had hurried ahead, not noticing them pause, and now danced back to them like a puppy.

'Quiet, lad: a man's dead.' As always, he spoke kindly to his son. 'Of course we never saw him much. If there was any business to be done, he would have sent poor wee Cocky Leckie. And Cocky would have called anyway, out of friendliness.'

'Will Aunty Chrissie be there?' Peter asked his

father, pointing to the cottage they were approaching.

'I dinna ken, lad. That's what we're here to find out. Sandy!' Geordie slapped the door. In the patch of land beside the cottage, a woman was pegging out washing, only her skirts visible behind swirling sheets. Murray, looking at the sky, thought she was being optimistic.

Geordie saw where he was looking.

'Ma!' he cried. The woman took her time pegging out a last towel, then bent and picked up the basket at her feet. She had a wiry, hard figure, which looked younger than her face. Two blue eyes like ice chips were set deep into leather skin.

'If you're looking your brother,' she started to speak when she was still at the line, 'you needn't expect sense from him. I needn't ask what time you think he got in last night: he had the whole house roused and the bairn greeting before he found his bed.'

'Aye, he was in a bad way.' Geordie briefly met Murray's eye. 'I'm sorry I couldna see him back myself, but you ken how things are.'

'Aye,' she said shortly. 'Hallo, there, Peter. Are you well?'

'Aye, Nan: I'm grand!' said Peter proudly.

'Well, away into the house then, and we'll have a bit of tea. You'll be the young gentleman from the Castle,' she said to Murray, eyes looking straight into him.

'Charles Murray, Mrs. Kinkell.' He bowed. She nodded, and led the way into the cottage.

This cottage was smoky, too, but the underlying smell was of baby: clean, well cared-for baby, fortunately. A pot of stew was over the fire, and Mrs. Kinkell went straight to it, giving it a quick, expert stir.

'Nathaniel Tibo's dead,' said Geordie quickly, as if he was afraid Murray would snatch his news from him. Mrs. Kinkell stopped and looked hard at her son, then turned back to push a kettle over the fire. 'He's murdered.'

'Murdered?' She bent to pick up the child that was squirming in its cradle, and sat on the bench under the window, the child firmly on her thin lap. She reminded Murray suddenly of Lady Scoggie, older and poorer, perhaps, but just as tough – or he would have said so, until Lady Scoggie's recent signs of weakness. 'Who killed him?'

'We don't know.' Murray jumped in before Geordie could say anything. Geordie opened his mouth to add something, but he was interrupted.

'Who the devil's that?'

The voice was slurred, and came from the curtained recess bed. Geordie's eyes rolled, and he took one long step across and swept the curtain back. There was a curse, and Sandy was revealed, his pimpled face blotchy, his red hair at all angles, clad only in the shirt he had worn last night, with a hand clutched across his eyes to shield them from the kitchen's dim light.

'It's me, Sandy. And the gentleman who took such good care of you last night when you called on his lordship, so you're no doing a good job of returning his hospitality.'

'He can go to Brigham, for all I'm fashed.' Sandy curled up like a worm disturbed. His bare legs did not make for an attractive view, but no one in the room seemed much concerned.

'Is your wife back, Sandy?'

'Can you see her? Aye, she's here in the bed with me, aren't you, Chrissie, my love?' He seized a scrawny pillow with passion, then sank back against the wall. 'Of course she's no back. She's still with her damned family, devil take the whole fish-fancying boiling of them.'

'You watch your tongue, laddie, or you'll feel the back of my hand,' snapped his mother.

'Ma, I'm a grown man!'

'You're neither dressed like one nor behaving like one. No, she's no back, Geordie,' she sighed, jiggling the baby a little. 'How could they keep her away from this wee one?'

Murray turned to Geordie.

'Lord Scoggie will want me to take this further. I shall visit the Farquhars,' he said, though the prospect did not appeal.

Geordie fetched the kettle off the fire, and poured

hot black tea for each of them, including Murray. Having a sick wife must have domesticated him, Murray thought, scalding his mouth with the drink. Sandy's lips must have been tougher, for he emptied the cup quickly and struggled off the bed. Just about upright, he clutched the wall for support.

'I'll come with you.'

'You'll no,' said his mother with certainty. 'You'll stay here at your home and do the work you need to do to put food in this bairn's bowl.'

'She's right, Sandy.' Geordie nodded firmly. 'You'll only get in a fight again.'

'I'm ready to fight, I am.'

'You're ready to fall over,' Geordie caught him as he wobbled. 'Lie down till you can stand up without help.' He turned to Murray. 'You'd better go now if you're going, before he gets his strength back.'

Murray nodded, and left with little formality. His visit was going to be difficult enough without trying to keep Sandy Kinkell out of trouble.

Outside the sky was heavier than before, and there was a suspicious mildness about the air that promised snow. Murray leaned into the fresh wind, automatically feeling to check that his pistols and sword were still in place. The wind brushed the smoke from his nose and eyes, and flapped at the tails of his coat as he made his way back along the narrow lane to the main village road.

The wind could not brush the questions from his mind. What was he going to say to the Farquhars, a family still in mourning? Where was Chrissie Farquhar? What was wrong with Lady Scoggie, and why would she not visit the Kinkells? Why was Lord Scoggie suddenly so interested in the Kinkells and their problems? What had he been burning in the library grate? Who was the fisherman last night? Was Keyes the intended victim? Why was Deborah going to meet Tibo? Who killed Tibo? The last question echoed round and round in his head, when the first one was the most urgent. Who had killed Tibo? and why had they done it last night? Opportunism? or planning? A chance encounter or a murderer who carried his weapon with him, pacing through the darkness to find his victim? Where was the household last night? Was the killer going to strike again?

He pictured the questions in his head, until his thoughts were completely tangled with the hooks of question marks. He hardly saw where he was walking, the wind filling his ears with bird cries and whirling leaves, until he was roused by the sound of a human voice. Startled, he stopped in his tracks. The end of the lane was narrow, with high banks, and he was almost upon it. Over the top of it, he recognised suddenly the top of Major Keyes' hat, and to his shame he ducked back instinctively, determined not to be caught up again. He pressed himself into the bank, and hid.

Major Keyes was not talking to himself: he was, as

he had hoped, escorting Lady Scoggie home from Tibo's house. There was a conscientious attentiveness in his attitude, ready for attack from any quarter, though Lady Scoggie herself seemed not to be concerned. Instead, she was frowning hard at the ground as she walked, while Keyes chattered on.

'And he knows nothing of the matter?' he was saying, as he passed the end of the lane.

'Of course not,' she turned on him fiercely, fortunately looking away from the lane. 'How could I tell him? After all this time?'

'Oh,' said Keyes, blithely, 'it's always best to tell. These things always come out.'

'It can't.' Lady Scoggie glared at the ground again. 'It mustn't.'

Then they were past. Murray stayed where he was, still as a waiting heron, feeling the damp ground through his coat. He counted to sixty before he moved, then slipped out of the end of the lane to follow them at a safe distance. He had one more errand to do before he went down to the village.

As he had hoped, Geordie Kinkell's cottage was deserted still apart from his wife. Murray knocked the door gently and went in. Mrs. Kinkell peered at his outline against the daylight, trying to work out who he was.

'It's Charles Murray again, Mrs. Kinkell, from the Castle.'

'Mr. Murray? My husband's still away out.'

'No, that's all right. It's you I've come to see, if you don't mind.'

A ghastly apprehension flickered over her face.

'It's no Andrew, is it?' she whispered.

Good heavens, he had forgotten. The cocky young servant was also a child of this house.

'No, no, not at all!' He hurried to reassure her. 'It's just – Lord Scoggie sent this.' He produced the unremarkable purse with its remarkable weight, and passed it to her. 'It's all in shillings,' he could hear Lord Scoggie explaining to him, 'anything bigger would be hard for her to use in the village.'

'Oh!' Recognition filled her eyes. 'I ken, of course. Poor wee Cocky's dead: he usually brings it for his lordship. I expected Mr. Tibo, but I'm sure he has more important things to be doing.'

'Aye, I'm sure,' said Murray blandly. 'You were a servant up at the Castle, then?'

The memory of a smile touched her lips.

'Oh, aye. Before the childer were born, you ken. Grand times, grand times.'

He smiled, and pulled his gloves back on.

'Now, if you're all right, I'd better get going.'

'Here,' she said, pulling a cloth bag out from under her pillow with some effort. She tipped the contents of the purse into it. 'There's the purse back. Though I doubt I'll live to see the next first of the month to take it again. Now, off you go, indeed, before Geordie comes back. He's gey proud, you ken?'

He bowed, again hampered by the low beams, and made his way back outside, making sure the door was firmly closed against the cold. No one was about. He turned, and hurried down the hill, into the wind, his head even more full of questions than before.

The main street was lined, on the inland side, with cottages, some rendered in grubby white, some left with their honey sandstone bare. Murray would have had little idea which one belonged to the Farquhars but for Lord Scoggie's careful directions: the third rig stair from the junction with the road down the hill, with the door and window to the left. Across the road, in the harbour, the boats were in, knocking hollowly at each other as the water surged and ebbed. A few men were bringing the nets back, hauling them from the chemical spring to the east of the town where they were dipped for their preservation. The ropes were reddish from the iron-laden water. They regarded Murray with suspicion, nodding at him but reserved.

The doorway was even lower than that at the Kinkells' cottage, probably to keep out the worst of the weather. A cry from inside was indistinguishable in the rising wind, but he assumed, optimistically, that it had been an instruction to enter, and pulled the rope latch on the door.

Again he found himself walking straight into a kitchen, but it seemed even smaller than those of the weavers. The outside walls were so thick it was like walking down a tunnel, and at the end of it the heat from the kitchen fire was intense, packed and folded round itself for so long that the room was probably never cold. Again there was a recess bed, curtains closed, and the requisite form and one or two creepy stools. Here, though, there was nowhere to sit down, even if he had been offered a place. On the bench sat a woman, large and miserable, wrapped into her plaid and black gown, as if she could bind up the wounds of her heart from the outside. Beside her was a young man with a drawn face, wearing fisherman's clothes, one leg stretched out deliberately across the floor. On a creepy stool sat the egg-bald Richie Shaw, whom Murray remembered from the meeting at the Castle, hugging his knees for balance. The other two creepy stools were occupied by three small children, presumably Hugh's younger siblings, solemn in the presence of grown-ups. In pride of place, though, in the Windsor chair, was Joe Baillie, just in the act of lighting his pipe. Murray, pursued by a gust of grey wind, entered the kitchen to be impaled on the stares of four pairs of eyes, and the first thing to move was Joe Baillie's hand, flicking a spill into the fire.

'His lordship's secretary, eh?' said Joe, establishing his authority in a moment. 'What do you want?'

'Forgive me for any intrusion.' Murray began with

as much courtesy as he could. 'And I am sorry for your loss, Mrs. Farquhar.' The large woman gulped a sob, and nodded, though her gaze dropped as soon as he looked at her. 'I have come on behalf of Lord Scoggie.'

'Aye, I thought Nathaniel Tibo would never come down here again. It was a wonder he darkened a door in the village the once. Send Cocky Leckie, aye, but when he's gone never dirty your fine gloves.' Joe eyed Murray's moderately fine gloves, which Murray obediently tugged off.

'Nathaniel Tibo is dead, Mr. Baillie.'

'Oh, aye?' Joe was calm, but the man with the drawn face twitched, and gave a little gasp of pain. Murray looked at him out of the corner of his eye. Was there something wrong with his leg?

'Aye. He was murdered last night.'

The woman breathed quickly, and Richie Shaw looked up sharply.

'I hadna heard that,' he said.

'Well, it's true. He was found dead by the lake at the Castle.'

Joe blew smoke out round the chewed stem of his pipe.

'Who would have done something like that?'

'Have you any suggestions?'

Joe laughed.

'If that's what you came here to ask, Mr. Murray, you've wasted a walk. None of us would ken anything of the goings on up yonder.'

'The weavers up the town thought you might have had something to do with it,' Murray tried.

'Oh, did they?' Joe caught the eye of first Richie, then of the man on the bench. There came a stirring from behind the recess bed curtain, and Mrs. Farquhar hurried to pull it back. A dark head, tousled and angry, looked out.

'The fellows up the hill would have more reason to do down yon lawyer than anyone down this end,' stated the stranger. 'We have enough to worry about. My son died at sea this week, did you no ken? We have no fisherman, and no boat.'

'Hush, Donald, the gentleman said he was sorry,' said Mrs. Farquhar, straightening the now visible bedclothes.

'Stop fussing, woman! What's this man here for, anyway?'

Joe, deferring for the moment to his host, nodded at Murray.

'What are you doing here?'

Murray cleared his throat and tried his best to look conciliatory.

'I'm sorry to bother you about this, but it's about your daughter Chrissie.'

In less time than it took to think, the man was out of bed. He flung himself across the kitchen, and dealt Murray a heavy blow on the chest. The wind knocked out of him, Murray sagged back against the door, while Richie and Mrs. Farquhar dragged the man back, panting.

'She's no daughter of mine!' cried Farquhar, leaning heavily on his wife. Out of the bed, he was small, with thin legs but a mighty chest, a minotaur scaled down to a recess bed. 'She left us for that pork-eating villain!' He seized his back with both hands, and let his wife lay him back on his bed.

'He hurt his back, four seasons ago,' Joe explained. 'That's why he canna go out on the boats. And now, as he says, he has no boat to go out on. James here is a bit young yet to feed the whole family, aren't you, lad?' He tapped the eldest of the children on the shoulder and puffed smoke in his face. 'They have enough mouths to feed here without Chrissie as well. She went back to her husband.'

'I'm afraid she didn't,' said Murray. 'She has not appeared there.'

Joe, for a moment, seemed disposed to disbelieve him, then changed his mind.

'She's no back?'

'No. When did she leave here?'

'She left on ... When was it, Margit?'

Mrs. Farquhar thought.

'It was the morning Hugh left. He took her back before you all went out.'

'Are you sure?' Murray asked quickly.

'Aye,' said Mrs. Farquhar. 'She packed her few things, and he took her off.'

'Well, he can't have taken her home.'

'Maybe he just took her a bit of the way?'

'He was gone an hour or more, Joe,' said Mrs. Farquhar. 'Where else would he have gone?'

'We'll have to organise a search,' said Joe, his face serious.

'We'll have to hurry. It's almost dark, and it's going to snow,' said Murray. 'I'll go back up and tell Lord Scoggie.'

'Aye, he'll help,' agreed Joe, sure of the laird's position in his world.

'I'll go along to our place and get some help,' said the young man on the bench. He shifted himself to his feet. 'Mr. Murray, are you ready to go?'

'Come on, then.' Murray opened the door, and looked back in time to see the young man lift a pair of crutches from against the wall. He manoeuvred himself to the door, skipping neatly around the children with a smile, and led Murray out on to the street.

Outside, the snow had begun, steady white streamers drawing the colour out of the street and the sea. The young man began to swing himself along, back the way Murray had come.

'I don't know your name,' said Murray, catching up with him in a couple of strides.

'Tom Baillie. I'm Joe's brother.'

'You use your crutches very ably. Is your injury an old one?'

Tom glanced at him, his eyebrows already white with snow.

'You'll ken Major Keyes?'

'Oh.' Murray understood. 'So what were you doing at the Castle last night?'

There was a sharp breath, somewhere between a gasp and a laugh.

'Do you think I killed Mr. Tibo?'

'I don't know. All I know is that you were seen there.'

'Oh, aye.' He swung on, but at the foot of the inland road, he stopped. 'Your way lies up there, and mine lies ahead.' He looked about him, watching the snow fall, then shivered. 'I was just there with a letter, that's all.'

'A letter? For whom?'

'For Major Keyes. I little thought, when he wrecked my leg, that I would end up running messenger for him.'

'Who wrote the letter, Tom?'

Tom smiled.

'Oh, aye, that would be telling!'

'Was it from someone down here? Or from someone up the town? Please tell me, Tom: it's very important.'

'It's no very important for me.' He turned away, then looked back. 'No, that's not really true. If it hadn't been important for me, I wouldn't have been hirpling up there after dark to take it. But it was from a friend of mine, and I had already left it late, so up I went.'

'Late? How late?'

'Later than I should have.' Tom was as obstinate as his brother. 'Now, away with you, Mr. Murray. We have a missing woman to find.'

It was the only thing which would have driven him home so quickly at that moment. The snow was teasing, heavy and light, sweeping carelessly along on the wind. If Chrissie Farquhar was out in it, she could be in serious trouble.

Slithering, clutching his stick as a support more than

a weapon, he climbed the hill back to the Castle. The sandstone walls were outlined in white, the scrub by the side of the road instantly remarkable. In the uneasy wind, the fir trees at the end of the dark grey lake made hapless remonstrations with their snow-laden branches. Suddenly the Castle seemed appealing again: as the sky darkened, he saw lights shine out from the narrow windows, the library, and Beatrix's room, and Lord Scoggie's own chamber. He made good time along the drive, on the relative flat, and in a moment was indoors, shaking the snow from his boots and coat.

He hurried into the library. To his surprise, Lord Scoggie was not there: instead, Lady Scoggie and Major Keyes were sitting by an unusually healthy fire. On the lower library table, the family papers he had been working on – quite some time ago, it seemed – had been moved aside, he noticed, and wondered what they had been looking at.

'Good evening, Mr. Murray. I hope you have not been out in the snow,' said Lady Scoggie. He was about to open his mouth to reply, but then he looked at her. It was extraordinary. She seemed to be aging visibly just at the moment – since Major Keyes' arrival, he suddenly thought. Beside her on the little table was a glass of what looked like brandy. As he stood staring at her, she lifted it, hands shaking, and took a large sip.

'Ah, um, I was looking for Lord Scoggie,' he managed to say at last. 'Is he about, do you know, my lady?'

She did not reply. Distantly, he heard, he thought, wheels on the gravel outside.

'Ah, I think he is upstairs. In his chamber,' said Major Keyes.

The door bell rang. As if he had been waiting for it, Naismyth's steps could be heard crossing the hall.

'In his chamber ... is someone coming for supper?' Murray asked.

'What?' Lady Scoggie jumped.

'Is someone expected for supper?' He could hear voices in the hall, but he had closed the door when he came in. In a moment, they had passed by, and in another, Naismyth was at the library door.

'My lady: the first guests have arrived for the dinner.'

'The what?' Lady Scoggie stared at him.

'The dinner, my lady. In honour of –' He jerked his head, as if he had spotted a likely worm. 'In honour of Major Keyes, my lady.'

'Tonight?' She leapt up with a little shriek. 'Not tonight?'

'Well, yes, my lady.'

She looked as if she was about to swoon. Keyes, Naismyth and Murray froze for a long second, ready to catch her. But she shook her head sharply.

'Is anything ready? Anything at all?'

'Why, yes, my lady,' said Naismyth, surprised. 'Mrs. Costane has been working hard all day. The staff are quite prepared.'

'Good, good,' she said faintly. 'And the family?'

'Lord Scoggie is ready in the drawing room. Miss Beatrix, I believe, is on her way down. Grisell has been waiting for you in your chamber, I think, my lady.'

'Oh, my goodness! Why did no one tell me?'

'Well, no one told me, either,' said Major Keyes, trying to seem humorous. 'Come along, cousin: a comb through your hair and a fresh shawl, and you'll do very well.' He rose and tugged her arm gently. 'We shall all be fine in a moment.' He led her out into the hall and towards the staircase. 'Come along, Murray: you'll need to look your best, too.'

The door bell rang again, and Naismyth hurried away. Murray and the others hurried upstairs, and in an extraordinarily short time they reappeared, brushed and washed, and in best dinner clothes. Keyes was in uniform, his buttons apparently already polished by Naismyth. Beatrix and Deborah, looking breathless, were already there, talking to the minister and a rather grand family from Elie, who had been the first guests to arrive. Beatrix broke away and came to greet Murray.

'Had you any idea about this?' she asked in a whisper.

'Not the least. Had you?'

'I thought we had cancelled it. The snow, and everything, and poor Mr. Tibo ... It must have been a dreadful shock for Lady Scoggie. She looks as if she has seen a ghost.'

'I know. Is she all right, do you know?'

Beatrix shrugged, but her forehead wrinkled with worry. Then, as if by a miracle, it cleared.

'Mr. and Mrs. Philip Bootham,' announced Naismyth from the drawing room door.

There were around twenty guests altogether, fewer than expected because of the snow. When they had all gathered and warmed themselves with sweet negus, Lady Scoggie, so brittle looking it seemed they could hear her bones rattle, led her guests down to the Great Hall, and saw them arranged around the table. A good fire had been lit, at which Lord Scoggie frowned. Murray, finding himself near his lordship's end of the table, suddenly remembered Chrissie Farquhar, but for the moment he could say nothing. They stood for Lord Scoggie's grace.

He kept it mercifully short, and with a rough scrape of chairs on the stone floor, they sat. Major Keyes seemed to glow in his scarlet by Lady Scoggie's side, ready to perform his show of hero for another audience. Lady Scoggie rang the little bell by her place, and the servants,

Naismyth, Andrew and Grisell, entered with the soup. The conversation lapsed a little in appreciation. Lady Scoggie glanced down the table as Naismyth removed the lid of the tureen in front of Lord Scoggie, and Andrew stepped forward with the dishes. Then she leapt from her seat, and screamed.

'This is your doing!' she shrieked down the table to where Philip Bootham was sitting, hair shining innocently. 'What is he doing here?'

Her shawl fell forgotten to the floor. Her outflung arm pointed unwavering, straight at Andrew.

CHAPTER EIGHTEEN

'I must confess, I have very little idea what you are talking about.'

Bootham spoke into the tingling silence with clarity and calm. Mrs. Bootham gave a little laugh, more nervous than amused, Murray thought. The eminent guests, the cream of the East Neuk of Fife, shuffled, but held their peace. At the end of the table, Lord Scoggie sat and stared, open-mouthed, at his wife.

Deborah was the first to move.

'I'm afraid my mother has not been well lately: she has been under a great deal of strain.' She hurried to Lady Scoggie's side. 'Mother, will you not sit down? Take a glass of wine.' She pulled at her mother's arm, but Lady Scoggie seemed fixed in place. She was still staring at Andrew.

'Where have you come from? Where did he find

you?'

Andrew was completely confused, and probably more conscious of Grisell's questioning stare than of anything else. He had the presence of mind to set down the soup plates, and bowed, less self-assured than Murray had ever seen him.

'My last place was Kirkcaldy, my lady. I started here a couple of weeks ago.'

'You have been in my house all this time?' She sounded faint. 'But what is your name? Who are your – your parents?'

'Mother.' Deborah tried again to pull her away. She looked to Beatrix for her usual support, but Beatrix only had eyes for Philip Bootham. 'Bea!' she muttered, but there was no response.

'My father is Geordie Kinkell, a weaver in the village,' said Andrew obediently. Deborah looked astonished.

'I knew it,' said her mother. 'You have brought this about!' She glowered again at Philip Bootham, who was regarding Andrew with curiosity.

'*He's* the one?' he asked. 'But I thought –'

'I think, perhaps, my dear, it would be most considerate to our guests to discuss this later.' Lord Scoggie had finally found something to say, though he still looked confused. Murray looked at him more closely.

There was more than that: there was a strain about him, as if he was waiting for something long expected.

'Come along, Mother: perhaps you had better lie down for a little.' Deborah tugged and tugged at her mother's arm, and finally pulled her towards the door. But Lady Arlingtoun, the most prestigious female guest, was up before she could reach it, and the gentlemen stood hurriedly in respect.

'It is clear that Lady Scoggie is much distressed,' she said with the authority that comes from making a good marriage. 'We shall, of course, make our departure as soon as our carriages can be brought.'

No other guest had any choice but to follow her example, even though one or two had begun to look as if they were enjoying the spectacle. In a remarkably short time, the guests had made some kind of farewell to their hosts and hurried out into the hall, where Naismyth and Grisell helped them into the cloaks they had so recently shed. Lady Scoggie shook Deborah off and sagged into her chair. The Boothams remained, as if they had been forgotten in the rush. Murray, sadly, glanced at the soup tureen still in front of Lord Scoggie. He was starving.

Deborah glared at the Boothams, and sank into an empty seat near her mother.

'Well, that will go down well in local society,' she remarked acidly. Major Keyes, who had managed to stay silent throughout, gave a wry chuckle.

'Would you like to explain, my lady, what caused

you to – to do as you did?' asked Lord Scoggie, formally, still at his own end of the table. Lady Scoggie, not meeting his eye, mumbled something. If the artist who had painted her portrait that hung above her had left a faint sketch of his work, an outline of bone and skin, it would have seemed more like her now than the portrait. 'What did you say, my dear?'

'I said,' she seemed to gather herself in, 'I had an – association.'

If the great vaulted ceiling had fallen in, still no one would have moved.

'With him,' she added. 'But he wasn't called Bootham then, were you?'

Mrs. Bootham gave a little scream, and ran out of the room.

'Was this – after we were married, my lady?' He seemed to have been on the point of saying 'my dear', but it stuck at the last moment.

'Yes.' Lady Scoggie's voice was faint again.

'What do you have to say to this, Mr. Bootham?' Lord Scoggie turned to his guest.

'I'm not sure what I have to say, my lord. Only that it is quite true.'

Deborah gasped, looking quickly from his cool face to her mother and back again, then, suddenly, to her hands clenched on the table. Murray, looking at her, was making the same calculation, he thought. Did she look like her mother? Did she look like Bootham? He had never thought of her looking like anyone but Lord Scoggie. He looked away, wondering, and his eye fell on Andrew, lingering uncertainly by the sideboard.

Andrew. Andrew with the golden hair.

Murray looked again at Bootham along the table from him. He was almost sure he was right, but how could that be?

'I was intrigued to find that I had a daughter,' added Bootham, looking at Deborah. 'Though you seem – you are not what I expected.'

'I should ask you to leave my house for such a remark,' said Lord Scoggie, 'but that I want to find out as much about this as I can.' He sounded very tired. 'My dear, tell me: is Deborah his child?'

'No, she is not.' Lady Scoggie spoke with great emphasis. Bootham raised his eyebrows. Lord Scoggie's shoulders relaxed a little, and Deborah looked up, an instant of hope in her eyes. 'But that boy is.'

Andrew stepped forward from the shadows. The confusion on his face was mirrored by that in Bootham's: the likeness was very striking.

'But I'm the son of Geordie Kinkell,' said Andrew. 'My lady,' he added, forgetting.

'No, you aren't,' said Lady Scoggie.

'How intriguing!' Bootham remarked. 'This servant is our son? You *exchanged* the babies? Why? It's like something from a fairy tale.'

'I did it for you.' But Lady Scoggie was not looking at Bootham: her eyes were fixed on her husband.

'I'm afraid I fail to understand, my dear.'

'I did it because I gave birth to a son. I could not have you wrongly thinking it was yours, your first-born son. How could you bear it if you ever found out? But a daughter – that would not matter so much. And the Kinkells ... needed a healthy son, after poor Peter.'

'And Henry and Robert?' Lord Scoggie asked, with great gentleness.

'On my honour, they are yours. I never made the same mistake again.' She looked with venom at Bootham. Lord Scoggie sat back, gaze thoughtfully on the table.

'I must say,' Bootham said, 'I'm delighted you're all taking this so well. I know it's difficult for people brought up in provincial life to react without unseemly emotion to news of this kind. I do hate displays of deep emotion.'

No one answered him. The air was thick with deep emotion, Murray thought: the man would have to have the sensitivity of lead not to notice. Even the family portraits, tacked to the high walls, seemed to watch tensely.

Deborah sprang from her chair and made a little

dash for the fire, where she stood with her back to them, rubbing her hands together.

'Am I the Kinkells' child, then?'

Major Keyes could not take his eyes off her. He had the hooded, watchful look of an officer who suspects that the enemy has somehow got round behind him. Lady Scoggie had found her shawl again and had wound it about her shoulders, arms clamped across her thin chest.

'You are, my dear.'

'Who knows about this?'

'Apart from us? Only Geordie Kinkell and his wife.'

'I think you're wrong,' said Deborah, still facing the fire as though her only strength came from the leaping flames. 'I think Mr. Tibo knew.'

'What are you talking about, my dear?' asked Lord Scoggie, who had been regarding her with raised eyebrows for some time. She did not look round.

'Last night, he told me he had found out something – about me, something he thought I should know, but it had to be told me in confidence. We arranged to meet outside, near the lake, between supper and the ball.' Murray could see her shaking. 'I went out, but I never found him.'

'Impossible,' muttered Lady Scoggie.

'Well, what was he going to tell me, then, *Lady*

Scoggie?' She spun to spit the words at the woman she had thought was her mother. 'What else could he have known about me, that I wouldn't know, that he would have to tell me in secret?'

'I think we should move to the parlour,' said Lord Scoggie suddenly. 'The smell of this soup is beginning to make me feel ill.' He stood up. 'Mr. Murray, will you be kind enough to go and apologise to Mrs. Costane for the ruination of her good dinner? Andrew, I think you had better come with us.'

Relieved as well as disappointed, Murray slipped out of the hall ahead of the family and darted down the passage to the kitchens. Halfway down he stopped, and leaned against the cool wall, breathing deeply. Tibo had a secret to impart to Deborah, but he was killed before he could talk to her. Was this the secret? If so, his killer must be kicking himself now. If not, what was it? It was the only good reason he had yet heard for Tibo being the intended victim of the murder. But who then was the murderer? He caught his breath. The most likely person, from the point of view of motive, had to be Lady Scoggie, the one person who had also really embraced the idea that Major Keyes was the intended victim. Could Lady Scoggie really have done it? To defend her reputation, her marriage, her children?

He had no idea where she had gone after she and Lord Scoggie had left the barn – in fact, had she left before her husband, while Lord Scoggie lingered to make sure that Murray could deal with Sandy Kinkell?

Oh, Lord, Sandy Kinkell!

Where was Chrissie?

He glanced out through the nearest window. The snow outside was falling thickly, silently. What hope did they have of finding her, and if they did, what state would she be in? He would have to try to tell Lord Scoggie, anyway, and see if anything could be done: it was not to be his choice.

He pushed himself away from the wall, and hurried on down the passage to the kitchens. He could hear the unusual quiet before he pulled open the door. Inside, Mrs. Costane, Hannah, Naismyth and Grisell sat round the table at which they usually ate, picking with their fingers at some particularly fine-looking food. His stomach lurched with hunger.

Mrs. Costane looked round, and everyone watched him as he walked towards them. He took a place on the bench beside Hannah, and pulled off a chicken leg, taking a large bite before looking at any of them.

'What's happening?' asked Mrs. Costane at last, unable to wait any longer.

'Lord Scoggie has asked me to apologise for the dinner being spoiled. This is delicious.'

'Oh, help yourself,' she said, sarcastically. 'There's more than we could eat, even if we had the appetite.'

'Thank you.' He pulled a plate towards himself, and

heaped it with fish in mushroom sauce. 'Wonderful.'

The others watched him as he ate, as if his appetite was something not quite morally proper.

'What's happening upstairs?' Mrs. Costane asked again when he had cleared the plate.

'Um.' Murray had been wondering what he should say, but the word would get out to the servants anyway, even if they persuaded Andrew not to talk. It would be better to get the story straight. 'Lady Scoggie had a child by Philip Bootham, but it's not Deborah: it's Andrew. Deborah is the daughter of Geordie Kinkell. The babies were exchanged at birth.'

'What?' The word was breathed out by all the others at once: he could not have distinguished between their voices.

'Andrew is up in the parlour with them now. Bootham is still here.'

'How is his lordship?' asked Naismyth grimly. It seemed clear whose side he would be on if the household split.

'He is quite calm at the moment. Everyone is quite calm.'

'Oh, aye, it's all right for the gentry,' said Hannah, sucking fruit cream from her fingers. 'It's no such a big thing for them.'

'Actually I think it's a huge thing for them. I think

it's devastating. But they're just managing to stay calm.'

'Aye,' said Mrs. Costane. 'Imagine what's going through Miss Deborah's head.'

They imagined it in silence. Then Grisell stumbled back over her bench and ran from the room.

'Aye, what effect is it to have on her and Andrew, that's another question,' Mrs. Costane acknowledged. She and Hannah managed to avoid looking at Naismyth, who made a huffing noise of dismissal.

'She'd be better off without the lad.'

'In the mean time,' Murray went on, finishing the mushroom sauce on some bread, 'Chrissie Kinkell is missing, and the Farquhars want us to get a search party together to look for her, and it's still snowing. I must go back to try to talk to Lord Scoggie.' He stood up, and stepped over the bench. Mrs. Costane, Hannah and Naismyth did not move, but remained much as he had found them. 'Thank you for the food.'

'Aye, you're a growing lad,' said Mrs. Costane.

He emerged from the servants' corridor again into the hall, and stopped to listen for an impression of where everyone was. For a moment there was silence, so they had moved from the Great Hall. Then he heard, or thought he heard, a sob.

He stood motionless. It came again. He thought it came from the library.

He stepped softly across the hall, and gently opened the library door.

Inside, the light was dim: only the upper half of the room, picking up light from the landing above, had colour. Down here, there were only shadows. He waited. It did not take long for one of the shadows to move.

'Who's there?' came a sharp, anxious whisper.

'It's me, Murray. Mrs. Bootham?'

She laughed, with another sob, and emerged from the darkness behind the high table. Snowlight from the windows slithered across the folds of her silk gown, and he held his breath.

'I'm not Mrs. Bootham.' He could not see her eyes, but he could feel them on him. 'My name is Jane Croft, spinster of this parish.'

'Then who is Mrs. Bootham?'

'I doubt there is one.' Her voice hardened. 'Marriage is not the kind of institution Philip would believe in. But I did believe – how could I be so innocent? – that I was his first love.'

If she had truly believed it, she certainly had been innocent. If Murray had met anyone who smacked of taking a pride in worldly experience, it was Philip Bootham. However, winged Cupid is painted blind.

'But what of your family?' he asked. 'Where are they? Did they not try to recover you?'

'My father knows where I am. You were there, I think, when I received a letter from him, addressed to my maiden name – my only true name. He believes I am here staying with a female friend, who does not exist.'

'And what would you have done as time went on?'

'I do not know!' The tears began again. 'I did not think beyond the moment! But now what am I to do? He has a child, he will be forced to acknowledge it. And everyone here will know what he has done. What am I to do?' She stepped closer to him, and he retreated, pressing himself against the library door. Candlelight from above played on her hair, hinted at the beauty of her face, the insidious power of her presence. If there had been a Bible handy, he would have grabbed it to protect himself.

'You knew nothing of this until now?'

'Nothing.'

'He never mentioned why he was so interested in Miss Deborah?'

'Never. He – he likes girls.' Murray was visited by a sudden image of him with Beatrix on his arm. His stomach turned. 'What shall I do, Mr. Murray?' she whispered. 'I need protection. My reputation ...' He felt, with alarm, her hand on his arm. He could not move. Her scent wove around him, a scent of wood and water, night and starlight. Her face turned up to his, her other hand reaching for the back of his neck, pulling him towards her.

He broke away, much, much later than he meant to,

and went to the fireplace to light a taper for the candles.

'It will do your reputation no good to be found in a darkened room with another man, Mrs. Bootham. Miss Croft. I should recommend that you go home and pack your possessions, and return to your father.'

'A strange contrast:' she gave a little laugh, 'last night I left here with him, and Mr. Tibo was alive, and the world was a different place.'

'Did he really leave with you?' He lit the last of the candles. The warm yellow light made her look a little more of this world, but he could feel, still, the pressure of her cool fingers on his neck. He tried not to look at her.

'Yes, he did.'

'And stayed at home?'

'You are not interested in me at all!' she cried. 'Will you at least see me to my carriage?'

'Certainly.' He reached over and rang the bell, and opened the library door wide, destroying their privacy before she could take advantage of it again.

'I have no idea whether or not he stayed at home,' she said quickly. 'As far as I knew he was up late writing poetry.' She invested the word with a degree of bitterness. 'He did not come to bed for several hours.' She caught his eye, but he looked away quickly, not wishing to be invited to think of her in bed.

Naismyth appeared in the doorway.

'Mrs. Bootham wishes to go home, Mr. Naismyth.'

'I shall call her carriage,' said Naismyth, bowing. He stood long enough to exchange a significant look with Murray before he went.

'Do you think he could have killed Tibo? Do you think he would have?' Murray asked, as soon as Naismyth had gone.

'I don't know!' Bootham would not have approved of her display of emotion, anyway. 'He's strong, but I have not known him to be violent. And anyway, I don't think he cares enough.' Her chin came up defiantly, and he knew she needed very little protection. She was strong. 'It means nothing to him that we are not married: I was the one who wished to be discreet about it. What would he find embarrassing about an affair that passed nearly twenty years ago?'

'Why did you come here? Whose idea was it?'

The thought had not struck her, he could see that, and it made her angry.

'It was his idea,' she said slowly. 'So all along he was expecting this to happen. He came back here to see her. Deliberately.' She met his eye, and there was nothing of seduction in it now: there was only revenge, and rage. 'I'm going back to that miserable house and I'm taking everything in it. I paid for most of it, anyway. Maybe that was all he wanted, my mother's money. And when he comes back – if he comes back – he can sleep on the doorstep, for all I care. I'm going home.'

Murray opened his mouth to reply, but was interrupted by the sound of carriage wheels on the drive outside.

'Your carriage, I believe,' he said instead.

In the hall, Naismyth was ready with her cloak and gloves. Murray handed her into the carriage and stood politely as it left. He had a feeling that he would never see her again, and it filled him with relief – and a little regret.

Naismyth closed the door, scowling, and disappeared back into the servants' corridor. Footsteps on the stairs made him turn, and he saw Bea coming to look for him.

'Who was that?' she asked.

'Mrs. Bootham. Or rather ... Bea, the Boothams are not married.'

'They aren't?'

To his dismay, all he could see in her face was a rekindled hope, none of the shock he had hoped to cause.

'Bea, he took her away from her family under false pretences, and deceived her for her money.'

'But he wouldn't do that to someone whom he really loved, who really loved him.' She had a little smile on her face, a kind he had never seen there before. He took her by the elbows, making her look into his face.

'If you went with him, he would only use you until

he tired of you. Then where would you be? What friends would you have? And would he take you, anyway? Lord Scoggie would never let your dowry go to him, not after this evening.' She did not seem to hear him. He gave her a little shake. 'Bea, you're worth more than him. Forget him. I'm sure he'll be going soon, anyway. You deserve better than that.'

'But I don't want any more than that,' she said at last. 'All I want is him. I would live with him in a ditch.'

'Bea, I think we can be fairly sure that there are no circumstances in this world in which Philip Bootham would condescend to live in a ditch.'

She pulled away.

'It's my decision, Mr. Murray. Don't make me angry with you.'

He sighed. There was no sense in pursuing it just now: there were more urgent things to think of.

'What's happening upstairs?'

'Nothing much. They're going round in circles. Lady Scoggie insists that the boys are hers and Lord Scoggie's, but Andrew is her son by Mr. Bootham. Lord Scoggie is asking her for all the details: it was when she was staying in London, just after they were married, when Lord Scoggie was up and down between London and Edinburgh. I think – I think maybe Major Keyes knew something about it. Lady Scoggie was staying with his mother at the time. Andrew was born here, though, because she came back, but Lord Scoggie was still away. Mrs. Kinkell was a maid here until just after she was married. That was how they knew about her.'

'How is Deborah?'

Beatrix shook her head, unable to describe Deborah's anguish. Then she looked up.

'Do you hear voices? Outside?'

Murray listened. He could indeed hear voices, and the crunching sound of many footsteps in the snowy gravel. He glanced out through one of the slit windows. A large crowd of men with torches was approaching the castle, looking unnervingly like a violent mob. At the front, he recognised the Kinkell brothers and Joe Baillie. With a gasp, once again he remembered the search party.

'Fetch Naismyth,' he hissed at Beatrix. 'I must run and warn Lord Scoggie.'

With a last glance at the crowd, he pushed her towards the servants' corridor and bounded up the stairs.

CHAPTER NINETEEN

Lord Scoggie left the parlour with the speed of a man looking for an excuse. Behind him, Murray could see Major Keyes, still staring at Deborah, whose face was the colour of chalk. Bootham, propped against the wall by the fireplace, looked entirely at home, and appeared to be asking Andrew some questions about his life. Lady Scoggie, a frail old woman, huddled into her shawl on a sofa.

'They're downstairs, my lord,' Murray explained, and followed Lord Scoggie down towards the servants' quarters.

'I should have asked you about this earlier,' Lord Scoggie muttered, annoyed with himself.

'I should have told you.'

'Too many things happening.'

In the kitchen, the men of both up and down town St. Monance were standing and sitting about the servants' table, eating, from cups and tankards, the wonderful asparagus soup that had been intended for higher guests than them. They straightened when Lord Scoggie came in, but the informality of the kitchen meant that several of them did not stand up until Naismyth poked them.

'Chrissie Farquhar is still missing, then,' said Lord Scoggie.

'We think they still have her,' Sandy Kinkell spat, pointing at Joe Baillie.

'We ken we don't,' said Joe Baillie, though Geordie Kinkell was already restraining his brother.

'Naismyth, will you go and rouse the gardeners and the stable lads, please. Murray, you are happy to go with them?'

'Of course, my lord.'

'And I shall go, too,' announced Major Keyes, from the kitchen door. 'I could do with some fresh air.'

'Good, good, Major. Now, I shall divide you into four groups, with fishermen and uptowners in each group, so that you can keep an eye on each other. You'll start up town. Come up and we'll look at a map of the parish.'

In the room with no name, Lord Scoggie spread a large map over the billiard table and directed operations like a general. The parallel may have occurred to him, too, for he turned to Major Keyes.

'Does this all make sense, Alec?'

'That seems grand, cousin, for all I know the land in question.'

'Is everyone else happy?' Lord Scoggie looked around the room: there was a warm smell of wet wool and asparagus breath.

'When do we do down the town?' asked Sandy, distrustfully.

'Do the up town, then come and report to me and have some breakfast. Then we'll start down town.'

'There are no so many houses up town,' Joe Baillie pointed out. 'Not if you count the salt workers' houses in with our end.'

'There are more sheds, barns and so on up here, though,' Lord Scoggie explained, indicating examples on the map. 'It's the middle of the night, so you'll wake fewer people up here for now.'

'They're all awake anyway,' said Geordie, one hand on Sandy's arm and the other drawing his son Peter back from the gun cabinets.

'Then let's keep them up no longer than we have to. Ah, Naismyth, have you brought the others?'

Naismyth, appearing at the door, nodded. Behind

him were the forces of garden and stables, and other outdoor servants, carrying unlit torches and lanterns and wrapped up against the snow.

'I have a taper ready for the lights, my lord,' he said.

'Very good. Now, your groups.'

In a few minutes he had sorted the two crowds into four mixed bands, fishermen and others, named leaders, and marked out on the map the borders of their search area. None of his decisions was disputed by anyone. One group was led by Joe Baillie, another by Richie Shaw, another by Geordie Kinkell, and the fourth, to his surprise, by Naismyth, who hurried away to find outdoor clothes. Murray and Keyes were allocated to Geordie Kinkell's group, and Murray was about to leave in the wake of Kinkell when Lord Scoggie drew him back quietly.

'Keep an eye on Major Keyes, will you? I don't want any of the fishermen ... thinking of old grudges.'

'I'll do my best, my lord.'

Lord Scoggie stood by the front door with Naismyth's taper, lighting each torch or lantern as they disappeared into the snow. By the time Murray's team was on the drive, the snow had been trampled flat and slithery, but more still fell, and they staggered close together, trying not to lose each other in the soft dark.

There then began a dreadful night. Every house had to be examined: every family roused from their sleep, every barn, loom house, shed or loft turned out as the owners shivered beside them, clutching coats over nightshirts with grey hands. Pig sheds were a bone of contention – the fishermen would not go into them, but did not trust the uptowners' accounts – until Mallie, the great butcher from down the town, finally agreed to go into each of them himself. Women pressed them to come in to the fire, to a hot drink and a moment of shelter, and in one or two places they agreed and stood, crushed and dripping, in tiny kitchens filled with pipe smoke and wide-eyed midnight children. But as the night went on, and they forgot what day and daylight looked like, or how it felt to be warm and dry, they began to avoid such encounters, to excuse themselves and press on. In between houses they searched ditches and hedges, poked their sticks under walls where the snow lay thick, held their torches for each other as they hunted amongst the roots of ancient trees, and upset sheep and cattle in the fields by chivvying them apart, in case she had hidden there for warmth. Sometimes they searched so hard they almost forgot what they were looking for, and overturned stones or peered up trees where no woman could hide. And all the time the snow fell, weighing on their eyelashes, slipping into their lungs with every breath, its irresistible, smooth descent making it look as if the world was slowly floating upwards.

When Murray finally sneaked a look at his watch by the light of a failing torch, he was surprised to find that it was six o'clock in the morning. He had lost most of the feeling in his fingers, toes and nose, and had also lost count of the number of times he had hauled Major Keyes to his feet, or foot, after a fall, but it was not that unusual: most of them had fallen once or twice. They were now on the road outside the gates of Aberardour Lodge, with only a few more houses to cover before they went to report to Lord Scoggie. They had already done the Lodge: Murray was interested to note that, according to the maid, Mrs. Bootham had packed a few personal effects and left for the inn at Elie, leaving instructions for the servants to refuse admittance to Mr. Bootham. To the marked disappointment of the maid and a manservant who lingered about the hallway, Mr. Bootham had not yet returned home to have admittance refused him: presumably he had been forced by the snow to stay at Scoggie Castle, a very welcome guest, no doubt. There was no trace of Chrissie Farquhar anywhere on the premises, even though Murray admitted to himself an unspoken longing to find something criminal about Philip Bootham.

Geordie Kinkell drew back to allow his group to search his cottage, which they did as quietly as possible out of respect to the sick woman asleep in the recess bed. Murray himself searched under the bed, taking a lantern to set beside him on the floor. There was nothing, which was hardly surprising. There was, if possible, less at his neighbour's house. The searchers gathered outside again in the road, and looked to Geordie for instructions.

'One more house to go,' Geordie said loudly, fighting the dampening snow in his face. 'Mr. Tibo's.'

'We can't search there,' said one of the fishermen. 'He's no buried yet.'

'Aye, we can.' Geordie only considered the question

for a moment. 'If she's there, and she's alive, she might be dead by the time he's buried.' There was a mumble of approval from some of the searchers.

'If we do it quiet-like, like we did in your place, Geordie,' suggested another fisherman, 'we should be in the right.'

'Aye, that's the way. On we go.' He urged the party on, but waited for Murray before falling into step with him. 'Will you talk to Mr. Tibo's brother, then?'

'Certainly,' Murray agreed, 'but why me?'

'Och, it needs someone of his own kind, ye ken? Since he's near a stranger to us, he's been away so long.'

'All right.'

There were no lights visible to the front of Nathaniel Tibo's house. The others in the group hung back while Murray climbed the few steps and rattled the risp. To judge by the snow, no one had disturbed the household for hours. In any establishment where they were not sitting up with a corpse, it would have taken much longer than these few seconds for the door to be answered. The windows on either side of the door were softly illuminated by candlelight, and the door shook as the locks were withdrawn. Then the man that Murray had seen in the carriage earlier opened the door, holding up the candle to see Murray's face.

'Who are you?' he snapped, without much sign of welcome.

'Forgive us for disturbing you, please,' said Murray, assuming a look that he hoped indicated worthy anxiety and polite respectability. 'We are looking for a missing woman. We're searching the whole parish, and we hoped you might give us your permission to search here. Indoors and out,' he added.

The dim candlelit circle had brushed the edge of the group of villagers behind him, and the man looked suspicious.

'Please allow me to introduce myself,' Murray added quickly. 'My name is Murray, and I am Lord Scoggie's private secretary. We are searching on his orders.'

'Oh aye?' said the man. 'And who's the missing woman? No his daughter?'

'No!' Murray was surprised. 'Her name is Chrissie Farquhar –'

'Hugh's sister?'

Murray had forgotten that this man must also have grown up in the village.

'That's the one, yes. She's been missing a few days, but no one realised till yesterday evening, so it's very urgent.'

The man considered.

'Aye, indeed,' he said in the end. 'Yes, your men may search where they will. You –' he jerked the candle at

Murray, 'come in and tell me why Chrissie Farquhar could go missing for a few days and no one notice – for if it's the same Chrissie Farquhar I remember, she's hard to miss.'

Murray looked back at Geordie, who nodded, with a wry smile. He led his men off to the back of the house. The snow was easing, and Murray watched them go, before he stepped into the hallway.

'You're soaking,' the man remarked. 'How long have you been out?'

'Since last night. And we've only done the up side of the village.'

'The weather has been devilish.' He led the way towards the back of the house. 'Do you mind sitting in with my brother? It's the only warm room in the house.'

'Ah ... no.'

In the main bedchamber, the air was so thick that walking in was like being smothered with a hot pillow. Nathaniel Tibo had been laid out smoothly on the bed and covered to the chin with a sheet, in a manner which would have satisfied even him. His brother was not up to the same sartorial standard. His cravat had been untied and his collar was loose, his coat flung on a chair and the top few buttons of his waistcoat were undone. His hair, dark with threads of the grey that had distinguished his brother, was tousled, and his face, though bearing a clear resemblance to Nathaniel, was at once less handsome and more approachable. He was closer to Murray's age, but a little older. There was a decanter of brandy on a table by the fire. Zachariah Tibo set the candlestick down beside the bed, and poured a glass for each of them: it was not his first.

'So tell me about Chrissie,' he said, handing a glass to Murray and nodding him into a chair nearby. Murray gave a quick account of Chrissie's injudicious marriage and her subsequent disappearance, and Lord Scoggie's part in the negotiations to return her to her family. Zachariah gave a dry laugh at the end of the story.

'So Hugh was the last to see her: what does he have to say about her?'

'Hugh was lost at sea during a storm a few days ago. The up town men think he hid Chrissie before he left for the fishing, but the down town men think she had been freed and either she is hiding up town to discredit them, or something else has happened to her. Mind you, I couldn't fault anyone's work last night. We must have searched every inch of the upper parish.'

'And now it's down town?'

'That's right.' Now that he was warming up, his toes were beginning to hurt, and he jiggled them inside his boots. 'After we've reported to Lord Scoggie.'

'So he's not out hunting?' Zachariah looked unsurprised.

'After your brother's murder, we've been careful about guarding the Castle,' Murray said defensively. 'The servants are all out with us, but he has stayed at home with the ladies.' And with Andrew and Philip Bootham, he added to himself. 'Even Major Keyes, who only has one leg, has come out with us.'

'Major Keyes? The hero of Seringapatam?'

'That's the one.'

'And the hero of the fight with Tom Baillie?' Zachariah added, with much more sarcasm.

'I believe so,' Murray agreed.

'Aye, I remember. I was here then myself. He made a real mess of Tom Baillie, you ken. He lost all control.'

'So I hear. But he seems to have mellowed over the years. He's to be engaged – ' he broke off. Would Major Keyes still wish to marry the daughter of the Kinkell household, rather than Miss Deborah Scoggie?

'Engaged? I don't envy the lady,' said Zachariah. 'Have more brandy. You look as if you need it.'

They sat for a moment in silence, looking into the fire.

'I was sorry about your brother,' Murray said at last. 'I hope we shall find his killer and bring him to justice.'

'Aye, well.' Zachariah wiped brandy from his mouth. 'It wouldn't have suited him to die in an untidy way. Appearance was important to him.'

'You didn't see the same way on things?' Murray

asked, thinking of his own brother.

'Ha! No, not really.' He leaned forward in his chair, and glanced back at the bed. 'Och, we got along well enough, I suppose. But I wanted to practise real law, to have different clients, that wanted different things. All he wanted was to be Lord Scoggie's toady, following in the great family tradition of Tibos through the ages ... It wasn't my idea of a life.'

'He seemed to be doing well enough out of it,' Murray remarked.

'Oh, aye, his lordship's trusted companion, writing out his best law hand, making up the numbers for grand dinners at the Castle, keeping his hands clean – and that gave poor wee Cocky Leckie a neat wee job – and set up to marry his lordship's daughter. He was doing very well out of it.'

'Oh, he told you about Deborah Scoggie, did he?' Murray asked, trying not to look surprised.

'Oh, aye. He seemed to think Major Keyes might be a rival, but not a serious one.' He gave Murray a quizzical look. 'Was he right?'

'Hard to say,' said Murray, blandly. 'Miss Deborah does not confide in me.'

'Of course, I only ever had Nathaniel's word on all these things.' Zachariah poured more brandy. 'A careful man would look out the evidence for the other side of the case, before making rash statements.' Regardless of the brandy, there was something about Zachariah that marked him out as a careful man. Murray tried to be as careful himself.

'I wondered if Nathaniel had ever mentioned any enemies to you?'

'Of course I've wondered that myself.' Zachariah spun the brandy in his glass, frowning into it. 'I could not remember anything. But I did wonder ...' he studied Murray instead for a moment, looking as if he wished he could stir him up like the brandy, see him from all angles. 'I wondered about Cocky Leckie's death. The two of them, in such a short time. Could it have something to do with my brother's apparently gentle work?'

'You said Cocky did his rougher work for him?'

'That's right. Not that there was anything very rough, but Cocky had an easier way with the villagers. I'll wager there were more people at Cocky's funeral than there will ever be at Nathaniel's.'

Murray gave a sharp sigh.

'But Cocky's death was definitely an accident. I was there.'

'Oh, of course you were. My brother mentioned you.'

'Did he?' Murray was unable to suppress curiosity. Zachariah grinned.

'Aye. You're the Master of Arts, aren't you?

Nathaniel didn't like you getting between him and Lord Scoggie.'

'Me? Good heavens.' As far as Murray was concerned, Tibo had always been closer to Lord Scoggie than he had. It was not something that had much bothered him.

'But you'll be pleased to know that he dismissed you as a rival for Miss Deborah,' Zachariah added.

'Well, he was right there,' Murray agreed, thinking briefly of Beatrix.

'But I still wonder about Cocky Leckie's death. My brother was his sole executor, you ken. He cleared out his cottage. What if he found something he wasna supposed to?'

'What like?'

'I don't know. See, I've been sitting here on my own all night, thinking about it, and it's the only thing I can think of that was different in my brother's life these last few weeks. His clerk died suddenly, then he did.'

It was certainly compelling.

'Did your brother still have the things he took from Cocky's cottage?' he asked.

'Aye, I think so. They're in his office yonder.' Zachariah stopped, then asked abruptly: 'Are you really interested in this, or have I just latched myself on to a good listener?'

Murray blinked.

'Lord Scoggie is keen for me to look into your brother's murder.'

'Lord Scoggie? Why? Are you any good at it?' Zachariah set his glass down. 'I'm sorry, that was not the right thing to say. I could never manage Nathaniel's elegance of speech. I mean, does he think you'll find the murderer? It's only that – well, I wonder if Lord Scoggie kens more about the matter than he's letting on.'

'You think Lord Scoggie had something to do with your brother's murder?' Murray shook his head. 'No, no. Surely not.' But he could not help remembering the time it took for Naismyth to fetch Lord Scoggie when the body was found. Why had it been so difficult to rouse him? What had Lord Scoggie been doing?

'I think we should look at Cocky's things.' Zachariah stood up, and looked over at the bed. 'I suppose we shouldn't leave him alone. You stay there, and I'll fetch them over. There's not much.' He left the door open and hurried off with the candlestick again, leaving Murray in a pleasant draught. Murray could hear him shifting things in the office at the front of the house, the other side of the hallway from the dining room in which he had spoken to Lady Scoggie. He was back in a few minutes, with the candle perched hazardously on top of a small deedbox. Murray was reminded of Lord Scoggie's family papers, and leapt up to seize the candlestick.

'I think my brother put them into this,' said

Zachariah, balancing the deedbox on the table by the fire. 'Cocky was a grand wee fellow, but I don't think he was the deedbox kind.' He fiddled with the lock, then reached for his discarded coat and felt in the pockets for a bunch of keys. He tried one or two of the smaller ones, and found one that worked. The box opened easily.

'Pensions ...' said Zachariah, pulling out the first couple of papers and glancing through them. 'Old servants still living nearby. This is the kind of thing Nathaniel would pass on to Cocky: no chance of him dirtying the seat of his breeches in some hovel. In his defence, of course, the pensioners would rather have a yarn with Cocky than stand on ceremony for him.'

'That's defence, is it?' said Murray with a grin.

'Aye.' Zachariah gave a nod of apology towards the bed. 'Och, it's not his fault he didna have the common touch. It's something you're born with: I don't think you can grow it on after.'

Murray wondered if he had it himself. He took a handful of papers out of the box and began to go through them. Zachariah was right: it was mostly pensions, for elderly villagers who had once worked at the Castle and were now past their time. One bundle, tied with string, seemed to encompass those who had died and gone beyond the reach of Lord Scoggie's charity: Murray recognised the family names, but not the individuals, and the dates of death were scrawled across the front of the folded papers.

'I cannot see how this is very useful,' said Zachariah, flinging his own handful of papers back into the box and sitting back in his chair.

'Would your brother have given all this work to Cocky?'

'Why, do you think it's a lot?'

'That's not what I mean.' Murray checked another document: a pension to a stableman with a broken leg. Lord Scoggie, as always, met his responsibilities. 'I mean, would any of it have come from anywhere else? Would Lord Scoggie, for instance, have bypassed Nathaniel for any reason, and given work straight to Cocky?'

A sly smile passed over Zachariah's face.

'That wouldn't have pleased my big brother, I can tell you.'

'Well, insulting your brother might not have been the intention, of course,' said Murray. 'I think Lord Scoggie really did hold him in high esteem. What if there was something he did not want him to know?' He flicked through a few more papers. Here was Mrs. Kinkell's pension, the one he himself had delivered the other day – yesterday. He opened up the papers to make sure he was right.

'Do you know something?' asked Zachariah, with the air of a born gossip. 'What has his lordship been up to?'

'Oh, I couldn't possibly tell you,' said Murray with another grin. Flat denial never worked with gossips. He looked through the pension contract for Mrs. Kinkell. It had been instituted eighteen years ago, in 1786. The words 'faithful servant' and 'loyal service' were standard for all the contracts, and the sum of money was the same as the one Murray had delivered yesterday. He wondered if he would be expected to take on all Cocky's customers for Lord Scoggie. Certainly a job for which a Master of Arts degree was essential. 'No, you're right. These are all pensioners. I can't see that it tells us anything.'

There was the sound of footsteps in the hall, and in a minute the door was tapped. It was Major Keyes.

'Just come to say we've finished our search here. Good evening, sir,' he added, and Murray introduced Zachariah to him. 'Nothing,' he added to Murray.

'Well, we didn't expect it, did we?' Murray set down his brandy glass. 'We must go now: Geordie will be eager to be off for his breakfast.'

'Geordie Kinkell?' asked Zachariah.

'That's right: he's leading our party of searchers.'

'A grand man,' said Zachariah. 'His wife was quite a charmer in her day. Is she still about?'

'She's not long for this world, I'm afraid,' said Murray, not meeting Keyes' eye. The Kinkells seemed to be becoming very prominent locally, all of a sudden.

'Aye, that's the way of things. Ten years ago, when I was sixteen or so, I could think of nothing but finding a woman like her. Well,' he pulled himself out of his chair, 'I shan't hold you back any longer. Thank you for your company, Murray.'

'We shall be at the funeral, of course,' said Murray, nodding towards the bed.

'Oh, aye. Tomorrow,' he said. Keyes looked round the door at the bed, and jumped.

'Forgive me, Mr. Tibo: I had my mind on other things.' He quickly paid his respects to the corpse, while Zachariah looked him up and down curiously, taking in the wooden leg and the inevitable presence of Tippoo the dog.

'We'd better go,' said Murray again. He led the way to the front door, and they made their farewells.

Outside the snow had stopped, and the dawn leaked apricot light across the world, smoothing it like silk. Lone thorns that had been huddled against the prevailing wind were now bolsters on the soft white pillows of the stone boundary walls. Sheep, nosing out the grass as best they could, looked dirty yellow in the pure white of their fields. The furrows, recently sown in the next field, were flat and even now, with no sign of the ploughman's passing. They followed their own shallow footprints back down to the gate, and turned uphill towards the Castle, and breakfast.

Even as they stepped through the front door, the castle had the air of an uneasy night. From the noise coming from the Great Hall, they could tell that they were not the first party back, and indeed when they had shed their outdoor clothes and gone in, Murray guessed from the numbers that they were the last party. For once the great table was full, and Lord Scoggie sat gloriously at its head, overseeing the breakfast of his guests. He saw Murray and Geordie Kinkell enter the hall, and beckoned them up to him.

'Any luck?' he asked, though he could already tell from their expressions. 'Well, we'll sort out a procedure for the lower town after you've all eaten. There's plenty: help yourselves.'

Murray led Geordie over to the sideboard and helped him to slices of beef and eggs: he noticed that neither fish nor pork was available. They returned to the table and found spaces side by side on two chairs brought in from the sides of the hall to seat the extra numbers.

'You'll be coming with us on the next search, then?' Murray asked.

'Oh, aye,' said Geordie. 'You ken I dinna trust the fishermen. Though last night went as well as it could, I thought.'

'I wonder which part we'll get.'

'Whatever it is, I want to call in on my wife first. See her settled. I wish I could leave Peter with her, too: I feel he's slowing us down, but my wife's not up to him.'

He nodded over to where Peter was crouched near the fireplace, tempting Tippoo with a slice of beef.

'I'm sure no one will mind if you go and see her.' He paused to eat an egg. 'Mr. Tibo's brother was sorry to hear she was ill.'

Geordie laughed.

'Oh, aye? He had a bit of fondness for her, I reckon, when he was a lad! I'll tell her. It'll make her smile.' He laughed again. 'She was a beautiful woman, though she could have been his mother, she was that age. Oh, I was lucky to get her.' Smiling, he seized bread and coffee as they passed from hand to hand round the table. Murray left it at that, but in the doziness brought on by food and warmth, he dreamed a little of Geordie Kinkell's lovely wife, a young mother, the mother, indeed, of the much-admired Deborah. A lovely woman as late as ten years ago ... eight years after her pension was granted to her.

All the other recipients of Lord Scoggie's pensions had been elderly or infirm, the stableman with the broken leg, or old Hunter, Naismyth's predecessor, hunched with age, or Mistress Farquhar, Hugh's aunt, who had been lady's maid to Lord Scoggie's grandmother and was widely believed to be over a hundred years old. Why had he granted a pension to a young woman making a decent marriage? It seemed overly generous. Could it have something to do with Deborah and Andrew? But the pension was from Lord Scoggie. Could he have known about the children all along?

Breakfast was drawing to a close, and Lord Scoggie indicated to the villagers that they might have a pipe where they were sitting, in the warm Great Hall. Murray thought he might take the opportunity to see how the boys were, but as he left the hall, Lord Scoggie hurried to join him.

'Going up to the schoolroom?' he asked. 'I'll come too. I haven't seen the boys this morning.'

Murray nodded, but he was not pleased. He wanted to see the boys on equal terms, not with Lord Scoggie's presence forcing courtesy on them – and indeed on him. For one thing, he did not know if they had been told the news about Deborah, or whether they were to be kept in ignorance. How would they feel about acquiring an older brother?

The boys were already in the schoolroom, and so, to the surprise of Murray, at least, was Lady Scoggie. The only time he had seen there before was when she had come to make sure he was doing his job properly, but this time he had a feeling that schoolwork was the last thing on her mind. She was in a low armchair, with her arms tightly round both boys, and had clearly been crying. The boys turned as the door opened: Henry looked upset, Robert merely puzzled. Their mother was not really the hugging kind.

When they saw who it was, they broke away from her and went to say good morning to their father, followed by some kind of courtesy to Murray. He looked at them carefully as they bowed to him: he was sure no one had told them what had happened at the abortive dinner last night.

'What have you said to them, my dear?' asked Lord Scoggie, not managing to look at his wife.

'Nothing. I was about to tell them –'

'You aren't thinking of leaving, are you?' Lord Scoggie spoke quickly. 'Please don't leave.'

'Leave?' Henry was thunderstruck. 'Mother, why would you leave?'

'Is it charity work?' asked Robert. Murray felt like boxing his ears. Robert was about as sensitive as the schoolroom table.

'I don't see what else I can do,' said Lady Scoggie. Her face was empty.

'Leaving with him?' Lord Scoggie cocked his head, presumably indicating Philip Bootham's position in some guest bedchamber.

'No!' She was shocked. 'That is not a mistake I would make twice. I promise you, my lord ...' She looked desperately at the boys. Lord Scoggie nodded impatiently. It was easier for him to accept her word that the boys were his sons than it was for her to feel worthy of belief. The boys looked bewildered. Murray wondered if he should take them quietly out of the room, or whether he should go himself. This was not his family.

Was this what had made a pretty, fashionable woman turn to charitable works and a shabby, dated appearance? He thought he saw, suddenly, how she had devoted herself to the needy and turned herself away from her family, the guilt that had driven her through all the years. What a contrast with Philip Bootham, he thought. Any implications of guilt seemed to slide off his smooth golden hair, though he knew and acknowledged what he had done. He would walk away from Jane Croft, too, with no regrets. He looked again at Lady Scoggie, nearly as ill as Mrs. Kinkell, nearly as thin. One of them eaten away, and one untouched. It seemed so unfair.

'You must not leave. Where would you go? It is unthinkable.' Lord Scoggie was trembling, Murray saw with shock.

'Will you tell them?'

'Tell us what?' Robert demanded.

'If I tell them – if we tell them – there is more to tell them than what you told us last night.'

'Tell us what?' Robert said loudly. Henry clutched Robert's arm, staring at his parents.

'I have told you everything, I promise,' insisted Lady Scoggie, her voice urgent.

'Not you,' said Lord Scoggie. 'Me.'

'What?' Lady Scoggie looked up at him, finally meeting his eye. He held her gaze. Murray's head was reeling. He could not take the boys away now. He could hardly move himself.

Lord Scoggie pulled a chair over from the table to sit in front of his wife, their knees touching. He reached a hand out to take her hand, then seemed unsure of himself and folded his hands in his own lap.

'You were away in London,' he began, as though feeling for the right thread. 'I was back and forth, London, Edinburgh, here ... The law case was not going well.' The stupid claim to the Marquisate of Ballavore, that was why he had been travelling around Murray suddenly realised the enormity of the damage the case had already done. 'You stayed in London with your aunt, and I was up here. You know when it was.'

'When I was – betraying you,' she whispered.

'When I was betraying you.' He repeated her words, and for a moment she did not understand. Then she stared at him.

'Who ... ?'

Lord Scoggie, even the little Murray could see of him from this angle, looked suddenly sheepish.

'Mary Kinkell.'

'Mary?' Lady Scoggie was breathless. She searched her husband's face, looking for a clue to this mystery. He nodded.

'She had a child. My child.' He took her hand now, as if he needed something to hold on to. 'I thought it was Andrew. Now I know – it was Deborah.'

'Deborah is your child?' Lady Scoggie was almost

inaudible.

'My dear,' He was still shaking. 'You exchanged the babies, and Mary never told me. You – tricked me into bringing up my own daughter, instead of your son.'

Emotions chased across Lady Scoggie's pale face, flickering with disbelief, anger, hope. She took a firmer hold of her husband's hand, clinging to him with her thin fingers and her bright gaze.

'What do you mean, your son?' asked Henry, who looked suddenly surprised that his voice had worked.

'Andrew is my son, Andrew Kinkell.' Lady Scoggie was not even looking at him, keeping her eyes on her husband. 'Mine and Philip Bootham's.'

The movement was too fast for Murray to catch. Henry hurled himself across the still room, and flung himself on his mother, beating her with his fists.

'How – could – you?' he cried. Lord Scoggie half-turned from his wife, and tried to push Henry back. Murray strode over to pull him away, but Henry's flailing arm lashed out sideways and knocked his father's face.

'Ow!' cried Lord Scoggie as Murray dragged Henry back, trying to pinion his wild arms. Lord Scoggie covered his mouth quickly with his hands, but Robert was staring, aghast. Slowly, Lord Scoggie lowered his hands, and discreetly spat something into them, cupping it secretly. Then he looked up, and gave a little embarrassed smile.

Murray felt his own mouth drop open. In front of him sat a completely different-looking man. Lord Scoggie's famous, gloriously protruding front teeth were gone.

CHAPTER TWENTY

Lord Scoggie was scarlet. Everyone else stood or sat with mouths wide open, staring either at the huge gap in Lord Scoggie's mouth, or at the odd bony thing clutched in his hands. Lord Scoggie looked from one to the other of them.

'You mean you really didn't know?' he asked, and a faint glint of delight came over his face. 'No one knew?'

Murray shook his head, but Lord Scoggie had turned to his wife.

'We had no idea ... What happened?' she breathed.

'When I was in Edinburgh – you know I had an accident in a chair ... I knocked my teeth out.'

'Oh, my dear!'

The boys involuntarily clutched their mouths, covering their own Scoggie teeth.

'But the people I was staying with recommended a man who makes these clever things.' He waved an embarrassed hand with the teeth in it. 'He glues the teeth into this wooden slip, then glues them into your mouth. But they come out at night, and they take ages to put in again properly: the glue has to set ...' Everyone looked a little sick. But Murray was thinking back to the night Tibo's body had been found. Lord Scoggie, roused from his bed by Naismyth's knocking, had taken a long time to appear. Murray had been tentatively picturing him removing traces of murder from his appearance, but was he simply trying to glue his teeth into his mouth?

'My lord, the search parties need to be making a move,' he said suddenly. 'Geordie has gone ahead to see to his wife ...' He stopped slowly, as Lord and Lady Scoggie looked at each other once more. 'I'll take the boys downstairs for now, shall I?'

There was no reply. He caught the boys by the shoulders, and guided them out of the schoolroom, wondering where he was going to take them out of the way. He was halfway along the passage with them when Robert looked round.

'Mr. Murray, you're wearing a sword!' He peered again at Murray's coat. 'And pistols!'

'Do you think you're going to have to fight to get Chrissie Farquhar back?' asked Henry curiously. He was still white in the face, and Murray was happy that he was not just asking questions about his mother's behaviour. It would take him a long time to get over that shock.

'No. Your father asked me to carry them until we find whoever it was murdered Mr. Tibo.'

Robert and Henry looked at each other, as they reached the stairs.

'If you find out who it was, will you kill him?' Henry asked, with a slight wobble in his voice.

'I shouldn't think so,' said Murray, surprised. 'Not unless he attacks someone else, and we have to defend them. Even then – '

'Would you kill someone who was trying to kill you?' Robert asked.

'I'm not sure,' said Murray. 'I daresay you'll find out, if you join a regiment.'

He heard Robert swallow. They were nearly at the bottom of the stairs.

'It's just,' said Henry, lagging behind a little, 'we think we know who killed him.' He looked up as he stepped off the last stair, and found himself in the hallway, crowded with the search parties. Major Keyes, with a nod at Murray, was gathering Geordie Kinkell's search party.

'He's off home to see that Mrs. Kinkell is settled,' the Major was saying, 'then he'll join us. So I think we should just follow him down there first, then we go on to the salt pans, I think.' He waved the party towards the door.

'I'll just –' Murray indicated the boys, and Keyes nodded. 'I'll catch you up.' He turned, and virtually walked into Deborah.

He almost did not recognise her. She was wearing an old, plain dress, with a thick and practical shawl, and her hair was pinned up in a simple roll. Her face had a bleak look.

'Did he say that Mr. Kinkell had gone home?' she asked, without looking at Murray.

'That's right. He wanted to take Peter home, too: the boy's exhausted, but he can't leave him with Mrs. Kinkell.'

'Then he can leave him with me. Peter is my brother, after all.' With a grim little twist of the mouth, she began pulling on her bonnet and cloak.

'Shall I take you there?' A new voice came from behind her, and Murray looked round again to find Andrew at her arm. 'Mother might find it strange, if you come unexpectedly.'

'Thank you, Mr. Kinkell.' She was ready, and turned to look up at him. 'You are very kind.'

Murray stood and watched them depart in the wake of the search parties, trying to sort out in his head what Deborah's position was now. She was Lord Scoggie's daughter, and presumably acknowledged, even if illegitimate. There was no reason to doubt that she would be allowed to keep her present status, and could still make a good marriage, even if Major Keyes would no longer take her. The only question was whether or not she would accept her place: Deborah's pride had been hurt, and she had the look of one who had been caught out in some shameful deception, even though she herself was not the guilty party.

And what of Andrew? As Lady Scoggie's illegitimate child, he had less chance of adoption into his mother's rank in society. Bootham would be unlikely to be in a position to help him, even if he wanted to. The chances were that, like many little accidents amongst the Scoggies' class, Andrew would spend his days in the family's service. Knowing Andrew, he would be able to use it to his advantage: he was not the kind to fail in life.

'What are we going to do today, Mr. Murray?' Robert asked, interrupting his thoughts. He looked down at the boys. Whatever had happened, their situation had hardly changed, and they still needed occupation and education. The schoolroom was busy: he took them across the hall to the library.

He pulled a copy of Shakespeare's *Henry V* off a shelf, and took it back to the table where the boys had found seats. He flicked through to King Henry's great St. Crispin's Day speech, and handed the book to Henry.

'I want you both to learn this speech and copy it out – here, there's paper, and here are some pens. I'll see how you've done when the search parties finish. And if you finish early – and mark, only if you really know the speech – you may go outside and play in the snow.'

Robert's eyes lit up, and he grabbed the book from Henry. Murray left them, smiling briefly, and returned to the hall to find his cloak in the chaos left by the search parties.

He was still looking for one glove when he heard light footsteps on the stairs. He turned, and found that it was Beatrix. She was wearing a pretty gown that Murray remembered seeing only a few days ago on Deborah, and over it had a blue spencer and a warm cloak. It was not fastened, and she had to set her bulging reticule down on the hall table to tie the strings at her neck and adjust her bonnet.

'Where are you off to? You look too elegant for charitable work,' he remarked, smiling in appreciation. She blushed.

'I'm just – going out.'

The blush made him suspicious.

'Where is Philip Bootham this morning, then? I did not see him at breakfast.'

'He took breakfast in his room. He thought it would be very crushed in the Great Hall.'

'I suppose he thinks he's going back to Aberardour Lodge today. He's going to find it difficult: the servants have orders not to admit him.'

She laughed lightly.

'Yes, I'm sure,' she said. 'Of course, he has no intention of going near the place. She can send on anything he needs.'

'So he's leaving, then? Good.' Something about the set of her shoulders suddenly made him ask: 'You're not going with him, are you?'

She spun round, and darted over to him. Her eyes were bright as stars, and she seemed to glow.

'Please, Mr. Murray, if we are friends, don't tell Lord Scoggie until we are far away!'

'Beatrix!' He sank back against the wall, his one glove forgotten in his hand. 'Beatrix, what are you doing?'

'Going away with Mr. Bootham. He has asked me to go to England with him.' An irrepressible laugh burst from her throat, as if what she was doing was perfectly proper, perfectly reasonable.

'When did you decide this?' He could think of nothing else to ask: his head was spinning. How did Bootham think he could get away with this? Beatrix had no money of her own. After last night, Lord Scoggie would never give her any, not to marry Bootham. And there was a question – was marriage what Bootham had in mind?

'He asked me last night. You told me he and – she – weren't married, so there was no question of him having any responsibilities towards her.'

'Beatrix!' He pushed himself upright. 'This is not you speaking. This is Bootham. How can you think this way?'

'Well, she has locked him out now, hasn't she? She clearly doesn't want him back, and I can – I can make him happy, I know I can.' She smiled, dreamily. Murray was disgusted.

'I just don't see how you can do this. Your home, your friends, your reputation ... and he hardly has a history of reliability, has he?'

'He says he loves me.' Her face was defiant, shining.

'And you believe –' He bit his lip. It was hardly tactful to express doubt.

'Well, I haven't much ground for comparison. No one else has said it to me.'

After a moment he managed to meet her eye. Suddenly she was looking cold and unfriendly, but more lovely than he had ever seen her. But he knew that there was nothing he could do for her. He had nothing to offer her, nothing more than friendship. He sighed.

'What?' she asked.

'I – I suppose I wish ... I wish things were different.'

'I don't.' She smiled again, but not at him. He

reached out impulsively, and took her gloved hand in his.

'Then I wish you every happiness. But Beatrix, please remember: if you ever need help, or a friend, for yourself, will you do me the honour of considering me for the position?'

She laughed, but he was earnest.

'Oh, very well. I shall remember,' she assured him. Then she turned, hearing footsteps on the stairs. 'Here he is!'

Philip Bootham paused on the stairs as they looked up at him, accepting the adulation of his audience. In the dim light, his hair was white gold, his hands, smoothing his gloves, long and suddenly spider-like. Murray shivered.

'Trouble, my dearest?' he asked Beatrix. She seemed to grow towards him, like a plant in the light.

'Not at all. But we had better go quickly. We are to walk to Elie,' she explained to Murray, 'to take the coach.'

'In this snow?' asked Murray.

'When there is no option,' began Beatrix, but Bootham interrupted her.

'What could be more romantic?' he asked. 'A brief struggle through the snowdrifts, to a warm fire and the beginning of our life together.' He opened the door, and ushered Beatrix out before him, making to follow.

'You have no shame, have you?' Murray hissed at him. 'Will you at least make an honest woman of her?'

'I cannot do that,' said Bootham smoothly. 'I believe, somewhere, my wife is still alive.'

'Jane Croft?'

'Oh, good heavens, no. Someone ages before that. I'm afraid I have lost track of her completely.'

Murray felt his hands twitch into fists, but Bootham, probably with years of experience, seemed to sense the danger and slid out through the door, pulling it firmly behind him.

By the time he found his glove and left the castle, Bootham and Beatrix were nowhere to be seen. To make sure he did not catch up with them, he hurried down towards the far end of the lake, over the snowy grass, and slithered over the gap in the wall where Tom Baillie had come in the evening of Tibo's death. Then he followed the crushed snow where the rest of the search party had headed down the hill towards Geordie Kinkell's cottage.

He caught up with them just as Geordie emerged from the cottage, on his own. He was frowning, and waved the party on ahead of him, pointing in the direction of the saltpans to the north, along the shore. Murray fell into step with him, one eye on Keyes up ahead.

'Are Andrew and Deborah with your wife, then?' he

asked quietly.

Geordie jerked his head round to stare at Murray, then shrugged.

'Aye, I suppose you ken the whole story.'

Murray thought that perhaps he did, but that Geordie himself did not.

'It's a bit of a guddle,' was all he said.

Geordie nodded.

'It seemed a grand notion at the time,' he said. 'We'd had Peter, you ken, and we thought if we had another son he might be the same – now, Peter's my son, and if anyone touched him I'd belt them, but I wanted someone who could support us when we were old ... When her ladyship wanted to exchange babbies, and the son she had was a grand strong one, I thought it was the right thing to do.'

'And Mrs. Kinkell?'

'Oh, aye, she agreed. She's always been fond of Andrew, as if he was her own. Well, he's a charmer, isn't he?'

Murray agreed. He took after his father.

'But did you ever wonder why Lady Scoggie wanted to exchange the babies?'

Geordie looked bland.

'I always thought there'd been a wee indiscretion, ye ken? She'd been away a gey long time in foreign parts, and his lordship hadn't always been with her.'

'But you didn't know who the father really was?'

'Not till the fella turned up in the parish. And even then ... well, you're not looking out for it, are you?'

They walked on together after the search party, saying nothing more of the matter. Murray was sure that Geordie thought he was Deborah's real father. How much longer he would remain ignorant was a moot point.

No one at the saltpans had seen Chrissie Farquhar. Staring silently at the search parties, the families of the saltworkers allowed them to search their thin new houses, finding nothing. They worked their way back along the shoreline, hunting between rocks and amongst fissures, the fishermen at least pleased to be off the snow and on the slippery shore instead.

They met the other search parties back on the main street, and they stood around, scuffling miserably, while the search party leaders debated what to do next, pointing out to each other the houses and outbuildings they had all searched. Murray moved over to Keyes again: there was snow down both sides of his cloak, where he had evidently fallen again. There was no stopping the man: Tippoo shivered by his side, as he balanced on wooden peg and stick to tap the snow out of his boot.

'Are you all right?'

'Oh, aye,' said Keyes, but his eyes were fixed on some point at the end of the main street, and his mind seemed to be elsewhere.

'It's looking a bit hopeless, isn't it?'

'Mmm.'

'Tempting to wait until the snow's melted: though it could be too late then, of course.'

'Aye. Has anyone searched the church?'

Murray turned to look at the church, squatting on its headland.

'I don't know. I'll ask Geordie.' He took two steps away towards Geordie and the other leaders, but Major Keyes was already away, limping towards the church.

'Geordie!' Murray called. 'Have we looked in the church?'

'Aye,' said Joe Baillie, clear eyes turning to take in Major Keyes. He watched the limping figure impassively.

'Major!' Murray called again. 'They've searched it.'

'But all of it?' the Major called back, not bothering to look round.

'Oh, aye, he has to ken best,' Murray heard Joe muttering. He and Geordie started after the Major, joined quickly by Sandy and Richie Shaw, and Murray, worried by the balance of this party, decided he had better go too. They hurried to catch up with Keyes, who was already perched at the crossing of the burn at the foot of the headland, trying to work out how to cross when the only large stepping stones were snow-capped. Murray grabbed his arm and dragged him across in two long strides, and the Major nodded and shook himself free to scrabble up the steep path. Tippoo was only just ahead, skittering through pockets of snow.

The headland was bleak and grey, the church a great black hulk in the centre with the crumpled lead sea beyond. The Major strode now across the kirkyard, managing to stay upright mostly by impetus, and made his way not to the door to the aisle in which the services were now held, but towards the old main door to the church, the place he and Murray had explored that first Sunday of his eventful visit. The doorway stood open, a dark hole at which the Major paused, staring into the void beyond, before plunging inside. Murray was next, stopping to let his eyes adjust, and the others were up with him before he stepped into the church.

Keyes was in the centre of the old building, listening carefully. The others stopped, too. All Murray could hear was the light, snowy wind outside, and the echo of gulls around the glaring gaps in the roof above them.

'What's that?' asked Joe Baillie suddenly. Murray concentrated harder, as the others around him strained to hear what Joe had heard. Dimly, there could be heard a thin scratching sound, and what could almost be a voice ...

Keyes swivelled on his peg. Ahead of him was the little door into the old kist room that he and Murray had looked at before, the one with no window, set into the thick wall of the old building. He snatched at the door latch, and pushed, but the door stuck.

Joe and Geordie were already with him. Joe snatched a great knife from his belt, and slipped it into the gap between the door and the doorframe, and pulled. There was a great crack, and the door shot open, a newish chain clattering to the floor, fallen from the rotten wood. There was a gasp, seemingly from all of them. The door swung right open, and Murray saw a figure inside, pale and thin, and for a second, motionless. Then it seemed as if they had let a whirlwind loose.

'Where is he? Where is he? I'll scratch the eyes out of his head!'

Chrissie Farquhar, her hair like a frayed rope end, eyes staring, came to a halt amongst them. Now Murray saw her clearly, he could see that she was not a young girl: there were lines on her thin face, though no doubt Sandy and her family between them had helped to score a few of them.

'Where's my fool of a brother?'

Joe Baillie stepped forward, a preparatory look on his face.

'Did Hugh put you in there?' he asked.

'Of course he did. Said he was going to take me

back home, and then tricked me in here! Oh, I could have kicked myself – after I'd kicked him! Where is he, the coward?'

'Chrissie, love,' her husband Sandy began, with a tentative hand on her arm. 'Hugh's gone.'

'Gone?'

'Lost, in the fishing,' Joe explained.

'What?' She looked disbelieving. 'When?'

'Probably the day he left you in here,' said Joe.

'Sandy?' She clutched at her husband's sleeve.

'Aye, love?' Sandy was looking at her as if he could not quite believe in her, either.

'We're going home. Is the bairn all right?'

'My mother's looking after him.'

'We'll soon put a stop to that.' She gave a wild look back at Joe Baillie, took a tighter grip on Sandy's arm, and shoved him ahead of her out of the church. Geordie followed, his face sombre. It was hardly the joyous moment that they had all expected, but at least Chrissie was safe.

With a satisfied look, Keyes turned away from the sight of her, and looked back into the kist room. Murray could see a blanket and a bottle and basket, the containers for the provisions she must have lived on since Hugh had gone missing. Keyes nodded to himself, and made to leave, but Joe Baillie had moved round to stand between him and the door. He nodded to Richie, who came to stand beside him, looking nervous.

'You've done well,' said Joe, nodding at Keyes. Murray found himself tensing. His hand drifted towards his sword, but apart from their sharp knives, he could see that the fishermen were not armed. 'You've done grandly, but you and I have other business, have we not?'

Major Keyes laughed.

'It's a long time since you and I had any business, Joe.' Murray glanced at him, and saw that he was not taking Joe's threat remotely seriously. 'I don't believe we've spoken for – oh, years and years, have we?'

'Oh, yes, Major. It's years and years all right: years and years since my brother Tom was able to earn a living, or support a wife or a family. Years and years since I lost my best man on my boat, because Tom could not go to sea.'

'Well, you'll be well used to it, then,' said Keyes with unbelievable carelessness. 'How is Tom these days? I see she did not wed him, anyway, yon Chrissie.'

Murray was stunned. He had had no idea that the woman they had been searching for, the wife of Sandy Kinkell, was the same woman that Keyes and Tom Baillie had fought over, all those years ago.

'No!' cried Joe. 'He did not! All ready to wed him,

she was, until you came along with your fancy red coat and caught her eye!'

'Oh, you're very kind, Joe, but the catching was all on her side,' Keyes insisted. 'She was a captivating little thing in those days. Hair like straw, blue eyes, and a wild temper. But she was gey fond of your brother, you know, Joe.'

'Not after you'd crippled him!' Joe shouted. He snatched up his knife, and Richie, shaking, drew his. Murray found his sword was in his hand, but he raised his empty left hand instead, and stepped forward.

'Now, Mr. Baillie, do you think this will do any good? Major Keyes here is crippled too, now. There is nothing more that you could do to punish him.'

'That's for me to decide. Draw your weapon if you want to, Keyes: I'll have you anyway!' He leapt forward, agile as if at sea. Keyes, surprised, flung up his arms to defend himself, then struggled to draw his own sword. Joe struck with his knife, but the thick cloth of Keyes' cloak muffled the blow. Murray, stepping forward, struck hard with the flat of his blade on Joe's shoulders, then on Keyes', trying to bring them both to their senses. They both staggered. Richie, fingering his knife handle, stood at the edge of the action, lips sucked in, too unsure to do anything, as Joe struck again and again and was parried by Keyes' sword. Tippoo started barking, a steady, insistent bark that echoed in the high church and seemed to strike as hard as any blow.

Keyes was just playing, Murray was sure of it. Joe was exhausting himself, without the reach of a sword. Then, just as Murray thought the fight would be over soon, Joe slashed down near Keyes' ribs, maybe by accident, and finally drew blood. Keyes stopped as if he had hit a wall. His face went white. Then he drew his sword back and brought down a mighty blow aimed directly at Joe's head.

'Keyes!' Murray cried, as Richie yelled 'Joe!' Murray flung himself forward at Keyes' legs, but slipped on the slimy floor and knocked the Major sideways. Keyes' sword flew from his hand and he cursed viciously, swiping at Murray's head with his fist, but Murray twisted aside. Joe slipped too, just as he tried to duck the sword blow. He fell hard.

Richie darted in to try and raise him, pulling him by the ankle in his haste. Murray bounced against the damp wall, spinning as he fell. Keyes had caught his balance again and was intent on Joe. He adjusted his stick, moved his foot to support him, and kicked hard with his peg leg, aiming for Joe's head.

Murray gasped at the force of the blow, and at the spced with which Joe defended himself, one hand clutching his head. They all heard the fingers crack as the peg leg hit them, and Joe grunted. Richie cried out and scrabbled again to drag Joe away, as Keyes drew back his leg for the next blow.

'Stop!'

A new voice, clear and urgent, came from the doorway. A slight figure stood against the light, clutching the doorpost.

Tippoo sat down and stared, mouth half-open. Blinking, Keyes caught himself, swaying, trying to see.

'Tom? Is that you?'

Tom Baillie swung himself in on his long crutches. He was flushed with the struggle of climbing the headland, snow flecking his bare head.

'Joe! What are you doing?'

Joe was breathing hard, still on the floor.

'I had to, Tom.' He used Richie's arm to haul himself on to his knees, then clutched at his broken hand. 'Look at yourself.'

'Aye, but Joe, that's me, not you.'

Joe looked up at Keyes, who was eyeing his sword. Murray stepped over and picked it up, helpfully, but did not, immediately, hand it back to Keyes.

Tom straightened from his brother, pale and thin, except where his shoulders had been hunched and toughened by years of crutch use. He glanced at Murray and took in the sword, point down, in his hand. Then he looked up at Keyes, a head taller than him.

'It ends here,' he said. 'Nobody gains anything by this, everyone just loses. Do you hear me?'

'He started it,' said Keyes, breathing deeply, but his mad surge of rage seemed to have died as quickly as it had the day he had scourged Tippoo in the library.

'I don't care. It ends. Joe?'

Joe was on his feet, but seemed disinclined to argue. He drew himself up and faced Keyes.

'Aye,' he said. 'I made my point.'

Tom paused for a moment, then asked:

'And you found Chrissie? Was she all right?'

'She was grand, Tom.'

Tom looked about him, then glimpsed the blanket in the dark kist room.

'In there? Why did I not think of that?' He shrugged, but looked deeply relieved. 'And you, did she not warn you to stay clear?'

For a moment it was not clear whom he was addressing, but then he looked straight at Keyes.

'She sent you all these letters – she knew her brother and Joe and Richie here would want a word with you. I suppose it was for old times' sake, eh? And for old times' sake, I delivered them for her.'

Not Hugh, but Chrissie. Chrissie had written the anonymous letters. But Chrissie had not tried to kill Keyes, and nor, to judge by their exchange just now, had the fishermen. So was it Keyes or Tibo who was the intended victim?

'Will you give me my sword, Mr. Murray?' Keyes asked, holding out his hand. Murray looked at Tom: the thin man seemed to be in charge now. Tom nodded. Murray turned the sword and handed it pommel first to Keyes. Keyes sheathed it, and straightened up.

'Aye, well,' he said. 'I don't think I'll be about in the parish for much longer anyway, lads, if it's any consolation to you. Are you coming, Mr. Murray? I think I'll go back to the castle.'

'In a while, Major,' said Murray. 'But don't wait for me: you'll need to get that cut tended to.'

'Aye.' He made his way slowly towards the door, playing a little, Murray thought, on his invalid state, though maybe he was only tired. 'I fancy a ride, though, while the snow's stopped. Do you mind if I take the boys out?'

Murray was surprised, but pleased enough.

'Certainly, take them out if they want to go. But please don't let Robert ride the gelding he took before.'

'Aye, I know.' He swung himself around, and disappeared.

Murray waited until he was sure Keyes was out of earshot, then cleared his throat.

'Lord Scoggie will want to know if you think you're

going to be all right,' he said, tentatively, to Joe.

Joe maintained his dignity.

'Aye, I will,' he said. 'I've had worse than broken fingers before now. But I suppose her ladyship will be round with the salves and the soup, all the same.' The corner of his mouth twitched.

'The soup's usually good,' said Murray mildly.

'Aye, I suppose.'

Murray rubbed his face with his hands, then found that he was covered in muck from the damp wall he had fallen against. His hat was dimly to be seen in a corner: he picked it up and inspected it in the light from the door. Richie was gathering the blanket and basket from the kist room.

'Mrs. Farquhar will want these back, I suppose,' he said apologetically. Now that the action was over, they all sounded tired. The old church was cold. Outside, a struggling sun was glinting on the snowy kirkyard, and casting soggy beams through the holes in the roof.

'I think he will be leaving soon, he spoke the truth,' said Murray, feeling he ought to say something. 'What he came for, he – I don't think he wants it any more.'

'Miss Deborah?' asked Joe, then added: 'Richie's wee lassie works in the castle.'

'Oh, Grisell, yes.'

'She told him about Mr. Bootham, and her ladyship, and young Andrew, and all. She's very upset,' he went on solidly, in case Murray would think she had only been gossiping.

'I have no doubt she is. I don't know,' said Murray honestly, 'how it will all work out.'

'Aye, well.' Joe eyed him for a long moment, then added unexpectedly, 'Will you come back for a cup of tea before you walk back up?'

Murray did not stay long at the Baillies' house, only long enough to warm himself and see that Mrs. Baillie was doing a fine job in bandaging Joe's broken hand. As Joe pointed out, it was the one from which he had already lost a finger, so there was less to break. Mrs. Baillie, a silent woman, sniffed with some emphasis.

He made hard work of walking back up the hill. He was dead tired, and hungry, and the thought of the castle was not a restful one. He would have to see to the boys, if they were not out, and report to Lord Scoggie, and he might have to answer for the fact that he had seen Beatrix leave, and had not stopped her.

Beatrix ...

He shook himself, and his mind wandered instead to the scene in the church. Heavens, if Major Keyes and Chrissie had ever married, if that had ever been a possibility, what a couple they would have made! The temper of either of them was frightening enough, without combining the two. He shivered. Keyes' temper really was disturbing. Deborah might well have had a lucky escape. He remembered the way Keyes had turned white, and then, with a chill, remembered too the vicious kick aimed at Joe's head.

He stopped in his tracks. He had seen a blow like that before – or rather, he had seen the injuries it had caused.

He began to walk faster, then to run. As the snow began to fall once more, he slipped and slid his way up the steep hill from the village, back along the road to the gap in the wall at the end of the lake. He scrambled over, and stood on one of the fallen stones, straining to see as far as he could, right round the park. In the uneasy wind, the fir trees bordering the dark grey lake made hapless remonstrations with their snow-laden branches. The park was bare. Was he too late? Please, no!

He sprinted up the slope towards the drive, dizzy with snowfall around him, feeling the flakes stick to his eyes and mouth, waving them away. On the drive he made better speed, but turned at the last minute and made for the orchard, and the path to the stables. There was no sense searching the park if the horses were all in their stalls.

They were. The stable boys looked oddly at him, but he snatched the door post to swing himself round and sped over to the kitchen door. It opened at last under his clumsy cold fingers, and he shot into the kitchen. Mrs. Costane and Hannah, busy preparing dinner, stopped and stared at him.

'Do you know where the boys are?' he demanded.

'They were here a minute ago, begging pies,' said Mrs. Costane sourly.

'Then where did they go?'

'The library, I suppose, they've been there all morning, but who knows? I ken nothing about what's happening in this house the day. I'm making dinner on blind faith!' she shouted after him as he pelted up the corridor to the castle entrance hall. Once there, he stopped and listened. The castle was silent. He tiptoed forward, pausing again to listen outside the library door, then, bracing himself, he opened it.

The library was empty. On the long table, the volume of *Henry V* lay abandoned, the chairs on either side of it pushed back.

His long legs took the stairs easily two at a time, pounding in the silence of the hallway. On the second floor he turned abruptly to the right, and found himself in the long gallery, dark now with the snow filling the tall windows.

He listened again. The castle was still. There was no distant noise of Deborah and Beatrix bustling around, or of Lady Scoggie hurrying out, or of the boys running and shouting. He swallowed hard, and tried to calm his racing heart. He stepped forward to the door of the third guest room, and knocked.

'Come in!' called a voice, and he turned the handle, and went inside.

Major Keyes was at the window, which he seemed to be struggling to close. Murray glanced quickly around the room. Apart from Tippoo, sprawled by the fire, the Major seemed to be alone.

'The room was stuffy, and I wanted a breath of air, but now I think the sash cord has caught,' Keyes explained with a rueful grin.

'Let me see if I can help,' said Murray quickly. He hauled down at the sash, but it would not move. In the process, he glanced outside. The snow-covered yard, far below the window, was empty. 'No chance to take the boys out then?' He nodded at the falling snow.

'No! Pity: I love a ride in the snow.'

'Have you seen Robert and Henry?'

'Not yet.' The Major was looking away. Giving up on the window, he had settled down on a chair at the little table he had been given as a desk. 'Is that why you're up here?'

'That's right.'

'I hope we don't have more missing bodies to search for!'

The use of the word 'bodies' was probably not supposed to mean 'dead bodies', but for a moment it was all Murray could picture.

'I'm sure they're around somewhere,' he said after a moment, trying to sound relaxed.

The room smelled of wet wool as the fire began to dry them both. The Major had had time to take his coat off and pull on a warm banyan: his coat, draped, Murray saw with surprise, on a spare peg leg, was propped against the wall by the door. The door itself had a long scar on it, from where Tippoo must have scratched to get out at some point.

'Take a seat, anyway, while you're here.' Keyes waved to a low armchair by the fire. Tippoo squirmed as Murray sat down and gave a yawn of contented greeting, bright eyes on Murray's feet.

'I wish I could just go off to bed for a few hours and get some sleep,' said Murray. 'Now that the excitement of finding Chrissie Farquhar is over, I'm dead on my feet.'

'Oh, you're a young man. Imagine how I feel!'

'And you've had a fight, too.' Murray looked down at Tippoo. 'I was interested by that kick you used. It never struck me that kicking was an option – for you.'

'An old soldier's trick,' said Keyes, though it seemed to Murray that there was a tension in his voice.

'You do it well.' Silence fell. Then Murray nodded his head at the door. 'I see Tippoo's left his mark, anyway.'

'He's a menace, sometimes. It's only if he's left

alone.'

'Do you know,' said Murray without expression, 'I can't think of a time since you came here that he has not been with you.'

'He does tend to follow me around, that's true.' Keyes had a laugh in his voice, but his eyes were assessing.

'So you would have brought him back up here, then, the night of the servants' ball, and closed him in? You wouldn't have wanted him following you, not that night.'

Keyes took a deep breath.

'Ah, I thought you were on to me. Damn you!' he added, fairly affably. 'I should have killed you, too, when I had the chance!'

'When did you have the chance?' said Murray, surprised.

'Oh, at the boxing lesson. I tried a shove in the direction of that great mirror, but Cocky broke your fall.'

Murray closed his mind to that for the moment: he had to concentrate.

'So you did kill Tibo. No wonder you disregarded my warnings that the killer might have intended you.'

'I was a bit surprised, it's true. Lord Scoggie had told me – at length – how intelligent you are. You'll have worked out then, by now, that I killed him because he was going to tell everyone about Deborah's birth, about her true parents. I couldn't allow Deborah to be hurt like that. You understand, don't you?'

'But the information came out anyway.' Murray was very still. Keyes, on the other hand, seemed relaxed, his usual, jovial self.

'Yes, that was unfortunate.'

'I don't think you did kill him because of that,' said Murray. 'For one thing, how did you find out what Tibo knew? Tibo hardly regarded you as a confidant.'

'He worked out somehow about my cousin and that Bootham man.'

'No, he didn't.' Murray felt vulnerable in the low chair. 'He didn't know about that. He knew who Deborah's real father was.'

'Do you mean my cousin had more than one affair?' Keyes looked shocked. 'That's the kind of statement I would have to ask you to prove, Mr. Murray, otherwise I should call you out.'

'No, Lady Scoggie is innocent of that charge.'

'The Kinkell woman, then.' Keyes sat back. 'No wonder she was happy to exchange the babies.'

Murray looked at him, taking in the easy face, the peg leg folded casually over the sound one, the hands crossed and forgotten on his lap.

'You killed him because you were jealous of him, didn't you? You killed him because he had gone out to meet Deborah.'

Keyes' head snapped round, his face suddenly white. Murray's heart took off like a firework. In a second Keyes was out of his seat, and Murray was pinned back so hard in his chair that the chair tipped over backwards. They crashed in a heap on the floor. There was no question of swords: Murray rolled painfully on to the hilt of his, and Keyes' was flung on the distant bed. Murray's pistols, too, were inaccessible, though he hardly thought of them. Floor wrestling was not Keyes' style, however: he pushed himself to his foot and peg, and hauled Murray after with horrible strength. He clutched Murray by the knot of his cravat, and punched him hard across the jaw. Murray's head swam, but he struggled to find his balance, and jabbed under Keyes' arms, in at his unprotected stomach – not a gentlemanly manoeuvre, but one the Pugilistic Chanticleer would have been proud of. Keyes jerked and folded, and Murray managed another blow to his left ear.

'Where are the boys?' he cried, beating off Keyes' fisted right hand. 'What have you done with them?'

'Damn the boys!' Keyes bellowed. 'Damn them! They saw me trying to kill you at the boxing, then they were at the lake that night!'

'So what did you do with – oof!' Murray doubled now, as Keyes caught him off guard. He kicked at Keyes' leg, but only hit the peg, a glancing blow that did nothing. Keyes seized him by the collar and struck again across his cheekbone. An astounding pain shot through Murray's head. Keyes swung again for another blow, and Murray wriggled, then let himself drop, out of Keyes' hands. He rolled rapidly out of the way as Keyes tottered. Keyes clutched the back of his upright chair, but now Murray had scrambled towards the door, panting, trying to clear his head. Tippoo circled him, barking and nipping. He was still on the floor. He turned his head. Keyes was close now: he had grabbed his stick, and balanced himself. He drew his peg leg back, ready to kick.

Murray felt behind him. He seized Keyes' spare leg, propped by the wall. Swinging it round fast, he hit Keyes' good leg a cracking blow. Keyes gasped, staggering. Murray pulled himself fast to his feet, his back to the door, then sprang forward as Keyes tried to steady himself for another attack. The room was small. Two strides brought them both to the window again. But Keyes still had his stick. He struck out with it, beating Murray's upper arms as Murray tried to use the spare leg to topple him again. Moments passed as blows rained back and forth, then there was a resounding crack. The spare leg, wielded by Murray, had broken the peg leg in two, in a jagged fracture. Keyes looked down, surprised, just as he was transferring his weight to the peg. There was a long second when neither of them seemed to understand what was happening. Then, in silence, Keyes toppled out of the window.

'No!' Murray lunged, trying to catch Keyes' arm, or his stick. But it was too late. He saw Keyes hit the ground, with a final crunch: a sprawling scar on the immaculate white snow.

Tippoo fell silent, staring at the window as if expecting his master to bounce back. Murray turned and ran.

Down the stairs and out the front door, and round the wing that would take him to the stable yard and then the tight angle of the castle where Keyes lay. If he hurried –

He ran straight into Lord Scoggie at the head of the stairs on the first floor landing. Lady Scoggie was with him, in companionable fashion.

'Keyes,' he gasped, as they took in his battered face. 'Fallen out of his window.'

'Keyes?' Lord Scoggie raised his eyebrows. His teeth were back in place.

'Don't know what he's done to the boys.' Murray glared at his employer, wondering why he did not seem to understand. 'Keyes murdered Tibo.'

'Is he dead?' demanded Lady Scoggie.

Murray shrugged.

'Have you seen the boys?' he demanded.

'Go and look for them,' said Lord Scoggie. 'I'll see to Keyes. Out of his own window, you say?'

Murray nodded, and wiped blood from his chin. He turned and ran back up the stairs, to Keyes' room.

There was no sign of the boys. He ripped off curtains and bed hangings, and knelt to look under the bed, but there was nothing. He stopped. Tippoo was heading out the door, but Murray could not believe that the dog had any interest in two small boys.

Where should he try next?

There was always the obvious.

He ran along the gallery, and turned into the school room corridor. He stopped, and drew his sword, then listened carefully.

There was no sound.

He tiptoed along the rush mat that floored the corridor. At the school room door, he paused again. Then, taking a deep breath, sword at the ready, he turned the handle.

Robert was sitting on the table, swinging his legs and eating a pie. Henry had a book propped in front of him, which by the look of it was their greasy copy of *Cook's Last Voyage*, and was licking his fingers thoughtfully. They were alone.

They jumped guiltily when Murray came in.

'We've learned it, sir, but it was starting to snow, so – '

'And it was warmer up here, sir. And Mrs. Costane gave us these pies ...'

'Do you want to hear the speech now, sir?'

Murray could not believe the relief that filled him on seeing his pupils alive and well. He leaned back against the door for a long moment, his head in his hands.

'What have you been doing, Mr. Murray? Your coat's filthy,' said Henry.

'And why do you have your sword out? Have you found Mr. Tibo's murderer?'

'Have you found Chrissie Farquhar?' added Henry. 'Someone's hit you on the face,' he added, as if Murray might not have noticed.

'Yes,' said Murray. 'Yes, yes and yes.'

'Yes, you want to hear the speech?'

'We've found Chrissie Farquhar, alive and fairly well. Someone's hit me on the face. We've found Mr. Tibo's murderer.'

'Major Keyes?' asked Henry, with a wary look.

'That's right.' He could ask them, angrily, why they had not told him. He was too tired.

'He pushed you down at the boxing lesson. We only realised afterwards, but he had gone all white.' Robert was quite pale himself. 'We thought he was just upset at Cocky. But then we thought he was really cross.'

'Why was he cross with you?' Henry asked.

'I don't know.' He sheathed his sword, and rubbed a hand through his hair. He took a chair at the schoolroom table. Had Keyes really thought that he, too, was a rival for Deborah? Keyes said Lord Scoggie had sung his praises. It fitted the pattern: the hot temper, combined with jealousy: jealousy over Chrissie Farquhar long ago, or over Deborah now. But Tibo's death had not been entirely impulsive. If Keyes had not planned something of the sort, he would never have left Tippoo behind, locked up.

'Sir?' Murray opened his eyes, and looked up.

'Henry's found another brilliant bit in Captain Cook, Mr. Murray. Do you think, if we pretended this table was the *Discovery* ...'

'Is there a bit in it where the captive natives fall asleep, at all?' Murray asked.

Henry and Robert looked at each other.

'*May*be,' said Henry, sensing a deal to be struck.

'Then I'll take it,' said Murray, and the game commenced.

About the Author

LEXIE CONYNGHAM IS a historian living in the shadow of the Highlands. Her historical crime novels are born of a life amidst Scotland's old cities, ancient universities and hidden-away aristocratic estates, but she has written since the day she found out that people were allowed to do such a thing. Beyond teaching and research, her days are spent with wool, wild allotments and a wee bit of whisky.

We hope you've enjoyed this instalment. Reviews are important to authors, so it would be lovely if you could post a review where you bought it!

Visit our website at www.lexieconyngham.co.uk. There are several free Murray of Letho short stories, Murray's World Tour of Edinburgh, and the chance to follow Lexie Conyngham's meandering thoughts on writing, gardening and knitting, at www.murrayofletho.blogspot.co.uk. You can also follow Lexie, should such a thing appeal, on Facebook, Pinterest or Instagram.

Finally! If you'd like to be kept up to date with Lexie and her writing, please join our mailing list and claim your free copy of three novellas here:

Murray of Letho

WE FIRST MEET Charles Murray when he's a student at St. Andrews University in Fife in 1802, resisting his father's attempts to force him home to the family estate to learn how it's run. Pushed into involvement in the investigation of a professor's death, he solves his first murder before taking up a post as tutor to Lord Scoggie. This series takes us around Georgian Scotland as well as India, Italy and Norway (so far!), in the company of Murray, his manservant Robbins, his father's old friend Blair, the enigmatic Mary, and other members of his occasionally shambolic household.

Death in a Scarlet Gown
The Status of Murder (a novella)
Knowledge of Sins Past
Service of the Heir: An Edinburgh Murder
An Abandoned Woman
Fellowship with Demons
The Tender Herb: A Murder in Mughal India
Death of an Officer's Lady
Out of a Dark Reflection
A Dark Night at Midsummer (a novella)
Slow Death by Quicksilver
Thicker than Water
A Deficit of Bones
The Dead Chase
Shroud for a Sinner

Hippolyta Napier

HIPPOLYTA NAPIER IS only nineteen when she arrives in Ballater, on Deeside, in 1829, the new wife of the local doctor. Blessed with a love of animals, a talent for painting, a helpless instinct for hospitality, and insatiable curiosity, Hippolyta finds her feet in her new home and role in society, making friends and enemies as she goes. Ballater may be small but it attracts great numbers of visitors, so the issues of the time, politics, slavery, medical advances, all affect the locals. Hippolyta, despite her loving husband and their friend Durris, the sheriff's officer, manages to involve herself in all kinds of dangerous adventures in her efforts to solve every mystery that presents itself.

A Knife in Darkness
Death of a False Physician
A Murderous Game
The Thankless Child
A Lochgorm Lament
The Corrupted Blood
A Day for Death
The Children's Party (a prequel novella)

Orkneyinga Murders

ORKNEY, C.1050 A.D.: THORFINN Sigurdarson, Earl of Orkney, rules from the Brough of Birsay on the western edges of these islands. Ketil Gunnarson is his man, representing his interests in any part of his extended realm. When Sigrid, a childhood friend of Ketil's, finds a dead man on her land, Ketil, despite his distrust of islands, is commissioned to investigate. Sigrid, though she has quite enough to do, decides he cannot manage on his own, and insists on helping – which Ketil might or might not appreciate.

Tomb for an Eagle
A Wolf at the Gate
Dragon in the Snow
The Bear at Midnight
The Fate of the Sea Stag

Other books by Lexie Conyngham:

Windhorse Burning

'I'm not mad, for a start, and I'm about as far from violent as you can get.'
When Toby's mother, Tibet activist Susan Hepplewhite, dies, he is determined to honour her memory. He finds her diaries and decides to have them translated into English. But his mother had a secret, and she was not the only one: Toby's decision will lead to obsession and murder.

The War, The Bones, and Dr. Cowie

Far from the London Blitz, Marian Cowie is reluctantly resting in rural Aberdeenshire when a German 'plane crashes nearby. An airman goes missing, and old bones are revealed. Marian is sure she could solve the mystery if only the villagers would stop telling her useless stories – but then the crisis comes, and Marian finds the stories may have a use after all.

Jail Fever

It's the year 2000, and millennium paranoia is everywhere.
Eliot is a bad-tempered merchant with a shady past, feeling under the weather.
Catriona is an archaeologist at a student dig, when she finds something unexpected.
Tom is a microbiologist, investigating a new and

terrible disease with a stigma.

Together, their knowledge could save thousands of lives – but someone does not want them to …

The Slaughter of Leith Hall and *The Contentious Business of Samuel Seabury*

'See, Charlie, it might be near twenty years since Culloden, but there's plenty hard feelings still amongst the Jacobites, and no so far under the skin, ken?'

Charlie Rob has never thought of politics, nor strayed far from his Aberdeenshire birthplace. But when John Leith of Leith Hall takes him under his wing, his life changes completely. Soon he is far from home, dealing with conspiracy and murder, and lost in a desperate hunt for justice.

Thrawn Thoughts and Blithe Bits and *Quite Useful in Minor Emergencies*

Two collections of short stories, some featuring characters from the series, some not; some seen before, some not; some long, some very short. Find a whole new dimension to car theft, the life history of an unfortunate Victorian rebel, a problem with dragons and a problem with draugens, and what happens when you advertise that you've found somebody's leg.